THE PRESENCE

BY JOHN SAUL:

Suffer the Children
Punish the Sinners
Cry for the Strangers
Comes the Blind Fury
When the Wind Blows
The God Project
Nathaniel
Brainchild
Hellfire
The Unwanted
The Unloved
Creature
Second Child
Sleepwalk
Darkness
Shadows
Guardian *
The Homing *
Black Lightning *
The Blackstone Chronicles
    PART 1: An Eye for an Eye: The Doll *
    PART 2: Twist of Fate: The Locket *
    PART 3: Ashes to Ashes: The Dragon's Flame *
    PART 4: In the Shadow of Evil: The Handkerchief *
    PART 5: Day of Reckoning: The Stereoscope *
    PART 6: The Asylum *
The Presence *

* Published by Fawcett Books

JOHN SAUL

THE PRESENCE

FAWCETT COLUMBINE · NEW YORK

A Fawcett Columbine Book
Published by Ballantine Books

Copyright © 1997 by John Saul

http://www.randomhouse.com

Library of Congress Cataloging-in-Publication Data
Saul, John.
The presence / John Saul. — 1st ed.
p.   cm.
ISBN 0-449-91055-5 (hardcover)
I. Title
PS3569.A787P73   1997
813'.54—dc21   97-14756

ISBN: 0-449-91055-5

Manufactured in the United States of America

First Edition: August 1997
10 9 8 7 6 5 4 3 2 1

To all my friends on Maui, and especially to the Maui Writers Conference and School, which has enriched my life not only as a writer, but in every other way as well.

As all of us know, *Maui No Ka Oi*—Maui truly is the best, a paradise on earth.

THE DISCOVERY

From above, the day was perfect.

A sky of sapphire blue, a sea of sparkling turquoise. A scattering of marsh-mallow clouds drifted across a vast expanse of azure.

The wind had died, and the ocean rose and fell gently against the shat-tered end of a lava flow that extended from the sea to a vent nearly halfway up Kilauea on the island of Hawaii.

The Big Island. Bigger by far than all the rest of the Hawaiian islands put together.

And growing bigger every year.

Today, though, even the earth seemed to have fallen in with the torpor of the air and water. The fires burning deep within the island's core seemed to have settled to a slight simmering, as if waiting for another time to push up through the rocky crust above and send trails of glowing magma snaking down the mountain's flank to push farther into the sea.

The kind of day for which the diving team had been waiting.

An hour after dawn, they were aboard the tug and barge that carried them out of Hilo Bay. Now the barge was anchored two hundred yards off the end of the lava flow, held in place by three anchors chained to heavy hawsers. The tug itself needed nothing more than a lunch hook to hold its position, and the surface crew—with little to do until the divers in the water signaled them—relaxed on deck, drinking beer and playing cards, as somnolent as the weather itself.

Perhaps if the wind and the sea hadn't conspired against them, someone would have felt the seismic blip and realized that the idyllic day's serenity was an illusion.

Beneath the thick tongue of lava that wound down from the distant vent, the pressure from the hot core far below the crust of the earth had built, cracking apart a great slab of rock.

It wasn't an explosive crack—nothing like the displacement that occurs when the locked edges of continental plates suddenly break free and hundreds of miles of solid-seeming earth jerk abruptly in opposite directions.

Nor was it the kind of crack in which, without warning, the floor of the sea heaves upward, sending a great tidal wave thousands of miles in every direction, towering over land, to drown whatever stands in its way.

This crack, occurring just below the surface, caused only the smallest of blips on the seismographs that monitored the mountain's movements. If anyone on the island felt it at all, it was to wonder a moment later if perhaps he had merely imagined it.

Beneath the lava flow, the fissure in the rock provided just enough room for a glowing column of molten rock to begin its rise to the surface, heat and pressure widening its path as it went, until at last the white-hot magma broke into the empty tunnel under the broad strip of lava on the top, where years ago the still-molten interior of the flow had simply drained out of the tube formed by its own fast-cooling surface.

Now, as the tug bobbed peacefully at the end of the flow, and the divers below worked in blissful innocence, the liquid fire streamed downhill, both hidden and insulated by the black rock above it.

Coming to the end of the tube, to the closed chamber where the last flow had finally been frozen by the sea, the lava pooled, more and more of it pouring in every minute, its weight building against the interior of the cliff's face, its heat relentlessly burning away the wall of stone that kept the boiling magma from the sea.

One hundred feet below the surface, the two divers, a man and a woman, worked with intense concentration to retrieve the object they had discovered a week ago.

Embedded in the layer of lava that covered the ocean floor, it was almost perfectly spherical, its color so close to that of the lava itself that the divers, coming upon it for the first time, almost missed it completely. Its shape was what had caught the woman's eye—a curve caught in her peripheral vision.

She had paused to take a closer look, because it struck her as an interesting formation of lava. Seconds after she bent to investigate it, her partner, sensing that she was no longer in her customary position to his right, turned back to make certain she was all right. Within less than a minute, he had become as interested in the sphere as she.

For nearly ten minutes they'd examined it. Though it was firmly anchored in the lava, they could see that it was not quite part of it. A geode of some sort. After photographing it and recording its exact position, they finished their dive, and later on that day reported the find to their employer.

Now, they had returned to the site of their discovery. They had been underwater for nearly an hour, carefully working a custom-made net around the sphere and fastening the net itself to a hook suspended from the end of a large crane mounted in the center of the barge's deck. The basket net, designed specifically for this purpose, resembled the macramé seines that generations of Japanese fishermen had once secured around glass floats, but it was woven from a plastic fiber stronger even than steel.

Having secured their net, and satisfied that the heavy mesh would not slip, the woman activated a signaling device fastened to her weight belt.

On the tug, the crew set to work to lift the geode from the ocean floor.

One of the men, catching a whiff of sulfur in the air, wrinkled his nose, then decided it was nothing more than the noxious odor the tug's bank of batteries sometimes threw off.

As they concentrated on operating the crane, none of the crew noticed the smoke that was starting to drift through the first tiny rifts in the face of the cliff two hundred yards away.

A hundred feet down, the two divers backed thirty feet away from the geode, then turned to watch as the cable from the crane tightened. For a breath-held moment nothing moved. Then the geode—nearly three feet across—abruptly came free from the lava, shooting upward a few yards before dropping instantly back almost to the bottom, like a yo-yo on a string. A momentary pause. Then it began a slow, steady vertical journey toward the surface, while the two divers made their way back to the place where it had lain.

The crane was just swinging the geode onto the deck of the barge when the face of the cliff gave way. As a gout of brilliant yellow lava spewed out, exploding into millions of fragments when it hit the surface of the sea a split second later, the crane operator screamed a warning. Within seconds the hawsers had been cut, the anchors and their chains abandoned, and the tug was running directly out to sea.

The water, dead calm only a few seconds before, churned around the tug, reacting to the explosive force of the fast-growing gush of lava now pouring forth from the crumbling face of the cliff.

"What about the divers?" someone yelled.

But even as he spoke, the terrified crewman knew the answer to his question.

The divers were just peering into the depression in which the geode had rested when they felt the first subsonic vibration. In the instant that surprise became panic and they reached for their belts to release their weights and make an emergency ascent, it was already far too late.

A rift suddenly opened in the ocean floor, and as the boiling magma burst into the sea, the water itself seemed to explode into a hellfire cauldron of sulfuric acid, boiling water, and steam. A fusillade of shrapnel-size fragments of volcanic glass shot in every direction. An instant after the divers had been killed by the steam, acid, and boiling seawater, their bodies were shredded by the silicate fragments, which tore through them like millions of white-hot scalpels.

Within seconds, nothing was left of them.

A mile out to sea, the crew of the tug gazed in awe at the spectacle behind them.

The shoreline had disappeared, lost in a dense fog of steam mixed with poisonous gases and volcanic ash that hung like a curtain where only a few minutes ago the face of the cliff had been. The sea, whipped by a building wind, was heaving, and overhead dark clouds gathered as if the forces that had unleashed the fury of the mountain now had summoned a storm.

Using binoculars, the crew scanned the water for any sign of the two divers, but even as they searched, they knew they were bound to fail. They had barely escaped with their own lives. As the storm built and the seas became great, heaving swells, the captain of the tug turned back toward Hilo and the safety of the harbor.

On the barge, three men secured the geode to the deck, silently wondering if it had been worth the lives it had cost to collect it.

PROLOGUE

LOS ANGELES

It wasn't supposed to be like this.

Everything was supposed to be getting better, not worse.

They'd promised him—everyone had promised him.

First the doctor: "If you take the pills, you'll feel better."

Then his coach: "Just try a little harder. No pain, no gain."

Even his mom: "Just take it one day at a time, and don't try to do everything at once."

So he'd taken the pills, and tried harder, but also tried not to do too much. And for a while last week things actually seemed to improve. Although smog had settled over the city so heavily that most of his friends had cut out of school early and headed for the beach, where an offshore wind might bring fresh air in from the ocean, he'd gone to all his classes. After the last bell he'd stripped out of his clothes in the locker room and donned his gym shorts before jogging out to the track to do the four warm-up laps that always preceded the more serious work of the high hurdles.

The event that just might, with a little more work, make him a State Champion on his eighteenth birthday.

One day last week, when he was alone on the field, the pills had at last seemed to kick in. He'd been expecting to lose his wind halfway around the first lap, but even as he rounded the final turn, he felt his body surging with energy, his lungs pumping air easily, his heartbeat barely above normal. On the second and third laps he'd kicked his pace up a notch, but still felt good—really good. So on the fourth lap he'd gone all out, and it was like a few months ago, when he'd still felt great all the time. That day last week, he felt greater than ever: his lungs had been sucking huge volumes of air, and his whole body had responded. Instead of the slow burn of pain he usually felt toward the end of the warm-up mile, his muscles had merely tingled pleasurably, his chest expanding and contracting in an easy rhythm that synched perfectly with his steady heartbeat. His whole body had been functioning in harmony. He'd even taken a couple of extra laps that day, exulting in the strength of his body, euphoric that finally the pills and the exercise were working. He'd set up the hurdles then, spacing them precisely, but setting them a little higher than usual.

He'd soared over them one after the other, clearing the crossbars easily, feeling utterly weightless as his body floated over one barricade after another.

When he'd started back to the locker room two hours after he began, he was barely out of breath, his heart beating easily and his legs feeling as if he'd only been strolling for half an hour instead of running and jumping full-out for two.

The next day it had all crashed in on him.

A quarter of the way around the first lap, he'd felt the familiar constrictions around his lungs, and his heart began pounding as if he were in the last stretch of a 10K run. He kept going, telling himself it was nothing more than a reaction from the day before, when he'd worked far harder than he should have. But by the time he finished the first lap, he knew it wasn't going to work. Swerving off the hard-packed earth of the track, he flopped down onto the grass, rolling over to stare up into the blue of the sky, squinting against the glare of the afternoon sun. What the hell was wrong? Yesterday he'd felt great! Today he felt like an old man.

He'd refused to give in to the pain in his lungs, the pounding of his heart, the agony in his legs. When his coach had come over to find out if he was all right, he'd tossed it off, claiming he'd just gotten a cramp, then rubbing the muscles of his right calf as if to prove the lie. The coach had bought it—or at least pretended to, which was just as good—and he'd gotten up and gone back to the track.

He made it through the four laps, but by the last one he'd only been able to maintain a pace that was little more than a fast walk.

The coach had told him to try harder or go home.

He'd tried harder, but in the end he'd gone home.

And each day since then it had grown worse.

Each day he'd struggled a little harder against the pain.

The day before yesterday, he'd gone to the doctor for the fourth time since New Year's, and once again the doctor hadn't been able to find anything wrong. Once again he'd answered all the questions: Yes, he was fine when he came back from Maui with his mom after New Year's. No, his father hadn't been there; he'd gone to Grand Cayman with his new wife and their baby. No, it didn't bother him that his dad hadn't gone to Maui with them—in fact, he was glad his mom had dumped his dad, since his dad seemed to like hitting both of them when he got drunk, which had been practically every night the last couple of years before he finally left. No, he didn't hate his dad. He didn't like him much, and was glad he was gone, but he didn't hate him.

What he hated was the way he felt.

The doctor had said maybe he should see a shrink, but he wasn't about to do that. Only geeks and losers went to shrinks. Whatever was wrong, he'd get over it by himself. But over the last two days the pain had become almost unbearable. He was having nightmares, and waking up unable to breathe, and his whole body had started hurting all the time.

This afternoon, when he started feeling like maybe it might be better just to die if he couldn't get away from the pain, he'd cut out after school and driven around for a while, until a cop stopped him and gave him a ticket for having a broken muffler. So now what the hell was he going to do? He couldn't afford to pay for the ticket, let alone get the damn muffler on the car fixed. Besides, what was the big deal? It didn't make that much noise, and hardly stank up the inside of the car at all. But his mom was going to give him hell for the ticket anyway, and his dad would only launch into an endless lecture about how much it costs to raise two families if he asked to borrow the money to fix the muffler.

What a mess!

Turning into the tree-lined block on which he'd lived all his life, he pressed the button on the sun visor that would activate the garage door opener while he was still two houses away, and turned into the driveway just as the door opened fully. Automatically starting the game he played against himself every afternoon,

he pressed the button again, trying to gauge it so the descending garage door
would just clear the back end of his car as he pulled it inside.

Today he missed, and the car jolted sharply as the garage door glanced off
the rear bumper. So now there would be scrapes on the car and the garage door,
as well as the ticket and the bad muffler.

And he still hurt.

Maybe, instead of going into the house, he'd just sit here awhile.

Sit here and see what happened.

A feeling of warmth began to spread through him, washing away the pain
he'd been enduring, and suddenly everything began to seem better.

Maybe he'd finally found the answer to his problems.

Without his mother.

Without his coach.

Even without his doctor.

The boy closed his eyes, breathed deeply, and for the first time in weeks felt
no pain.

For the woman, the day had been no better than it had been for her son, starting with an early call from her ex-husband suggesting that they renegotiate his
child support payments. Translation: the bimbo he'd run off with wanted more
money to spend on herself. Well, she'd disabused him of that idea pretty
quickly. At noon she'd discovered that an associate who was a full year junior to
her was going to get the partnership slot that should have been hers. So now she
was faced with a decision: Sit it out for another year, or start job hunting? But
she knew the answer to that one: she wasn't going to be made a partner, ever, so
she might as well start checking with the headhunters.

Then, when she'd decided things couldn't get any worse, the doctor called to
recommend a good psychiatrist for her son. Well, before she sent him off to a
shrink, she'd have him checked out by someone else. Except the HMO probably
wouldn't pay for it, and the trip to Maui at New Year's had strained the budget
as far as it would go.

Still, she'd figure out something.

Turning into the driveway, she jabbed the remote on the visor, bringing the
car to a complete stop as she waited for the garage door to open.

It was the noise of the engine more than the fumes that poured out of the garage that told her something was wrong. Slamming the gear lever into Park with one hand as she opened the door with the other, she slid out of her car and ran into the garage.

She could see her son slumped inside his car, his legs up on the front passenger seat, his back resting against the driver's door. His head was lolling on his chest.

Stifling a scream, she grabbed the driver's door handle.

Locked!

She ran around the car and tried the other door, then called her son's name.

Nothing!

Wait!

Had something moved inside the car?

She cupped her hands over her eyes and peered into its shadowy interior.

His chest was moving! He was still breathing!

Coughing as the fumes in the garage filled her lungs, she fumbled for the extra key that hung from a nail under the workbench, shoved open the door to the kitchen and grabbed the phone. "My son!" she cried as soon as the 911 operator answered. "Oh, God, I need an ambulance!"

A carefully measured voice calmly asked for her address.

Her address!

Her mind was suddenly blank. "I can't—oh, God! It's—" Then it came back to her and she blurted out a number. "On North Maple, between Dayton and Clifton. Oh, God, hurry! He locked himself in the car in the garage and—"

"It's all right, ma'am," the calm voice broke in. "An aid car is already on its way."

Dropping the phone on the counter, she raced back to the garage. She had to get the car open—she had to! A hammer! There used to be a sledgehammer at the end of the workbench! Squeezing between the front of her son's car and the wooden bench, she uttered a silent prayer that her ex-husband hadn't simply helped himself to the big maul. He hadn't—it was right where she remembered it. Grasping its handle with both hands, she hoisted it up, then slammed its huge metal head into the passenger window of her son's car. The safety glass shattered into thousands of tiny pieces, and the woman dropped the hammer to the floor, snaked a hand through the broken window, and pulled the door open. Reaching across her son's body, she switched the ignition off, and the loud rumble of the motor died away, only to be instantly replaced by the wail of a fast-approaching siren. She grasped her son's ankles and tried to pull him out of the car, but before she'd managed to haul him even halfway through the door, two white-clad medics were taking over, gently easing her aside, pulling the boy out of the car and clamping an oxygen mask over his face. As he stirred, her panic at last began to ease its grip.

"He's coming around," one of medics assured her as they carried him out of the garage and put him on a stretcher. "Looks like he's going to make it okay."

Her son began struggling as the medics put him into the ambulance and started to close its rear door.

"I want to come," the woman begged. "For God's sake! He's my son!"

The door to the ambulance reopened, and the woman scrambled inside. With the siren wailing, the ambulance raced toward Cedars-Sinai Hospital, nearly twenty blocks away.

The ride seemed to take forever, and the woman watched helplessly as her son struggled against the two medics, one of whom was trying to hold the boy still while the other kept the oxygen mask pressed firmly over his nose and mouth. Clutching her son's hand, the woman tried to soothe him, and finally his struggles eased. But just as the ambulance pulled to a stop at the hospital's emergency entrance, she felt his hand suddenly relax in hers. His whole body went limp on the stretcher.

She heard one of the medics curse softly.

Her body went numb, and when the doors were yanked open from the outside, she climbed out of the ambulance slowly, as if she'd fallen into a trance.

The crew rushed her son into the emergency room, where a team of doctors waited to take over for the medics.

She followed the stretcher into the hospital.

Silently, she watched the doctors work, but already knew what was coming.

And in the end, she heard the same words she'd heard first from her son's doctor, then from the ambulance crew: "I don't understand—he should be doing fine!"

But her son—her sweet, handsome only son—wasn't doing fine.

Her son was dead.

CHAPTER 1

NEW YORK CITY

"Whatcha tryin' ta do, Sundquist? Kill ya'self?"

A harsh laugh followed the mocking words, ricocheting off the bare concrete walls of the high school gymnasium, echoing louder in Michael Sundquist's ears as it resonated. What should he do? Abandon the bench presses he was doing and confront the jerk?

Not a good idea. The jerk, whose name was Slotzky—first name unknown, at least to Michael—was about a foot taller than he, and outweighed him by maybe fifty pounds, all of it solid muscle. Confronting Slotzky would be a good way to get his ass whipped, and getting his ass whipped was definitely not high on Michael Sundquist's priority list this morning.

Finishing the bench presses, however, was very high on the list, as were doing fifty push-ups and fifty chin-ups, followed by as many laps around the track on the gym's mezzanine as he could manage before the ten-minute bell sent him to the showers. If he ignored Slotzky, avoided a fight, and kept his mind firmly on his work, he could easily achieve his goal.

A varsity letter.

That was all he really wanted.

He would never be tall enough for basketball, or heavy enough for football. He suspected it was way too late for him to take up baseball. That left track. And the thing he'd always been best at was running. Even when his asthma had been so bad he could barely breathe, he'd still been able to beat the rest of the kids in his class in short sprints. In fact, it had been kind of a joke: don't bother trying to beat Sundquist off the block, just keep trotting along behind him and sooner or later he'll run down like a broken watch.

The joke had been all too true. Only a year ago he'd often found it impossible to run more than a quarter of a mile. Though he invariably led at the beginning of races, he never quite managed to win a fifty-yard dash, and in the hundred he always came in dead last.

But even when the asthma was at its worst, he never *ever* gave up. When his mother claimed it was no big deal—that no one on either side of his family had ever been an athlete—it only made Michael more determined. What did she know, anyway? It was a guy thing. The kind of thing his father would have understood if his father were still alive.

Whenever Michael ran, battling for breath, forcing his body beyond its capacity, determined to conquer the frightening condition that had held him in its power ever since he'd been a little boy, he imagined his dad cheering him on. Though his father's face was becoming cloudy, and sometimes he could barely remember that deep, booming voice, Michael clung to his vision of his dad. And kept at it until finally, last year, he'd begun to outgrow the asthma.

Finishing the bench presses, he dropped to the floor to do fifty quick push-ups—still barely breathing hard—then started toward the high bar to begin his chin-ups, glancing as he passed at his reflection in the wire-mesh window that separated the gym from the coaching room. Yes, his chest was deepening—he could see it.

Every day, bench press by bench press, push-up by push-up, lap by lap, his work was paying off.

The other guys weren't laughing at him anymore, except for Slotzky. And even Slotzky would stop tormenting him if he could actually make the varsity track team.

And not as a sprinter, either.

No, Michael had set his sights on a higher goal—long-distance running, where endurance counted every bit as much as speed, if not more.

He finished the last of the chin-ups and checked his respiration again. He was breathing a little harder than at the start of the hour, but he wasn't anywhere near panting, no sign of the onset of those terrible attacks that used to grip him in clammy, gasping terror. He loped over to the metal stairs leading up to the track that was suspended from the walls twelve feet up, just below the rafters and well above the basketball hoops. Taking the stairs two at a time, he glanced at the clock on the far wall.

Twenty minutes left. He could run a couple of miles before heading for the showers.

He broke into an easy jog, pacing himself carefully so he wouldn't have to break his stride as he approached the sharp turns at each of the gym's four corners. There was no one else on the track; the rest of the class was on the floor below, some of them playing a game of basketball, a few lifting weights, but most of them just sprawled out on the floor, waiting for the hour to end.

"Hey, Sundquist," Slotzky yelled, an ugly grin splitting his lips. "Ain't ya afraid ya might pass out up there?" As Slotzky's friends laughed obediently, Michael, stopped by Slotzky's shout, spontaneously raised the middle finger of his left hand.

Big mistake.

Slotzky's grin disappeared. He rose from the floor and started up the stairs, three of his friends following him. As he searched for an escape route, Michael wondered what misguided impulse had led him to do something so stupid.

He also wondered if there were any truth to the rumor that Slotzky had once thrown someone off the roof of a building.

As Slotzky and one of his friends approached him from one direction, the others circled around the opposite way, catching him in a heavy-duty pincers.

"Whatcha gonna do, chickenshit?" Slotzky taunted as he advanced on Michael, closing the distance between them.

Michael glanced at Slotzky, then at the bully's friend. There was only one way out. Dropping down onto his stomach, he swung his legs out over the edge of the track, then lowered himself until he was hanging by his fingers. Slotzky was running toward him now, and though the bigger boy was still thirty feet away, Michael could already feel the soles of Slotsky's Nikes grinding down on his fingertips. Without so much as glancing down at the floor below, he released his grip and let himself drop, falling into a rolling tumble the moment his feet touched the hardwood planks.

A twinge of pain shot through his shoulder, but he ignored it, scrambling to his feet and looking up to see what his pursuers would do.

Slotzky leaned over the rail, glowering at him. Then, with a skill perfected by years of practice, he spat on Michael. "See ya after school," he said.

Wiping Slotzky's slimy glob from his face, Michael backed away a few paces, then turned and trotted off toward the showers.

He wondered if Slotzky would be carrying a knife or a gun after school today.

Or both.

Katharine Sundquist knew she should be concentrating on the work at hand. Before her, on the desk in her office in the Natural History Museum, was a fragment of a hominid jaw that had arrived from a dig in Africa a week ago. Not that there was much work to be done: she had tentatively identified the specimen as *Australopithecus afarensis* the moment she'd seen it, and her subsequent examination failed to suggest that it might be anything else. It had been discovered in an area where *Australopithecus afarensis* was, if not common, certainly not unheard of, and excavated at a depth that, barring something unusual turning up in the carbon dating of the site, generally corresponded to the level where that particular precursor of Homo sapiens might be found. The problem was, she kept getting distracted by a series of photographs that had arrived the day after the australopithecine jaw.

There were half a dozen pictures, along with a letter describing the site more fully. The name on the letterhead—Rob Silver—had caught Katharine's attention immediately, for though she'd seen Silver only a few times in the twenty-odd years since they'd been in graduate school together, she still had a clear mental image of him: tall, muscular, with an unruly mop of light brown hair and blue eyes that had—at least for a while—never failed to set her heart beating faster every time she saw him. The romance, though, had quickly faded when his interest in Polynesian culture and hers in early man had sent them in opposite directions, putting not only a scientific gulf between them, but an entire planet as well. Within four years she'd met and married Tom Sundquist and given birth to Michael.

When Michael was six, Tom Sundquist had died.

Died in Africa, on a perfect summer morning, a decade ago. But the image of it was as clear in her mind now as if it had happened only yesterday. Tom was leaving for Nairobi to catch a flight to Amsterdam, where he was scheduled to read a paper on the dig they'd been developing together for the past five years. She and Michael were staying on at the dig, where Katharine would supervise the work in Tom's absence while Michael happily played with the African children with whom he'd made fast friends. She and Michael had stood together, hand in hand, as Tom's single-engine Cessna accelerated down the dirt landing strip and rose into the morning sky. As always, the pilot swung around to pass over them one final time, but that morning he'd decided to show off.

As Katharine and Michael watched—she with growing apprehension, he with growing excitement—the pilot put the little plane through a series of twists and loops, then sent it straight up until it went into a stall, flipped over, and plunged toward the earth in an accelerating nose dive.

Katharine had seen it before—it was one of the pilot's favorite stunts—and it always terrified her. At the last second the pilot would pull out of the dive, waggle his wings, and head off toward Nairobi, flying low enough to send the herds of animals below him into panicked stampedes.

But that morning, as she and Michael watched, the plane smashed nose first into the ground, instantly exploding into a ball of fire.

She and Michael had left the dig that day and never returned.

Within a year Michael's asthma attacks began, triggered, Katharine was convinced, by what he'd seen on the morning his father died. In the years since Tom's death, Katharine had concentrated on only two things: her son's health and her work. For most of that time, it had been enough. But lately, especially the past few months, when Michael seemed finally to have freed himself from the crippling attacks, she'd been wondering if she wasn't turning into just another of the fossils she spent so much of her time studying.

And then, last week, the letter from Rob Silver arrived, along with the photographs. The site, he explained, was on the flank of Haleakala, on Maui. For the last five years he'd been working in Hawaii, studying the evolution of Polynesian architecture as it moved from the South Pacific into the Hawaiian Islands. But the site in the photographs, he wrote, bore no resemblance to anything he'd ever seen in Hawaii. He had money in his budget for a consultant, and wanted to know if Katharine would be interested.

She kept returning to the pictures, peering at the images of the site that had been discovered beneath a thick layer of vegetation.

She'd gone through the museum's library, comparing the photographs to every other image she could find of early Hawaiian ruins.

There was no comparison.

Yet the only way she could truly analyze the site would be to see it.

Now, once again putting aside the drab grayish fossil, and the photos of the equally drab grayish site from which it had been excavated, she again picked up the pictures of the site on Maui.

Though the site itself appeared to be little more than a collection of rough stones, it was surrounded by a lush forest of towering trees and flowering shrubs and vines, and while in some of the pictures the turquoise-blue of the Pacific Ocean could be seen in the distance, in others there were glimpses of a waterfall tumbling into a crystal-clear pool, a setting so beautiful it could have come straight from a Hollywood set designer's vision of Eden.

Had Rob deliberately given her those seductive glimpses of the paradise surrounding his site?

And why was she even daydreaming about tropical flowers and trade winds? It was the *site* that counted!

But as she glanced around the windowless cubicle in the dismal cave that was her office, and remembered just how miserable the weather outside was, she knew exactly why she was as tantalized by the lush surroundings of Rob Silver's site as she was by the discovery he had made.

She picked up the letter once more.

Thirty thousand dollars.

Rob Silver was offering her thirty thousand dollars to spend three months working with him on Maui.

Plus expenses.

She remembered the tense meeting she'd had with the museum's director last week. Her budget alone was about to be slashed by thirty percent.

The grant from the National Science Foundation—the grant she'd been counting on to fund fieldwork this summer—was "approved but not funded."

So there, but for the offer on her desk, was the future: no fieldwork and a budget that was all but nonexistent.

The major problem was that Rob Silver needed her by the first of the month, which was as long as he could hold up his dig. That would mean taking Michael out of school—and away from the track team he'd become so enamored of lately—which she suspected he wouldn't like at all. Well, maybe when she told him where they were going, his objections might evaporate.

She picked up the phone and called the director. "I may want to take a leave of absence," she said. "Three months." She hesitated, then spoke again. "Without pay, of course." As she hung up the phone five minutes later, she wondered if Michael would be as easily convinced as the director had been.

When she got home that afternoon, though, and saw the cut on his arm and the ugly yellowish purple bruise that surrounded her son's painfully swollen left eye, Katharine knew that the decision was made. Three months away from New York was just what both of them needed.

CHAPTER 2

Pedro Santiago's eyes snapped open as the 747's attitude changed slightly, beginning its descent into Honolulu. Pedro hadn't meant to sleep on the flight; ever since the moment the man in Manila had handed him the locked Louis Vuitton makeup case, he'd been determined to stay wide-awake through the entire trip to Hawaii. Not that he had actually been asleep, he reassured himself. Not really. His eyes had perhaps been closed, and his mind might have slipped into that state of relaxation that was almost as refreshing as true sleep, but he'd still been perfectly aware of his surroundings.

He'd heard the woman across the aisle order a third mai-tai, then a fourth, and, a few minutes ago, a fifth.

He'd listened to the man in the row ahead of him snoring.

His feet had rested against the makeup case tucked beneath the seat directly ahead of him, where the sleeping man unknowingly guarded it from the front as securely as Pedro himself guarded it from his position.

He'd bought two first-class seats for his trip. He hated having to make polite conversation with strangers on airplanes, but more important, an empty seat acted as one more buffer in his carefully unobtrusive security system.

An occupant of the seat next to him might, if he—or she, Pedro carefully reminded himself—were extraordinarily clever, be able to lull him into lowering his guard just long enough to . . .

To what?

Kill him?

Possibly. Certainly such things had happened before. Two members of his fraternity had died in the last three years, suffering "heart attacks" on airplanes, expiring quietly in their seats with no one but their killers any the wiser until the planes were preparing for landing. Poison could be delivered in so many ways:

A fresh drink, prepared by a stewardess who was momentarily diverted from her work by an overly friendly passenger.

A tiny needle, expertly placed in the neck by someone who seemed accidentally to lose his footing while making his way to the rest room.

Pedro Santiago always took a window seat, and drank only from cans he opened himself.

Still, the instincts of his profession had told him that this would be an easy run. If danger awaited him, it would strike on the return trip, after the delivery, when the fee had been paid.

He raised the window blind and peered out into the bright morning. Far below, a solid bank of clouds obscured the sea and all but the very tops of three large volcanoes. Pedro shrugged; Hawaii's scenic splendor was of no interest to him. As the intercom came alive, announcing the imminent landing of the plane, Santiago picked up the makeup case and cradled it in his lap.

"All carry-on items must be stowed under the seat or in the overhead bin, Mr. Jennings," the flight attendant reminded him as she moved down the aisle with the last tray of empty cocktail glasses.

He smiled, nodded, put the case back under the seat in front of him.

The plane touched down, slowed, then taxied to the gate.

Pedro Santiago emerged from the jetway into the gate area and ignored the sign that directed him toward Customs.

One thing Santiago had never done in his professional career was risk carrying one of his packages past a Customs inspector. That kind of work was reserved for the mules—the stupid college students who would risk years in jail for less money than he could spend on an evening with a whore in Amsterdam.

While the other passengers flooded toward the Customs area, Santiago approached a man in a blue uniform who stood a few yards from the flight's arrival gate. "I believe you might be waiting for me," he said in an English as accent-free as was his Spanish, his Portuguese, and his Turkish.

"I believe you might be right, Mr. . . ." The man let the end of the sentence hang between them.

"Jennings," Pedro Santiago finished, completing the innocuous code that had been established when he'd agreed to deliver the Vuitton case.

"If you'll follow me."

The man in the uniform led Santiago to a locked door, punched a series of numbers into the combination plate, then held the door open to allow the courier to pass through ahead of him.

At the foot of a short flight of stairs, an electric golf cart waited. The man in the blue uniform steered it toward a helicopter waiting a quarter of a mile away. Following the man's lead, Santiago climbed into the chopper, pulled the door closed, and strapped himself securely into the seat. The engine ground for a second or two, then caught and roared to life. Above him the helicopter's huge rotor began to turn.

The pilot revved the engine, the rotor's speed increased, and the aircraft lurched up, tipped forward, and sped off across the field, staying low as it crossed the shoreline. Once over water, it shifted course slightly, briefly following the coast toward Honolulu before veering off to the southeast toward Molokai and Maui.

Forty minutes later Pedro Santiago peered down through the Plexiglas bubble in front of him as the helicopter swept across the rugged southeast coast of Maui and the dark blue surface of the sea was abruptly replaced by the undulating green carpet of the rain forest. The chopper dropped low, until it seemed to Santiago as if it were barely clearing the treetops. Then the trees gave way to a clearing dotted with several buildings whose green-tile roofs would make them invisible from any altitude higher than that at which the helicopter hovered.

Quickly, expertly, the pilot let the big aircraft settle onto a lawn surrounded by several buildings. As Santiago unstrapped himself from the seat and opened the door beside him, a man emerged from one of the buildings, but did not come toward the helicopter.

Instinctively recognizing his employer, though he'd never met him before, Santiago ducked his head protectively low as he dashed out from under the helicopter's downdraft, cradling the Louis Vuitton case in both his arms.

"Mr. — Jennings," the waiting man said, hesitating just long enough before using the alias to let Santiago know he felt the use of the code name bordered on the moronic. Santiago couldn't have cared less — code names had kept him alive and fattened his Swiss bank account beyond the dreams of most men who had been born in the slums of São Paulo. Nodding curtly, he followed the other man into the building, down a corridor, and into a small, windowless room bare of any furniture save a small table on which sat a case identical to the one Santiago carried.

The man nodded toward the table, and Santiago set his case down, then tried the lock of the duplicate. The latch snapped open and he lifted the case's lid. Though his instincts told him all the money would be there, he nonetheless took the time to count it.

It was in fifty-dollar bills, as he'd requested.

He'd had no particular interest in whether the serial numbers of the bills were sequential, but as he began counting them, he noted that they weren't.

Whoever he was dealing with knew what he was doing.

He finished his counting and looked up. "Two hundred thousand."

"Exactly as we agreed," the man replied.

Pedro Santiago packed the money back into the makeup case, changed its combination, and snapped its latch closed. "Then we're finished."

The man nodded and extended his hand. Santiago ignored the gesture, turning back toward the single door that provided the only access to the room. Accepting that Santiago had nothing more to say, the man escorted him back to the outside door and waited while the courier got back into the helicopter, closed the door, and strapped himself in. As the craft rose up from the lawn and moved back toward the sea, the man remained near the door, watching.

The moment the man disappeared from Pedro Santiago's view, Santiago began thinking about his next job, a run from South Africa.

That job, he suspected, would be a lot more interesting than this one had proved to be.

As the helicopter disappeared over the green horizon of the rain forest, the man reentered the building and closed the door behind him. Returning to the room where he had completed his transaction with the person he knew only as "Mr.

Jennings," he closed and locked the door, then opened the Louis Vuitton makeup case.

His hands trembled as he lifted the lid.

Inside the makeup case there was a single object.

A skull.

Its empty eyes stared up at him.

The hairs on the back of Pedro Santiago's neck suddenly rose and a tiny alarm sounded in his head.

Danger!

The helicopter was five miles off the coast of Maui, and though he couldn't have said what it was that set off his internal alarm, something had changed inside the cabin.

Not a movement—at least not a movement of the aircraft itself.

The pilot?

He couldn't be certain.

Being careful to give no sign that he was now on full alert, Santiago glanced over from the copilot's seat, but the pilot was staring straight ahead, seeming almost to have forgotten his passenger's presence.

Or was he looking for something?

Santiago's eyes left the pilot, sweeping the panorama of sea and islands that lay beyond the Plexiglas bubble that formed the cabin's front. A few boats were scattered over the ocean's surface, and except for a single airliner far in the distance, the sky was empty.

Yet Pedro Santiago's internal alarms were sounding louder than ever.

His body tensed, though he still had no idea what the threat might be, nor from what direction it would come.

Once again his eyes darted toward the pilot, and now he could see the tension in the other man's body: the narrowing of his eyes, the tightening of his grip on the helicopter's joystick.

Suddenly, a flicker of movement was reflected in the curve of the Plexiglas, a flicker so faint and distorted that Santiago almost missed it. Then, as his body tensed, he understood.

Behind him!

Someone was behind him!

But it was already too late. Even as Pedro Santiago instinctively started to duck away, the man who had hidden himself in the back of the helicopter during the few minutes the craft waited in the clearing released the latch on the door with one hand, while he freed Santiago's safety belt with the other.

At exactly the same instant, the pilot pulled hard on the joystick, and the chopper yawed over to starboard.

Even before he quite realized what had happened, Pedro Santiago was tumbling toward the sea, four hundred feet below.

CHAPTER
3

Michael stared down at the islands that had finally appeared out of the endless expanse of sea. Three months! Three whole months! What was he supposed to do here for three months? A couple of weeks, sure! But three months? He could barely believe his mother had actually yanked him out of school just as he was about to make the track team. Still, he sort of knew why she'd done it.

It was the black eye and the cut on his arm that had made up her mind. If he'd just managed to give Slotzky the slip that day . . .

But he hadn't, so now here he was, out in the middle of the ocean! He didn't know anybody at all, and he'd never really been very good at making friends, always afraid that his asthma would get in the way. So what was he supposed to do while his mom was working the dig? From what she'd said, there wasn't even a city on Maui—only a couple of little towns, and they weren't even going to be living in one of them! On the other hand, the islands *did* look beautiful, and there was always the possibility that maybe his mom would finally let him learn to scuba dive. Even now, he could remember his father promising to take him diving as soon as he was strong enough to pick up the tanks. But then . . .

A vision of the burning airplane in which Tom Sundquist had died filled Michael's mind, and he felt the familiar sick sensation that still came into his stomach whenever he remembered that morning when his whole life had literally blown up in front of his eyes. And now, just when it seemed like things were starting to go okay, his mom had made him come out here! "Will you at least let me learn to dive?" he asked, peering out the window at the islands below.

There was a bleakness in her son's voice that twisted Katharine's heart. It hadn't been as easy as she'd hoped to convince him that this was going to be a great adventure. Still, Michael had finally accepted the fact that they were going to go, and switched from trying to talk her out of the trip to attempting to convince her he should be allowed to go scuba diving. Rather than refuse outright, she'd taken the coward's way out. "We'll see," she now said yet again, wondering how much longer she could put off the inevitable confrontation that would occur when she finally told Michael she hated the idea of his risking his life under a hundred feet of water. But when he winced at her equivocation, she knew he'd already figured out what her final answer would to be. Now, trying to steer him away from the subject, she leaned across her son and looked out the window.

A chain of islands lay spread beneath the plane. The day was perfectly clear, and a snowcapped mountain peak glistened against a sky that was somehow even bluer than the sea. As the plane began its descent, the islands grew clearer, and then the pilot's voice came over the intercom, identifying them.

"To the right of the plane, we're getting a terrific view of Oahu today, while passengers on the left can see the peaks of Mauna Kea and Mauna Loa on the Big Island of Hawaii. In a few minutes we'll be able to look down into the craters of both Mauna Loa on the Big Island and Haleakala on Maui. I doubt any of you will have trouble figuring out which one is the active volcano."

As the plane descended, Katharine glimpsed the smoke boiling up from one of the active vents on the flanks of Kilauea, but then her attention was diverted by the pilot's voice.

"As we make the turn around Maui, passengers on the right side of the plane will be able to see the southwest coast of the island, with the resort areas of Wailea and Kihei stretched along what many people — myself included — believe to be the best string of beaches in the state. For those of you who are visiting, may I be the first to wish you aloha. For those lucky enough to live here, welcome home."

The plane swept lower and banked into the final turn. Through the window Katharine could see the coastline winding up toward Lahaina, and then the wildly rugged, green-clad buttresses of the West Maui mountains came into view. Below, a carpet of green spread across the valley floor.

The plane touched down, slowed, and turned to taxi up to the long, low building that housed the airport at Kahului. Michael was out of his seat the moment the DC-10 came to a stop, working his way around Katharine's legs in his anxiety to retrieve their carry-on bags from the overhead compartment. Three minutes later, Katharine stepped out of the plane and felt the first naturally warmed air she'd experienced in months. She walked quickly through the jetway into the gate area. Michael was already outside the glass doors, and when he turned, she could see the wide grin on his face. She took a deep breath as the doors slid open in front of her, and as the fragrant air filled her lungs, a single word came into her mind.

Soft.

It was the only word to describe the caress of the gentle breeze.

Soft.

"We're sure not in New York anymore, are we?" she heard her son say.

She glared at him with an expression of exasperation that was only slightly exaggerated. "I don't believe it! We're in paradise for three months, and all you can say is it's not New York?"

"Come on, Mom! I didn't say it was terrible! Actually, the weather's not too bad. It's—"

But Katharine was no longer listening to him, for she'd spotted a familiar figure at the far end of the long walkway.

A figure she hadn't seen since graduate school, but whom she nevertheless recognized instantly.

Rob Silver.

He was as lithe and muscular as he'd been twenty years earlier, but his face had weathered into a rugged handsomeness, and his mop of unruly hair had grayed slightly. His eyes, however, sparkling as they fixed on her, were every bit as blue as she'd remembered them. As he dropped a sweet-smelling lei over her shoulders, he echoed aloud the words that had popped into her head the minute she'd seen him: "My God, you're even more gorgeous than I remembered!"

While she tried to cover the flush that had come into her cheeks, he stuck his hand out to her son. "Hi," he said. "You must be Michael. I'm Rob Silver."

Michael hesitated, his eyes moving from Rob to his mother. He frowned, as if trying to puzzle something out, and when he at last took the hand that had been extended to him, Katharine could sense his reluctance. "Nice to meet you," he said.

As they headed toward the baggage area, Katharine knew that despite his words, Michael wasn't sure if he was pleased to meet Rob Silver or not.

She suspected that he was leaning toward "not."

"They actually pay you to work out here?" Katharine asked as Rob Silver turned his dusty Ford Explorer onto a four-lane highway that seemed to lead straight up the vast mountain that made up the southeastern half of Maui. The car's windows were wide open, and though the trade winds were blowing, the breeze held none of the bite of the harsh winter gale that had been lashing through the streets of Manhattan when they'd left the day before.

Rob gave her a mischievous glance. "Can I take that as an offer that you'll work for free?"

"Fat chance," Katharine replied. "I'm a poor working mother, remember? The happily starving student you used to know is long gone."

"Oh, I don't know," Rob drawled. "Doesn't seem to me like you've changed at all." Catching the look that came into Michael's eyes in the rearview mirror—a look made up of equal parts suspicion and disapproval— Rob dropped the flirtatious note from his voice. "Actually, I'm not sure what'll happen when I'm done with my project out here. I've got some feelers in at the university, but I suspect there are at least ten people I'd have to kill to get to the top of the list."

"How much longer does your grant run?" Katharine asked.

In the backseat, Michael turned and gazed out the window at the cane fields that lined both sides of the road, tuning out the conversation droning on in the front seat. Couldn't they ever talk about anything but money? Sometimes it seemed like that was the only thing his mother and her friends were really interested in.

Except for Rob Silver. From the moment he'd seen the way Rob Silver looked at his mother, Michael was pretty sure he knew what that man was interested in. And he was very sure that Silver and his mother hadn't just been friends back in college. He'd also understood that as far as Rob Silver was concerned, nothing had changed.

Funny how his mother hadn't said anything about *that* when she'd been trying to convince him that coming to Maui was such a great idea. Now, as the Explorer rolled through the fields, he was beginning to understand what she'd meant. Sure it was great for her—she got a good job, and plenty of money, and a man he could tell she was interested in, based on the way she'd looked at him at the airport.

So here he was, in a place where he didn't know a single soul except his mother, and with only about three months of school left. Too much for him to talk his mom into letting him skip the rest of the year—he'd already tried that one—but not enough to give him time to make any friends, despite what his mother had said. He could still hear her: "Of course you'll make friends. It's not like New York. It'll be easy."

But it wouldn't be easy. Easy? Michael wished his mom could understand how hard it really was to meet a whole new bunch of kids. Kids who might not like him. Or who might make fun of him the way they used to when he was sick all the time. Well, he wasn't sick anymore, so maybe things would be different. Maybe he wouldn't be quite as lonely as he thought. He sure hoped not.

His reverie was interrupted by the sight of a great plume of smoke billowing off to the left. "What's that?" he asked.

"Sugarcane fire," Rob Silver explained. "They burn the fields to make it easier to harvest the cane. That way they're not hauling a lot of extra vegetation around. You'll get so you automatically close the windows whenever you see it."

"How come? It's gotta be half a mile away." Just then a blob of black soot blew in the open window, smearing across Michael's shirt as he tried to brush it away. As he heard Rob laughing in the front seat, he felt his face redden.

"It's called Maui snow," Rob told him.

As the car climbed the flank of Haleakala, the cane fields were replaced by pineapple, and a few miles farther on, the pineapple, in turn, gave way to pastureland. But they were pastures that looked nothing at all like the farms of upstate New York. Here the pastures were an emerald-green, and dotted with jacaranda trees covered with lavender flowers.

A few miles farther on Rob turned off to the left. "That's where you'll be going to school," he said, tipping his head toward a cluster of buildings that lay off to the right. Peering out the window, Michael saw a campus that bore no resemblance to the school he'd attended in New York. Instead of a huge brick block of a building with a fenced-in, asphalt-paved lot next to it that served as an athletic field, this school consisted of a group of single-story buildings shaded by enormous trees, set in a spacious lawn. Beyond were a baseball field, basketball and tennis courts, and a full track as well as a football field.

Half a dozen guys were on the track, and as they drove past, Michael studied their speed and pacing, measuring his own abilities against the runners.

His mother turned in the front seat. "Do I get credit for being right about them having a track team?"

Michael tried to suppress the grin that was threatening to lighten his mood, but failed miserably. "I guess so," he admitted. "And I guess I can't really say the school in New York had a nicer campus, can I?"

"Hallelujah!" Katharine exclaimed. "Maybe there's going to be life after New York after all."

Less than a mile farther on they came to a tiny town. "This is Makawao," Rob said. "It used to be a cowboy town, but now it's the New Age capital of Maui. More different kinds of therapy than there are residents. All the most interesting people live up here, myself included." As the Explorer slowed to make a right turn, Katharine looked to the left and saw a two-block-long stretch of false-fronted buildings that looked as though they'd come out of a Western movie.

"Are they real?" she asked.

Rob nodded. "They've been fixed up, but they're pretty much the way they were when they were built. Except instead of selling saddles and bridles, now they have herbal teas and homeopathic remedies."

Just beyond Makawao, the street they took narrowed and wound steeply up the mountainside in a series of hairpin curves. Soon the tropical growth around the town yielded to groves of eucalyptus, then pines and cedars began cropping up. "Where are we going?" Katharine finally asked.

"To your house," Rob replied. "I found a place for you pretty close to the site. It's not very grand, but the school bus stop is only about a quarter of a mile away." He glanced in the rearview mirror once again. Michael, if he was even listening, said nothing, and when Rob looked over at Katharine, she only shrugged. "I hope you'll like it," he said.

"It seems like it's kind of far away from everything, doesn't it?" Michael asked from the backseat. "I mean, I can't drive, and it seems like it's an awful long way from the town, doesn't it?"

"How about a bicycle?" Rob suggested.

Michael gazed out at the steepening road. "That might work going downhill, but how do you get back up again? You'd need about fifty gears, wouldn't you?"

Rob winced as he realized Michael had a point, and that when he'd looked at the house, he hadn't thought about how Michael might get around. "Maybe I goofed," he admitted. "Actually, I guess I just picked the one I liked best. So if you hate it, you can find something else. Okay?"

Michael shrugged, but didn't say anything more.

Emerging from the cedars, they slowed for yet another hairpin curve, and finally turned onto a long, narrow, eucalyptus-shaded lane. Along both sides were scattered a few small, weathered wooden houses. After a quarter of a mile they came to the end of the lane, where a narrow driveway had been cut through a fence constructed entirely of eucalyptus logs stacked between the trunks of still-living trees. Inside the fence was a shady clearing, in the middle of which stood the most charming house Katharine had ever seen.

A single story, it was completely surrounded by a wide veranda. The roofline over the porch broke and became slightly steeper as it rose to a peak over the center of the house. Even at first glance Katharine could see that the building was perfectly rectangular, each face of the roof pierced by a small dormer. The posts and beams that supported the veranda were all adorned with latticework that gave the house a Victorian aura, despite its essentially Polynesian architecture.

Inside, there was a large living room, a kitchen, two bedrooms, and a bathroom. Outside the kitchen an area of the veranda had been closed in to make a makeshift laundry room.

Beyond the house, and the eucalyptus grove, a pasture spread down the mountainside like an undulating carpet, broken here and there by stands of eucalyptus and a few jacarandas. Beyond the pasture, the vista widened to include both coasts of the island, the valley that separated them, and the West Maui mountains, their wind- and rain-eroded flanks carved into a rugged wilderness.

Katharine stood on the veranda, exulting in the cool, eucalyptus-perfumed air. The sun was lowering in the western sky, birds were singing, and everywhere she looked there was a rainbow of colors provided by a lush profusion of tropical flowers.

She turned to Michael, who was just coming out of the house, a folder clutched in his hand. "Well?" she asked. "What do you think?"

Michael glanced at the view, and she could see him struggling to resist the beauty of the panorama spread beneath them. But finally he gave up and shook his head. "Okay, so maybe I was wrong," he said. "Maybe this isn't the worst place in the world after all. Okay?"

"So you don't hate your old mother?"

"I don't hate you," Michael replied, smiling at her exaggerated expression of relief. "And you're not old. Okay? And if you really want me to throw in the towel and agree you were right about this whole idea . . ." He let his voice trail off as he held out the folder. "Can I sign up for it?" he asked. "Please?" His voice held a plaintive note, half hopeful, half already resigned to the answer he expected.

Katharine took the folder. She knew, even before she looked at it, that it had to be an advertisement for scuba-diving classes. Her first instinct was to refuse flat out, but before she could speak, Rob appeared in the doorway behind Michael.

"It's really very safe," he said. "Hundreds of tourists do it every day, from little kids to people in their eighties."

Katharine looked up from the brochure, briefly meeting Rob's gaze before turning to Michael. Memories churned in her mind—nightmare memories of her son waking up in the middle of the night, gasping for air, barely able to breathe. What if he had an attack while he was fifty feet underwater? What would he do? If anything happened to him . . .

It was as if Michael had read her mind. "I'm not gonna drown, Mom. And I'm not going to have an asthma attack, either. I promise."

Still Katharine hesitated, but then she remembered something else: Michael's father, who had fallen in love with scuba diving long before his son had been born. Tom Sundquist had loved skiing, surfing, and sky-diving, and half a dozen other sports that terrified Katharine. And if he were here now, she knew exactly what he would say. Taking a deep breath, she spoke the words that Tom could not: "Go for it. You only live once, right?"

Michael, with a gleeful war whoop, gave her a bone-crushing hug, then disappeared into the house to set up a scuba lesson.

Rob spread his hands apologetically. "Maybe I shouldn't have picked up that brochure—" he began, but Katharine shook her head.

"I'm glad you did, Rob. He hasn't been at all happy about this move. Maybe this will help."

"I think I know where he's coming from," Rob said. "What is he, fifteen? Sixteen?"

"Sixteen."

"Tough time for a boy. I was just about his age when my mom met my—" Falling silent, Rob seemed to fumble for a moment, then awkwardly changed course: "Well, with a kid that age, you just have to cut him a little slack, you know? Part of him wants to try new things, but part of him doesn't want anything to change."

In her own mind Katharine finished the thought that Rob himself had been unwilling to say. *When my mom met my stepfather,* he'd been about to say. As the sun began to drop toward the horizon she stood on the veranda, gazing at him.

Rob's blue eyes searched her face.

Neither of them spoke.

Neither of them had to.

It was nearly two A.M. when Katharine awakened from a restless sleep. For a moment she didn't know where she was, but as she realized the traffic noises of New York had been replaced by the quiet sounds of chirping insects, and the parched air of the apartment had been displaced by a soft tropical fragrance, she remembered. Getting out of bed, she shivered in the chill of the high altitude as she pulled on a thick terry-cloth robe. On the veranda, she found that Michael had awakened and come outside, too. She stood quietly next to him for a moment, gazing up into a sky strewn with more stars than she'd seen since she had been in Africa. Finally she reached out and put her hand on Michael's shoulder. "It's not really so terrible, is it, sweetheart?"

Michael hesitated, then shrugged, and when he spoke, there was more pain than anger in his words. "No, it's not terrible. In fact, it's beautiful. But it's just that things were finally going good in New York, Mom. I mean, really good! And what if I can't make friends out here, or can't get on the track team, or—"

"Or what if you just give it a chance?" Katharine broke in. "Tomorrow you go scuba diving, so it isn't *all* so awful, is it?"

They stood quietly in the darkness for a few more minutes, and Katharine finally decided that his silence was at least better than the answer he could have given. When he didn't pull away from her good-night kiss, she decided that maybe, after all, things were going to be all right.

Michael, though, remained leaning on the veranda railing for a long time after his mother had gone back to bed, a confusion of emotions warring inside him. He hadn't meant to complain to his mom, and he was a little ashamed to have revealed his fears like some big baby. But he was still scared of facing a whole new school on Monday. And how was he going to live all the way up here for a whole three months?

Couldn't they at least have found a place at the beach?

CHAPTER
4

Michael glanced surreptitiously at the half-dozen people gathered around the diving instructor and wondered if any of them felt as nervous as he did. Yesterday, even this morning—hell, even half an hour ago!—diving in the ocean had seemed like a cool idea. But this morning he'd been in a swimming pool, where there was no surf, the water was shallow, and all that was in it were three novice divers and Dave, who instructed them while someone else stood on the edge of the pool, watching, just in case something bad happened.

Something bad, like starting to drown.

Now there were six people besides himself, which meant Dave wouldn't be able to watch everyone, and the Pacific was a lot bigger than a swimming pool. Plus, the wet suit had been pretty hard to pull on, its fit was uncomfortably tight, and it was getting really hot with the sun beating down on the black rubber. He was already starting to sweat and get itchy where the tiny rivulets of perspiration were creeping down his back.

The equipment looked a lot clumsier now than it had this morning, too. The tank was heavier than he remembered it, and once it was strapped onto his back, it seemed to pull him way off balance. Still, he'd come this far, and he wasn't going to chicken out now. Picking up his fins and mask, he checked the air regulator one more time, then started down to the beach.

The waves, which hadn't looked like much of anything a few minutes ago when they'd climbed out of the van and started carrying the equipment down to the little park above the beach, seemed suddenly to have swelled into huge crests, even though he was sure they hadn't.

Pretty sure, anyway.

Behind him, someone spoke: "This is your first dive, isn't it?"

Michael stiffened as he heard what sounded like a hostile note in the speaker's voice, and an image of Slotzky's sneering face rose in his mind. But Slotzky wasn't here—he was back in New York, where, Michael hoped, he was freezing his ass off. Still, Michael wasn't about to admit that this was his first dive and that he'd only had his pool training this morning. "I've done it a couple of times."

"I've been diving since I was ten," the voice said, and now Michael heard the lilt that he'd already come to recognize as the local accent. "The first time I was scared shitless, though. I mean, except for when I learned in the pool."

They were on the beach now, and finally Michael got a good look at the guy. He wasn't part of their group, and Michael could tell right away he wasn't a tourist, either. Though the guy was about his age, he was a little shorter and had a body that looked wiry even under the bulky wet suit. His eyes were almost as dark as his black hair, and when the boy grinned at him, his teeth looked almost unnaturally white.

Michael couldn't tell whether the grin looked friendly or not. "You diving by yourself?" he asked.

"Sure," the other boy said. "I do it all the time."

Michael remembered what Dave had said this morning about never diving without a buddy, but the boy didn't look like the kind who wanted to hear any advice from a beginner. He was pulling his fins on now, and Michael leaned down to follow suit. But even before he'd gotten his foot into the fin, it had filled up with sand, and by the time he struggled both of his feet into them, he'd almost lost his balance twice.

At least he hadn't collapsed onto the beach like one of the other guys had.

"See you in the water," the dark-haired guy said. Pulling on his mask and clamping his regulator in his mouth, the boy walked backward down the beach until he was waist-deep in the surf, then lay back in the water, rolled over, and disappeared.

Five minutes later Michael and the rest of the group were finally ready, and Dave led them into the water.

Michael was paired with a man named Les, who was about thirty and barely acknowledged his presence. Turning around to back into the water the same way he'd seen it done only a few minutes earlier, Michael nearly tripped three times before he finally got deep enough to try submerging himself. He put the regulator in his mouth, checked the valves to make certain everything was operating properly, and finally put his face mask in place. Then he took a deep breath, lowered himself and rolled over.

In an instant the world changed.

The wet suit no longer felt the least bit clumsy—in fact, it felt like a second skin, protecting him from the cold of the water, but hardly restricting his movement at all.

The water was crystal clear. Sand moved and swirled over the bottom, making it look almost as if the ocean floor had turned to liquid.

When he felt a slight pain in his chest, he realized he was still holding his breath. He forced himself to let it out, then slowly breathe in. His lungs filled with fresh air from the tank on his back. Taking a second breath, he looked around and spotted Les about twenty feet ahead of him, already swimming away from the beach. Michael's first instinct was to yell at him to wait up, but he realized that even if he could have shouted, there was no way the guy was going to hear him.

Better just try to catch up.

Michael swam, kicking hard with his legs, his hands clasped across his stomach just as Dave had taught them in the pool this morning. Aided by the fins, he surged ahead, leaving a small stream of bubbles from the regulator behind him. As he left the surf line, the bottom came into focus, the sand showing a gently rippled surface that sloped slowly deeper as he swam farther from the beach. With each stroke, he felt the tension inside him drain away, and a quiet peacefulness he'd never had began to enfold his spirit. The water around him glowed brightly with diffused sunlight, and suddenly a pair of fish, perhaps eighteen inches long, swam lazily across his path, coming so close that Michael could reach out and touch them. Then they darted away with no more than the slightest twitch of their tails.

He was closing in on Les now. The older man was turning to the right, and when Michael, too, made a turn, he caught his first glimpse of the reef.

From the surface it had looked like a finger of nearly black lava reaching out into the sea, but from below, Michael could see the bright reds and blues of coral heads, with hundreds of fish darting among them, some of them so pale they were nearly translucent, some so brilliantly colored they seemed to be acting as beacons in the sea. As he neared the reef, a group of parrot fish gathered around him, looking for food. When he produced nothing, they quickly swam off, heading off toward a woman who was floating on the surface a few yards away, breathing through a snorkel tube and holding out a handful of frozen peas that the fish snatched right out of her fingers.

Michael watched the feeding fish for several seconds, wishing he'd brought something along to attract them as strongly as the peas obviously did. The fish finished the food, then, as if by magic, disappeared. He had no feeling of having watched them go; it was as if they'd been there one second and vanished the next. He turned, looking for them, but saw only empty water.

Water empty even of Les, the man who was supposed to be his dive buddy.

Michael's first impulse was to surface and call for help, but then he realized that was exactly the wrong thing to do.

"Never let panic scare you to the surface," he remembered Dave telling them this morning. "On the first dive this afternoon, you won't be going deep, so there won't be any danger of getting the bends. But on a deep dive, a fast rise is the worst thing you can do. Come up too fast, and the best you can expect is pain like you've never felt before. The worst is that you could die." Dave had paused, letting the warning sink in. "But it's not just that," he went on. "If you find yourself alone, it could mean that your buddy is in trouble. Don't go looking for help. Remember, you're supposed to *be* the help. Only go to the surface if you have no other choice."

Throwing off the panic that was starting to coil around him, Michael filled his lungs with air, as much to reassure himself that he could still breathe as to gain the steadying effects of a deep breath.

Calmer, he looked around for Les. There was no trace of his assigned buddy, which could mean either of two things: Les was in trouble, or had simply gone his own way, never bothering even to glance back to see if he was still with him.

Either way, it wasn't a good situation, for if Michael got in trouble now, there was no one to help him.

Panic, sensing another opportunity, crept closer, but Michael brushed it away more easily this time. He had plenty of air, he wasn't in deep water, and his fins made him a much stronger swimmer than he normally was.

He turned toward the reef a dozen yards away, an expanse of lava covered with bright orange coral. There were several snorkelers hovering above it, and three divers at its base.

Three? Maybe he'd finally found Les!

He kicked his legs, and the fins sent him smoothly and quickly through the water. A few seconds later he was with the divers and recognized Les through his face mask.

And a second after that, without even acknowledging Michael's presence, Les moved farther down the reef.

The fear that had reached out to Michael earlier congealed into anger. What was the bastard up to? Whatever it was, it obviously didn't involve keeping an eye on him. What should he do? Give up the dive and head back to the beach? Or stick with Les, even though it was obvious he couldn't count on him if he himself got into trouble?

Then he remembered the other guy his own age, who was diving alone. Maybe he could find him, and the two of them could buddy up. He looked around. Les had disappeared.

Should he go look for him again? He told himself he shouldn't bother, then decided it didn't matter whether Les was going to watch out for him or not. He'd agreed to accept Les as a buddy—not that he'd been given much choice—and that was that.

Once again he started looking, this time moving higher in the water to swim over the top of the reef. There were fish everywhere now, triggerfish moving in large schools, a few brilliantly colored humahumas searching for food in the coral, and the ever-present parrot fish, nibbling at the coral itself.

But no sign of Les.

He dropped deeper in the water, swimming along the base of the reef, but still found no sign of Les. He was about to turn to search the other side of the reef when he suddenly saw something.

The end of a swim fin. It was just a single flipper, sticking out from the reef, its bright neon-green strip glittering in the sunlight. Had someone lost it?

Then it moved, kicking violently.

What the hell?

And suddenly Michael knew.

Someone was in trouble. It wasn't Les—his dive buddy had been wearing a pair of black fins identical to his own.

Kicking hard, Michael swam toward the fin, then came around a finger of the reef that jutted out from the main flow and saw what had happened. There was a hole in the reef, and the person whose foot was in the fin must have gone inside to take a look and gotten stuck. Now that he was closer, Michael could make out the person's legs. The second fin was dug into the sand in what Michael could see was a useless attempt to gain leverage. The sand was only swirling away, leaving a depression where the fin was searching for a toehold. Reaching out, Michael took hold of one of the fins. Sensing that help had arrived, the person caught in the small cave stopped kicking.

Nothing.

Michael moved up and reached into the cave, then knew why the diver couldn't get free: his tank was wedged in the coral lip at the top of the small cave. Moving cautiously closer, Michael tried to work the tank free, but the cave was so dark that he couldn't see it at all; indeed, he could barely reach it. Finally he did the only thing he could do: feeling for the buckles on the tank's straps, he worked them loose, then took a deep breath, braced his feet against the reef on either side of the small opening, grasped both of the diver's ankles, and pulled.

The person trapped in the cave slid out from under the tanks, and by the time he was out of the cave, Michael was ready. Taking one more deep breath, he pulled the regulator out of his mouth and pushed it toward the other diver's face.

It was the kid he'd talked to on the beach.

The kid who was diving by himself.

The other boy's face mask had come off as Michael pulled him out of the cave, but he felt the regulator Michael was offering him, slipped the mouthpiece between his lips, took a deep breath, and returned the regulator to Michael, pointing to the surface as he pulled the emergency cord on his life vest, inflating it. As the Hawaiian boy started to rise through the water, Michael inflated his own vest. Seconds later he was bobbing on the surface, face-to-face with the other boy.

A frightened gasp erupted from the guy's mouth.

"You okay?" Michael asked. "Can you make it to the beach?"

The boy nodded. "Where's your buddy?"

"He kept disappearing. I was looking for him when I found you."

They started swimming, the boy he'd rescued pacing himself in order to allow Michael to stay close to him until they were near the beach. Then the boy ducked his head under the surface. When he reappeared, he was standing in water that was only chest deep, although they were beyond the breaker line.

"Take your fins off," the boy told him. "Then we'll get your tank off your back."

Michael dropped in the water, pulled both his fins off, and stood up. He felt the other boy lift his tank so he could slip out of its straps. "What about yours?" he asked.

The boy shrugged. "I'll go get it later. At least I know where it is, and it's sure not going anywhere." As they plowed through the surf toward the beach, the boy stuck out his hand. "I'm Josh Malani."

"Michael Sundquist," Michael replied.

"Mike?"

"Michael," Michael corrected him. "Nobody ever calls me Mike."

Josh Malani's face lit into a wide grin. "Someone calls you Mike now. Get used to it. How long you gonna be on Maui?"

They were on the beach now. Dropping Michael's tank on the sand, they started peeling out of their wet suits. "I just moved here."

Josh's eyes lit up. "You mean you're not a tourist?"

Michael shook his head. "My mom's working here. We just got here yesterday."

"Not too bad, man," Josh told him. "Only here a day, and you already got a best friend!"

Michael bent down to pick up his tank, but Josh already had it and was starting across the beach toward the small park. Michael stayed where he was. "What if I don't like you?" he called after Josh. "What if you turn out to be a complete jerk?"

Josh glanced back over his shoulder, his trademark grin even broader. "Lots of people think I'm a jerk. But my grandfather's Chinese, and in China, if you save someone's life, you're responsible for him. You're stuck with me. Get used to it."

CHAPTER
5

Katharine was just putting the last suitcase on the shelf in her closet when she heard a horn honk and glanced out the window to see Rob Silver's Explorer emerging from the eucalyptus grove into the clearing. Her eyes flicked to the clock on the nightstand, and she noted with satisfaction that Rob's habit of perfect punctuality hadn't changed since graduate school. Two o'clock was what he'd said, and two o'clock it was, right on the dot. She picked up the battered canvas backpack that had served as her field purse since her days in Africa and went out to the veranda just as he swung out of the Explorer's cab.

"Let me guess," he said, with a wide smile. "You just put the last of the suitcases away as I was driving in, right?"

"Okay, so we're still the two most compulsive people we know." Katharine laughed as she got into the Explorer. "Although I still prefer to think of it as perfect timing. Do I need to lock the house?"

Rob shook his head. "Not up here. Did you find the keys? They were on the kitchen counter, I think."

"Got 'em," Katharine replied. "Let's go. I'm dying to get a look at this mysterious site of yours."

Rob swung the car around in a wide U-turn, maneuvered it along the narrow track through the eucalyptus grove, and turned down the hill. "You'll have a car this afternoon," he told her as they came to Makawao a few minutes later and he turned right to drive out toward Haiku. "Actually, it's pretty much like this one, just a little more beat up. But it's free."

Katharine's brows arched. "A salary that's twice as much as I usually get paid, travel expenses for me *and* my son, a house, and now a car. Who's funding you? It sure isn't the National Science Foundation!"

"You're right," Rob agreed. "It's not the NSF. It's a guy named Takeo Yoshihara. Ever heard of him?" Katharine shook her head. "His headquarters are in Tokyo, and he operates all over the world, but he spends a lot of his time here."

"How'd you find him?" Katharine asked. "And is there another one just like him who's interested in early man in Africa?"

"He found me," Rob explained. "He's interested in everything having to do with the Pacific Rim, including the native cultures. He's got quite a setup, which you'll see on the way to the site."

They'd passed through the loose collection of buildings that formed the town of Haiku, and a few minutes later emerged onto the Hana Highway. Rob turned right. After a few miles the road narrowed severely, winding through a series of tight turns that hung perilously close to a straight drop into the sea one minute, then plunged deep into the rain forest the next. "This is the weather side of the island," Rob explained. "The road's like this for another thirty-five miles. In the rainy season there are waterfalls and streams in every ravine you go through." He turned sharply off to the right, into a narrow lane that Katharine was certain she'd have missed entirely if she'd been driving herself. Paved only with two strips of concrete, the track wound through a dense forest of vine-covered trees, finally coming to a gate constructed of heavily patinated bronze and copper in bamboo forms that blended almost perfectly with the surrounding vegetation. The gate opened as the car approached, apparently of its own volition.

"All the cars that are authorized for entry carry beacons that activate the gate," Rob explained in answer to Katharine's unspoken question. When she turned to look back, the gate was already silently closing.

"What's he afraid of?" she asked.

Rob smiled. "I have a feeling Takeo Yoshihara isn't afraid of anything. He just likes his privacy. Believe me, he can afford it."

Katharine settled back in her seat as the car made one more turn and emerged from the rain forest into a scene that nearly took her breath away, not only in its unexpectedness, but in its sheer beauty.

The area that spread before her covered perhaps five acres. It seemed as if nature itself had sculpted the landscape out of the forest, though Katharine knew that was impossible. Still, the basic contours had to have been there from the start. Takeo Yoshihara's estate had been constructed on a broad terrace backed by a sheer face of fern-covered rocks, down which cascaded three separate waterfalls—bright silver ribbons that flowed from a ledge high above, filling the air with soft, babbling music as they tumbled into a pool below. In front of the pool was a lawn as perfectly kept as the fairways of the most exclusive golf course, an expanse of emerald interspersed with vividly colored beds of tropical flowers. Banks of towering red flowering ginger were counterbalanced by the most delicately colored stems of orchids Katharine had ever seen. There were rocks, too, great lava boulders, placed so artfully that for a moment Katharine was certain that nature herself must have laid them out. But as the Explorer moved along the gravel drive to which the twin concrete strips had now given way, she realized that she was seeing a Zen garden laid out on an enormous scale, for as the car passed among them, the rocks almost seemed to move, appearing and disappearing in an ever-changing pattern.

There were several buildings scattered around the perimeter of the huge garden, which she now realized formed a large courtyard. The buildings had an Oriental cast to them, but reflected the old Hawaiian culture as well. While the roofs were tiled in a green harmonious with the lawns and surrounding rain forest, she could easily imagine them thatched with palm fronds, and though the walls were covered with stucco, the huge supporting posts, exposed at every juncture, hinted at the ancient Polynesian boathouses from which the structures had taken their inspiration. As the car rolled to a stop in front of the largest building, a man stepped out onto the wide veranda that ran along the building's entire length.

Katharine knew without being told that this was Rob's benefactor, Takeo Yoshihara. He was tall and lean, and even before he strode down the two broad steps to meet her, his right hand outstretched in greeting, she sensed that she would find little of the rather stiff formality she'd come to expect in the few dealings she'd had with the Japanese over the years. Part of it, she knew, was the way he was dressed: a brightly flowered shirt, open at the throat, white cotton pants, and sandals.

"Dr. Sundquist!" Yoshihara's voice was as warm and friendly as the grip that closed on her hand as he stuck his own hand through the open window of the Explorer. He grinned as he added two more words: "I presume?"

Yoshihara's smile made up for the weakness of a joke Katharine had heard so many times before that it had long ceased to elicit more than a polite chuckle from her. This afternoon, though, as her eyes swept the dense rain forest that protected Takeo Yoshihara's estate from the outside world, she found herself breaking into a genuine smile. "Finally uttered in the proper surroundings," she offered. "And I suspect I'd be as lost as Livingston if I ever ventured very far into that forest."

"Why do I doubt that?" Yoshihara asked. "Could it be because Rob tells me you're one of the best field people he's ever met?"

Katharine saw no point in mentioning that she and Rob had barely seen each other for twenty years. "I hope I don't disappoint!"

Yoshihara stepped back from the Explorer. "I'm sure you won't. And I shall be very interested in hearing what you think of our little discovery."

After maneuvering the Explorer another mile along a pair of ruts so rough that they tested even the four-wheel-drive vehicle's toughness, Rob pulled to a stop in a second clearing in the rain forest. This one, though, bore no resemblance to the one they'd just left. Here there were no traces of manicured lawns, artfully arranged rocks, perfectly planted gardens, or beautifully designed buildings, but the scene that presented itself to Katharine was far more familiar:

There were a couple of large tents, little more than tarpaulins strung between trees, with additional sheets of canvas lashed to their edges to form makeshift walls that could be folded back whenever the weather was good enough. This afternoon, with the sky having turned leaden with the threat of a tropical shower, most of the walls had already been lowered, though in the wide gaps between the hanging canvases, Katharine could easily see the same kind of plank-and-sawhorse worktables that she herself had used so often. The clearing itself looked newly created, dotted with fresh-cut stumps of trees. At its edges there were piles of cuttings that were just beginning to rot, and on the opposite side of the clearing from where Rob had just parked the Explorer a shirtless man was hacking away at the undergrowth with a vicious-looking machete. A few yards to the man's left Katharine spotted what looked like a trailhead. "Does that lead to the site?"

Rob nodded. "From here, we walk. It's about another two hundred yards farther, but there's no way to get a headquarters any closer to the actual dig."

"Before we go up, may I take a look at what you've found so far?"

"Absolutely." He led her into one of the tents, where two large tables had been set up. One of them was still empty, and the other displayed only a dozen artifacts, consisting of little more than roughly worked pieces of lava.

"How long have you been working here?" Katharine asked, picking up a smoothly worn oblong object that looked no different from hundreds of other primitive grinding stones she'd seen.

"Two months," Rob told her. "And I've been pretty much on hold since you agreed to come. Been spending most of my time on a village out past Hana."

Katharine picked up another of the objects, turned it over, and again saw nothing particularly unusual about it. "Let's go up and see what you've got."

The path leading up to the site was steep and rocky. "How'd you ever find it in the first place?" Katharine asked as she stepped over a rotting log and tested the solidity of the ground on the other side before she shifted her full weight to it.

"I didn't. One of Yoshihara's gardeners was looking for a particular kind of fern up here, and he found one of the artifacts you saw back in the tent. Even after he brought me up, it took us a week before we were really sure we'd found something."

Fifty yards farther on they came into yet another clearing. This one, though very small, had been carved meticulously out of the rain forest, and Katharine could tell at a glance that the crew who had cleared it had been careful to disturb nothing on the floor of the forest. Except that the site wasn't actually on the floor of the forest at all, but on a ledge high up in one of the myriad tiny ravines that scarred this side of the mountain. A few yards farther up Katharine could hear the sound of a waterfall cascading into a pool—the alluring cascade in Rob's photos, she decided. The stream that drained the pool twisted through the bottom of the ravine.

"There was a vent up here, back when Haleakala was active," Rob explained. "Most of the ravines in this area are the result of erosion, but this one's different. It seems to have been formed by the volcano itself." He pointed to some yellowish deposits on an overhanging rock. "You can see the sulfur, which wouldn't be here if it had been formed by erosion."

Katharine moved closer. "You can still smell it! Are you sure the vent isn't active?"

"This is the year they declare Haleakala extinct," he told her. "There hasn't been any activity for two hundred years."

"Two hundred years is nothing, geologically speaking," Katharine reminded him.

"A nanosecond on an archaeologist's clock. But if the volcano boys say it's extinct, who am I to argue?"

Shrugging, Katharine shifted her attention to a rough circle of stones. It had not yet been completely uncovered, but even half buried, it was clear the rocks formed a fire pit. "You're going to want to be careful excavating that," she warned Rob. "You should be able to get some very datable material out of it."

"What do you mean, 'I should be careful'?" Rob asked. "I specialize in architecture, remember? Polynesian *architecture*." His glance scraped the rough rocks. "And I don't call this architecture. I call this a campsite." He smiled, his eyes taking on their mischievous twinkle. "Which is why I called you, and why I am paying you a king's ransom. Time to get out your little picks and brushes, Kath." His smile broadened into a wide grin. "And be careful as you excavate it," he added. "Someone told me there might be some very datable material in it. But the real reason you're here is this," he said, his tone serious now, as he stooped down to peel back a sheet of plastic that had been spread over an area a few yards from the fire pit.

Katharine exhaled sharply.

Bones.

No more deeply excavated than the fire pit, they barely showed above the surface, but even what little earth had been peeled away revealed what Katharine instantly recognized as the occipital area of a skull and part of a jaw. When she dropped down to her hands and knees to explore the bones with a slender dental pick she fished out of her backpack, Rob crouched down next to her.

"What do you think?" he asked.

Katharine, already concentrating on the nearly buried bones, hardly heard him, and several seconds passed before she answered his question.

Seconds during which a strange feeling gripped her.

Though she had no clear idea why, and though she could barely see them yet, she was certain that there was something wrong with these bones.

Something very wrong.

CHAPTER
6

"You're sure you don't want me to drive you?" Katharine asked.

Michael stifled a groan. It had been bad enough on Friday, when she insisted on going with him to the school to register. It wasn't like it was any big deal—all he had to do was fill out a couple of forms, and then they transferred all his records from New York through the computer. She'd only had to sign one form, and he could have brought it home, had her sign it over the weekend, and taken it back this morning. But no—she'd had to stand there peering over his shoulder like he was in the fourth grade or something, while all the kids who'd come into the office stared at him like he was some kind of geek who couldn't even get himself into school without his mommy holding his hand.

And now she wanted to drive him to school on the first day.

"I think I can walk to the bus stop, Mom," he said. "It's right at the end of the driveway, remember?"

"Just asking," Katharine told him, glancing at the clock and picking up her backpack. "I can drop you at the bus stop if you're ready."

Michael shook his head. "I've got half an hour before the bus."

"Then you can clean up the kitchen, okay? And I'll see you tonight." Kissing him on the cheek, she made her exit before Michael had a chance to argue.

A moment later he heard the engine of the nearly worn-out car that Rob Silver had loaned them grinding in protest as she tried to start it. For a minute it sounded as if the battery was going to give up before the engine caught, but then he saw a great puff of exhaust burst from the tailpipe, and the battered four-wheel-drive Explorer jerked down the drive toward the road.

Finally safe from the embarrassment of having his mother drive him to school, Michael cleaned up the breakfast dishes, ignored the mess in his room, stuffed his gym clothes, running shoes, and a notebook into his book bag, and got to the end of the driveway just as a mud-streaked yellow bus appeared around the uphill bend.

Climbing onto the bus, he spotted an empty seat near the back of the crowded vehicle and started down the aisle.

He felt every eye on the bus watching him.

Watching him, and sizing him up.

He could almost hear the word that was going through their minds:

Haole.

"White."

Josh Malani had warned him it was going to happen. "Some of the kids even got a special day here," he'd said on Saturday while giving Michael his first lesson in body surfing. "Kill a *haole* day. 'Course they don't actually kill guys with skin like yours. They just sorta try to change its color. Make it black and blue, instead of white."

"You're kidding," Michael had replied, though he was pretty sure Josh wasn't kidding.

Josh shrugged. "Hey, you guys came out here and stole everything, and ran everything your way for a couple hundred years. Times have changed."

Still, Michael had hoped Josh wasn't serious.

Now he knew he was.

Walking down the aisle, he suddenly felt like he was back in New York, with Slotzky looking for an opportunity to pick a fight. Except now there were half a dozen Slotzkys just on this bus, and God only knew how many waiting for him at school.

Should he look them straight in the eye?

That was the last thing you ever wanted to do in New York. If someone was looking at you, you just looked the other way, avoiding any direct eye contact.

Meeting someone's eyes was a challenge.

Better assume it was the same here, he decided. Keeping his eyes carefully on the floor ahead of him, Michael worked his way down the aisle to the nearest vacant seat, slid onto it, and tried to make himself inconspicuous.

The bus continued down the hill, making three more stops. Though he could feel every single person who got on the bus staring at him, no one spoke to him.

It was going to be every bit as bad as he'd thought.

The bus finally pulled to a stop in the school parking lot, and as it began disgorging its passengers, Michael sighed with relief: maybe nothing as bad as Josh had predicted was going to happen.

Maybe they were only going to ignore him.

But then, as he started up the aisle toward the door, he stopped. Two boys—each of them much bigger than him—had hung back, apparently looking for something they'd stuck under the seat in front of them.

How dumb did they think he was?

And why the hell couldn't Josh Malani have been on the bus with him?

Finally deciding they weren't going to leave until he did, Michael started for the door again. As he approached their seat, one of the boys moved into the aisle. For a moment Michael thought he was going to block him.

Instead, the other boy started toward the door.

Michael hesitated. He didn't want to look as if he were afraid of them. So what if they were both three inches taller than he was and outweighed him by at least forty pounds apiece? Looking scared was just what they wanted.

Michael kept moving. The second boy fell in behind him.

Right behind him—so close he could feel the boy's breath on the back of his neck.

"Why don't you pricks stay where you belong?" he heard the boy behind him mutter, not quite loudly enough so the bus driver would be able to hear. As the guy behind him spoke, the one in front of him stopped short.

The one behind him gave a hard shove.

"What the fuck you doin', asshole?" the guy ahead of him demanded, whirling around to cast malevolent eyes on Michael. "You *haoles* all think you own the world. Well, you can eat my shit!"

Michael knew nothing he said was going to get him out of this. He braced himself for the fist that was about to plunge into his gut. Then he heard another voice.

"Not till you're off my bus," the driver said, standing and fixing Michael's tormentor with a baleful glare.

The boy in front of Michael hesitated a moment, then turned and got off the bus. Michael, with the second guy crowding him from behind, had no choice but to follow. He readied himself for the confrontation and prayed that Josh Malani might appear. Even if Josh turned out to be no better than he at fighting guys twice his size, he might at least be able to talk these creeps out of killing him.

By the time he was out of the bus, the situation had changed, if only slightly. For the moment, at least, they were surrounded by a couple dozen other kids. Whatever Michael's two tormentors were planning seemed to get put on hold, at least temporarily. The bigger one gave Michael the same kind of stomach-churning stare he'd seen in Slotzky's eyes the day he'd gotten his black eye and the cut on his arm. "After school," the boy said in a grating voice. "Or maybe tomorrow. But don't worry, *haole*—we're gonna put your face in it." Then he turned away, and both he and his friend disappeared into the crowd of milling students.

As he watched them go, Michael wondered how much more of a punch this guy packed than Slotzky had back in New York.

Probably a lot.

The slight shift in the crust of the earth beneath the island of Hawaii was so small, and occurred so slowly, that for several hours it went unnoticed by anything except the machines.

The machines, of course, noticed everything, for that's what they had been designed to do. Sensitive instruments perceived the small tremors that resulted as a new fissure opened deep in the bowels of the great volcano Mauna Loa, recording those tremors and reporting them to other machines.

No alarms sounded, no sirens wailed warnings of the tidal waves that can be generated by the sudden major shifts that sometimes occur on the ocean floor.

Instead, the machines whispered among themselves, passing the news of the activity beneath Mauna Loa from one information nexus to another, until, long before any man was aware of the movement, the computers of the world were already building models to project what the slight shifts might mean for the future of the planet.

Deep beneath the mountain, the magma, molten and seething, made its way toward the surface, oozing through the cracks and crevices the pressure from below had caused, widening them and filling them, gathering force from below to propel the climb upward to the surface.

And as the magma moved, the mountain gave way to it, and the tremors increased.

Men, as well as machines, began to notice.

Among the first on Maui to note the trembling in the earth beneath their feet were the technicians tending the array of telescopes at the top of Haleakala. Their computers were programmed specifically to alert them to volcanic activity. Despite the massive concrete blocks on which the telescopes sit and the shock absorbers that are designed to protect them from the smallest vibrations, tremors in the earth wreak havoc with observation of the universe beyond the planet's bounds.

When the earth moves, nothing stops it.

And astronomical observation stops instantly.

Phil Howell was annoyed. Experience told him that these tremors almost certainly would continue, at least for the next few days. It meant there would be no more observation of a star he'd been watching deep in the Whirlpool Galaxy, fifteen million light-years away.

Howell was fascinated with the star for two reasons. The first was that it seemed to be the source of a signal that various radio-telescopic antenna arrays had begun picking up a few years ago. So far the signal existed only in fragmented bits and pieces that he was only now beginning to assemble into a whole.

The other reason for Phil Howell's fascination with the star was that it was going nova. The radio signal, he was almost certain, would eventually prove to have been a precursor to the star's impending destruction.

But now the computer had alerted him that the unrest in the earth was going to postpone his observations of the sky indefinitely. Leaving the computers to continue their work on the fragments of radio signal, he decided to take the rest of the day off and drive out to see the site Rob Silver had been talking about for the last month. Rob's discovery was intriguing; even more intriguing was the opportunity to meet Katharine Sundquist, the woman who seemed to fascinate Rob Silver every bit as much as the distant star fascinated Phil. Leaving the computers to tend to the universe, he locked his office and headed out toward Hana.

Click!

The shutter snapped, the automatic film advance hummed, and Katharine adjusted her position slightly, as oblivious to the flies that were hovering around her as she was to the sweat that was running down her face in muddy rivulets. Every bone in her body ached from the hours she'd spent crouched over the skull—now nearly fully exposed—but she was no more aware of the pain in her joints than of the heat and the insects.

The important thing was to get the pictures, to have the visual proof of the position in which the skull, and the rest of the skeleton, had been found.

She pressed the shutter release again.

Click!

Another whir, another painful adjustment in her position.

Another photograph.

Another document to prove eventually that despite the fact that what she was uncovering made no sense, it had, in fact, been found in exactly this position, at exactly this location.

She'd been laboring on the excavation for two days now, carefully scraping away the deposits to expose the remains, with no sense yet of when the body had been buried. From what she'd seen so far, it could have been a year or a decade or a century.

A thousand years? Four thousand years? Certainly no more than that, for man hadn't been on Maui—or anywhere else in Hawaii—any longer than that, and no animal except man built fire pits.

Undoubtedly the site was much younger than a thousand years—probably only a few hundred, given how shallow it was.

She'd refused to let Rob's crew help with the excavation of the skeleton, assigning them to the area around the rudimentary fire circle. The contents of the circle itself were still undisturbed. Having decided to work on the skeleton first, Katharine immediately ordered the fire pit covered and declared it off limits. Once she'd exposed every one of the bones, photographing them at every stage of their excavation until she was satisfied that she had a complete record of their recovery and would feel comfortable about moving them to a lab, she'd turn her attention to the fire pit.

"I want every layer kept separate," she'd explained to Rob. "Even if I have to peel it down a millimeter at a time."

"What is it you think you've got here?" Rob asked, realizing she was dead serious about doing all the excavation herself.

When he first asked the question, she had no answer for him. She'd been acting purely on instinct—that intuition born of experience that told her that she'd never seen a site quite like this one.

As she began exposing the skull, though, her motives for not telling Rob what she was thinking had changed.

The fact was, what she was thinking made no sense.

As she'd first begun uncovering the skull, it had been clear that it was some sort of primate. That alone was strange enough, because she was well aware that there were no primates native to Hawaii.

In addition, the positioning was problematic: you wouldn't find a chimpanzee or gorilla—or any species of primate, for that matter—next to a fire circle. Not unless someone had killed the animal and left it there.

A scenario, she knew, that was possible, but unlikely, given the location.

But as she kept digging, patiently cleaning the skull with dental tools and brushes, she began to realize that it didn't look like a primate at all.

What it most closely resembled, in fact, was some of the early hominids.

That, of course, was impossible.

First, early man hadn't existed in Hawaii.

Second, this particular site hadn't existed at the time of early man.

Therefore, the skull had to be something else. Whatever it turned out to be, she was determined to have a perfect scientific record to back up the assertions she would eventually make.

She took one more photograph, and as the camera began rewinding, she stood, stretched, and took a deep breath, wincing as her nostrils filled with the sulfurous odor that seemed to be hanging over the site more strongly than usual today. She was reloading the camera when she heard Rob's voice.

"Kath? Got a visitor who wants to meet you!" Looking up, Katharine saw Rob step into the clearing. Behind him was a second man the same age as Rob. "This is Phil Howell. He's the head stargazer up at the top of the mountain. Phil, this is Katharine Sundquist."

Phil Howell stepped forward, extended his hand, then lifted his brows as he got a whiff of the scent of rotting eggs. "My God! What are you excavating with, sulfuric acid?"

Katharine shook her head. "Just deposits around an old vent. But it seems to be worse today."

The astronomer frowned. "Are you sure?"

Something in his tone set off an alarm in Katharine's head. "I think so," she said. "I assume it has to do with the rain we had this morning."

"Or maybe the earthquakes opened up a pocket of gas," Howell replied.

Katharine's gaze shifted worriedly to Rob. "Earthquakes?" she repeated. "What's he talking about?"

"The volcano," Phil Howell said before Rob could speak. "Looks like it's getting ready to kick up again."

Katharine's heart skipped a beat and she looked at Rob again. "You said it was extinct!"

"It is," Rob assured her. "He's talking about Kilauea on the Big Island." He could tell by the look on her face that Katharine wasn't convinced. "Tell her, Phil. She obviously doesn't believe me."

Katharine listened silently as Phil Howell explained the volcanic movement under the Big Island. "It's not just the earthquakes," he finished. "If it really gets going, it spews so much dust into the air you can't see anything even if the scopes are holding still." He paused. "Makes you wonder if mountaintops are really the best places for observatories, doesn't it?"

Katharine made no reply, but as she began showing the site to the astronomer, she found herself glancing toward the hole in the side of the ravine that marked the ancient volcanic vent. All but lost in the tangled vegetation of the rain forest, it certainly looked harmless enough.

As she tried to concentrate on what she was saying, she kept thinking that the smell of sulfur was growing stronger.

Should she mention it to Rob and Phil? But no, they seemed unconcerned. It must be her imagination.

It had to be.

The hostility from the two guys on the bus followed Michael around all day long. Wherever he was, they seemed to be there, always together, always watching him. During the break between his last two classes, they'd shoved him up against a locker.

"Another hour," the bigger one had growled. "Then you're dead meat, *haole*." So far, though, they hadn't actually tried anything, and if they were planning to wait for him after school, they were going to have to wait a long time, for today Michael was going to do something he'd never done before. Today, for the first time in his life, he was actually going to go out for a team.

He made up his mind during gym class. He'd been checking his breathing all day, and there hadn't been any problems. In fact, he felt better than ever. "Just wait," Josh Malani told him as they'd jogged around the track. "Sometimes the trades die down, and they start burnin' the cane fields, and the mountain on the Big Island goes off. Man, you could choke to death around here!"

But his breathing had been deep and easy, and even after he'd finished three laps, he barely felt it. So when he'd seen the track team practice schedule posted on the bulletin board in the locker room, he decided. Today was the day.

Now, as the final bell sounded and he left his last class, instead of heading out to the side of the school where the buses—and the two guys—would be waiting, Michael went the other way, toward the locker room.

Stripping off his clothes, he put on his gym shorts, still damp from P.E. class that morning. He laced up his shoes carefully, making sure they weren't so tight his feet would start swelling before he even got warmed up, then left the locker room and trotted out to the field, where the track team was already starting their warm-up calisthenics.

Should he go over and join them, or warm up by himself?

What if he went over just like he was one of them, and then didn't make the team when he tried out? Better just to take a couple of laps around the track.

He finished the first lap and was a hundred feet into the second when he felt a sharp elbow dig into the ribs on his right side.

"What do you think you're doin', jerk?" a familiar voice said.

Michael glanced over without turning his head. It was the bigger of the two guys from the bus. And he was wearing a track suit.

Saying nothing, Michael kept running.

The other boy, towering half a foot over Michael, shortened his stride enough to match Michael's pace. "Can't you talk, asshole?"

Michael remained silent, but kept running, concentrating only on his pace, determined neither to change it nor to break stride. If the guy was going to shove him off the track, so be it. But he wasn't going to quit.

They rounded the last turn. As Michael dropped his pace back to a walk and approached the coach, the other boy kept going, stepping up his own stride with an ease that made Michael question whether he shouldn't just head back to the locker room, take a shower, and go home. Then he saw the other guy from the bus, his lips curled into a contemptuous sneer, as if the guy knew exactly what was going through his mind.

With perfect clarity, Michael knew that if he walked off the field now, he'd hate every single day he had to come back to Bailey High. Taking a deep breath, he walked up to the coach. "I'm Michael Sundquist," he said. "I want to try out for the team." He felt the coach look him over with appraising eyes, and easily read the doubt in his face. "I'm a sprinter."

"I think I can make up my own mind about what you can do," the coach said. The team, except for the one guy who was still running around the track, laughed, and Michael tried to ignore the burning in his face. But when he didn't flinch from the words, the coach relented. "Okay, what do you want to try?"

"The hundred meter, or the two hundred," Michael offered.

"How about the four hundred?" the coach asked.

Michael bit his lip, then decided he'd better tell the truth. "I had asthma. I'm not sure I can last that long, full-out."

The coach raised a brow, but when he spoke, his voice carried no note of judgment. "Okay. I'll tell you when to go." Pulling a stopwatch out of his pocket, he set it, then handed it to the second of the guys from the bus. When the timer had reached the mark a hundred meters down the track, the coach nodded to Michael, who moved out to the starting blocks. "On your mark."

Michael dropped to a crouch, putting his left foot against the block.

"Set."

Michael tensed, ready for the coach to utter the final word.

And waited.

What on earth was going on? Was the coach pulling some kind of joke on him? His legs began to ache. Jaw clenched, determination tensing every muscle, he crouched low to the track. His left foot still braced, he remained tensed to take off. Then, as he heard feet approaching from behind him, he understood.

Sure enough, just as the guy who'd elbowed him a few minutes ago passed him, the coach shouted, "Go!"

As Michael launched himself off the block, he could see the bigger boy, already ahead of him, increase his pace. Swell! Not only was he going to have to try to catch up with someone who had a head start and was bigger, but he was going to have to eat dust, too.

Well, if that was the game they wanted to play, fine!

Sucking air deep into his lungs, Michael lunged forward, hitting his full stride in the first two steps, then pouring on as much speed as he could muster.

After he'd gone ten steps he realized the runner ahead of him was no longer widening the distance.

In fact, the gap was narrowing.

Then he heard a voice yelling from the bleachers and glanced over to see Josh Malani jumping up and down. "Go, Mike! Go!"

Clenching his fists as if to squeeze even more energy out of his body, Michael focused on closing the gap. After they had run forty meters, there were only four meters between them.

At seventy meters, Michael was only a foot behind.

He came abreast of the other runner at eighty meters, and when he crossed the finish line he was at least a full meter ahead.

Slowing down, he waited for the consequences. The guy already hated him just because of the color of his skin, and now he'd beaten him in front of his friends. Great!

Josh Malani was out of the bleachers, jogging across the track. "Way to go, Mike! You left him in the dust!"

Without warning the guy he'd just beaten, who'd earlier looked as if he was ready to smash Michael's face, stopped short, his expression confused. "You're Mike Sundquist?" he demanded.

"Michael," Josh said immediately. "He hates it if you call him Mike."

"So that's why you call him Mike?" the guy with the stopwatch demanded. "I thought he pulled you out of the reef!"

"He did."

"So show a little respect!" He turned to Michael. "Malani gives you any trouble, you let me know. I been wantin' to kick the shit out of him for years, but he's too small to bother with. Even smaller than you. But he can't run!"

Michael's head was swimming. What was going on?

"How'd you do that?" the defeated runner was asking now. "Jesus, man! I was ten meters ahead of you, and goin' full speed when you started!" Slinging an arm around Michael's shoulders, he started back toward the coach and the rest of the team, calling out to the boy with the stopwatch. "Hey, Rick, how fast did he do that hundred?"

"A little more than eleven seconds," the timer replied.

"That's a whole second faster than anyone we've ever had," the other one said. "I can do the long stuff, but it's a bitch getting up to speed."

Michael eyed him suspiciously. "I thought I was supposed to eat shit!"

The huge boy grinned. "That was when you were nothin' but a stinkin' *haole*. I'm Jeff Kina." He stuck out his hand, then turned to call to the coach, "Hey, Mr. Peters, he's on the team, isn't he?"

"He is, but I don't know how much longer you will be. How'd you get beaten by someone half a foot smaller than you, when you had a head start?"

An enormous laugh rumbled from Jeff Kina's throat. "Hey, I can't do everything, can I? So what I can't do, Michael will take care of, and this year we'll kick everyone's ass. Right?"

For the first time, Michael began to think that coming to Maui might not have been such a bad idea after all, and when he called home an hour later— his first track practice behind him—he didn't even bother to pretend to be cool.

"It's me, Mom," he said when the answering machine picked up his call. "Guess what? I did it! I made the track team! Can you believe it? I *made* it!" He paused for a second, then rushed on, his words spewing out in a torrent of excitement. "I've met a whole bunch of new guys, and they're really great. Except that one of them was gonna—" He cut himself short, then quickly changed course. No use getting his mother all upset by telling her some-one had threatened to beat him up this morning. Besides, that was all over now. "Anyway, I'm gonna go out with Josh and a bunch of guys from the team. We're going over to Kihei and grab a burger and go to a movie or some-thing, to celebrate. I'll be home by ten-thirty, maybe eleven. Isn't it great that I made it? See you later!" Hanging up the phone, Michael grinned at Josh Malani and Jeff Kina, who were waiting for him by the door. "Where're the other guys?"

"They took off already," Josh told him.

"Then let's go!" Michael said, picking up his book bag. "Anybody know what movies are playing?"

But as they were leaving the locker room and heading toward the parking lot, Josh Malani came up with another suggestion—one that had nothing to do with movies. As he listened, Michael felt a knot forming in his stomach.

Part of it, he knew, was excitement at the idea Josh was proposing.

But another part of it was fear.

"Night diving?" he asked as he tossed his book bag into the back of Josh's Chevy pickup. "Isn't it dangerous?"

Josh grinned at him. "A little, maybe. But so what? You're gonna love it!"

Maybe I should call Mom back, Michael thought as he and the two other boys piled into Josh's rusting pickup truck. Maybe I should tell her what we're really doing. After all, if something happens . . .

Forget it, he told himself. All she'll do is worry.

CHAPTER 7

"You sure this is a good idea?" Michael asked again. He, Josh Malani, Jeff Kina, and two other guys from the track team—Rick Pieper and someone named Kioki, whose last name Michael didn't remember—had grabbed hamburgers, fries, and Cokes at a place called Peggy Sue's. As they ate, Josh explained how they would equip themselves at Kihei Ken's Dive Shop: "He leaves the key under the barrel behind the back door."

"What's that got to do with it?" Michael asked, though by now he thought he knew Josh well enough to be certain that whatever peculiar illogic his friend might come up with, he would manage to make it sound reasonable.

"Ken's my friend, and he'd say it was okay."

"Why don't you just call him and ask him?" Michael asked, which only netted him one of Josh's patented looks of complete scorn.

"He's off-island, for Christ's sake. He's over on Lanai and won't be back till tomorrow. Come on, Mike, don't give me a hard time! I'm your best friend."

"You're also crazy," Michael reminded him.

Josh's affable grin spread wide. "That's not news. But you still saved my life, so I wouldn't mess you up, would I?"

At the time, the final logic had seemed impeccable. Now that he was actually standing at the back door of Ken's Dive Shop with three guys he'd known only since that afternoon, and one good friend who was—according to everyone who had known him a lot longer than Michael—certifiably crazy, he wasn't so sure.

What if an alarm went off?

What if they got caught?

What if they got taken to jail?

But even as the questions rose in Michael's mind, Josh Malani fished the key out from under the barrel in back, unlocked the door, and flipped on the lights.

"Jeez, Josh! Shut off the lights!" Jeff Kina demanded.

"Why?" Josh asked. "We're not doing anything wrong. Come on in and help me find what we need."

It didn't take nearly as long as Michael thought it would: within ten minutes they had enough gear for all five of them in the bed of Josh's truck. But as Jeff Kina started loading air tanks, he swore.

"What's wrong?" Michael asked.

"There's only one full tank," Jeff said. "Any of you guys know how to work the compressor?"

Everyone shook their heads and shrugged helplessly, and Michael felt a moment of relief, thinking they might have to bag the whole plan. But just as he was about to suggest they haul the gear back in from the truck, Josh found five more tanks on a shelf next to the door that separated the back room from the shop. His new friends loaded four of them into the truck, with the full tank from the first batch of tanks they found, then the boys all piled in.

They drove south on Kihei Road, through Wailea and out past Makena Beach. The road narrowed and grew bumpy, and finally they came to a tiny cove where the water glittered in the light of an almost full moon. Michael began to relax, then realized Josh wasn't going to stop. "What was wrong with that bay?" he asked, peering back over his shoulder. Even in the darkness, the inlet looked reasonably safe.

"LaPerrouse?" Josh asked. "That's for tourists. We're goin' to the goldfish bowl."

They kept moving farther south. Finally, the dense thickets of kiawe that lined both sides of the road gave way to what at first looked to Michael like a huge field of freshly plowed earth, hundreds of acres of it, spreading away from the road in both directions. Then he realized he wasn't looking at a field of earth at all: he was looking at raw lava.

Lava so desolate that practically nothing grew on it. In the darkness, it held a forbidding aura that made him shiver despite the warmth of the air.

They were deep into the lava field when Josh pulled the truck off the road into a narrow parking area.

Michael looked around, seeing nothing but the vast expanse of lava. "Where's the goldfish bowl?" he asked.

"At the end of the flow," Josh told him. "There's a path a little further down the road, but this is as close as you can park to it. Practically nobody knows about it." The five boys scrambled out of the truck, slung their air tanks onto their backs, and picked up the bags they'd filled with regulators, masks, fins, and life vests. Josh led them down the road two hundred yards, then stepped over a pipe that ran parallel to the asphalt pavement.

"What's that?" Michael asked.

"Water pipe," Jeff Kina told him. "It's too hard to bury it in the lava, so they just lay it along the surface next to the road."

They were picking their way through the lava now, but Michael saw no sign of anything that looked like a path until they came to a sign that warned them against overnight camping. "This is really a path?" he asked as he gingerly made his way across lava that looked sharp enough to slash him if he so much as touched it.

"That's the neat thing," Josh explained. "If you don't know exactly where it is, you can't find it."

"I know where it is, and most of the time I still can't find it," Rick Pieper muttered. "Last time I came out here, I almost tore my feet off."

"Quit bitchin'," Kioki told him. "It's easy." Then, a second later, he lost his balance, instinctively put a hand out to steady himself, and howled in pain. "Goddamn it, I hate this stuff!"

"So go back and wait in the truck," Josh told him.

"No chance," Kioki shot back. "I'm okay."

Forty minutes later they came to a small cove that was almost completely landlocked by a long tongue of lava that protected it from the open ocean. While the pool itself lay serenely still, no more than twenty feet away the heaving sea clawed at the embracing arm of rock. It was as if a hungry animal were attempting to dig its prey out of a protective burrow. The surf snarled, and angry fountains of foam spewed into the sky like the anticipatory saliva of a beast about to feed. For a long time Michael stared at the spectacle, wondering how safe the pool really was.

"It's okay," Josh Malani told him, once again accurately reading his thoughts. "There's only one channel into the pool, and it's over on the other side, in the lee. There's hardly even any current, and I won't be more than a couple yards away from you. Okay?"

Michael nodded, still unsure if he wanted to go into the water, which seemed to have darkened even as he stared at it. He told himself it was only his imagination, since the moon was shining as brightly as ever. The other guys were already stripping their clothes off, and soon all of them were naked and helping each other strap on their tanks and check their regulators. Then, one by one, they went into the pool, until only Michael and Josh were still on the beach.

"You want to skip it?" Josh asked. There was nothing of his usual mocking tone now, and Michael guessed that if he decided to chicken out, Josh would make sure the other boys thought it was his own idea to stay out of the water. In fact, he suspected Josh might even go as far as to slash his foot on the lava, if he thought that's what it would take to convince everyone that Michael hadn't lost his nerve.

He looked at the water once more, then punched Josh on the shoulder. "Let's do it," he said.

They backed in until they were up to their waists, then Michael checked his regulator one last time, lowered himself, stretched out, and rolled over.

The water closed around him, and, as it had on his first dive, the world changed.

It was nothing like the daytime dive. The sunlight was gone, and with it the Day-Glo colors of the coral and the fish. Now the water was infused with a silvery glow from the moon, and the fish that darted among the shadows of the pool appeared as no more than phantoms. Here and there phosphorescent creatures glowed, and occasionally a fish glimmered brightly as the moonlight caught its scales.

Josh Malani turned on a flashlight, and everything changed once more. The ocean came alive with creatures attracted by the light, and the water that only a moment ago seemed populated by nothing more than a few ghostly floating shapes was transformed into a whirling kaleidoscope of lemon tangs, damselfish, and butterfly fish. Beyond the brilliant cone emanating from Josh's flashlight, there was only an inky blackness, and suddenly Michael wished Josh hadn't turned on the light at all. He was about to signal Josh to turn it off when a large shape drifted into the light, startling Michael for a moment before he recognized it as a sea turtle. The turtle swam gracefully toward them, hovered in the light for a few seconds, then turned away, disappearing into the surrounding darkness. Maneuvering close to Josh, Michael motioned for him to kill the light, and a second later both boys were plunged momentarily into total blackness.

Michael's night vision slowly returned as the pale glow of moonlight filtered through the curtain of black. With Josh just ahead of him, Michael drifted through the water, feeling lazily disconnected from the world beyond the crystalline basin. The water was no more than fifteen feet deep, and even in the dim moonlight the bottom was clearly visible. The tendrils of anemones waved gently in the nearly still water, and the dark spines of sea urchins protruded from holes in the lava.

Time seemed to slow as the ghostly shapes of fish floated around him.

A large sea snail crept along the lava floor of the pool, antennae extended, mantle partially covering its bright shell. Michael dove deeper, intent on getting a closer look at the snail, when something else attracted his attention.

There was a crevice in the lava, with something protruding from it.

Michael changed course, moved closer to the crevice, then recognized what he was seeing.

A moray eel! Its rows of sharp teeth glistened in the moonlight as it slowly flexed its jaw.

Carefully, trying to move slowly enough not to disturb the eel, Michael inched closer.

The eel, seeing him coming, opened its jaw wide. Its entire body seemed to tense.

It waited, watching, ready to strike.

Josh Malani hovered about six feet beneath the surface, watching an octopus that appeared to be staring right back at him. Twice he'd reached out to try to touch the small cephalopod, but each time it shrank away from him, and Josh had the eerie sense that the little creature felt as strange in the moonlit water as he did himself. The fact was, he kind of wanted to turn the flashlight back on, if for no other reason than to regain the sense of familiarity that the bright colors of the coral and the fish would bring him. Being in the dark was kind of like wandering in a graveyard: he was sure there wasn't anything in the pool that could really hurt him, but the shadowy water alone was enough to make him nervous. Thus, when the first touch came, he was so startled he almost yanked on his emergency cord.

Then he realized it had to be Michael, letting him know he was there.

Then the second touch came.

Not gentle like the first, but sharp—as if claws had raked across his side.

Reflexively jerking away, Josh once again had to resist the instinctive urge to jerk on the emergency cord that would release the CO_2 cartridge, inflating his life vest and shooting him to the surface. Forcing himself not to give in to the surge of panic that shot through him at the clawing touch, he twisted around in the water, searching for the source of the attack.

At first he saw nothing. Then, out of the corner of his eye, he spotted a shape moving toward him. For an instant he felt the strictures of panic close once more around him. But then he realized what the shape was.

A turtle! Nothing but the sea turtle coming back for another look at the odd-looking creatures that had invaded its environment. Probably the same one he and Michael had seen a little while ago.

Michael!

Where was he? Josh looked quickly around but saw no sign of his friend. He'd just been there, right behind him, just a couple of feet to the right!

Hadn't he?

Suddenly he remembered the octopus. How long had he been watching it? You tended to lose track of time underwater; everyone did. And the darkness only made it worse. Damn! How long had it been since he'd actually seen Michael?

Josh twisted frantically in the water now, searching for a glimpse of Michael. What the hell had he been thinking of, bringing Michael out here in the middle of the night? Just because Michael had managed to pull him out of the reef didn't make him an expert diver! He should have known better. And he sure shouldn't have let Michael out of his sight, even for a second.

He switched on his flashlight and shined it around.

Nothing.

Now he aimed the beam downward, raking it back and forth across the bottom, silently praying that when the light picked Michael out of the darkness, he would be moving, not just—

Before the words could form in Josh's mind, he saw him.

Michael was twenty to twenty-five feet off to the left, and ten or twelve feet below. And he was moving.

Josh's panic subsiding now that he'd located Michael, he automatically sucked in a breath of air in preparation for the dive down to make sure his friend was all right.

But the familiar pressure from the regulator had disappeared, as if the tank had run out of air. That didn't make any sense—they'd only been in the water for maybe forty minutes, and the tank should have held enough air for an hour.

Unless it hadn't been full when they'd started.

But he'd checked it! He could distinctly remember checking the tank he was wearing, as well as Michael's and Jeff Kina's.

He looked down again. Was Michael really moving?

Suddenly he couldn't tell.

What if Michael had run out of air, too?

What if he'd forgotten what to do, and panicked?

His fear for Michael flooding back, Josh reached back and jerked the lever over to the reserve position, then frantically dived down toward Michael. He was just coming into the murky part of the water when he saw Michael drop his weights and pull the cord that activated the CO_2 cartridge on his life vest. The vest instantly inflated, and Michael popped to the surface, shooting past Josh. Not bothering with his own emergency cord, Josh swam quickly to the surface, pulling the regulator out of his mouth the second his head popped out of the water.

"You okay?' he asked. But even in the dim light he could see that something had happened to Michael.

"I—I think so," Michael stammered. "I just—I don't know—all of a sudden I couldn't breathe!"

"Damn it!" Josh Malani exclaimed. "Let me see your gauge." He maneuvered himself around behind Michael, switched on the flashlight and shined it on the gauge. "It's the damned tanks," he told Michael. "Mine's running out, too! I was going down to get you when you pulled the cord. Let's get back to the beach and make sure the other guys are okay."

Inflating his own vest to make swimming on the surface easier, Josh started toward the beach, keeping pace with Michael. It wasn't until they were scrambling out of the water onto the beach that they saw Jeff Kina trying to get a small pile of kiawe burning in a makeshift fire pit.

"What happened?" Josh asked. "How come you're out already? You're always down till you start breathing water."

"And that wasn't very long ago," Jeff replied. "The gauge said the tank was full when I went in, but I ran out of air ten minutes ago." He scowled in the moonlight, then glared at the offending tank. "And we can't even complain to Ken about it, since he didn't exactly rent this stuff to us!" He struck another match. The small pile of kindling under the kiawe branches sputtered, then burst into flame.

A few minutes later, as the fire crept up through the kiawe, which burned brighter every minute, Rick and Kioki emerged from the water, too. "What happened to you guys?" they asked.

Josh shrugged. "Tanks weren't full."

Kioki frowned. "Yours, too? I figured it was only mine."

Rick Pieper glanced at his buddy. "What are you talking about? You had trouble, too?"

Kioki nodded. "I think the gauge on mine was screwed up. I had to switch over to the emergency real early on."

"Why didn't you give me a signal?" Rick demanded. "My air supply was okay. Jeez, Kioki, if we'd been down deep, you coulda been in real trouble."

An expression of sudden fear came over Michael's face, and Josh spoke quickly. "But we *weren't* deep. We're all fine, and all we have to do is put this crap back in the dive shop and make sure that next time everything works right. Okay?" He looked from one face to another, as if daring anyone to challenge him.

"Don't you think we ought to tell Ken?" Rick finally ventured.

"Tell him what?" Josh demanded. "That we snuck in and borrowed his stuff?" His voice took on that edge of sarcasm already familiar to Michael. "That'd be a real good idea, wouldn't it?"

"So what do we do?" Jeff Kina asked.

Josh shrugged. "What we were always planning to do. Nothing happened, so we take the stuff back, clean it up, and go home. Or do you all want Ken calling the cops on us?"

As they moved closer to the fire, letting its warmth drive the chill of the water out of their bodies, no one said anything.

No one had to.

Michael gazed past the campfire's flames at the dark pool of water, and shivered as he realized how close to danger they had come.

But nothing *had* happened. He hadn't panicked, and he'd gotten the weights off, and . . .

And he wished he'd never come on this dive.

CHAPTER
8

Rick Pieper glanced at his watch—it was 11:35. If his folks were still up, there'd be hell to pay, since he'd sworn he'd be back no later than eleven. But it had taken longer than they thought to get all the equipment back into the dive shop, and even when they were done he was pretty sure Ken would notice in the morning, no matter what Josh Malani had said. Well, if Ken figured it out, Malani would just have to find some way to get them all out of it. One thing about Josh—he could always figure out something. Now, as Rick slowed his car to make the left turn off the highway to the village in the cane fields where Kioki Santoya lived, he tooted his horn at Josh's beat-up truck, which sped on up the mountainside.

"Want me to drive you all the way home?" Rick asked a few minutes later as they approached the intersection where he'd have to turn to drop Kioki at his house.

The other boy shook his head. "My mom'll wake up. Seems like she can hear a car a mile away. Just let me out up here, and I'll walk the rest of the way."

Rick Pieper pulled the car over close to the ditch. As Kioki opened the door, he felt something funny, like a wave of dizziness. Hesitating, he wondered if maybe he shouldn't have Rick drive him the rest of the way home after all. But the feeling passed as suddenly as it came on. Kioki slammed the door shut behind him. "See you in the morning," he called. Rick popped the clutch on his car, taking off with a screech of wheels and a cloud of dirt that kicked up into Kioki's face. Flipping his friend the finger, Kioki started along the narrow road.

He hadn't gone more than a hundred yards when the strange feeling came over him again, a dizziness, then a pressure in his chest. Suddenly, he felt just as he did when they burned the cane fields at night and he forgot to close his bedroom window.

Coughing, he stopped and looked around, searching for the fire, but saw nothing except the sweep of stars across the sky and the sinking moon, dropping toward the horizon.

Nor could he smell the acrid fumes that boiled off the fields when they burned them, or hear the crackling of the blazing cane that always sounded like it was right outside the house even when it was a mile away.

His coughing subsided, but the pain in his chest got worse.

What the hell was going on? He was never sick!

Kioki began to walk again, but within a few yards had to slow down. His whole body was starting to hurt now, and his breath was coming in short gasps.

Home!

He had to get home!

He lurched on, straining to make the muscles in his legs work, but lost his balance and pitched forward, sprawling facedown into the road. He threw his hands out to break his fall. A rock scraped the skin on his left hand, and a piece of broken glass slashed deep into his right palm.

Kioki grunted at the stab of pain, pulled himself into a sitting position, and tried to get a look at his bleeding hand.

The cut extended from the base of his thumb across to his little finger, and was already starting to throb.

Clutching his right hand with his left, Kioki struggled back to his feet, staggering with the effort. Now his heart was starting to pound, and every breath he took was agonizing.

He tried to force his body into a run, but he felt the dizziness descend again. After only a single step his legs buckled beneath him and he collapsed onto the ground. Falling too close to the edge of the irrigation ditch that ran along the edge of the road, he slid down its steep bank and sank into the stinking water and the thick layer of mud that lay three feet beneath its surface.

The shock of the water closing over him galvanized Kioki for a moment, and he hurled himself back onto the bank, clawing at the dirt with both hands, ignoring the pain that was throbbing up his arm and the blood gushing from his right palm.

His legs seemed mired in the mud, and he could barely breathe, but at last he heaved himself free from the muck, scrambled up the bank, and sprawled out by the side of the road.

Kioki lay still, exhausted, his whole body hurting now.

He stared up into the sky, waiting for whatever had struck him to pass, his breath coming in ragged patches.

Now his vision blurred, and as he felt his stomach cramp with nausea, he rolled over to keep from puking all over himself.

As the retching began, the uncontrollable spasms sent him sliding back into the irrigation ditch.

This time he couldn't find the strength to pull himself out, and clawed ineffectually at the bank as the pain in his chest and stomach spread through him, his dizziness grew worse, and vomit began to boil up out of his throat.

A few minutes later, alone in the blackness in the middle of the cane field, Kioki Santoya sank into the arms of death.

Ten more minutes.

Katharine decided to wait ten more minutes—until the clock on the mantel showed exactly midnight—before she started making her calls.

She'd already written down the phone number of Maui Memorial Hospital, as well as the number for the main police station in Wailuku and the substation in Kihei. So far, she'd been unable to get a listing for Josh Malani's parents.

A movie. That's where Michael had said he was going.

A perfectly reasonable and harmless thing to do.

But she knew why she was worried: Josh Malani. Although she hardly knew him—and kept trying to convince herself that she shouldn't judge a sixteen-year-old boy on first impressions—all her instincts warned her that the handsome teenager whose life Michael had saved was a dangerous companion for her son. He'd struck her as cocky, and the fact that he'd gone diving by himself told her he was supremely lacking in common sense. And who else was Michael with? Some kids from the track team.

Kids whose names he hadn't even bothered to mention.

"Would it make any difference if he *had* left their names?" Rob had asked with a logic that had done nothing to allay her fears. "You wouldn't know any more about them."

"It would have given me more people to call if he's late!"

Rob had eyed her from across the table in the restaurant where they'd had dinner. "That would make him real happy," he observed archly. "Teenage boys love to have their moms call their friends, looking for them. Besides, this is Maui, not New York. He'll be fine."

Through the rest of their dinner and during the drive home she'd managed to hold her worries in check, but in the house alone an hour later, when Michael hadn't arrived home, she'd called Rob. "Give him until eleven-thirty at least," he'd counseled. "If he's still not there, then call me and we'll figure out what to do. Unless you'd like me to come over?"

"No," Katharine had sighed. "I'll be okay. But thanks for offering."

She'd done her best to stay calm, telling herself there were any number of plausible reasons for Michael's lateness.

The movie could have run later than they'd thought, or the theater could be far enough from Makawao that it was taking longer for him to get home than he'd thought. After all, neither of them really knew their way around the island yet, and if anyone had asked her how long it took to drive from her house to Kihei, she wouldn't have the slightest idea what the right answer might be.

By eleven-forty, though, all her rationales had turned hollow. By a quarter to twelve, a nightmare image had invaded her mind:

Michael trapped in a wrecked car, struggling to get out.

When the clock's gears began to grind softly as it prepared to strike midnight, Katharine reached for the phone to dial the hospital. Before her fingers had touched the first button on the key pad, however, the glint of headlights coming down the driveway struck the wall opposite the front windows.

Her hand dropped away from the telephone as the clock chimed. As Michael came through the front door, the bubble of fear that had been swelling inside her broke, exploding into anger at his lateness.

"Do you have any idea what time it is?" she demanded even before he'd closed the door.

Michael's eyes darted toward the clock, and he winced as he saw how late he was. "We just sort of lost track of time," he said. "We were playing video games and—"

"Video games?" Katharine interrupted. "I thought you said you were going to the movies."

"We were," Michael said quickly, improvising as fast as he could. "But the only one we wanted to see was sold out, so we started playing video games, and just lost track of time. I'm really sorry, Mom. I—"

"Why didn't you call me?" Katharine interrupted. "Do you have any idea how worried I've been?"

The repentance in Michael's eyes vanished. "Jeez, Mom, I'm only an hour late! What's the big deal?"

"The big deal, as you put it, is that I've been worried sick!" Katharine shot back. "Anything could have happened to you! You could have gotten into an accident, or someone might have mugged you, or—"

"This is Hawaii, Mom, not New York! And I'm not a baby anymore. Nobody else had to call his *mommy*!"

"Maybe nobody else has a *mommy* who cares," Katharine snapped, deliberately mimicking his tone. "I don't even know who you were with, except Josh Malani, and I can't say I'm nuts about him!"

Recoiling from the sting of his mother's words, Michael struggled against the tightness that had suddenly constricted his throat and the wetness welling in his eyes. "I was just with some other guys from the team, okay? Jeez, Mom! I made the track team, and I'm making some friends out here. I thought you'd be happy for me!" Katharine's anger dissolved in the face of her son's pain, but it was too late. "I'm not dead," he went on. "And I'm not hurt." His eyes fixed on her, as if challenging her to say anything more. "And I'm going to bed!" he finished. Stalking from the living room into his bedroom, he slammed the door behind him.

Left alone, Katharine dropped tiredly onto a chair. Why had she yelled at him? Why hadn't she at least listened to his explanation before she'd jumped all over him? In fact, now that she thought about what he'd said, she realized he had a point. Part of the reason he'd always been home on time in New York was because he'd been by himself. The asthma that had kept him out of school so much had seen to that. Until a year ago, when he'd made up his mind to make the track team, Michael had never been part of a crowd, rarely even had friends to hang around with for more than a few weeks at a time. And then, just as he'd been on the verge of realizing his goal, she'd moved him out here.

And he'd succeeded. How could she have started in on him before she'd even congratulated him on making the team this afternoon? It had to have been one of the happiest days of his life, and what had she done? She'd spoiled it, simply because he was an hour late getting home.

Rob was right—she should have controlled her own fears, and been happy that for once in his life Michael was just one of the guys instead of the skinny, wheezing kid who always stood on the sidelines.

He must have been so excited, she should count herself lucky that he'd called her at all!

Katharine went to his door, knocked softly, then opened it a crack. "Michael? May I come in?" When there was no answer, she spoke again. "Tell you what. I'll forgive you for being late if you'll forgive me for forgetting that you made the team today. I'm really sorry I yelled at you."

She waited, hoping he'd turn on the light and tell her to come in, but after a long silence, he only spoke briefly out of the darkness. "Okay, Mom," he said. Then: "See you in the morning."

Katharine pulled Michael's door closed again.

In his room, Michael lay staring up at the ceiling in the darkness. Should he have told her the truth about where he'd really been and what he'd been doing? But if he had, she would have yelled at him some more.

Better just to leave it alone.

Still, it took a long time for him to get to sleep that night.

He could feel nothing except the still coolness around him.

It was dark, the kind of darkness that could wrap itself around you like a shroud, bringing with it claustrophobia. All around him was blackness, and he was suspended in midair.

Slowly, just as the space around him started closing in—so slowly Michael was at first uncertain that it was happening at all—the blackness began to fade into silvery gray.

The water!

He was back in the water again!

As if to prove the thought, a fish swam by. A beautiful fish, striped in startling hues of bloodred, electric-blue, and a green so bright it was almost blinding.

Michael had never seen such a fish, and he turned to look at it. As if sensing his interest, the fish circled slowly in the water, almost as if it were deliberately exhibiting itself to him. With a kick of his fins, Michael moved toward the fish, but it countered his move, pulling away from him at exactly the same speed with which he was approaching.

He stopped.

The fish stopped.

He swam closer, and this time the fish hesitated before moving away and dropping deeper into the water.

Michael tried the maneuver again, but this time moved very slowly, hoping the fish wouldn't notice his careful approach.

He got within a few feet of the fish before it dived away and stopped below him, as if challenging him to follow.

Michael stayed where he was. Time itself seemed to slow as he floated in the water, gazing down at the fish, now as immobile as he. In the ghostly gray, silent water, he realized that his friends were gone.

He was alone.

Slowly, inexorably, the fish drew him deeper below the surface, moving closer to him whenever he hesitated, backing away from him just before he could quite reach it with his fingers.

Luring him.

The fish moved deeper into the water, and Michael, powerless to resist, dived after it. Deeper. Deeper and deeper they went. Michael, mesmerized, followed the brilliantly colored fish. Then it stopped, abruptly twitched its tail, and disappeared.

Startled, Michael turned in the water, searching for the fish, but it was nowhere to be seen.

And suddenly he realized that the bottom seemed to have fallen away. No moonlight penetrated the water from above. The darkness had returned. The sea itself was pressing in on him. It was getting harder to breathe.

It felt as if metal bands were fastened around his chest, squeezing him. He struggled against the tightening bonds, but it didn't help.

Panicking, he struggled harder.

Breathe. *Breathe!*

But he couldn't!

No matter how hard he tried, he couldn't get any air into his lungs.

The tanks!

Something had gone wrong with the tanks!

He sucked at his regulator, trying to pull air from the tank on his back into his lungs, but nothing happened.

Empty!

The tank was empty!

But there was a reserve supply! All he had to do was reach back and turn the lever and he would have ten more minutes of air.

He started to reach back; his arms wouldn't move.

He was sinking now, dropping into the darkness, into the great yawning void below—

He fought to reach the emergency valve, struggled to suck more air out of the tank, but now his lungs began to feel as if they were filling with water.

The surface. He had to get to the surface!

Drop the weight belt! Drop the weight belt, and pull the cord on the CO_2 canister. His vest would inflate: he would pop to the surface.

But he couldn't move!

He couldn't even feel his fingers anymore.

Terrified, he struggled again, dislodging the regulator from his mouth.

He had to get it back in!

But his hands wouldn't obey him. The regulator dangled from the air hoses, just out of reach.

If he could just get his mouth close enough . . .

He struggled to move his head, but even that was useless.

Now he could feel water seeping in through his nose. He tried to exhale, but there was nothing left in his lungs to expel.

His mouth opened and he tried to breathe.

Water flooded into his mouth, down his throat, into his already choking lungs.

He was going to die.

Die here, alone, deep under the surface of the sea.

No!

Loose! He had to get loose!

Even as he felt his lungs flooding and the blackness of death begin to close around him, Michael thrashed against the milky shroud that was still tightening around him, and a great scream built in his throat.

Frantic, he kicked out, twisting his body in a futile struggle to escape, struggling to gather enough energy for one last effort before the blackness closed around him forever.

Then, suddenly, the shriek in his throat erupted.

Michael jerked awake.

He was tangled in the bedding; the panic still clutched him. He could barely move, barely breathe.

Then, slowly, he began to understand.

A dream.

It had been nothing but a terrible dream.

The light in the middle of the ceiling flashed on, blinding him.

"Michael?" he heard his mother say. "Honey, are you okay?"

His chest still felt as if it was constricted by the bands that had tightened on him in the dream, and Michael wasn't sure if he could speak. When he finally formed the words, his voice was barely audible. "A nightmare," he said. "It was terrible. I—" He cut his words short as he realized where the dream had come from, what had triggered it.

"You were having trouble breathing," Katharine said, coming over to the bed to gaze anxiously at her son's face. "I was afraid you were having an attack—"

"I'm not," Michael told her, working himself loose from the sheets and sitting up, sucking the fresh night air so deep into his lungs that he started coughing. A moment later, though, he got through the coughing fit and flopped back against the pillow. "It's okay, Mom," he insisted as she started to speak. "It was just a bad dream, that's all."

Katharine leaned over and kissed his forehead. "You're sure?" she asked, her eyes still worried. "I know you thought you were all over it, but—"

"But nothing," Michael told her. "I'm fine." He glanced over at the clock on the nightstand; it was nearly five, and outside the window it was almost as dark as it had been at the end of the nightmare. "Let's just go back to sleep, okay?"

"Maybe you shouldn't have stayed out quite so late last night," Katharine suggested, but laid a hand on Michael's cheek to keep the words from stinging.

Michael sank lower in the bed. "I'm sorry," he said. "I guess when I knew I was going to be late I should have found a phone. Okay?"

"And I'm sorry I overreacted," Katharine told him. "And congratulations on making the team. I'm really proud of you." For the first time since he'd come home, a smile came to his lips. "Sleep tight." She kissed him once more, and turned the light off as she left the room. But as she went back to her own room, the worry stayed with her. Had it really been only a bad dream that awakened him? Or was it the beginning of yet another siege of the disease they both had thought he'd conquered?

She got back into bed, but for a long time didn't sleep. Instead, she listened, silently praying not to hear the rasping sound of asthmatic lungs struggling to fill themselves with air.

In his room, Michael was no longer in his bed.

Instead he was sitting beside the open window, breathing deeply of the fresh night air, trying to rid himself of the terrible choking feeling he'd had in the dream.

Yet even now that he was wide-awake, he still couldn't quite get rid of it, couldn't quite catch his breath.

CHAPTER 9

Alice Santoya slid the stack of pancakes onto her son's plate, put the plate on the table, then called out for the fourth time, "If you don't get up right now, Kioki, you're never gonna get the bus, and I'm not gonna drive you!" When she still got no answer, she went to her son's door, rapped loudly on it, then shoved it open. "Kioki, I'm tell—"

The words died on her lips as she saw the empty bed and realized that he hadn't come home at all last night.

But Kioki always came home! He was a good boy, not like that Josh Malani he hung around with sometimes. And when he'd called, he promised to be home early. He was just going to a movie with Rick Pieper and Josh and—

Josh!

She'd bet every penny she had that Josh Malani had gotten hold of some beer and talked Kioki into going out to a beach somewhere and getting drunk. And then he'd been scared to come home.

Just wait till she got her hands on him!

Going back to the kitchen, Alice picked up the phone and called Rick

Pieper's house. "Maria?" she said when Rick's mother picked up the phone. "It's Alice. Did Kioki come home with Rick last night?" A moment later, when Rick came on the line and told her he'd dropped Kioki off at the intersection, her anger dissolved into fear. If they'd been drinking . . .

"Did you boys get drunk?" she demanded. "If that Josh Malani got my son drunk—"

"He didn't," Rick Pieper insisted, then Maria Pieper was back on the line.

"Rick came in just before midnight," she told Alice. "Believe me, I know. I was waiting up for him. He said they were playing video games and lost track of time."

"Hah! If Josh Malani was with them—"

"They weren't drinking, Alice," Maria Pieper assured her. "Rick was fine when he got home."

As she hung up the phone, Alice Santoya tried to tell herself that there were a dozen good reasons why Kioki might not have come home last night.

But she couldn't think of a single one.

The one image that kept flashing into her mind, though, was of her husband, who had been walking home from the night shift at the mill in Puunene. They'd lived only two blocks from the mill, and it should have been safe.

But that night as he'd been crossing the road from Kihei—only half a block from the house—a car had come out of nowhere and smashed into Keali'i, killing him instantly.

Kids, getting drunk in the cane fields.

Like the cane fields all around this house.

Her anxiety mounting, Alice Santoya left her house and got into her car. She was going to be late for her job at the hotel out in Wailea, but it didn't matter. If Kioki was lying out there somewhere by the side of the road—

No!

He was all right!

Something else had happened, and he was fine!

But as she drove along the narrow track that led to the road half a mile away, she began to get a sick feeling in the pit of her stomach, a feeling of foreboding that she could not shake off.

It had rained during the night, and the road was slick with red mud. Apprehension tightened her hands on the wheel.

And then she saw him.

He was on the left, maybe fifty yards away.

He was lying facedown, his arms stretched up over his head, his legs in the irrigation ditch.

Choking back a scream, she braked to a stop a few feet from Kioki. Leaving the engine running, she scrambled out of the car and ran over to her son. "Kioki!" she cried. "You're all right! You're going to be—"

Kioki didn't move.

Unconscious!

He was unconscious and couldn't hear her.

Dropping down onto her knees in the mud, she reached out and touched him. "Kioki, it's Mama. . . ."

Her voice died away as she felt the coldness of his skin.

"Kioki?"

For a long time Alice Santoya crouched on her knees in the mud, willing her son to wake up, to move, to whimper, to do anything that would be a sign telling her that what she knew to be true wasn't true at all.

An image of her husband flashed into her mind, but now, instead of seeing Keali'i's face, it was Kioki who stared at her through a mask of death.

"No . . ." she finally moaned. "Oh, no, Kioki. Oh, no, please . . ."

Slipping her hands under her son's shoulders, she pulled him from the irrigation ditch. Sitting in the mud, she cradled his head in her lap, stroking his forehead with her fingers, tears flowing down her face, a keening sound issuing from her throat.

After a while a car approached, slowed to a stop, and its driver got out. Then another car arrived, and another.

A little while after that, the police arrived, and an ambulance.

But Alice Santoya was barely aware of the activity around her.

Her heart broken, her spirit destroyed, she sat in the mud and cradled her dead son in her arms.

Ken Richter knew something was wrong the minute he unlocked the back door of the shop that morning. A methodical man—who had christened himself "Kihei Ken" when he'd opened the dive shop two years ago on the strength of his reputation and a loan from Takeo Yoshihara—he had always believed that there was a place for everything, and that everything should be in its place.

This morning, everything was not in its place.

It was nothing obvious; indeed, when he first stepped into the back room of his store, it was little more than a feeling. But when he turned on the lights and looked around, the feeling grew stronger.

Then he saw the puddle in the middle of the floor.

Ken Richter did not leave puddles in the middle of floors.

Finding a towel, he began mopping the puddle up, already rehearsing the speech he would give to Nick Grieco for locking up last night without making sure the place was clean.

He and Nick had arrived on Maui as surfing buddies a dozen years ago, and though they were still friends, Nick now worked for Ken, spending just enough hours each day tending to the shop or taking tourists out on dives to pay the rent on his one-room apartment in Kihei and keep gas in the rusty Volkswagen van that took him and his surfboard out to wherever the waves were breaking best, the perfect wave being his single-minded pursuit. Last night he obviously hadn't been working much. Not only was there a puddle in the middle of the floor, but the equipment that should have been ready for this morning's dive didn't look as if it had been checked over.

Which annoyed Ken Richter even more, since he'd told Nick just before taking off for Lanai yesterday afternoon to double-check everything. The last thing he needed was to mess up a dive that had been arranged by Takeo Yoshihara's office. This one was important enough that a truck had arrived yesterday with brand-new equipment.

Finished mopping, Ken Richter turned his attention to the equipment, wondering if Nick had even looked at it, let alone made sure it was all in perfect condition. He was just starting to inspect the fins and masks when the back door opened and Nick himself appeared, along with Al Kalama, who was going to be helping Nick with the dive.

"Am I asking you to do too much around here?" Ken asked, his voice tight. "Because if I am, just tell me, and I can get someone else." His eyes fixed angrily on Nick. "That would be instead of you, though, not in addition to you."

Nick glanced uneasily at Al Kalama. "What're you mad at me for?"

Ken Richter's eyes swept the storage room. "Does this place look the way it should? I already cleaned up the mess you left on the floor."

"What are you talking about?" Grieco asked. "There was no mess!"

"Didn't I ask you to check all this stuff out before you left last night?" Ken demanded, ignoring the other man's question. "What did you think—I was kidding?"

"I did check it out," Nick Grieco insisted. "Fins, masks, regulators, tanks. Everything!"

Ken Richter's gaze shifted to the five tanks that he himself had lined up on the third shelf yesterday. "You checked all of them?" he asked.

His tone was enough to make Nick Grieco's eyes follow his boss's, and as he saw that four of the tanks were registering empty, he felt a flash of uncertainty.

Had he checked the tanks?

He tried to think back.

It had been pretty quiet most of yesterday afternoon, and he'd closed the shop up maybe half an hour after the last of the rental equipment had been returned.

And he'd had a couple of beers with his dinner. Better not mention *that* to Ken. But he'd come back after dinner and opened up again, just like he was supposed to.

He'd even sold a couple of bathing suits, and a snorkel set.

Then, around seven, he'd closed up for the night, but not until he'd inspected the equipment for this morning's dive, just like Ken had told him to.

But had he actually checked every one of them, or—

His thoughts were interrupted by a loud banging on the front door.

"That'll be the bunch Yoshihara set up. Go let 'em in, and see if you can stall 'em for a little while. Maybe sell 'em some sunglasses or something, while Al and I take care of these tanks."

"I can do it—" Nick protested, but Ken cut him off.

"Yeah, right. That's what you said yesterday, but it didn't happen, did it?"

As Nick Grieco went into the front of the shop, Al Kalama swung one of the tanks off the shelf and took it over to the air compressor. "You know," he said cautiously, not certain quite how angry Ken was, "it might not be Grieco's fault. If the tanks are faulty—"

"Four faulty tanks?" Richter cut in. "Get real, Al. One maybe, or even two. But not four. Not from Yoshihara. Everything he's ever sent down has always been perfect. Face it—Grieco screwed up."

"But—"

"Can it, Al," Ken said. "Let's just get these tanks filled and checked, and get these kids going. The last thing I need is having them go whine to their folks that they had to wait around for an hour because there was something wrong with the equipment." When the first one was filled, Ken nodded toward the barrel of water that stood just outside the back door. "Sink it in there for a minute, just in case. I've never sent a leaky tank out yet, and I'm not about to start now."

Taking the newly filled air tank to the barrel, Al Kalama lowered it into the water, then searched for any sign of air bubbles that would betray a leak.

Nothing.

He repeated the process with the other three tanks after Ken had finished filling them. All four tanks checked out perfectly.

There were no signs of leakage, and all the gauges now read full.

"Take them," he said. "Who knows? The guys up at Yoshihara's probably sent them over empty, and Nick just didn't notice."

The tanks were packed into the van, the van departed for the beach, and Kihei Ken proceeded with the business of the day. But he'd still have it out with Nick Grieco later on, because whatever else he'd done last night— or not done—he should have made damned sure of the condition of those tanks.

Faulty tanks could kill people.

Michael knew something was wrong the minute he got on the school bus that morning. "What's going on?" he asked, sliding into the seat next to Jeff Kina.

Jeff glanced around uneasily, and when he spoke, he kept his voice low enough that only Michael could hear him. "Kioki didn't make it home last night."

"What do you mean? Wasn't Rick going to drop him off?"

Jeff shrugged. "Didn't happen. Rick said it was gettin' so late, Kioki didn't want to wake up his ma. So Rick dropped him at the corner instead of taking him all the way home."

"When did you talk to Rick?"

"Just before I left for the bus stop. Kioki's ma called his ma, and he called me right after they hung up."

"What happened to Kioki?"

"Don't know," Jeff replied. "But it's only like half a mile from where Rick dropped him to his house, and there's nothin' out there."

"Maybe he got caught doing a drug deal," a voice from the seat behind them said.

Jeff Kina turned and glared angrily at the boy in the seat behind them. "Kioki? No way."

"What if he ran into some other people doing a deal?" the other boy pressed.

Jeff scowled. "Get off it, Jimmy. Just because you're always out there doesn't mean everybody else is."

"I never did—" Jimmy began, but Jeff stopped him.

"Don't give me that crap. Everybody knows you're the biggest dealer in the school. But you never sold anything to Kioki, did you?" Jimmy glowered angrily, and Jeff rose out of his seat, turning around to tower over the boy behind him. "Did you?" Jeff demanded.

"Sit down back there," the bus driver called, glaring at Jeff in the rearview mirror. As the bus slowed, Michael pulled Jeff back into his seat.

"Forget it. He's not even as big as Josh!" Jeff sank reluctantly back into his seat, and the bus sped up again. "Maybe Kioki was going to meet someone," Michael suggested. "Does he have a girlfriend?"

Jeff shook his head. "Never had one. He's always real shy around girls."

As the bus pulled into the parking lot, Michael and Jeff saw Rick Pieper waiting for them, his face ashen. A crowd of kids had gathered around him. Michael could see them whispering nervously among themselves.

"Shit," Jeff said quietly. "Come on." Rising from his seat, he wriggled past Michael and surged down the aisle, with Michael right behind him. "What happened?" he asked Rick as he stepped out of the bus.

Rick seemed dazed as he looked at Michael and Jeff. "His mom found him," he said. He hesitated a moment, then spoke again, his voice breaking. "He's dead."

Michael and Jeff stared blankly at Rick.

Though neither of them spoke a word, both of them were experiencing exactly the same thing: an oddly sick feeling, which spread through them, numbing their bodies as well as their minds.

It wasn't possible—they'd been with Kioki only a few hours ago, and he'd been fine.

And now he was dead?

Instinctively, Jeff, Rick, and Michael drew closer together as they began moving slowly toward the school. The whispering voices of their classmates swirled around them, and though nearly every person who whispered the news to someone else had an explanation for Kioki's death, none of them knew the truth.

Michael walked to his locker as if in a trance, and stared stupidly at the lock, its combination having vanished from his head. Then, from behind him, he heard Josh Malani's voice.

"We gotta talk," Josh said. "All of us."

Michael turned and gazed at his friend. "What happened?" he said. "What happened to Kioki?"

Josh Malani's eyes narrowed. "I don't know," he said. Then he quickly looked around, as if checking for anyone who might be listening. When he spoke again, his voice was barely more than a whisper. "But it's got nothing to do with us," he said. "Nothing at all."

Michael stared at his friend for a long time, wishing he could believe him.

Deep down inside, though, he couldn't.

CHAPTER 10

Katharine was genuinely annoyed with herself. The bones of the skeleton, fully exposed now, were laid out in precisely the position in which they'd been found. She'd had to move a few of them as she'd cleaned away the sediment that covered them, but in addition to the endless rolls of 35mm film she'd shot, there were dozens of Polaroids as well—a complete photographic record of the excavation and an essential aid to reconstructing the skeleton *in situ*. Now, as she stared down at the skeleton, her impatience with herself grew.

She should know what she was looking at.

In fact, she should have known what she was looking at yesterday, right after the skull and mandible had been fully excavated. But no matter what came to mind—chimpanzee, gorilla, gibbon, or any of a dozen other apes and primates—there was always something wrong: the skull not prognathic enough, or the mandible too wide, or the teeth showing the wrong configuration. The devil, she decided, was definitely in the details on this one, because it was the details that didn't add up.

"So, have you decided what it is?" Rob Silver asked, emerging from the rain forest to stand next to her.

"Well, I'm absolutely certain it's an anthropoid," Katharine said, attempting to mask the crankiness she was feeling, but failing to fool Rob. "And I'm fairly certain it died from a blow to the head."

Rob squatted down. "May I pick it up?"

"Be my guest," Katharine said, crouching down next to him. "I have to tell you, right now I'm thinking you're wasting a lot of Takeo Yoshihara's money on me. Either that, or I'm missing something that's staring me right in the face."

"Don't be so hard on yourself," Rob told her. "If this was going to be an easy one, I wouldn't have needed you at all, would I?" He held the skull up, rotated it, then stuck a finger through the hole that had been pierced in the left parietal bone. "What do you think caused this?"

That, at least, was something she felt confident about. "A spear. I've seen exactly the same kind of wound in hundreds of skulls in Africa. And you can see by the position of the skeleton that while this head wound appears to be the mortal blow, the body was moved."

"*You* can see that," Rob countered. "Explain, please?"

"For one thing, it's lying on its back. If you assume someone threw the spear that killed it, it would have just collapsed."

"So whoever threw the spear pulled it out."

Katharine nodded. "But someone also laid the body out," she went on. "See how the arms are? They're not just lying at its sides." With a forefinger, she traced along the right humerus, which lay parallel to the spine. But the arm bent at the elbow, with the radius and ulna angling inward toward the center of the pelvis. The bones of the left arm mirrored their counterparts on the right, and the small bones that had made up the hands and fingers were jumbled together, as if one hand had been placed on top of the other.

"Like it was laid out for burial," Rob suggested.

"Exactly," Katharine said.

"Sounds as if we have a murder mystery on our hands," Rob said, laying the skull carefully back in the exact position in which it had been resting. "Someone killed this guy, and then his family brought him up here and buried him."

Katharine shook her head. "Doesn't add up," she said. "First, he wasn't buried. Everything I scraped away was natural debris, the kind of stuff that builds up in a hurry in rain forests. I don't find any evidence of burial. Just laid out, and then left here. And the Hawaiians didn't do that, did they?"

"Absolutely not. They have a great respect for their dead. The burial grounds are sacred, no matter how old they are. And bodies were always buried."

"So what went on here?" Katharine asked.

"Whoever killed this guy laid him out, then walked away?"

"Maybe," Katharine agreed, straightening up from her crouch, but keeping her eyes fixed on the skeleton. "But that's not my biggest problem." Rob looked up at her. "My biggest problem is that I can't figure out what it is."

"It's human, isn't it?" Rob asked.

"Not from what I know of humans," Katharine replied. "It's barely four feet long, which makes it awfully small for a full-grown Homo sapiens."

"Maybe it's a child."

"The skull doesn't look like a child's skull. It seems to be fully developed." Stooping again, she traced her finger along the seams between the parietal and occipital plates. "See? The bones are fully fused, which means the head is pretty much full size. Yet it's no larger than your average six-year-old's. Also, look at the forehead—way too sloped for Homo sapiens. The mandible's all wrong, too."

"So it's some kind of primate," Rob suggested.

Katharine fixed him with a withering look. "First, there are not now, and never were, any primates on these islands, except for the ones in the zoo in Honolulu. But more important than that, when a chimpanzee or a gorilla dies, you don't lay it out as you do a human."

Rob chewed thoughtfully on his lower lip. "If it was a pet—"

"Forget it," Katharine interrupted, her annoyance toward herself now widening to include Rob. "Believe me, I've thought about that. This was no pet."

"So what is it?" Rob asked, deciding to ignore her annoyance. "Come on, you've got to have some idea."

Katharine took a deep breath. "All right," she said. "Since it's just you and me, I'll tell you. But you have to promise not to laugh." Rob's brows rose in a noncommittal arch, which Katharine suspected was as far as he'd commit himself. "What it looks like is utterly impossible. You won't believe it any more than I do."

"Try me," Rob suggested.

"Early man," Katharine said.

Rob shook his head. "You're right. Not possible. Aside from the fact that there was no such thing as early man in this area, these islands weren't even formed when early man was poking around the planet. Even if Maui was here—which I seriously doubt—what we're standing on wasn't. This is a volcanic island, Kath. Layer after layer of lava. I'll bet the layer we're standing on isn't more than a couple of thousand years old, and probably a lot younger than that."

"I didn't say I believed it," Katharine said. "And I can add half a dozen other reasons why it's impossible, starting with the fact that every early man specimen I've ever seen—and I mean *every* one—is a fossil. And these bones, in case you haven't noticed, aren't fossils. They don't look more than a few hundred years old, if that."

"So what do we have?" Rob asked.

"I wish I knew," Katharine sighed. "What I'd really like to get my hands on is a computer, so I could check some things out on the Net."

"Well, at least that part's easy," Rob told her. "Come on."

The funny feeling started almost the minute Michael emerged from the locker room and trotted out to the field for his fourth-period gym class. At first he hardly noticed it, but as he jogged across the grass toward the spot near the far end zone of the football field where his class was falling in for the morning's round of calisthenics, he felt it again. It was like last night, when he'd awakened from the nightmare and felt as if there was something in his lungs that wasn't quite letting him catch his breath, or fill his lungs with air.

Asthma.

But even as the word popped into his consciousness, he rejected it.

It didn't feel like asthma, and besides, he was over that—he hadn't had an attack in months!

Ignore it, he told himself. It'll go away.

He fell into place in the loose formation just in time to yell out a loud "Yo!" when the teacher called his name, then dropped down to the ground for the set of ten quick push-ups that opened the gym class. The class was quiet this morning, and everyone knew why.

Kioki Santoya.

All morning, people Michael didn't even know had come up to him, asking if there had been anything strange about Kioki last night. What was he supposed to say? He'd hardly even known Kioki—even this morning he had still been having trouble remembering his last name. Now, as he did his push-ups, he could sense the other guys watching him, wondering if there was something he wasn't talking about. He made it through the push-ups, and though the odd sensation in his chest was still there, it didn't seem to be any worse. Along with the rest of the class, he scrambled to his feet and starting doing jumping jacks. By the time they'd finished a set of twenty-five, Michael was starting to sweat and he could feel his muscles warming up.

"O-*kay!*" the teacher said. "Run in place!"

Michael's arms dropped to his sides as he began running, lifting his knees high with each step, working his legs like two pistons. This was one of his favorite exercises, for in the long months it had taken to build his lungs, his legs had developed, too, and he'd almost come to think of their strength as a kind of barometer, proof positive that his entire body was growing stronger every week, forever throwing off the terrible grip in which his disease had held him.

This morning, though, after only a few steps, the muscles in his legs started to burn. But that was crazy—he was barely getting warmed up! At this rate, a single lap around the track would wear him out.

"Okay, let's do it!" the teacher yelled. "One lap, and the first two around choose up sides for baseball!"

The class broke ranks and headed out onto the quarter-mile track that circled the football field. Two of the guys—Zack Cater, who was in Michael's English class, and someone whose name Michael thought was Sky, and who lived down the road from him—took off in the lead. Instantly, Michael knew he had no chance of beating them. He might be able to put on enough speed in the first hundred yards to pull ahead of them, but by the second hundred he'd have fallen behind. Then, most of his energy having been spent on the first sprint, he'd wind up straggling in at the very back of the class.

Not good for someone who had made the track team just yesterday.

Worse would be the humiliation that followed when Zack and Sky left him until dead last to be chosen for the baseball teams.

Better to pace himself and finish somewhere in the middle of the pack.

Glancing around, he saw that there were only two other boys behind him, so he increased his pace slightly, quickly passing three runners, then closing on two more. Once he'd left all five of them behind, he steadied his pace, falling into an easy gait that should have carried him comfortably through the turn at the end zone, then back along the opposite side of the field.

Except that the strange feeling in his chest was getting worse and the muscles of both his legs were burning like crazy, and threatening to cramp up any second.

But he'd done a full lap yesterday, then whipped Jeff Kina in a sprint! What the hell was wrong?

Once again, as it had every few minutes this morning, his mind went back to the dive last night.

But it wasn't just the dive he was thinking about. It was also the long hike across the rough lava, stumbling with every step.

And the fight with his mother, and the hours of sleep he'd missed. So what did he expect? All his body was doing was punishing him for last night.

A strange thought flickered through Michael's mind: Was that what had happened to Kioki Santoya, too? If they hadn't gone on the dive at all—if they'd just gone to a movie, and then come home early, as they'd first planned—would Kioki still be alive?

But that didn't make any sense. It wouldn't have made any difference what they'd done last night—what had happened to Kioki . . . had just happened.

For himself, though, the hike and the dive and the loss of sleep were costing him. Well, fine. If he had to pay for what he'd done, so be it. But he still wasn't going to let himself finish last.

Determined to ignore the discomfort in his chest and the pain in his legs no matter what, Michael held his pace through the curve around the end zone, and started down the long straightaway. One of the boys he'd passed on the first stretch came up on his right and fell in beside him.

"Thought you were supposed to be real hot shit," the boy said. Laughing loudly, he pulled away from Michael, deliberately twisting his feet to kick up a cloud of dust from the cinders that paved the track.

Michael tried to turn his head away, but couldn't avoid sucking in some of the dust, and braced himself against the fit of coughing he was sure would seize him. But then he was through the gray cloud and suddenly felt himself building up speed.

He'd been right! Whatever it was, all he'd had to do was work his way through it! His legs were starting to feel a little better, and his chest was getting back to normal, so he notched up his stride and started to close on the boy ahead of him for the second time. They pounded down the track with Michael just a pace behind, and though the dust behind the other boy was starting to make Michael's eyes sting, he could feel his strength surging back. As they headed into the last curve, Michael pulled ahead.

Now the finish line was just yards away. Michael poured all the energy he could muster into the final sprint. He passed one more boy, then crossed the line, his chest heaving and his legs burning again. It wasn't until he dropped his pace back to a walk and turned to join the rest of the class that he realized the gym teacher had been watching him.

"What's going on, Sundquist?" he asked. "Jack Peters told me how good you were yesterday afternoon, but I'm sure not seeing it this morning. You feel okay?"

Michael hesitated. Should he say anything about the funny feeling he'd had his chest? Or the fire in his legs? But if he did, it was a sure thing the gym teacher would do the same thing the ones back in New York always had: send him to the nurse.

He wasn't about to start that again. No way!

"I'm okay," he said. "I just stayed up too late last night, that's all."

"Don't let Peters hear you say that," the teacher told him. "You want to stay on the team, you keep yourself in shape. Got it?"

"Got it," Michael agreed, silently suspecting there was a rule somewhere that said gym teachers had to be jerks. He was about to turn away when the teacher spoke again, and Michael wondered if he'd known what he was thinking.

"Then take a few more laps. And while you're running, you can think about the value of a good night's sleep."

While the rest of the class split up into teams for baseball, Michael started around the track.

He steeled himself against the pain as his legs began to burn again, determined that no matter how bad it got, he wouldn't give in.

He'd built himself up, and he'd made the track team, and whatever was causing the funny feeling in his chest, he'd get through it.

Or die trying.

Katharine gazed in awe at the office Rob Silver had been given on Takeo Yoshihara's estate. Housed in a large pavilion that blended almost perfectly with the hillside abutting its far end, the two-room suite lay behind a beautifully carved koa-wood door. The smaller of the two spacious, airy rooms was equipped with a desk and filing cabinets, while the larger was filled with tables on which photographs, drawings, and models of native Polynesian buildings were laid out in a manner that was perfectly reflective of the innate tidiness they both shared. Beyond a set of French doors, she could see the gardens that spread across the estate. Aside from the view, Rob's work space was at least eight times the size of her office at the museum in New York, and apparently whatever equipment Rob might need, Takeo Yoshihara supplied. Against one wall of the larger room was a second desk, supporting Rob's computer, along with several printers, a scanner, and an array of other equipment Katharine didn't recognize.

"Can you get me online?" she asked. "I want to start by looking at some files at the museum. I remember something that looks a lot like our skull—"

"I've got a better idea," Rob said. "Let me have those Polaroids."

Puzzled, Katharine fished the pictures she'd taken of the skull out of her bag, and watched as Rob placed them on the bed of a scanner, brought up a program that allowed him to manipulate images, and began rapidly entering instructions on the keyboard and clicking the mouse. A few minutes later eight views of the skull they'd uncovered in the rain forest appeared on the screen, each depicting it from a different angle.

Six more depicted the mandible.

Rob stood up. "What I want you to do is pick a few things that are unique, that you'd be looking for if you were hunting for similar skulls and mandibles."

Lowering herself into the chair, Katharine experimented with the mouse and soon got the hang of zooming in on first one image, then another. Five minutes later she'd made her choices, and Rob showed her how to copy the small areas she'd outlined with the cursor so they lay on a blank screen like so many pieces of a jigsaw puzzle. "But they're just fragments," Katharine objected. "Even if you put them all together, you wouldn't get a complete skull."

Rob grinned. "Want to bet?" His tone was enough to warn her it was a bet she'd lose. "We're going to tell the computer to search for graphic matches to these shapes," he explained. "It'll comb every database on the Internet and—"

"Are you crazy?" Katharine objected. "That'll take months!"

"Maybe it would at your museum," Rob placidly replied, "but this computer is hooked up to one of the two most powerful computers in the world."

"You're kidding." But one look at his smug expression said he was not.

"It was put in to handle all the data from the telescopes up on top of the mountain," Rob explained as he typed in a series of instructions to initiate Katharine's search for a match to the skull they'd unearthed. "The Air Force has a big project up there that tracks spy satellites and space garbage and asteroids, and God knows what all."

He hit the Enter key to start the search, the screen went blank for a moment, and then lines of type began scrolling down so fast that Katharine couldn't read them. Reaching out, Rob hit the Pause key. The screen froze.

Katharine found herself gazing at a series of Internet addresses, each of them ending in file names that indicated one or another of half a dozen types of graphic formats. Each was followed by a percentage number.

On the screen Katharine was watching, the percentage numbers ranged from 1 all the way to 100.

Rob hit the Enter and Pause keys again, and more files appeared.

"My God, there's hundreds of them," Katharine said.

"Bad search," Rob told her, hitting the Escape key, then typing in more instructions. "It was matching every image individually. We'll narrow it down so it doesn't give us anything that doesn't have at least four matches for the skull and three for the mandible." He ran the search again. Within a few seconds a list of 382 files appeared, each with its attached percentage-of-match rating. "Let's rearrange these according to the match rate," Rob said, his fingers flying over the keyboard. A moment later the screen blinked, and the list of files reappeared, this time with the closest matches at the top. "Okay, let's see what we've got," Rob said, double-clicking on the file at the top of the list. A graphic image appeared of a large fragment of jawbone very similar to the one they had unearthed. It was in a collection in a university in Sweden, and had been discovered in Africa forty years earlier.

Katharine stared at it in shock. "I've never seen that before." She studied the image and its caption, which identified it as a hominid collected in the Olduvai Gorge. Though the fossil was not ascribed to a species, Katharine thought she saw a definite resemblance to *Australopithecus afarensis*.

She clicked on the second file.

This time an image of a skull appeared.

A skull that looked to Katharine very much like the one they had unearthed.

The image bore no identification other than that it had been collected on the slopes of Mount Pinatubo, in the Philippines. Other than the image and the brief notation, all that appeared in the window was a link to another file.

Frowning, Katharine double-clicked on the link. A second later a new window opened, and a new picture appeared.

This one, though, wasn't simply an image.

It was a movie or video, obviously made by someone whose skills with the camera were no further advanced than Katharine's own. The crudeness of the photography, though, did nothing to lessen the fascination with which Katharine and Rob watched what unfolded on the computer screen.

The camera was trained on something that looked unlike anything either Katharine Sundquist or Rob Silver had ever seen before.

It appeared to be some kind of humanoid, and though it was impossible to be certain, it gave the impression of being a young male.

His prognathic ridge jutted forward while his brow sloped sharply back. His features were large and coarse, his eyes peering fearfully from deep sockets. His jaw looked underslung, and his body, clad only in a loincloth, appeared to be almost covered with a light coat of hair.

Formed in a loose circle around the boy—if they could really call him a boy—was a group of perhaps fifteen tribesmen. The men seemed to be warily watching the boy they had encircled, as if they weren't certain what to expect of him.

As Katharine watched, the circle tightened, and she could see the boy in the center tense, his eyes darting from one person to another. Then, in a movement that came so quickly it was little more than a blur, the boy darted out of the circle and disappeared into the jungle. Stunned into momentary inaction by the sudden movement, the tribesmen appeared to talk animatedly among themselves for a few seconds, and finally vanished into the jungle themselves, obviously intent on tracking the fleeing boy.

The screen went black, and for a moment Katharine and Rob thought the video had come to an end.

They were wrong.

After several seconds the computer screen filled with a jungle scene. The village was gone, and for a moment, as the image on the screen hovered in stasis, Katharine wondered if perhaps whoever had made the video was merely checking his camera. But then the lens zoomed in, and finally Katharine saw it:

The face—the hominid face of the boy, if that was truly what he was—gazed out from a thicket of vines in a way that made Katharine shiver as a wave of déjà vu passed over her. Then she realized what it was: not déjà vu at all. The image on the screen was triggering a genuine memory, a memory of a museum exhibit she'd seen years ago, depicting a family of Homo habilis, perhaps the earliest of the hominids to make tools.

The being on the screen, but for the color of its skin and the pattern of hair on its face, might have stepped out of that diorama and into the jungle scene she and Rob Silver were watching.

But of course it was impossible; Homo habilis had been extinct for two million years.

Therefore, what they were watching was a hoax.

"Can you pause it?" Katharine asked as the camera lingered on the face.

Rob reached out and clicked the mouse on a button on the screen. The image froze. Katharine leaned forward, examining the face. This had to be an actor expertly made up, a work of cosmetic wizardry worthy of a Hollywood special effects team. But how had they managed to slope his forehead so perfectly? It would have been a simple thing, of course, to add anything necessary to give the actor's features the proper look, but enough prostheses to lend the boy such authentic features should have enlarged his head.

Yet it seemed to be in perfect proportion to the body.

Reaching out to manipulate the mouse herself, Katharine restored the picture to its former size and set it running again.

A split second later the first spear struck.

The lens of the camera was still in close-up, and the look of shock that came into the boy's eyes was perfect. They widened, then moved, as if searching for the source of the stick that protruded from his chest.

A second and third spear struck, and the boy's expression of shock twisted into an agonized grimace of pain so genuine that Katharine was glad the video had no sound track—even in the silence of the room she could almost hear the howl that must have torn from his throat.

His mouth gaped open, and then he pitched forward onto the ground, twitched spasmodically for a few seconds, and lay still.

Rob reached over and took Katharine's hand as they watched the rest of the video unfold:

The men and boys of the tribe gathered around the body, poking at it until they were certain it was dead.

They tied it to a pole, securing it by its hands and feet, letting it hang as they carried it back to their village.

In the village, the men dressed the corpse, slitting open its belly and throwing the entrails to a pack of dogs who snatched them up, fought over them, then settled down to gobble their feast in an atmosphere of uneasy suspicion.

The men roasted the body over a fire as the tribe gathered around to share in the unexpected delicacy.

For a moment the camera settled on the face of a woman who stood apart from the rest, her eyes glistening as she watched.

The tribe ate, but instead of throwing the bones to the dogs, they tossed them into a large kettle, where the remaining flesh would simmer into a rich broth.

The scene changed again, and now darkness had fallen over the village.

A form moved in the darkness, and Katharine had to strain to make out the details.

It was the woman. As Katharine watched, the woman used a net to lift the bones from the kettle, and piled them on a cloth she had spread on the ground. She kept fishing until she was certain there was nothing left to find. The woman began folding the cloth around the bones, and for a moment the camera lingered on the grotesque pile.

The woman seemed to have found all the bones but one.

The skull was missing.

The window in which the video had been playing abruptly closed. Once more, Katharine and Rob found themselves staring in silence at the image of the skull.

The implication was clear.

It was Rob who finally broke the silence. "What do you think? Any chance at all that the film was real?"

Katharine shook her head. "Absolutely not. Nothing like that has lived—" But then she cut her own words off as she remembered the skeleton that even now lay by the fire pit only a few miles away.

The skeleton that could have belonged to the very creature they'd just seen on the computer screen.

Yet she still couldn't believe it. The video had to be an elaborate fake. "Let's look at the film again," she said.

Rob reached for the mouse to click on the link a second time. But even as he was moving the cursor across the screen, the window displaying the skull closed. "Damn," he said softly. "Sorry about that." Where the window had been a second ago, now only the list of files appeared. Rob once more manipulated the mouse, trying to highlight the file name again.

The file name, like the window, had vanished.

"Where is it?" Katharine asked.

They hunted for the vanished file for an hour, but finally gave up. It was almost as if the file had never been there at all.

☆   ☆   ☆

In his private office, Takeo Yoshihara leaned back in his chair, staring at the skull that had been delivered to him by the courier from Manila. He'd photographed the skull himself, using a digital camera, and transferred the contents of the videotape that had accompanied the skull into a digitized graphics file. The videotape itself was now locked in the safe in this very office, to which only he had the combination.

Before he left his office, the skull would join the videotape.

The graphics files in his computer were equally secure, protected by security codes known only to himself and the few trusted lieutenants to whom he had transmitted copies of the files an hour ago.

The money he had spent on the skull had been well worth it. It was too bad, though, that the boy had to die.

Still, no progress came without a price, and what was the harm in spending a few lives, given what he was trying to accomplish?

CHAPTER 12

Sergeant Cal Olani had just come on duty that morning when he'd gotten the call sending him out to the lonely stretch of road where Alice Santoya had found her son's body. As he'd driven out, he assumed he'd find the victim of a hit-and-run. Five minutes after he'd arrived at the scene, though, he'd known that no hit-and-run had been involved. The absence of tread marks, in itself, didn't mean much, since the rain last night could have washed them away. But the condition of the boy's body revealed nothing to confirm such an accident.

Except for a gash on his right palm, the boy exhibited none of the gross trauma that would have been apparent if he'd been hit by a car hard enough to kill him.

Olani had worked alongside the crew of medics who attempted to revive the boy despite the fact that it was obvious from his temperature alone that he'd been dead for hours. He'd stayed at the site until the photographer had come and gone, and searched the area for any clues.

Olani had tried to take a statement from Alice Santoya, but she'd been pretty incoherent as she sobbed over the loss of her only child.

After an hour, he was finished at the scene, having found no evidence that any crime had been committed. But Kioki Santoya had stayed in his mind all through the day as he'd dealt with one petty disturbance after another. There'd been a domestic squabble up in Paia. He solved that one by parking out in front of the house and tooting the horn a couple of times to let Lee and Rosie Chin know that if they didn't settle down, he'd have to come in and do it for them.

Then there'd been a minor fender-bender in which he had to convince the owner of a rusted-out 1974 Chevy Impala that he probably wasn't going to get much of a settlement out of the tourist who "rear-ended me, man! I got whiplash real bad!" The problem for the Chevy's owner was that three witnesses backed up the tourist's story that he'd been waiting for a light to turn green when the car ahead of him suddenly slammed into his front end. If he hadn't had his foot firmly on his own brakes, he probably would have crashed into the car behind him.

After sorting that out, Olani cruised up and down Front Street in Lahaina for a while, just showing the colors to let the troublemakers know he was around.

Through it all, he'd been unable to stop thinking about Kioki Santoya. Now, with only another hour before the end of his shift, when he could go home to Malia and the twins, he decided he might as well swing by Maui Memorial on his way back to the Sheriff's Department. The hospital was barely a quarter of a mile from headquarters, and he knew he wouldn't stop thinking about the teenage boy who had died last night until he found out exactly what had killed him.

He pulled the car into the nearly empty parking lot next to the hospital, and went in through the emergency entrance that was almost hidden in the L-shaped building's corner. Jo-Nell Sims, the nurse on duty, looked up. "Ten minutes," she said as she recognized him. "That's all I have left on my shift." Putting on an expression of exaggerated annoyance, she shook a finger at him. "Don't tell me you're bringing someone in, Cal. Please, just don't tell me that."

"Relax, Jo," Olani told her. "All's quiet out there. I just stopped by to find out what happened to the boy they brought in this morning. Kioki Santoya."

Jo-Nell's eyes lost their sparkle. "Isn't it terrible? I just feel so sorry for his mother."

"Have they finished the autopsy on him yet?" Olani pressed.

Still shaking her head in sympathy for Alice Santoya's loss, Jo-Nell scanned a schedule. "Laura Hatcher was on it," she said. Picking up a phone, she spoke for a moment, then waved Cal through the doors leading to the examining rooms. "She'll meet you in a couple of minutes. First door on your left."

Five minutes later Laura Hatcher came in. No more than five feet one inch tall, she couldn't have weighed more than ninety-three pounds, and looked to Cal Olani to be about twelve years old. Except that he'd dealt with her many times before, and knew that behind that incredibly slender and innocent-looking facade was the tough mind of a very well-trained pathologist.

"So what about Kioki Santoya?" Cal asked. "Any idea what killed him?"

Laura Hatcher flipped open a metal-covered clipboard she was carrying, riffled through a few sheets, then found what she was looking for. "Well, I can tell you what didn't happen," she said. "Nothing much in the way of external trauma at all—a few minor abrasions on his left palm, and a deep cut on his right one."

"I saw that. Looked more like the kind of cut you'd get from a piece of broken glass than a knife wound."

Laura Hatcher nodded. "No argument there. And it wasn't nearly bad enough for him to have bled to death through it."

"How about alcohol?" the policeman suggested. "The way some of the kids drink these days—"

"I thought of that right away. Nothing."

"So what are you saying? He just died? Kids that age don't have heart attacks, do they?"

"Actually, it's not impossible, but in this case there wasn't any evidence of it. The only thing that looked even slightly abnormal was his lungs, but until I get some results back from the lab, I won't even know if that's what killed him." She spread her hands helplessly. "I wish I could be more specific, but I can't tell you much right now. It could have been a virus—one of these new bugs that have been cropping up lately—but he doesn't seem to have manifested any symptoms of illness prior to death. His mother says he was fine."

"But you can't be sure of that, either." Olani sighed, knowing the caveat the doctor was certain to add.

Hatcher nodded her agreement. "Sorry. I wish I could be more help." She glanced down at her notes. "Do the names Rick Pieper, Josh Malani, and Jeff Kina mean anything to you?"

"There've been a couple problems with the Kina kid. He's big, and has a chip on his shoulder when it comes to *haoles*. And Josh Malani tries to act tough, but it's mostly for show. Why?"

"According to Alice Santoya, her son was out with those three boys last night. He left a message saying he was going to a movie with them. Depending on what comes back from the lab, someone might want to talk to them."

Cal Olani wrote the three names in his notebook. Maybe he'd just drop by the school and have a talk with those boys.

Ten minutes after Cal Olani finished his conversation with Laura Hatcher, a man stepped into the small room that served as the hospital's morgue. Making certain no one had seen him come in, he locked the door, then opened the drawer containing the remains of Kioki Santoya. Having to deal with dead people was the worst part of being an orderly. Elvis Dinkins had never really minded the rest of the job—emptying bedpans and changing linen didn't bother him.

Even sick people didn't bother him.

But dead people . . .

Despite his revulsion at having to deal with the corpse—or maybe *because* of it—Elvis Dinkins's eyes fixed on Kioki Santoya's face. The boy's eyes were open, and his face looked bloated. His mouth was open, too, and it looked to Elvis like the kid's tongue was all swollen up. His stomach churned as he saw the place where Dr. Hatcher had cut away a slice of it to send to the lab.

As he pulled on the surgical gloves he'd swiped from the scrub room, Elvis wondered if maybe he should take a slice of the tongue, too. But that would mean actually reaching into the dead boy's mouth, and Elvis wasn't sure he could do that.

It was going to be bad enough just taking pieces of tissue from the wound that Dr. Hatcher had cut when she'd opened the kid up to do the autopsy. Elvis shuddered. The sight of blood did tend to make him feel sick.

In fact, it made him feel sick enough that he was thinking about looking around for another job.

Maybe one working for Takeo Yoshihara, who he'd heard paid a lot better than anyone else on Maui.

And that, at least indirectly, was why he was in the morgue today.

A few days after he started working at the hospital, he'd been cleaning up one of the rooms when a doctor came in. Although Elvis Dinkins had been at the hospital less than a week, he'd already known who this doctor was.

Stephen Jameson. Personal physician to Takeo Yoshihara.

Someone to pay attention to.

Therefore, Elvis Dinkins had listened carefully when Dr. Jameson suggested that if he ever came across anything in the hospital that seemed unusual, he would appreciate it if Elvis would let him know.

At the time, of course, Elvis hadn't really known what might be considered unusual in a hospital. He'd waited, keeping a sharp lookout, but nothing "unusual" had come his way. Until now.

A teenage kid who'd died for some reason that even Dr. Hatcher hadn't been able to figure out—now that was something else again! It was just lucky for him he'd been in the emergency room a few minutes ago when Sergeant Olani came in.

He'd hung around in the hall while the cop talked to Hatcher, and then clocked out at the end of the shift, right after Jo-Nell Sims. Except instead of leaving, he'd waited until Dr. Hatcher left, then printed out a copy of the autopsy report she'd done. For a minute he'd thought maybe that was all he would give Dr. Jameson, but then he remembered the doctor talking about how the lungs looked funny. That was when he'd decided to collect a sample of the kid's lungs, too.

Now, though, as he stared at the loose stitches Dr. Hatcher had used to close the huge Y-shaped cut she'd made to gain access to the interior of Kioki Santoya's body, he wondered if he could actually do it. His hands were starting to shake, and he hadn't even cut the thread.

Gripping the handle of the scalpel he'd picked up in the operating room, Elvis Dinkins steeled himself and bent closer.

One by one he sliced through the stitches, until the corpse's torso was gaping open.

Elvis Dinkins gazed down at the jumbled organs that had been packed back into the body after the autopsy was completed. His stomach churned again, and he had to struggle to keep from throwing up right there. But as he sank the scalpel deep into the tissue of the left lung, he told himself it wasn't much different from cutting up the liver his mother used to fry with onions.

His nausea eased a little.

A few seconds later he had hacked a piece of the lung out and dropped it into one of the plastic specimen jars he'd found in the same cabinet as the scalpel. Of course, he had no idea what Jameson might find in the sample, but he thought it might be important.

Really important.

And if it was . . .

As he slipped out of the hospital, Elvis Dinkins was already dreaming about the future. Maybe after he got a job working for Takeo Yoshihara, he'd find a new apartment.

Hell, if he was lucky, the contents of the plastic bag might change his whole life!

The thought that they might also end his life never entered Elvis Dinkins's mind.

Jack Peters wished he knew what to say to the dozen teenage boys clustered around him. There was none of the laughter and playful jostling that ordinarily preceded track practice; this afternoon they all seemed lost in their own thoughts, and as the coach's eyes moved from one face to another, he saw one common element.

Fear.

None of them knew why Kioki Santoya had died last night, and because they didn't know, they were frightened.

He could almost hear what they were thinking:

What if Kioki had one of those new diseases, like ebola, where if you got it, you were dead in a few hours, puking your brains out, and bleeding everywhere?

What if someone killed Kioki?

What if . . . ?

But there were so many "what ifs" that Jack Peters knew there was no way to answer all of them; indeed, until they *knew* what had happened to Kioki, there was no way to answer any of them. "I guess none of us feels like practice today," he finally said. "I know I don't. And I know a lot of people say that when something like this happens, the best thing is to stay busy, to do anything just to keep from thinking about it. But I miss Kioki, and . . ." His voice trailed off while he tried to clear the lump that had formed in his throat. "I just want to remember him, I guess. So I'm canceling track practice today. Any of you who want to hang around and just talk, I'll be here. If you don't want to, that's fine, too." Once again his eyes roamed over the team. "I guess that's all I have to say," he finished.

For a few seconds no one moved; it was as if each of them was waiting for someone else to act. But finally Rick Pieper, shoulders slumped, hands in pockets, started back toward the locker room. Kioki, Peters knew, had been Rick's best friend. A moment later, Jeff Kina and Michael Sundquist followed Rick. As if taking their lead from the three who had been the last to see Kioki alive, the rest of the team began drifting back toward the locker room. The silence that had hung over the dozen boys on the field stayed with them as they stripped off their gym shorts and began pulling on their street clothes.

Ten minutes later, still together, Michael, Jeff Kina, and Rick Pieper emerged from the gym. Josh Malani was waiting for them.

"You wanta go get something to eat?" Josh asked, and Michael could tell by the uncertainty in his voice that Josh was wondering if any of them blamed him for Kioki's death.

"I'm not very hungry," Jeff said.

Josh's eyes narrowed slightly. "Look, what happened to Kioki wasn't our fault."

"No one said it was," Jeff replied. "I just wish I knew what happened. I mean—" He fell silent as he saw a police car turning into the school parking lot. "Uh-oh."

The other three boys turned to follow Jeff's gaze.

"You think they already figured out we broke into Ken's Dive Shop?" Rick Pieper asked as the squad car pulled to a stop.

"We didn't break in," Josh Malani said quickly. The policeman was out of his car now and coming toward him. "And there's no way he could know. All we'll tell him is that we were at the arcade out in Kihei. Okay? Just playing video games."

A moment later Cal Olani had ambled up to them, and Michael saw a glint of hostility flare up in Josh Malani's eyes.

Cal Olani saw it, too. "Take it easy, Josh," he said. "I'm not here to hassle you. Just wanted to ask you and your friends a couple of questions about last night." He studied each boy's face in turn, his eyes finally coming to rest on Michael. "Don't think I know you." He stuck his right hand out. "I'm Cal Olani."

"Michael Sundquist," Michael replied, automatically shaking the officer's hand.

"So, were you with Kioki Santoya last night, too?"

Michael nodded.

"Mind if I ask you a few questions?"

Michael shrugged.

"What'd you guys do?"

Michael felt a knot of fear tightening in his stomach. He was certain the cop would know the moment he told the first lie. But before he could say anything, Josh Malani began talking.

"Come on, man, all we were doin' was hangin' at the arcade over in Kihei."

"That true?" Olani asked Michael.

Michael could feel Josh's eyes boring into him. Finally, telling himself that if he didn't actually say anything it wasn't really a lie, he shrugged noncommittally and did his best to mimic the slightly sullen look that had come over both Jeff Kina's and Josh Malani's faces the moment the cop appeared.

Olani turned to Rick Pieper. "You were the one who dropped the Santoya boy off?"

Rick nodded. "I offered to drive him all the way home, but he didn't want my car to wake up his mom. So I dropped him off at his road."

"He seem okay?"

Rick frowned. "You mean like was he sick or something?"

When the cop nodded, Rick shrugged. "I guess he was okay. I mean, he didn't say he wasn't, and he didn't want me to take him all the way home, so I guess he must have been okay, huh?"

Cal Olani's eyes drifted from one boy to another. "How about you guys? You okay?"

"Since when do you care how we feel?" Josh Malani demanded.

Before Cal Olani could respond, Rick Pieper cut in. "Is that what happened to Kioki? He was sick?"

Olani hesitated, knowing any answer he gave would race through the school—and from there through the whole island—faster than an epidemic of flu. And Laura Hatcher hadn't actually said what had killed Kioki; she'd only been willing to rule certain things out. "Don't know yet. But he didn't seem to have any injuries." His eyes fixed on Josh again. "Look, Malani, I don't have any axes to grind. I'm just trying to find out what happened to your friend so it doesn't happen to anyone else. So just take it easy, okay?"

Josh shoved his hands deep in the pockets of his pants. "I'm cool," he said. "We just don't know anything."

Once more Cal Olani's eyes scanned the faces of the four boys. There was something, he was sure, that they weren't telling him. On the other hand, he couldn't remember the last time he'd talked to any kid on the island when he hadn't felt the same thing, to one degree or another. And until he knew exactly what had killed Kioki Santoya, there wasn't any use in trying to lean on them. Another day, maybe, but not now. "All right," he said. "Stay out of trouble, okay? I don't come back on shift until tomorrow."

"What do you think?" Jeff Kina asked as Olani drove out of the parking lot. "Does he know we borrowed Ken's stuff?"

" 'Course he doesn't," Josh insisted. "If he did, he wouldn't have left." He turned to Michael. "Want a ride home?"

Michael hesitated, still not sure they shouldn't have told the officer exactly what had happened last night. And when the guy had asked them if they were feeling okay, he'd instantly remembered gym class, when—

But he'd gotten over that!

Except he hadn't. At least not quite. Even now he could still feel something in his chest—nothing bad, really, but just not quite right. And if the other guys felt okay, he wasn't going to be the whiner. "Sure," he said, finally answering Josh's question. "Let's go."

But five minutes later, as they were coming into Makawao, he knew Josh had felt his hesitation. "You pissed at me?"

Michael shrugged. "I don't know. I just—"

"You never had the cops hassle you, did you?" Josh asked. Michael looked over at his friend, but Josh was staring straight ahead. "You never had them want to know what you were doin' on the beach in the middle of the night, and not want to tell them 'cause you didn't want to admit your dad was drunk and you just didn't want to go home."

Michael bit his lip.

"You never had to sit in the police station all night because your folks wouldn't come and get you, did you?"

Michael shook his head, but still said nothing.

"Okay, so maybe we should have told him," Josh finally admitted. "But I just get tired of being hassled, you know? So don't be pissed off at me, okay?" He paused, then: "Come on, Mike, let's just go do something!"

"Like what?" Michael asked warily.

Josh hesitated. When he spoke, his voice sounded almost shy and he continued to stare straight ahead out the windshield. " 'Spose your mom would mind if you showed me what she's digging up?"

Michael turned to stare at his friend. "You're kidding. *You* want to see an archaeological site?"

Josh Malani reddened. "Why wouldn't I?" he demanded. "I'm not stupid, you know."

Michael started laughing. "Well, sometimes you sure act stupid," he said. Then he spotted a pay phone outside one of the buildings in Makawao. "Pull over there."

Josh pulled over. "So are we still friends, or what?"

"Of course we're still friends," Michael assured him. "I've just got to call my mom so she can meet us at the gate."

"The gate?" Josh echoed. "What gate?"

"Ever hear of some guy named Takeo Yoshihara?"

Josh's eyes widened. "Is that who your mom works for?"

Michael cocked his head. "Is that some kind of big deal?" he countered.

Josh nodded. "Around here it doesn't get any bigger. Nobody ever sees him, and nobody really knows what he does. And hardly anybody's ever seen where he lives."

"Well, get ready," Michael said. " 'Cause we're about to see it all."

Not likely, Josh Malani thought as Michael swung out of the truck to call his mother. Not likely at all.

"Holy shit," Josh whispered as his truck, following Rob Silver's Explorer, emerged from the rain forest into the vast garden that was Takeo Yoshihara's estate. "Will you look at this? What do you think it cost?"

Even though his mother had described the estate to him, Michael was no more prepared for the reality of it than Josh. As his eyes darted from a pond to a waterfall to a Zen garden, he found himself unable to really look at anything. "Ten million?" he guessed.

"A lot more'n that," Josh said. "Look at those buildings. That's all koa wood, man. Stuff costs a fortune." He slowed the truck to a crawl, staring first in one direction, then in another. Suddenly an albino peacock appeared from a grove of trees, stopped short, and spread its enormous tail into a huge white fan. "I don't believe this, man," Josh breathed. "How many people do you suppose it takes to take care of it?"

Michael grinned. "Maybe we can get summer jobs as gardeners."

"Right," Josh groaned. "Except I hear you practically have to be a landscape architect just to mow the lawns in here."

A minute later they were through the estate and onto the bumpy track that led out to the site two miles farther on.

Stephen Jameson stared, unseeing, out the window of his office in the long, low-slung building that stood on the far side of the gardens from his employer's private residence. Though his eyes had unconsciously followed the progress of the Explorer and the ancient pickup that followed it as they wound through the gardens, a minute after they passed he wouldn't have even been able to say for certain what color either vehicle had been, so focused was his mind on the problem at hand.

On his desk lay the copy of the autopsy report. Next to it stood the jar containing the specimen of Kioki Santoya's lung that the orderly had carved out of the corpse. For a moment Jameson considered arranging to have the corpse transferred from the hospital morgue to the estate, but then realized that would only serve to draw more attention to the body than was already being paid. Besides, what would be the point? Jameson was already certain he knew the exact cause of the boy's death. He had already had a cursory look at the tissue sample through the microscope in his office. The full lab analysis that would be performed on the sample would, he was sure, only confirm his preliminary findings.

The question was, how had Kioki become exposed? And, just as important, had the three boys mentioned in the memo accompanying the autopsy report also been exposed?

Stephen Jameson picked up the phone on his desk, dialed a four-digit number, and began speaking the moment the phone at the other end was answered.

"Dr. Jameson here. I have three names: Jeff Kina, Josh Malani, and Rick Pieper. All three of them sixteen or seventeen years old. All three are to be kept under surveillance. If anything should happen to any of them—if they should get sick—bring them here. Is that clear?"

The man at the other end read back the three names. Stephen Jameson was about to hang up when another thought occurred to him. "There's one more name," he added. "Elvis Dinkins. He just left the estate a few minutes ago. It would be best if he didn't make it back to Wailuku."

By the time they'd gone only a quarter of a mile from the main part of Takeo Yoshihara's estate, Josh Malani had skidded off the rutted road twice, and the second time Rob Silver had to tow Josh's truck back onto the track.

"Maybe we better leave your truck here and go the rest of the way in the Explorer," he suggested as he unfastened the tow rope from Josh's front bumper.

"I can make it," Josh insisted. "I've been on lots worse roads than this one."

The look in Josh's eye told Rob that argument would be useless, so he tossed the rope into the back of his Explorer and continued along the road, glancing in his rearview mirror every few seconds to make sure Josh's rusty pickup was still behind him.

Miraculously, Josh managed to keep on the track the rest of the way, finally lurching to a stop in the clearing where the canopies had been set up to shelter the worktables. Josh gazed around, his disappointment at finding nothing more interesting than some worn rocks clear on his face. "This isn't actually the site," Katharine told the boys, coming out of the shelter of one of the canopies. "It's up that way. Come on."

As she led them along the steep trail into the ravine, Michael once again felt the strange sensation in his chest.

Not a pain, really.

Just a funny feeling, as if he were about to run out of breath, even though he was breathing just fine right now.

Weird.

Steeling himself against the odd phenomenon, he continued along the trail until at last they came to the ledge on which the fire pit and the skeleton lay.

"Jeez," Josh whispered as he gazed down at the remains that still lay in exactly the position in which Katharine had uncovered them. "What is it? A chimpanzee?"

"Not a chimpanzee, and not a gorilla," Katharine told him. She knelt down and began explaining the features of the skeleton, but Michael was no longer listening, for the moment he'd seen the skeleton, a feeling even stranger than the one in his chest had come over him.

A feeling that ran over his spine like fingers of ice.

A feeling almost like fear, but not quite.

He stood staring down at the skeleton, transfixed, then slowly forced himself to look away.

He glanced around.

Maybe it was just that it reminded him of someplace else—someplace he and his mother had been to years ago, some other dig, somewhere in Africa.

But most of the places they'd been in Africa hadn't been anything like this. They'd been in dry, desert areas, places where rain was so scarce that practically nothing grew at all, while here they were surrounded by rain forest, with trees towering overhead, vines climbing up their trunks, ferns sprouting from the vertical faces of the ravine, mosses everywhere.

Nothing like the part of Africa he'd been to—or anyplace else he could remember, either.

His eyes returned to the skeleton. He stooped down, and reached out a hand, laying it on the steeply sloping forehead of the skull.

Why? he thought. *Why did I do that?*

"Careful," he heard his mother say.

Jerking his hand away almost guiltily, he looked up at her. "What is it?" he asked.

Katharine's brows furrowed and her lips twisted into a quizzical half smile.

"Haven't you been listening? I was just telling Josh that so far it doesn't seem to quite fit with anything I've seen before."

But Michael's eyes remained on the skeleton. Again he felt the strange, cold shiver, the tightness in his chest. Involuntarily, he reached out, but before he could touch the skull again, his mother's voice cut through his reverie.

"Michael? Honey, are you all right?"

Michael pulled his hand away from the skull and straightened up. How could he tell his mother what he was feeling? How could he tell anyone, since he barely understood it himself? Finally tearing his eyes away from the strange skull, he looked up into his mother's face.

"What is it?" she asked again. "What's wrong?"

Michael's mind raced, but before he could reply, he heard Josh answering his mother's question.

"One of our friends died last night."

Katharine's mouth dropped open. "One of your friends?" she echoed. Her eyes shifted from Josh to Michael. "You mean one of the boys you were out with last night?"

Michael nodded. "Kioki Santoya," he said. "He was on the track team."

Katharine sank down onto a large boulder. "How?" she asked. "What happened?"

Slowly, Michael and Josh told her the little they knew about Kioki's death.

"And he just died?" Katharine asked as they finished. "In the middle of a cane field?"

As Michael and Josh nodded, Katharine instinctively stood and put her arms around her son. "How awful," she said. "You must feel—"

"I'm okay, Mom," Michael said, his face reddening with embarrassment as he pulled himself out of her embrace. "I—I hardly even knew him." His eyes darted toward Josh, and he was instantly sorry for how the words must have sounded. "I mean—" He floundered for a moment, then: "Oh, Jeez, I don't know *what* I mean!" Turning away, he stumbled up the trail toward the deep cleft in the face of the ravine that was the ancient fumarole. A moment later, almost hidden by the dense foliage that surrounded him, he dropped onto a fallen tree.

Shit!

What the hell was *wrong* with him? Why had he said that?

Suddenly, he saw a movement a few yards down the trail. Great! Now his mother was coming after him, like he was still ten years old.

Or still had asthma!

But a second later it was Josh Malani who appeared, and once more Michael felt himself flush with embarrassment. "Look, I didn't mean that about Kioki. I mean—"

"It's okay," Josh told him, dropping down onto the log next to him. "I say things I don't mean all the time."

Michael felt the heat in his face dissipate a little. "Still friends?"

Josh grinned. "You're not getting rid of me that easily." The two boys sat quietly for a minute, listening to the singing of the birds and the splashing of the waterfall. Then Josh spoke again. "How come you didn't want your mom to hug you?"

Michael's brow furrowed. "I'm not a little kid anymore," he groaned. "I mean, Jeez, Josh! Do you like it when your mom hugs you in front of your friends?"

Josh turned to look straight at Michael. "I wouldn't know," he said. "My mom never hugs me." He stood up. "Maybe we better go back down there, huh?"

Michael and Josh were just starting down the trail when Rob Silver appeared from around the bend. "Hey, what are you two up to?"

"Nothing," Michael said. "Just talking."

"Up here?" Rob asked, wrinkling his nose against the sulfurous fumes that filled the air. "How can you stand the stink?"

Michael and Josh looked at each other. "What stink?" Michael asked.

"That fumarole," Rob replied. "Can't you smell the sulfur? Your mom and I have been practically choking on it all afternoon."

Michael was about to say something, but once again Josh spoke before he had a chance.

"It's not so bad. I've smelled a lot worse."

Rob Silver rolled his eyes. "Not unless you live in a landfill. Come on, let's get out of here."

They walked back down to the clearing where the skeleton was, and Michael, unable to stop himself, gazed at the skull once again, the odd feeling washing over him stronger than ever, as if commanding him to stoop down once more, to take a closer look. Then, as he forced himself to back away, he realized that the strange feeling in his chest—the feeling that he was about to lose his breath—was gone.

Five minutes later, as they were getting back into Josh's truck, Katharine called out to them. "You guys want steaks for dinner?"

Michael glanced at Josh, who nodded. "Sure."

"Will you stop in Makawao and pick some up on the way home?"

"No problem!" Josh called. Gunning the engine, he popped the clutch and shot out of the clearing.

Katharine watched the truck disappear, shaking her head. "Do you suppose he always drives that way, or was he just showing off?"

Rob slung his arm around Katharine's shoulders. "Will you stop worrying? Believe me, Josh knows exactly how to drive that truck. I only had to pull him back on the road once on the way out here."

Katharine couldn't tell from Rob's tone whether he was kidding or not.

Michael hung onto the dashboard as the pickup bounced along the ruts, wishing it at least had seat belts. "Will you slow down?" he complained. "What if we break an axle?"

A peal of laughter rolled from Josh. "We won't! But even if we do, so what? From here, we could hike to your house!"

"Are you nuts?" Michael shot back. "We're miles away."

Josh shook his head. "We just circled around. If you went the other way when you left the clearing, you'd come to a path. All you have to do is climb over a couple of fences, and you come out about half a mile up from where you live. I've been out here lots of times. Sure never knew there was somebody buried up there, though."

Dusk was falling as Josh finally pulled out of the eucalyptus grove and parked the truck in front of the Sundquists' house. But instead of getting out of the cab, Michael sat thoughtfully gazing out at the fading panorama of the valley far below. "Hey, Josh?" he asked.

Something in his voice made the other boy pause. "Yeah?"

"Up there at that sulfur vent," Michael went on, his eyes finally shifting to look at his friend, "did you really smell anything?"

Josh hesitated, then shook his head. "I didn't smell a thing."

"So why did you lie?"

Josh shrugged. "Didn't feel like arguing. I just figured it was better to agree with him."

"You think Rob really smelled it?"

Josh frowned. "Sure. Why would he lie?"

Michael felt a shiver of apprehension. "Then why didn't *we* smell it?" he asked. "How come we didn't smell anything at all?"

A quizzical expression spread across Josh Malani's face. "What's going on with you? You sound like you're scared or something."

Michael shook his head. "I'm not scared, exactly. But I just keep thinking about Kioki, and—"

Josh jerked on the door handle and swung out of the cab. "Will you quit worrying all the time? I'm telling you, whatever happened to Kioki doesn't have anything to do with us. Everything's fine!"

But as Michael got out of the truck, he still kept wondering:

If everything was so fine, how come Kioki was dead?

CHAPTER 14

Smoke and steam were billowing up from a great tear in the surface of the mountainside, and a curtain of fire hung against the black night sky. It was as if the entire mountain were ready to explode. Katharine shuddered as she stared at the image on the screen.

Rob Silver, sitting next to her on the sofa, picked up on her fears instantly. "Take it easy," he said. "It looks a lot worse than it is."

For half an hour they'd been watching the live coverage of the new eruption on the Big Island, and although it was the third time Rob had reassured her, Katharine still sat staring, nearly frozen in horror, at the hellish images being broadcast from the next island—an island that suddenly seemed much closer than it had only an hour earlier.

"I know that's what you keep telling me," she replied. "And I understand that these aren't the kind of volcanoes that explode. But you have to admit, it's very, very scary-looking."

Josh Malani, sprawled out on the floor next to Michael, gazed at the fiery scene as if mesmerized. "Wouldn't it be neat to be there? You can go right out onto the lava flows and look down into the crevices where it's still red hot."

"Maybe we can fly over there," Michael suggested. "Maybe—"

"Maybe Josh can go home, and you can go to bed," Katharine interrupted, shutting off the television with the remote. "You both have school tomorrow, remember?"

"Come on, Mom, turn it back on," Michael pleaded. "It's only a little after ten, and—"

"And it's 'educational'?" Katharine interrupted, reading her son's mind. "I don't think we need to go through that one, do you?"

Josh Malani, hearing the slight edge that had come into Katharine's voice, scrambled to his feet. "I think I better get out of here," he said. A couple of minutes later, as he and Michael were going out to his truck, he said, "I like your mom."

"Yeah, right," Michael groaned. "She just kicked you out, and sent me to bed."

"So what?" Josh countered. "She let me come up here for dinner, and no one got drunk and started yelling."

Michael studied his friend. "Is that what happens at your house?"

"Not every night," Josh said a little too quickly, wishing he'd kept his mouth shut. "I guess it happens to everyone, though, doesn't it?"

"Sure," Michael replied, though certainly nothing like that had ever happened to him. Then: "Hey, if you want, you can stay here tonight."

Josh hesitated, then shook his head. "I better go. Don't want your mom thinking I'm moving in." His smile flashed. "Besides, I'm not sleepy. I think I might just drive around for a while. Wanta come?"

Michael rolled his eyes. "Like my mom'd let me."

Josh shrugged, gunning the engine. "Okay. See you tomorrow." Shoving the transmission into reverse, he whipped the pickup around, shifted into low, and shot away, laughing as he watched Michael try to duck away from the plume of dirt his spinning tires kicked up. But as he turned down Olinda Road, his laughter died away, and the strange restlessness that had been creeping up on him all evening came over him once again.

Except it wasn't exactly that he felt restless.

It was something else—something he couldn't quite get a grip on.

Part of it was his chest, which felt kind of funny. It didn't hurt, exactly, and didn't feel congested, like he was getting a cold.

It just felt—weird!

Coming out onto Olinda Road, he turned up the hill. Though the night was getting chilly, he left the windows wide open. Finally, near the top, he turned left and began winding back down toward Makawao. As he came around a curve, his headlights swept across a familiar figure.

Jeff Kina, his huge frame hunched over, his head down, was walking along the side of the road. Josh slowed the truck as he came abreast of Jeff. "Hey! Whatcha doin'?"

Jeff, startled, squinted in the darkness, then recognized Josh's truck. "Just walkin'," he said. "Didn't feel like going to bed, and—I don't know—I just felt sort of weird. Like if I couldn't get out of the house I was gonna go nuts or something." He fell silent for a moment, then: "I don't know. Maybe it's what happened to Kioki, you know?"

"Nobody knows what happened to Kioki," Josh reminded him. "Hey, want to go do something?"

Jeff shrugged. "Might as well," he agreed. Pulling open the passenger door, he climbed into the truck and Josh continued down the hill toward Makawao.

Neither of them paid any attention to the car that was pulled off the road just below the next curve.

The driver, though, noticed them, and as soon as Josh's truck passed him, he turned his car around. In accordance with the orders he'd been given a few hours earlier, he continued following Jeff Kina.

The driver of the pickup—whoever he was—was somebody else's problem.

Josh turned onto the Haleakala Highway, utterly unaware of the car that was following his truck. In the distance he could see the glow of a burning cane field. The smoke roiling into the night sky brought an image of the volcano on the Big Island into his mind. At the same time, a thrill of anticipation raced through his body.

"Ever been close to a cane fire?" he asked Jeff. When the other boy made no reply, Josh glanced over at him. Jeff's eyes—like his own a moment ago—seemed to be fixed on the distant flames. "Jeff?" he said more loudly, and finally Jeff turned to look at him, though for a moment Josh wasn't sure his friend was actually seeing him. "You okay?"

Jeff nodded. "You ever been close to a cane fire?" he asked, his words exactly echoing the question Josh himself had asked only a moment before.

Josh, deciding not to question his friend's odd behavior, shook his head. "Want to go see it?"

Again Jeff nodded, but he said nothing and his eyes went back to the cane fire that was quickly spreading in the distance. Josh pressed his foot on the accelerator, and the truck lunged forward, picking up speed as it tore down the nearly deserted highway.

The driver watched the truck surge ahead, then punched one of the two memory buttons on his cell phone. He waited impatiently until the phone was answered at the other end. "My guy may have spotted me," he said. "Anyway, something just spooked him, and the guy he's with took off like a jackrabbit with a firecracker up its ass. Do we have anybody in Kahului?"

"You're covered," the man at the other end replied. "Just give me the description."

"It's a pickup truck, real old, real rusted, and beat-up. Two kids in the cab."

"Got a license?"

"Couldn't get close enough." Cutting off the connection, the man pressed on the gas pedal, speeding up just enough to keep the taillights of the racing truck visible.

Josh swerved the truck into a narrow lane that headed through the fields toward the spot where the blaze was still growing.

"Jesus," Jeff whispered in the seat next to him. "Did you ever see anything like that?"

"We've seen it a million times," Josh replied. But even as he spoke the words, he knew that tonight it was different.

Always before he'd done his best to avoid cane fires, closing the windows tightly against the smoke and soot, even shutting the air vents to keep the acrid fumes out of the car.

Once—only a couple of months ago—he'd had to drive past a burning field on his way down from Pukalani. For a minute he'd considered turning around, although detouring meant going nearly twenty miles out of his way. And when he was about halfway past the burning field, he'd wished he'd done it. The heat on his face had felt like it was searing his skin, and the roar of the fire had scared him almost as much as the crackling flames.

But tonight the blazing inferno of the field fascinated him even more than the images of the erupting craters on the Big Island.

He pressed his foot on the accelerator, and the truck shot forward.

"Yee-*hah!*" Jeff Kina whooped in the seat next to him. "Let's go!"

The truck surged ahead, the dust from the road mixing with the black ash that was raining from the sky to swirl in through the open windows. The air was thick with smoke now, and Jeff, still howling next to him, was sucking it deep into his lungs.

Josh drove on. The truck roared into the burn area. Now the fields on both sides of them were ablaze, the stalks of cane charred black, the smoldering foliage glowing an angry red. Josh brought the truck to a halt and sat gazing, awestruck, at the inferno around him.

The strange, constricted feeling that had been growing in him all evening was suddenly gone.

Jeff Kina stared at the whirlwind of fire racing through the fields around him. Everywhere he looked there were flames, and as he sucked the smoky air deep into his lungs, he felt a wave of exultation break over him, setting every nerve in his body on edge and heightening every one of his senses. His skin thrilled to the heat of the fire, and he could taste the sweetness of the burning cane in his mouth. The flames danced around him, and as smoke streamed up from the charred cane of the field, he nearly imagined he could see strange, wraithlike forms dancing above the inferno. It was almost like being stoned, and a great feeling of well-being spread through him, pushing out the peculiar restlessness that had driven him from the house an hour ago. Then, as the fiery tempest swirled higher and hotter around him, he heard another sound—the seductively whispering song of a siren.

It was as if the siren was speaking to him, urging him to leave the truck and join in the dance the flames were performing in the fields.

The smoke itself seemed to beckon to him. Jeff Kina opened the door of the truck and slid out. . . .

The screaming sirens interrupted the reverie Josh Malani had slipped into, and the truck door slamming drove the last vestiges of it away. "What are you doing?" he yelled as Jeff stood by the truck, staring at the flames as if he'd been hypnotized. Sliding across the front seat, he reached out and grabbed Jeff's arm as the warning siren grew louder and the flashing lights of an approaching truck became visible through the miasma of smoke. Jeff was trying to pull away from him now, but he tightened his grip on the other boy's arm. "Jesus, Jeff! Get back in the truck! The fire crew's coming! What the hell's wrong with you?"

The yellow truck slammed to a stop directly ahead of the pickup, and while one man jumped out of the passenger seat, two more leaped from its bed. As two of the men grabbed Jeff's arm and began pulling him toward the yellow truck, the third one yelled at Josh.

"Are you kids crazy? Get this damned truck out of here before it blows up!"

Sliding back into the driver's seat, Josh slammed the truck into reverse and began backing down the road. An ember flew through the window and seared his forehead, and as he momentarily lost his grip on the steering wheel, the pickup swerved sharply to the right. For a split second Josh tried to regain control, then he let the wheel spin. The truck slewed around, its rear end leaving the dirt road and skidding into the burning field, but even before it came to a stop, Josh had shoved the transmission into gear and smashed his foot against the gas pedal. The rear tires spun, then caught, and Josh shot forward, not slowing down until he reached the paved highway.

Jeff!

Where was Jeff!

Should he go back and try to find him?

A set of headlights flashed on in front of him, and for the first time Josh realized that there was a car parked across the road. Then, as the car's engine roared to life and it shot down the road Josh had just emerged from, he saw another car racing toward him, this one coming from Kahului.

Blue lights were flashing on its roof.

Cops!

Shit! What was he supposed to do?

What *could* he do?

Taking a last look down the road, but seeing no trace of Jeff Kina, or the truck the two men had been dragging him toward, or the car that had been parked on the other side of the highway, Josh made up his mind.

Jeff would be all right. Those guys must have been a fire crew. They'd get Jeff out of there.

But it was time for him to get out of *here*. Slamming the truck into gear, he started down the highway. A few seconds later he passed the speeding car with the flashing blue lights, never noticing that it wasn't a police car.

As soon as it passed, he looked in the rearview mirror, certain that the cops would turn around to chase him. But the car turned off the highway into the burning cane field.

CHAPTER 15

Katharine came totally awake in an instant, her motherly instincts on full alert, knowing without doubt what had awakened her.

After all, how many times before had she been jolted from sleep exactly this way, sound asleep one moment, wide awake the next?

More than she wanted to remember.

She lay in the darkness, praying that she was wrong, praying that it wasn't happening again. And listening.

Then she heard it—the sound that must have awakened her.

It was coming from Michael's room, and it was the terrible racking gasp of someone who is unable to fill his lungs with air.

Getting up from her bed and snatching a thin robe from the chair in the corner, she raced for her son's room.

There was a silvery glow all around him, and he knew he was in the water again.

He also knew it was night.

And that he was alone.

Fear shot through him: you were never supposed to dive alone.

He turned in the water, trying to orient himself.

Where was the bottom? He gazed downward, peering into the depths, but the silvery glow seemed to go on forever. There were no fish, no heads of coral, no sandy bottom rippled by currents.

He rolled over, peering upward.

No glimpse of the surface. All he could perceive was the same silver-lit expanse spreading endlessly away.

He felt his heart start to beat faster, could even hear it in the silence of the deep.

How deep?

But how deep could he be? He wasn't wearing a diver's suit—not even a wet suit.

The pulse of terror pounding in his ears, he realized that not only were his friends not with him, but he wasn't in the safe confines of the small pool at the end of the lava flow, either.

He was alone in the vastness of the ocean.

Except he wasn't alone.

There was something else—some presence—nearby.

He could feel it, just out of his range of vision.

Panic reached for him with the grip of tentacles grasping their prey.

He twisted around in the water, searching for the unseen presence, catching just a flicker of it: a figure, ghostly pale in the water, gazing at him.

The tentacles wrapped themselves around him.

He felt the presence again, closer this time, and whirled in the water.

Again he caught just a flash of it before it vanished.

And then he saw another and another: Ghostly wraiths in the water, almost without shape or form, but starting to close in on him.

He had to get away from them.

He started swimming, but the water seemed to have turned to sludge, and he could barely move his arms and legs. Then he felt something clammy on his leg, felt one of the beings touch him, and tried to jerk away.

They were all around him, surrounding him, wrapping themselves around his body so tightly that he couldn't move, couldn't breathe.

Air!

He was running out of air!

He redoubled his efforts to thrash out against the wraiths, but they were twisted around his chest now, squeezing tighter and tighter until he knew it no longer mattered if there was any air left in his tanks, for he no longer had the power to breathe.

He was going to die, drown alone in the sea!

He thrashed out once more, lunging this time with enough force to jerk himself out of the nightmare world in which he'd been entrapped.

Coming awake, he rolled off the bed and onto the floor, and lay still for a moment, struggling to catch his breath, wrestling against the wraiths that still constricted him.

His sheet!

He tore at it, finally pulling it loose and shucking it off, but still he couldn't catch his breath.

It was as if the nightmare were still upon him, though he knew he was wide-awake.

Suddenly the darkness of the room was washed away by a blinding glare, and in the sudden whiteness he saw one of the apparitions from the sea, nearly invisible in the surrounding brightness, looming over him.

With a great agonizing gasp, Michael finally succeeded in sucking air into his constricted lungs. Jerking the window open even as he rose from the floor, he fled out into the night.

"Michael!" Katharine called as her son dove through the window. "Michael, don't! Let me help you!"

If he heard her, he gave no sign, and by the time she reached the window a second later, he was gone, swallowed up by the darkness as completely as if he'd vanished from the face of the planet.

Wrapping her robe more tightly around her, Katharine found a flashlight and went out onto the veranda, snapping the porch light on, but turning it out again immediately as she realized it blinded her to anything beyond the circle of its own illumination. As her eyes readjusted to the darkness, she switched the flashlight on and played its beam over the small clearing in which the house sat.

Nothing.

Nothing except the shadowy grove of eucalyptus, the ancient trees surrounding her like giants out of a dark fantasy. As the light passed over their twisted trunks they seemed to come alive, moving in the darkness, their limbs reaching out to her.

No! she told herself. They're just trees.

"Michael!" she called again. "Michael, come back!"

Again there was no answer, but she was almost certain he must still be able to hear her. And if he was running through the eucalyptus grove, why couldn't she hear him?

But of course she couldn't—his bare feet would be all but soundless on the thick carpet of leaves that covered the ground, so sodden from the frequent rain that they barely cracked under the leather soles of shoes.

She circled the house, then went to the edge of the clearing and circled the area again, using the beam of light to penetrate as deeply as she could into the dense stand of trees.

Finally she returned to the house, but stood on the veranda, trying to decide what to do.

Search the forest?

To go alone into the eucalyptus grove and the rain forest beyond would be to risk getting lost herself.

Call the police?

And tell them what? That her asthmatic son had run away in the middle of the night? When they heard how old he was, they would tell her to call back in the morning.

But what had possessed Michael to run from her that way?

Obviously he'd had another nightmare, and this one must have been far worse than the first. Although she'd barely had a glimpse of him in the moment before he bolted through the open window, she'd seen the terror on his face.

His eyes were wide and his mouth stretched into a rictus of fear as if he were gazing upon the evil countenance of a demon that was attacking him.

But it had been only her, clad in her white robe, reaching out to him.

Then he was gone, diving headfirst through the window, rolling once on the veranda before leaping to his feet and sprinting across the clearing, disappearing into the blackness of the night even before he reached the forest.

If the forest was where he had headed.

And wearing nothing but a pair of Jockey shorts.

For the first time, she despised the isolation of the house. Why had she ever taken it? There were neighborhoods all over the island where there were streetlights, where she would have seen him running, known at least in which direction he had gone.

Where there were neighbors who might have seen him, too, and been worried about a boy running through the night in nothing but a pair of undershorts.

But up here there was nothing but darkness in which he could easily hide, with only a scattering of houses he could skirt around if he didn't want to be seen.

Maybe she should just wait.

Maybe, when the terror of the dream had finally released him from its grip, he would come home again.

As Katharine turned to step back into the house through the French doors, she noticed her eyes were stinging. Then, as she rubbed them with her fists, she noticed something else.

The winds had died, and the rustling of the leaves of the eucalyptus trees had stopped. Other than the faint chirping of a few frogs and insects, the night was silent.

And the air had turned heavy, laden with the dust and gases being spewed out from the eruption on the Big Island.

If it was making her eyes sting, what must the vog be doing to Michael? Was that what had happened? Had he awakened to find his lungs choking on the pollution that, until a moment ago, she herself hadn't even noticed?

She moved through the French doors, closing them behind her, then went through the house and switched on every light, both inside and out, turning the little bungalow into a beacon in the night.

If Michael tried to come home, at least he would be able to see the house.

Then she sat down to wait, already wondering how long she could stay here alone, worrying about him, and whom she would call when finally she could stand it no longer.

But of course she already knew whom she would call.

Rob Silver.

And he would come, and help her, and help Michael.

If, that is, they could find Michael.

CHAPTER
16

Michael moved quickly through the dark shadows cast by the dense groves of trees that lined the road. He'd lost track of time—had no idea how long it had been since he'd fled from the house, no idea what time it might be now.

He could barely remember scrambling through the window, jumping over the railing around the veranda, and dashing across the clearing toward the darkness of the eucalyptus grove, so gripped had he been by the terrors of the dream. His only motivation had been to escape the light, and the apparition that appeared in it. But even after he'd escaped into the protective darkness, he kept running, dodging between the trees until he emerged from the woods and burst out into a grassy field. He'd dropped down to the ground, breathing hard.

Escape!

He had to escape.

But where? Even as the question formed in his head, so also had the answer: in his mind he saw the cleft in the ravine above the place where his mother had unearthed the strange skeleton.

That's where he would go.

But how would he find it?

As the terror of the dream began to loosen its clammy grip, he remembered what Josh had told him that afternoon. Somewhere up the road, there was a trail.

He was still more or less following the road, keeping to a few of its twists and turns, but more often than not scrambling up the steep slope where the hairpins were so tight it would take him far longer to follow the pavement. He'd passed half a dozen driveways, and even something that looked like it might be a footpath, but some voice inside him had told him to keep walking, to go farther up. A few yards farther on, though, he stopped abruptly.

For a moment he didn't know quite why he'd stopped, but a second later he saw it: a narrow track leading off in the general direction of where Takeo Yoshihara's estate—and his mother's dig—must lie. But how could he know? What if it was the wrong path? What if it took him in the wrong direction?

Despite his doubts, he began moving along the trail, something inside of him sure that he was going in the right direction. Twenty minutes later the path ended at a rough track. Not hesitating, Michael turned left.

He broke into a trot, the certainty that he was going in the right direction growing stronger with every step. A little farther on he came to a gate, climbed over it, then scrambled over the fence he encountered a few minutes later. It was as if he was following a beacon, though the darkness of the night was barely softened by the dim moon above, its light cut by scudding clouds.

Finally, though, as he came to the clearing that housed the worktables and their canopies, the last of the fear that had gripped him during the nightmare disappeared.

He moved on, a moment later coming to the ancient campsite where the skeleton lay. Michael knelt for a moment. His eyes fixed on the fleshless features of the skull, and as a silvery ray of moonlight found a tear in the clouds and illuminated the long-dead being's empty eyes, Michael felt once more the strange sensation come over him, as it had that afternoon, composed partly of familiarity, partly of fear.

Then the ray of moonlight disappeared behind the curtain of clouds, releasing him. Michael rose to his feet and moved into the protective shelter of the long-dead vent.

Tonight the vent was warm—far warmer than the air outside—and

Michael felt a soft mist envelop him. He sank down, slumping against the moss-covered rocks.

Soon he was drifting into a dreamless sleep.

He had no idea what woke him up; perhaps a sound, perhaps some sixth sense.

Nor did he have any idea how long he'd been asleep.

But the moment Michael came awake, all his senses were fully alert. He pulled himself into a tight crouch and held perfectly still, listening.

The moon had nearly set and the clouds had thickened. Even so, he could easily make out the shapes of the trees around him, and see the lithe form of a mongoose slip past on the narrow trail that had brought him to the lair in which he hid.

He made no movement, for above the chirping of the insects and the faint mumblings of sleepy birds, another sound was coming to him.

Voices.

Human voices, so low he couldn't quite make out the words.

But they were coming closer.

Michael rose to his feet, his senses practically tingling with the sensation of gathering danger.

He strained his ears, and finally he could make out a sentence.

"About a quarter of a mile ahead—up where that friend of Dr. Silver's is working."

Him!

They were looking for him!

Instinctively, Michael shrank back deeper into the cleft in the ravine's wall, but a second later realized the trap. If they knew where he was, he'd have no escape.

Darting out into the darkness, he shivered for a moment against the cold of the night, then pushed the chill from his mind, concentrating on only one thing.

Escape.

He moved quickly—far more quickly than when he'd come—leaving the path only a few feet from the entry to the cleft, snaking his way through the dense tangle of the rain forest until he came back to the track a hundred yards from the main clearing where the worktables stood.

He could still hear the voices, but as he listened they became less distinct, and he knew they were no longer coming toward him, but searching for him where he'd been only a few moments ago.

Seizing the opportunity, he turned and fled, loping along the rutted track with an ease that belied the darkness.

Coming to the fence, he climbed over it, then vaulted the gate a minute later. He kept running, his legs pumping in a steady rhythm, his feet making barely any sound as he flew along the track. He came to the path that led off to the right, but instead of turning, he went on, then left the track and made his way across the mountain's slope, only coming back to the path when he was a few yards from the point where he'd left the pavement—

When?

How long had it been?

He had no idea.

Suddenly he was exhausted. The muscles in his legs were starting to burn, and his knees and ankles felt as sore as if he'd been running for hours. He was panting, and as he stopped to catch his breath, he listened.

He heard nothing.

Once again he was alone in the night.

As he emerged from the narrow lane leading through the eucalyptus trees, Michael could see his mother standing on the veranda, still clad in her thin white bathrobe. The moment he saw her, he understood part of the panic he'd felt earlier.

What he'd seen in his room hadn't been one of the apparitions from the dream.

It had only been his mother, switching on the light.

Stupid!

How could he have been so stupid?

Taking a deep breath, he walked out of the grove of trees and into the circle of light that spread from the veranda out into the clearing.

Katharine's eyes widened and her mouth dropped open. "Michael?" Then: "*Michael!* My God, are you all right?" A second later she was off the veranda. "Michael, what happened? Oh, God, I've been so frightened! When you went out the window—"

"I'm okay, Mom," Michael broke in. "I just—I don't know—it was really weird, and—" They were back on the veranda now, and his mother was clinging to his arm. "I'm really sorry," he said.

Katharine pulled Michael into the house and looked anxiously into his face. "Are you sure you're all right?" she asked again. "I've been so worried. You sounded like you could hardly breathe, and the way you took off—"

Michael pulled away from her grip. "I really feel dumb," he said, sinking down onto the sofa. He looked up at her. "And you're gonna be really pissed at me."

Katharine dropped into the chair opposite him. "Just tell me what happened."

He tried to tell her about the nightmare, but most of it had vanished from his memory. Still fresh, however, was the vision he'd seen when his terror had finally driven him out of his sleep. "It was you," he finished. "In that bathrobe. I was barely awake, and that robe makes you look like one of the things that was chasing me in the nightmare."

"But that's crazy!" Katharine objected. "I was trying to help you! All I wanted to do was—"

"It doesn't matter, Mom," Michael said. "I'm really sorry I scared you."

"But where did you go?" Katharine asked.

Should he tell her? How could he? He barely understood what he had done himself. Suddenly it seemed almost impossible that he'd not only found the trail Josh had told him about, but followed an unmarked route to the dig as well.

And what about the people who'd been looking for him? Suddenly he knew who they must have been and how they'd known he was there.

The dig was on Takeo Yoshihara's property, and he probably had a surveillance system everywhere on it.

They must have been watching him from the minute he climbed that first gate. And if they'd caught him . . .

Jesus! His mom probably would have lost her job!

But they hadn't caught him—he'd gotten away!

He made up his mind.

"I didn't go anywhere, really," he said. "When I finally came awake—I mean really awake—I was out in a field." He hesitated. "And it was kind of fun being outside in the middle of the night. So I lay down to look at the sky for a while and I guess I fell asleep." Did she believe him? He couldn't tell. "I guess you're pretty mad at me, aren't you?"

Katharine took a deep breath, then let it out in a long sigh. "I don't know," she finally admitted. "I was so frightened at the way you were breathing, and when you didn't come back . . ." She shook her head. "You're really sure you're all right now?"

"I'm fine," Michael insisted.

"If you're 'fine,' then why were you having such a hard time breathing?" Katharine demanded, her fear giving way to anger as she remembered the torment she'd gone through. "And do you have any idea how many times I picked up the phone to call the police?"

Michael stifled a groan.

"But I didn't," Katharine went on. "I kept reminding myself that you're not a little boy, and that I have to stop thinking of you as if you were still sick all the time." Her eyes fixed on his. "So I didn't call them. Instead I sat here and worried myself half to death."

"I'm really sorry, Mom," Michael began again. "I don't know what I can tell you. I—"

"Don't tell me anything," Katharine interrupted. "Just don't argue about going to see a doctor in the morning, all right?"

A glare of headlights appeared through the window. "I thought you said you didn't call anyone." Michael, already on his feet, was starting toward his room, suddenly embarrassed about being clad in his underwear.

"I didn't call the police," Katharine told him. "But I had to call someone."

A car door slammed, and a moment later Rob Silver appeared at the front door. "I've changed my mind," he began. "I really think we ought to call the police. If he's out—"

"He's back," Katharine told him. "He came in about five minutes ago. And he seems to be okay. But I'm taking him to see a doctor in the morning."

Rob nodded. "I'll call Stephen Jameson first thing," he said. "He's the best doctor on the island, and he works for Takeo Yoshihara."

"All he's going to do is tell you I'm fine, and then you really are going to look like an overprotective mother," Michael groused. "Why don't you just drop me off at school?"

"In case you didn't notice," Katharine observed archly, "we're going in exactly the opposite direction. And as for me being overprotective, we're just going to have to agree to disagree. Given your medical history, I think your difficulty breathing last night is a perfectly legitimate cause for concern. And since Dr. Jameson agreed with me, that settles it."

The argument had been going on ever since breakfast, when Rob Silver, who had spent the rest of the night on the Sundquists' sofa, had called Stephen Jameson, then turned the phone over to Katharine. Michael had listened in silence as she set up the appointment, and wondered if someone at Takeo Yoshihara's estate might have seen him last night and would recognize him this morning. After all, *something* had told them he was there last night, and brought the guards looking for him.

What if they actually had pictures of him?

There were cameras that could do that—cameras that could photograph things in a lot less light than there'd been last night.

But wouldn't they have called the police if they had pictures?

Though he'd done his best to talk her out of it, and knew he was now skating on pretty thin ice, Michael figured he might as well take one last shot at it. "There's a school bus stop right up there," he said, pointing to a yellow sign a hundred yards farther along the road. "If you just drop me off—"

"I'm not going to drop you off, and I'm getting tired of arguing about it," Katharine cut in.

Michael, watching the bus stop slide by, and hearing the finality in his mother's voice, gave up the argument and reached out to turn on the car radio. An announcer was just finishing a report on the mayor's assessments of the island's economic condition, and Michael was about to change the station when the newscaster's voice took on a somber note. "Two local men died in the scheduled burning of a Maui sugarcane field last night. Their bodies were recovered this morning from a field off the Haleakala Highway. Their names are being withheld pending notification of their families. In an unrelated incident, a Makawao boy has been reported missing by his mother. Jeff Kina left his home around nine o'clock last night, and police confirm that he was one of three boys questioned in relation to the death of Kioki Santoya, whose body was found early yesterday. Though there is currently no evidence connecting the Kina boy's disappearance to the death of young Kioki Santoya, police are not yet ruling out the possibility that these two incidents are related. Anyone who might have seen Jeff Kina, who is described as being six feet two inches tall and weighing 225 pounds, should contact the Maui Sheriff's Department immediately.

"In other news . . ."

But Michael was no longer listening.

What was going on? Jeff was missing? He glanced over at his mother. Should he tell her he knew both Jeff and Kioki? That they'd both been with him the night before last?

But then he'd have to tell her everything. And when she found out he'd not only gone out diving at night, but broken into a dive shop—

No! Josh had known where the key was, and they hadn't broken in!

But they might as well have.

He was still struggling with what, if anything, he should tell his mother about Kioki and Jeff when he saw the gate to Takeo Yoshihara's estate swing open. But his mother hadn't pressed any buttons on the sun visor, or anywhere else that he could see. "Where's the remote control?" he asked, a knot of apprehension forming in his stomach.

"There isn't one," Katharine told him. "The car has some gadget on it that the gate can sense."

"You're kidding," Michael breathed. His eyes were already searching for signs of the cameras that he now was certain must be keeping watch over the grounds. "Does it know who you are, too?" He tried to keep his voice casual. "Or do they have cameras?"

Katharine glanced quizzically at Michael out of the corner of her eye. "I hardly think they need cameras," she said. Yet as they went into the lobby of the building she'd been in yesterday with Rob Silver, her eyes—almost of their own volition—scanned the corners where security cameras would most likely be.

They were there.

But why wouldn't they be, she wondered, given the collection of art housed in the lobby? There were at least half a dozen sculptures scattered through the vast space, cabinets filled with priceless artifacts stood against the walls, and the painting that hung behind the desk where a private security officer sat looked like it might be a Vlaminck. The security guard himself—the same one who'd been on duty yesterday when she and Rob had gone to Rob's office to use the computer—looked up, then smiled as he recognized her.

"Morning, Dr. Sundquist. Dr. Jameson's already in his office." He gestured in the opposite direction from the wing in which Rob Silver's office was located. "Third door on the right."

A beautiful Eurasian woman of perhaps thirty sat at a desk behind the door the guard had indicated. "I'm Jade Quinn," she said, standing up and offering her hand to Katharine as they came into the spacious office. "Steve Jameson's nurse, secretary, and all-around gofer." She smiled at Michael. "You must be Michael, but you certainly don't look very sick."

"See?" Michael said to Katharine. "I told you. Can we go now? If we hurry, I won't miss second period."

"Not quite that easily," Katharine observed. "Is Dr. Jameson here yet?"

"In the building, but not quite in the office yet," the nurse replied, smiling apologetically. She rose and led them to a door leading to an inner office. "If you'll just make yourselves comfortable, I'm sure Dr. Jameson will be here in a minute or two."

Katharine and Michael stepped into a room that looked nothing like an ordinary doctor's office. Decorated like a comfortable den, its three interior walls were paneled in koa, and the outside wall was made up of French doors opening onto an elegantly laid-out Zen garden. The gravel was perfectly raked, and the stones, though apparently natural at first glance, had actually been subtly carved into abstract forms that both arrested and soothed the eye. Just as Katharine and Michael were about to seat themselves on a deep leather-upholstered sofa, the door from the receptionist's office opened and Stephen Jameson stepped in.

"Dr. Sundquist," he said, taking Katharine's hand in his and gripping it warmly. "So nice to meet you. Sorry to be late—I was just finishing something up in the lab downstairs. And you must be Michael," he continued, releasing his grip on Katharine's hand to extend his hand toward Michael. "Steve Jameson."

"Hi," Michael said, briefly shaking the doctor's hand. "Look, I'm really sorry Mom called you—"

"Suppose I be the judge of whether she should have called me or not?" Jameson interrupted. He tipped his head toward a door set into a wall that was otherwise filled with bookshelves. "Why don't you go in there and take your shirt off, then we'll have a look." When Michael was gone, he gestured Katharine into one of the two chairs in front of his desk, dropped something that looked like a plastic card into the top drawer of a credenza, then seated himself in the chair opposite Katharine. "Why don't you tell me what happened last night?"

Katharine related the story as briefly as she could as Jameson jotted a few notes. Then she waited in the office as the doctor followed Michael into the next room. Half an hour later, Dr. Jameson's examination of Michael finished, he lowered his large frame into the chair behind his desk and waited until Michael, still buttoning his shirt, emerged from the other room and took the chair next to his mother. Jameson winked at him, then turned to Katharine.

"Well, I've done as much poking, prodding, and peering as I can, and I've listened to practically every inch of his lungs. I had Jade take a set of X rays, which she should be finished cooking in a few more minutes. The blood and urine samples will take a little longer, but unless something unexpected shows up, I don't see anything for you to be worried about."

"But last night—"

"Last night he had a nightmare, and bad dreams can make for some of the worst noises you've ever heard," Jameson interrupted. The door to the examining room opened and Jade Quinn appeared, holding a large sheet of film which she placed on a light box built into one of the walls. "Why don't we take a look?" the doctor suggested.

As far as Katharine could tell, the picture showed Michael's lungs looking no different than they had the last time they'd been X-rayed in New York. "Considering his history of asthma, they're in remarkably good shape," she heard Jameson say. "And his lung capacity, though not quite up to where I'd like it to be, isn't anything to worry about, either. All in all, I'd have to say he's in very good health."

Katharine felt a surge of relief.

"Then can I go to school now?" Michael asked.

"As far as I'm concerned, you can."

"And my mother can stop worrying about me every second of the day?"

Jameson smiled. "I'm just a doctor," he said. "There are some things even I can't stop."

Katharine stood up. "I guess maybe I overreacted last night," she said, extending her hand to the doctor. "I can't thank you enough for taking a look, though."

Jameson spread his hands in a dismissive gesture. "Glad to be of service. And please feel free to call me anytime." He walked them to the door of the office, nodded a final good-bye as they left, then returned to his desk and picked up the phone.

"I've finished my examination of the boy," he said when the call was answered at the other end. "It appears that he, too, has somehow been exposed to the project."

"How is that possible?" Takeo Yoshihara demanded.

"I'm sure I don't know, since security is not my department," Jameson replied. "But nonetheless, it seems to have happened."

For a long moment Takeo Yoshihara said nothing. Then: "For now, we will take no action. We will watch him, as we are watching the others. We're far too close to success to run any risks now," he said. "If it becomes necessary, we will dispose of him."

CHAPTER
18

"You're really sure you're all right?" Katharine fretted as she pulled the Explorer to a stop in the school's parking lot. Despite the doctor's assurances, she couldn't convince herself that her son's terrible wheezing last night had been caused by nothing more than a bad dream.

"I'm fine," Michael insisted for at least the fourth time since they'd left the estate. Grabbing his book bag from the backseat, he swung out of the car and slammed the door. Then he opened it again and stuck his head back in. "Look, I'm really sorry about what happened last night, Mom. I didn't mean to scare you, and I won't do it again. But you've got to stop worrying about me every minute of the day. I'm really okay now."

Katharine sighed and stretched in the driver's seat. Her whole body felt as tired and sore as if she'd already been crouching over the skeleton up in the ravine all day, instead of still having that job to look forward to. "I'll try," she agreed. Before she could say anything more, Michael glanced at his watch, waved to her, then turned and started toward the building. She watched him until he'd disappeared inside, still unable to shake the feeling that, despite his assurances, there was something he wasn't telling her, something he was keeping to himself. But as she started out of the parking lot a moment later, she told herself that maybe the problem wasn't Michael at all.

Maybe it was her.

She hadn't gotten more than an hour's sleep last night—maybe two—and she felt bone weary already. And she still had an entire day of work ahead, moving the skeleton from the site in the ravine into the safety of Rob's office. But the very thought of spending the rest of the day stooped over the bones, carefully freeing them from their shallow grave, only made her feel even more exhausted. Finally she pulled her cell phone out of her bag and called Rob. "I've got a deal for you," she said. "If you can get the skeleton collected without me, I'll fix you dinner tonight. I think I'm getting too old to stay up all night and then work in the field all day."

"Not a problem," he replied. "Go home. By this afternoon I'll have it all moved indoors. See you later."

Dropping the phone back in her bag, Katharine pulled out of the parking lot, remembering as she was starting up the road toward her house that the only things in the refrigerator were a half gallon of milk, a few eggs, and a six-pack of Cokes. Taking a deep breath, she made a right half a mile farther on and headed for the market in Kula, wondering whether Rob would prefer steak or chicken.

Hearing her name half an hour later as she was pushing the cart through the last aisle of the grocery store, Katharine looked up in surprise. The man who was smiling at her looked familiar, but for a moment she couldn't quite place him.

"Phil Howell," he said, reading her confusion. "Astronomer? Friend of Rob Silver's?"

"Of course," Katharine assured him, her memory finally putting it together. "Sorry—I'm afraid I was up all night. In fact, I'm on my way home to sleep the entire day."

"Lucky you," Howell sighed. "I've been on top of the mountain all night, and now I've got about five hours of work on the supercomputer down in Kihei."

Katharine cocked her head. "Kihei? Isn't that down by the water on the other side of the island? I thought the computer was up on the mountain."

"I wish," Howell sighed. "But our guys only use a little tiny part of it. Most of it's being used by everyone else. Schoolkids, business types—you name it. It's an amazing machine—you can do anything with it if you know how."

Katharine went silent, the image she'd seen on the monitor in Rob's office popping into the forefront of her mind: the skull, and the strange video file that had been linked to it, both of which had mysteriously vanished from the screen, defying even Rob's ability to reconstruct the file. Now an idea was forming in her mind. "How good are you with that computer?" she asked.

"A lot better than I wish, actually," Phil Howell said wryly. "I spend far more time on the computer than I do with my telescopes these days. What do you need?"

Katharine told him about the file that had disappeared yesterday. "Do you think there's any way of finding out where it came from?" she asked.

Howell thought for a moment. "I'm not sure," he mused. "But practically everything that goes through the Net gets cached one place or another. If we can find the right cache record—"

Suddenly, the exhaustion Katharine had felt only a moment ago evaporated. If Phil Howell could find that file for her again—or even just the location of it—she'd at least have a chance of figuring out what the strange skull she'd uncovered in the ravine might be. "Could we do it this morning?"

"If we don't do it this morning, I suspect there's practically no chance we'll find it," Howell told her. "The caches are all timed to dump after a set period of time, which I suspect isn't any more than twenty-four hours. But it could be a lot less."

"Then let's go," Katharine said. Abandoning the rest of her shopping, she headed for the checkout stand.

If dinner wasn't very interesting, Rob and Michael would just have to deal with it.

Josh Malani's whole body hurt.

Instinctively trying to escape the pain, he drew his knees up to his chest, but that only hurt more. Then, as he came fully awake and felt the heat of the sun on his face, he knew why he hurt.

He wasn't in bed. He wasn't even home.

He was in the back of his truck, which was parked in the lot at Makena Beach.

Slowly, as if he were thumbing through a stack of snapshots, the memories of last night came back to him.

Feeling kind of funny when he'd left Mike Sundquist's place.

Picking up Jeff, and taking off into the night.

The burning cane field that had been vomiting fire and smoke into the air.

The images flashed faster: glimpses of Jeff, getting out of the truck.

Another truck coming toward them.

Losing his nerve, and driving away. But if the police had caught him—

But they hadn't caught him. He hadn't dared to go home last night, afraid that someone in the car with the flashing lights that raced past him on the highway might have written down his license number. If the cops came looking for him at home, and his dad was drunk, the mess would only get worse. So instead he'd come out here to Makena, parked the pickup under the trees, and finally fallen asleep on the hard metal surface of the truck's bed.

He sat up. The sun was already above the mountain, so he was way late for school. Maybe he should just cut the rest of the day and hang out here at the beach.

But what about Jeff? He remembered the crazy way Jeff had been acting— getting out of the truck as if he were going to run right into the flaming field.

What if he was dead? What if he'd choked to death, or tried to get away from the fire crew in the truck and run into the cane field?

Josh shuddered as he imagined Jeff charging through the burning cane. If he tripped . . . Josh shut his eyes against the image that came into his head. Why the hell had he left? If anything happened to Jeff . . .

But nothing had happened to Jeff, he told himself. Jeff was okay. Jeff had to be okay.

He was kidding himself, he knew. How the hell would he know if Jeff was all right? He sure hadn't stayed around to find out. What would have happened if Mike Sundquist had just swum off the day he'd gotten caught under the reef, instead of trying to help him?

He would be dead now.

A hot ember of shame starting to burn deep inside him, Josh Malani moved from the bed of the truck to the cab, started the engine, and set off toward his house. Maybe, if no one was home, he'd grab a quick shower and change his clothes. Then, even if he didn't get there till noon, he'd go to school, find Jeff, and apologize to him.

If Jeff was still speaking to him.

An hour later he slowed down as he neared the run-down house he and his parents had moved into six months ago, after his father had lost his last job. Seeing his dad's rust-eaten Dodge sitting in the driveway—and his father himself slouched on the sofa in the living room, staring at the TV—he sped up and drove on by. He'd take a shower at school, and put on the same clothes he'd been wearing since yesterday. Better that than having his dad yelling at him; if the old man had been drinking, he might even take a swing at him.

Still accelerating as he squealed around the corner at the end of the block, concerned only with getting out of sight before his father noticed he was there, Josh never saw the brown sedan that pulled out of its parking space three houses down from his own, falling in behind him as he continued on to school.

In the stillness of the black-glass building in Kihei, the more than six hundred nodes that comprised one of the world's two most powerful computers were hard at work. Yet as Katharine Sundquist gazed through the large window that gave anyone in the building's lobby an unobstructed view of the immense machine, nothing betrayed the furious electronic activity going on within.

She saw a reel of tape spinning now and then, and a few lights occasionally blinking.

The machine worked in an oddly eerie solitude, monitoring itself, curing most of its own ills long before any of the humans involved in its maintenance were even aware that anything had gone wrong.

Beneath the false floor of the machine's perfectly air-conditioned chamber, a maze of wires connected each node of the computer to all the others. In its turn, the entire mass of processing units and wiring was connected to cables that snaked from the building, to connect to the immense fiber-optic cable that lay deep beneath the surface of the Pacific, the essential aorta that supplied the machine with its lifeblood.

Data.

Billions upon billions upon billions of bytes of data, a seeming infinity of information, flowing through the computer's systems; billions upon billions of connections every second, twenty-four hours a day, seven days a week. Though Katharine had a vague understanding of how it worked, her mind could no more truly grasp the reality of it than it could the concept of infinity.

Too much happening in too little time and with no apparent effort.

Not like archaeology at all.

Turning away from the window, she crossed the lobby and pushed through the doors into the terminal rooms, where dozens of monitors and keyboards sat in the small carrels into which the rows of tables in the room had been subdivided.

Most of the monitors were idle; only a few people were quietly tapping at keyboards.

At the sixth carrel in the fourth row, Katharine found Phil Howell, looking as if he hadn't moved at all during the few minutes she'd been stretching her aching muscles. The exhaustion that had dissipated so quickly when she thought there might be a chance of locating the vanishing file had quickly returned as Phil began setting up a search program that would pore through every cache in the enormous computer, searching for references to graphics files that had passed through the computer yesterday afternoon.

"Maybe between two and three," Katharine had told him when he'd asked what time she and Rob had seen the file. "Maybe a little earlier—maybe a little later."

The first list the computer generated seemed to scroll on endlessly. Even if the files they were looking for were there, she thought, it would be like searching for a needle in forty acres of haystacks.

As Phil patiently narrowed the search, Katharine felt both her excitement and her energy ebb.

Then, as she leaned a little closer to the screen, an electronic beep sounded and a window opened.

She felt a rush of adrenaline. "Is that it?" she asked.

"It's something," Phil told her. "But it's mine, not yours." With a flick of the mouse, he blew the window up to fill the screen. "I've been doing a search of my own," he said. "A lot of people have been picking up strange radio signals from somewhere near a nova I've been watching. They're just scraps, but they're really weird. So I've had the computer run a search, looking for any more signals that might match, but that I haven't heard about." He grinned at the puzzled look that came over Katharine's face. "It's sort of like hunting for the score to an entire symphony, when all you've got to match it to is a few notes. Frankly, I didn't really think I'd come up with anything." He turned his attention to the computer screen, which was now displaying another box:

> **Data Search Report:**
>
> **Project Name: Star Bright**
> **Requested By: Phil Howell**
> **Search Begun: 17:46:24**
> **Search Ended: 22:06:58**
> **Analysis Begun: 22:06:58**
> **Analysis Ended: 10:37:13**
> **Report Generated: 10:37:14**
> **See Starbrit.rtf**

Tapping at the keyboard, he brought up the report the computer had generated. A list of the files the computer had copied from all over the world scrolled down the screen, followed by another list, nearly as long, of the files upon which the report was based.

Each file was annotated as to its size, the date it had been created, the computer on which it had been stored, and the source of the raw data contained within the files.

Phil felt the first flush of excitement as he noted that the second list of files contained only data gathered from radio telescopes.

Next came the results of the computer's attempt to put the files together in a cohesive string.

His heart began to race as he saw that the signal appeared to have been coming in steadily for a period of months, starting more than two years ago. But then, 79 days after it had begun, it abruptly ended. After a silence of 142 days, it reappeared, and was picked up by one or another of dozens of radio telescopes for a period of 209 days. Then there had been another 142 days of silence. It had been detected again for a period of 132 days, ending last Saturday at noon, GMT.

Phil Howell gazed at the screen in something near disbelief: If the signal had been received for as long as the computer claimed, and by as many telescopes as the computer claimed, why had there been almost nothing written about it?

But then, as he studied the data further, he began to understand.

The signal had been picked up in so many bits and pieces that they simply went unnoticed in the sea of data being received from the universe every day.

Then he noticed something else, and he felt his skin go clammy with excitement.

The signal had not been consistently picked up on a single frequency. Instead, it was picked up on hundreds of frequencies, as if it had been blasted out by some kind of cosmic shotgun.

A normal radio signal emitted by a star or a quasar was carried on a single frequency.

Stars, obviously, had no technology that would allow them to change the frequency of a broadcast.

Nothing did, as far as Phil Howell knew, with a single exception.

And that exception was mankind.

"A planet," Phil breathed, almost inaudibly. "My God."

Katharine frowned. "A planet? What are you talking about?"

Howell's eyes never left the computer screen as he spoke. "It's this transmission," he said, his fingers touching the numbers on the screen almost as if he would be able to feel the signal they represented. "It stopped coming in twice, each time for a period of 142 days. That pause is very significant. And one explanation for it is if the signal was being broadcast from a planet rather than pulsating out from a star. If the planet's orbit was in the right plane, then the signal would be blocked from our telescopes whenever the planet was in the shadow of its own sun."

Katharine gazed at him, trying to absorb the full implication of the report on the screen. "But that means—"

She stopped, leaving it to the astronomer to finish her thought.

"If I'm right," Howell finally said, "it means there was someone out there."

"*If* you're right?" Katharine echoed. "You just said the only explanation—"

"I said, it's *one* explanation," Howell interrupted. "And certainly my favorite," he went on, a wry smile twisting his lips, "since finding someone out there would make me the most famous astronomer on the planet. But unfortunately I have a feeling there are about a hundred other explanations, all of them far more probable than what I just told you." His eyes returned to the computer monitor. "Look, don't say anything about this to anyone else, okay? There's not much chance I'm right, and the opposite of being known as the most famous astronomer on the planet is being known as the stupidest. Okay?"

"But if you're right—" Katharine began, and again the astronomer interrupted her.

"If I'm right, you can testify that you were here when the discovery was made. But I'd just as soon prove it first before talking about it." He looked up at her. "Deal?"

"Deal," Katharine agreed.

Another soft electronic signal sounded, and both of them looked back at the monitor to see that another window had opened in the lower right quadrant of the screen Howell had been studying.

"Well, look at that," he said. "This morning we both get results."

Katharine studied the two file names that appeared in the box, both of them stark in their simplicity.

Skull.jpg

Video.avi.

Both of them were annotated with their domain of origin, which was listed as *mishimoto.com*.

"I'm almost sure the file names were a lot longer than these," Katharine said. "It's as though the computer looked for names that matched what I saw, instead of content."

Phil Howell shook his head. "You said there was a link on the page with the skull that took you to the video. The file name you saw was probably the one for the page that contained the graphic of the skull, and the link. These would be the files themselves."

"But how do I find the files themselves?"

"Go back to Rob Silver's office," the astronomer told her. "Mishimoto is the name of Takeo Yoshihara's company, which should mean that mishimoto dot com is the name of his private domain for e-mail purposes. Which means that those files are somewhere on one of Takeo Yoshihara's own computers."

"Can you find them from here?"

Howell shrugged. "Maybe, if I were an expert hacker. But it shouldn't be too hard to find them from Rob's office, since he's already inside Yoshihara's network. As for me, I'm going back to work on my signal. And remember," he added, nodding toward the computer screen that was still displaying the results of his own search. "Not a word about this. Please?"

"Not even a hint," Katharine promised. "And thanks for helping me out. If I find anything, believe me, I'll let you know."

"Great," Howell replied. But by the time Katharine was back in her car less than a minute later, the astronomer had already dismissed the two files from his mind. To him, the strange radio signal from a star fifteen million light-years away was far more interesting than any image of an earthbound skull could ever be.

CHAPTER
19

He was back in the cane field.

The fire was crackling around him, and though he could see no flames, its glow suffused the darkness with a reddish tinge.

He could feel it, creeping toward him from every direction. It was as if he were encircled by hunters so sure of their kill that they no longer felt any need to conceal their presence with silence.

Despite the approaching hunters, he was unafraid.

He could smell the first tendrils of smoke as they slithered into his nostrils and down his throat to his lungs.

But it didn't smell like smoke—not quite.

Smoke had always made him choke, made his eyes sting and run, left a bitter taste in his mouth.

He breathed deeply of it, drawing it into his lungs as if it were fresh salt air blowing in from the sea on the trade winds. As it flowed into his body, he felt something he'd never experienced before, an exuberance, an exultation that infused his body with a strength and well-being that made him feel invincible.

The crackling of the fire grew louder, but he could hear something else now. A strange moaning sound, as if someone were in great pain. No, not a moaning, but the whoosh and crackle of the fire, gaining strength as it swept through the cane field, feeding on everything in its path, building on itself. It was like a living force now, rampaging across the earth, creating a great swirling, howling upward draft that sucked every molecule of air in from the surrounding area to feed the growing monster, huge now and continuing to grow, continuing to spread.

Yet still he couldn't see the flames.

Then, at last, they came.

Only glimpses at first, barely visible flickerings of orange, like the exploring tongues of serpents, poking through the dense thicket of cane that surrounded him.

He felt the first warmth of the fire on his skin, but it was like no fire he'd ever felt before.

This fire seemed to fuel him, to impart its strength to him rather than consume him. Then, as he felt his own being thrive upon the closeness of the throbbing monster's breath, the foliage around him began to quail before the beast. Everywhere he looked, the leaves and stalks withered before the advancing heat, then burst into flames as they succumbed to the rampaging marauder.

The tendrils of smoke thickened into the bodies of serpents, winding around his body, wrapping him tightly in their coils, but instead of struggling against their grasp, he reveled in the sensation, drawing as much vitality from the tightening spirals of smoke as from the fire itself.

The howling of the maelstrom filled his ears, and the darkness of the night was banished by the shower of embers exploding from the field. Smoke and flame intertwined, whirling around him like a living being.

Entranced, he reached out as if to gather the force of the firestorm to him, and a great cry of ecstasy rose from his throat.

He was no longer the hunted, but now, becoming as one with the inferno around him, he felt the spirit of the fire itself enter his soul.

He stretched to his full height, his legs spread, his arms flung out, and the cry of the hunter bellowed up from the core of his being. . . .

✳   ✳   ✳

Jeff Kina's whole body jerked spasmodically in response to the shout that issued from him and yanked him from the thrall of the dream. Yet as he came
awake, the dream stayed with him. The fire's heat he'd felt only a moment
ago was gone, but the smoke was not. The second he opened his eyes, he
could see it swirling around him, a gray-brown fog so thick he instinctively
closed his eyes against it.

He lay still, his eyes clamped shut, his heart pounding, but no longer from
the exultation of the dream.

Now it was pounding with fear.

The dream had been so real, it was exactly as if he'd been back in the cane
field, back in the vortex of the fire, just before the men from the yellow truck
had grabbed him, and Josh Malani had taken off in his pickup.

In those few seconds—those few moments while he'd stood next to Josh's
truck—he'd felt different than he'd ever felt before in his life.

Part of it had been the fire itself. There had been something about the way
the flames ebbed and flowed and danced together that reached into his mind,
touched something deep inside him, made him feel almost as if he'd been
hypnotized. And as the smoke had filled his nostrils, he'd felt something else.

The restlessness that had plagued him all evening disappeared, and his
whole body tingled exactly as it did when he was finished with his warm-ups
at a track meet and ready to run a race.

Then the men from the yellow truck were on him, yelling at him, grabbing him, trying to drag him away from the fire.

He was bigger than they—much bigger—and his right arm had come up,
jerking loose from the hands of one of the men so his fist could plunge into
the face of the other. Now, his eyes still closed, he remembered the blood
that spurted from the man's nose, the look of surprise that came into his eyes,
and the man's enraged shout.

But after that, everything was confused. Lights had hit him in the eyes,
brilliant halogen lamps that blinded him as thoroughly as if someone had
thrown a bag over his head.

After that, his memories were nothing more than impressions.

More lights.

The sound of engines; voices yelling.

Suddenly, more hands were on him, and he was on the ground, pinned
down by someone on his chest, someone else on his legs.

Something was pressed over his face, and he struggled to turn his head away, but couldn't.

Blackness had begun closing around him, and he'd known he was dying.

But now he was awake, and he was not dead.

He lay perfectly still, listening.

He could hear sounds he'd never heard before.

His own heartbeat, pumping blood through his veins. Though he knew it wasn't possible, he even imagined he heard the sound of his blood itself, whooshing softly as it coursed through his arteries, the sound changing with every contraction of the chambers of his heart.

He took an inventory of his body, testing every muscle, but moving each of them so slightly as to appear utterly immobile.

Nothing was broken; nothing even hurt.

And he was naked.

He turned his attention away from his own body to the environment around him. Though his eyes were still closed, he could sense there were walls around him, very close by.

And he was alone.

The air around him was moving, and unfamiliar scents were wafting through his nostrils.

Not unpleasant scents, but unfamiliar ones.

At last he opened his right eye—no more than a fraction of an inch—the movement so perfectly executed that no observer could have seen the slight flicker.

Fog.

The same brown fog.

But not fog, for he felt nothing of the cool dampness of fog against his skin.

His eye moved beneath its hooded lid, scanning the area around him, though he was far too uncertain of where he was or what might be nearby to betray himself by any but the slightest movement.

He saw nothing.

He opened both his eyes then, opened them wide, the lids snapping open in an unblinking stare.

He gazed straight ahead, his mind analyzing the data his eyes and ears and nose were gathering, searching for an as-yet-unnoticed enemy that might be lurking in the miasma.

Why didn't his eyes hurt?

Why weren't they stinging from the smoky haze, and streaming with tears?

Why wasn't he coughing and choking on the fumes that swirled around him?

No answer came to him.

He lay inert, only his eyes moving, flicking first in one direction, then in another.

Nothing he saw, nothing he heard, nothing he smelled, betrayed the presence of any other living thing.

Yet he was being watched.

He could feel it with a certain knowledge he'd never experienced before. Despite the evidence of his eyes, and his ears, and his nose, his skin was tingling and his nerves were on edge.

Then he saw it.

Far up, above him, and off to the right.

A camera.

He turned his head to it, staring straight into its lens like a wolf staring into the telescopic sight of a gun.

His eyes never leaving the camera, Jeff Kina slowly gathered himself into a crouch, every movement so subtle and smooth it was barely perceptible.

Had he been in a field of tall grass, barely a blade would have stirred.

He froze, his eyes fixed on the camera, waiting.

Then he sprang, launching himself from the floor on which he lay, his body extending with the grace of a leaping cat, his arms stretching outward as his hands reached for the camera, his legs extending behind him as they hurled his huge frame upward.

And in a split second he slammed against an unseen barrier.

A grunt escaping his lips, he fell back to the floor, pain shooting though his right hip and his left knee as they struck hard against the surface of the tile beneath him.

He lay still, waiting for the pain to ease, then slowly got to his feet and began moving cautiously, his hands and fingers reaching out to explore the strange surroundings.

He was in a box.

A large box, transparent, not cold to the touch.

Plexiglas.

The thick gray-brown fog that swirled around him had kept him from see-ing it before, but now, as he made his way around its perimeter for the second time, he could see it as well as feel it.

He was trapped, imprisoned in the box, which seemed to have no entry or exit, except for two vents through which the foglike atmosphere swirled, and a small air lock, with a door on each side.

He could open the inner door, but not the outer one.

He was imprisoned, like a wild animal.

And to the men who watched the image the camera above him was cap-turing, a wild animal was exactly what he appeared to be.

A feral creature, pacing the confines of its cage.

Michael was just closing his locker before going to the cafeteria for lunch when he heard the voice behind him.

"I don't know about you, but I'm starting to get scared."

Michael didn't need to be told what Rick Pieper was talking about; he'd been growing more and more worried himself all morning, ever since Josh had not turned up at the break after second period and even after hearing the radio report of Jeff's disappearance, he'd still half expected to see the big Hawaiian under the banyan tree where the rest of the track team hung out. But when Jeff failed to appear . . . "Did you try to call Jeff?" he asked as they started toward the cafeteria.

Rick nodded. "I talked to his mom just before third period. She said he went out around nine last night and didn't come home. She said she called the cops around four in the morning."

Michael stopped short just outside the cafeteria door and waited until the kids behind them had gone inside. "Maybe we should call them ourselves," he said. "I mean, after what happened to Kioki—"

"We don't *know* what happened to Kioki," Rick countered.

"What if someone saw us break into that dive shop the night before last?" Michael pressed, searching for an explanation—any explanation—for what had happened to Kioki, and could now explain why Josh Malani and Jeff Kina had disappeared. "I mean, what if someone told the guy who owns the shop who it was that broke in?"

Rick Pieper's eyes widened as the implication of what Michael was saying sank in, but a moment later he shook his head. "Ken Richter wouldn't do something like that."

"How do you know?" Michael demanded. "In New York—"

"This isn't New York," Rick said sharply. "If Ken was going to do anything at all, he'd call the cops, and the deputy who talked to us yesterday didn't say anything about breaking into the dive shop."

"So what else could it be?" Michael demanded. "Were Josh and Jeff in any kind of trouble?"

Rick hesitated.

"What?" Michael prompted him.

"Jeff wasn't in any trouble," Rick said carefully, "but Josh Malani's always in some kind of mess—"

"Oh, yeah?" a voice asked, and Rick spun around to see Josh Malani himself coming around the corner of the cafeteria, his eyes glinting angrily. "Just because I don't suck up to everyone like—"

"Well, I guess we can stop worrying about Josh," Rick cut in, his voice turning cold and his expression tightening. Before either Michael or Josh could say anything else, Rick stalked off into the cafeteria.

Michael stared at Josh's rumpled clothes and the smears of dirt on his face, seeing in an instant that Josh hadn't been home since last night. "What's going on?" he asked. "Where's Jeff?"

"Oh, Jeez," Josh whispered. "He isn't here?"

There was something in his friend's voice that made the apprehension Michael had been feeling all morning congeal into fear. He shook his head and told Josh what he had heard on the radio and what Rick had just confirmed.

"I ran into him after I left your house," Josh said. He glanced around nervously. "Maybe we better get out of here, huh?"

"You mean just cut school for the rest of the day?" Michael asked. "Come on, Josh! Just tell me what's going on, okay?"

"Not here!" Josh said as the cafeteria door opened and two kids came out, looked uncertainly at them, then hurried on. "What's wrong with them?" Josh asked as they disappeared around the corner.

"Have you taken a look at yourself? What did you do last night?"

Josh felt a flicker of anger. Why was Mike quizzing him so much? It wasn't as if he was asking much. . . .

But if he got pissed off at Michael, where could he go? Who could he even talk to? And he was starting to feel bad, too. But why wouldn't he, after breathing all that smoke in the cane field last night, then sleeping in his truck? "Look, let's just go over to the locker room. At least I can take a shower, and I'll tell you what happened last night. But you gotta promise not to tell anyone, okay?"

Dropping several quarters into the vending machine outside the cafeteria door, Michael got a couple of Cokes, a bag of Fritos, and two packages of stale-looking cookies. Popping the top off one of the Cokes, he handed it to Josh, who took a long swig from it as they started toward the locker room. But as Josh lifted the Coke to his lips for a second drink, he was seized by a fit of coughing.

"You okay?" Michael asked.

Josh shook his head. "I feel like crap."

In the locker room, Josh stripped out of his clothes and went into the showers. As he stood under the steaming water, scrubbing the soot and dirt from his skin, he finally told Michael what had happened last night.

"You just left him there?" Michael asked as Josh finished his shower and grabbed a towel.

"Well, what was I supposed to do?" Josh shot back as he started to dry off, his temper flaring again. "He wouldn't get back in the truck, and the fire was all around us, and those guys were coming, and—" His words were cut short as another hacking cough doubled him over.

"Maybe you better go home," Michael said.

"Home?" Josh demanded as the coughing subsided. "That's real easy for you, isn't it, Mike? Your mom doesn't get drunk and start pounding on you, like my dad does, and—" Suddenly Josh could barely breathe. Choking, he stumbled out of the locker room and shambled toward the rest room.

Michael hurried after him, and by the time he got to the rest room, Josh had sagged to the floor, his face pale. Frightened by the sudden change in his friend, Michael reached out and touched Josh's arm.

His skin was cold and clammy.

Josh was gasping for breath. "What is it?" Michael asked. "What's wrong?"

Josh peered up at Michael out of eyes that seemed to be glazing over. "D-Don't know," he gasped. "C-Can't breathe . . ."

Michael's eyes widened. Asthma? Could Josh be having an attack of asthma? His atomizer—the one his mother still made him take with him all the time, even though he hadn't had an attack of asthma in over a year . . . where was it?

His locker.

Or should he run and get the nurse?

He didn't even know where the nurse's office was!

"I'll be right back," he said. "I'm gonna try to find the nurse, and I've got something in my locker that might help you breathe."

"Not the nurse," Josh gasped. "I don't want—" But it was too late; Michael was already gone.

Struggling to catch his breath, Josh scrambled back to his feet, steadying himself with the knob of the closet door he'd been leaning against only a moment earlier. He took a tentative step, started to lose his balance, and jerked on the doorknob.

The door came open, revealing a jumble of boxes, cans, and bottles—the cleansers and disinfectants the janitor stored in the closet.

Instinctively moving back a step, Josh stared at the array of bottles and containers spread out in front of him. Then, reacting to an impulse that had suddenly seized him, he reached out, picked up a bottle of ammonia, opened it, and tentatively held it to his nose.

Sucking the fumes deep into his lungs, he felt an instant rush of energy, as if a shot of adrenaline had been injected into his bloodstream.

He breathed in again; an almost electric tingle ran through his body.

A moment later, when Michael Sundquist reappeared, his inhaler clutched in his hand, Josh Malani's entire demeanor had changed again.

His complexion looked healthy, his eyes were bright, and he seemed to be breathing perfectly normally.

As Michael looked on in astonishment, Josh once again raised the ammonia bottle to his nose and inhaled its fumes into his lungs. "Jeez, Josh, what are you doing?" Michael cried, grabbing the bottle from Josh's hand. "What's all this mess?"

"Give it back!" Josh demanded. "I was just sniffing it."

"Are you crazy? That stuff's poisonous! It can kill you."

Josh reached for the bottle once again. "Just give it to me!"

Shoving Josh away from the closet, Michael slammed the door shut, then leaned against it, the bottle of ammonia clutched in his hands. Josh glowered at him, and for a moment Michael was afraid he might be about to slug him. But then Josh shook his head. "The hell with you," he muttered. Turning his back on Michael, he barged out of the rest room. By the time Michael had put the ammonia away and gone after him, Josh was almost dressed again.

"Come on, Josh," Michael pleaded. "I'm just trying to help you."

Josh barely looked at him. "I don't need you helping me. I don't need anyone helping me." Then he was gone, shoving Michael aside as he left the locker room and headed for the parking lot. Michael caught up with him just as he was getting into his truck.

"I'm going with you," Michael said, heading toward the passenger's side.

"The hell you are." Starting the engine, Josh slammed the truck into gear and screeched out of the parking lot.

Michael stood in the cloud of dust the truck had kicked up, staring after his friend. Tears were welling up in his eyes, and in his stomach he felt a hard knot of anger and pain, all twisted together so tightly he couldn't even begin to unravel it. *He'll get over it*, he told himself as he finally turned away and started back toward the locker room. By the time school's out, he'll get over it. *It'll be okay*.

But even as he silently uttered the words to himself, he knew he didn't believe them.

CHAPTER
20

Josh Malani had no idea where he was going as he roared out of the school parking lot. All he knew was that he had to get away.

Already the tingling he'd felt in his body when he breathed in the ammonia was fading away, but so was the fury that had boiled up in him when Michael had torn the bottle from his hands.

What the hell was he doing, getting pissed off at Michael? Michael was his best friend.

Michael had saved his life.

Michael had only been trying to help him.

And what had he done? Blown his stack and taken off.

Terrific!

So now what?

Home was out—no way was he going to go there until at least five, when his mom would be home from work and he wouldn't have to be alone with his dad.

Maybe he'd just go to the beach for a couple of hours. He always felt a lot better after going for a swim, and then he'd come back just before school let out and find Mike.

He'd apologize, and then they'd figure out what to do about Jeff Kina. Maybe Mike was right—maybe they really should go tell the police where they'd been the night Kioki died.

By the time Josh came to the floor of the valley between Haleakala and the West Maui mountains, the strange discomfort in his chest had started up again, and as he headed out toward a park on the windward side where few people ever went during the week, another fit of coughing gripped him. Then, with the same frightening breathlessness that had come over him at the school once again descending on him, he pressed hard on the accelerator, determined to get to the beach, where he could take in the trade winds blowing in from the ocean. So focused was he on his struggle to overcome the choking airlessness that Josh never noticed that the car behind him sped up, too, keeping perfect pace with his truck.

The ammonia, he thought. *Michael was right.* His chest was aching painfully now, and no matter how hard he tried, he couldn't seem to get enough air into his lungs. As he pulled the truck to a stop in the empty parking lot behind the beach, he was gripping the wheel hard with both hands, partly against the terrible fiery pain spreading through him, but even more to keep himself steady.

His knuckles, already white with tension, were starting to turn blue, and now, when he looked out to sea, he could barely even see the horizon.

Everything seemed to be getting blurry, and the brightness of the afternoon was fading, even though a moment ago there hadn't been a cloud in the sky.

Out.

He had to get out of the truck and down onto the beach. If he could just get that far, he'd be able to breathe again, and lie down and rest for a while, and then this strange attack would pass. He'd be okay again. He fumbled for the door handle, found it, and slid out of the driver's seat. But instead of landing on his feet, his knees buckled beneath him and he crumbled to the ground, sprawling out in the dust.

He was panting, gasping for breath, but with every movement of his diaphragm, it felt as if his lungs were being seared from inside with a blowtorch.

Dying!

He knew it now, knew it with a terrible certainty.

The darkness was closing around him, and the pain was growing worse, and he couldn't breathe at all.

He reached out, flailing, searching for something—anything—to hang on to, to cling to, as if the act of clutching something in his hands could stave off the horrible suffocation that was claiming him.

He tried to cry out, tried to scream for help, but all that emerged from his throat was a whispered moan.

Then, as the darkness closed around him and the last of his strength deserted him, he felt a new sensation.

It was as if he was being lifted.

Lifted up, and carried away.

His beleaguered lungs still struggling for breath, Josh Malani surrendered to the blackness.

"My Jeff is a good boy," Uilani Kina insisted. "My Jeff wouldn't just take off. Something's happened to him."

Cal Olani nodded sympathetically, but the gesture was nearly automatic. After fifteen years as a cop, he'd long since learned that there wasn't a mother alive whose son wasn't "a good boy." It made no difference what the charge might be, or how damning the evidence.

"My son is a good boy," Mrs. Kina said again.

Still, as he looked around the tidy house that Uilani Kina kept, he didn't see any of the typical signs that a teenager was likely to be a troublemaker. On a side street above Makawao, the frame house sat in the midst of a well-kept garden. The patch of lawn in front was mowed, and though a few chickens pecked at the ground in a coop next to the house, they weren't running wild. Uilani's husband operated a small garden supply shop down the road in Makawao, where Jeff worked after school except during track season. Aside from a couple of incidents when he'd threatened a few *haoles*—but hadn't actually done much to make good on his threats—Jeff had never been in any serious trouble. Still, he was at the age when boys start wanting to show their independence, and had it not been for the discovery of Kioki Santoya's body yesterday morning, Cal would probably have tried a little harder to reassure Uilani Kina that her son would turn up by the end of the day. As it was, though, he had to take the boy's absence more seriously. "I'll put out an official missing persons report this afternoon," he promised, though he knew the news was out about Jeff all over the island. He closed his notebook and, putting it back in the inside pocket of his uniform jacket, he said as gently as he could, "Just try not to get too upset, Mrs. Kina."

"If it wasn't for Kioki—" Uilani Kina began, but couldn't bring herself even to finish the thought. A slim wraith of a woman with soft features framed by flowing black hair, she shook her head sadly. "I don't know what Alice is going to do. He was all she had, and now . . ." She struggled to compose herself. "What were those boys doing that night?" she asked, her eyes searching Cal Olani's face for an answer. "Did something happen? Did they get in a fight or something? Was someone mad at them?" She shook her head, clucking her tongue softly. "Who could get mad at them? Such good boys." Her voice changed, and Cal Olani had the feeling she was talking more to herself than to him. "Even Josh Malani. What can you expect with parents like that? I feel so sorry for him. . . ." Her voice trailed off again, but her liquid-brown eyes remained fixed on the policeman. "Find Jeff for me," she pleaded. "Please find him for me."

Back in his car a few minutes later, with the memory of the distraught woman's plea still fresh in his mind, Olani kept hearing echoes of her question: *Did something happen?*

And he also remembered the faces of the four boys he'd talked to at the high school yesterday afternoon. The way their eyes had darted toward Josh Malani before they answered his questions, as if seeking his advice or his permission before they spoke.

And the new boy—the one Cal couldn't remember having seen at all before yesterday—hadn't actually answered his questions with anything more than a noncommittal shrug. Glancing at his watch, he saw that it was just about time for school to be letting out. Maybe he'd swing back there and have another talk with those three. But just as he made the decision, the radio in the car came alive and he heard the dispatcher calling him.

"Car five here," he said into the microphone.

"I have a report of an abandoned car, Cal," the dispatcher told him. "Down in the park near Spreckelsville. You anywhere close?"

"Above Makawao," Olani replied, then told the dispatcher what he was planning to do next.

"I think you might want to take this abandoned car report," the dispatcher told him. "We've run the plates. It's an eighty-two Chevy pickup, registered to Joshua Malani."

Olani felt an uneasy chill ripple over him. "How long's it been there?" he asked.

"Not very long," the dispatcher replied. "The woman who reported it says it wasn't there this morning."

"Then why is it being reported as abandoned?" Olani asked. Who would report a truck the first time he saw it? After a day or two, maybe, but . . . The dispatcher's voice cut into his thought.

"The keys are in the ignition, and his wallet was left on the front seat."

The uneasy chill that had come over Cal Olani congealed into a feeling of dark foreboding. "Ten-four," he said. "I'm on my way."

"It certainly took you long enough." The woman was sunburned and over-weight and swathed in a wildly patterned muumuu in a particularly hideous shade of lavender. She made no effort to hide her displeasure as Cal Olani swung out of his patrol car nearly half an hour after he'd received the dispatcher's call.

"Now, Myrtle," her husband said, trying to soothe her. He sported a shirt that matched his wife's muumuu, and a sunburn even more purple. "You have to remember, this is Maui, not Cleveland." He offered his hand to Cal Olani. "I'm Fred Hooper, and this is my wife, Myrtle. We're staying in a condo down that way about a mile." He gestured vaguely in the direction of Spreckelsville. "I told Myrt she shouldn't bother you with this, but—"

"Nobody goes off and leaves a truck with the keys hanging in the ignition, and their wallet just lying out on the seat where anyone could come along and pick it up," Myrtle Hooper broke in, silencing Fred with a single quick gesture. "At least they don't in Cleveland, and I just don't believe things are that much different out here." As Cal Olani started toward Josh's truck, both Hoopers trailed after him, Myrtle still talking. "Something isn't right about this. I know Fred thinks I'm being silly, but a mother knows these things." They had reached the pickup, and as Olani turned to look questioningly at Mrs. Hooper, she pursed her lips. "We looked in the wallet, of course. We thought we might find a telephone number or something." She sighed deeply. "Just seventeen. Such a shame."

"Now, Myrt, we don't know what happened," Fred began, but once again his wife silenced him with a sweep of her hand.

"Of course we know what happened," she said. "It's happening to kids all the time now. Teenage suicide. I read about it in *Time* magazine." She shifted her gaze to Cal Olani. "His clothes are on the beach," she said. "At least I assume they're his clothes. There's no one else around here. And we put his wallet back on the seat of the car, exactly the way it was when we found it," she added as the policeman peered into the truck's open window.

Just as the woman had said, a worn wallet was lying on the seat of the truck, and the keys were hanging in the ignition. Picking the wallet up, Olani checked the driver's license himself.

Josh Malani.

There were a few dollar bills, a student identification card, some worn pictures, and various scraps of paper with girls' phone numbers written on them, but little else.

Moving on to the beach, Cal Olani found a pile of clothes, also just as Myrtle Hooper had described. There were a pair of worn jeans, a T-shirt, Jockey shorts, socks and shoes.

The jeans were on the bottom, then the T-shirt and the underwear, with the shoes resting on top of the pile, the socks tucked inside them.

Very neat.

Very tidy.

And from what Cal Olani knew of the boy, not at all like Josh Malani.

Unless Josh had been trying to say something.

Wordlessly, Olani went back to the truck. Shoved behind the driver's seat was a slightly damp towel, wrapped around an equally wet bathing suit.

Even if Josh had a dry bathing suit, wouldn't he have taken his towel down to the beach if all he was planning to do was go for a swim?

Of course, as Myrtle Hooper had pointedly implied, if the boy was plan-

ning to go into the water and not come out, what would be the point of having the towel on the beach?

He searched the cab of the pickup once more, looking for a note, but even
as he hunted he knew he wouldn't find one. A little too reckless, always a bit
too wild, Josh Malani wasn't the kind of kid who'd leave a note behind. Not
the kind of kid, either, who'd commit suicide. Yet the evidence seemed pretty
strong that that was exactly what he'd done.

He went back to the beach, where Mrs. Hooper waited for him, a faintly
smug expression on her face. Cal Olani found himself disliking her intensely:
a woman who was more concerned about having her opinion validated than
she was about what might have happened to a seventeen-year-old boy.

"There's some footprints, too," he heard Fred Hooper say. "We were careful not to disturb them."

Olani moved closer to the neatly folded clothes and looked down at the
sand. A single set of footprints led toward the water, disappearing where the
surf—gentle today—had washed them away. Shading his eyes from the sun's
glare on the water, he peered out at the ocean, searching for signs of someone
swimming, but saw no sign of Josh or anyone else. Not that he had expected
to; his gut was already telling him that Josh Malani was dead.

"It's tough for them," Fred Hooper said softly, his eyes, like Cal Olani's,
fixed on the sea. "Not like when I was a kid. We didn't have to worry about
anything. Grow up, raise a family, retire, and come to places like this. But
what do the kids have to look forward to now? Drugs, and gangs, and getting
shot at when you're just minding your own business." He was quiet for a moment, then: "I wish we'd gotten here a little earlier. Maybe if he'd just had
someone to talk to, it would have helped, you know?"

Cal Olani rested his hand on the man's shoulder. "Maybe it would have,"
he said. But as he started taping the area off to keep the people who'd been attracted by the presence of his squad car from messing up the site before it
could be photographed, he wondered. Would talking to someone really have
helped?

Yesterday, neither Josh Malani nor any of his friends had been interested
in talking about anything.

Now Kioki Santoya was dead, Jeff Kina was missing, and Josh Malani had
apparently drowned himself.

What the hell was going on?

CHAPTER
21

Katharine Sundquist was excited when she returned to Takeo Yoshihara's estate, convinced she held the key not only to the missing computer files, but to the mystery of the skeleton in the ravine. Arriving just as Rob and one of his workmen were transferring the last of the carefully tagged bones from the back of the Explorer into his office, she'd barely been able to hold her impatience in check until the entire find had been carefully laid out on a lab table in the room that adjoined Rob's office.

The sharp edge of her excitement had been blunted, though, when the files proved less easy to locate than she'd hoped. It should have been so simple: they had the file names, and Phil Howell was certain they were somewhere on Takeo Yoshihara's computer. But when Rob brought up a directory of the drive, no such file names appeared. Sensing Katharine's disappointment, he'd tried to reassure her. "Not to worry. This is only one drive, and there have to be a lot more than that. I'll run a search."

The search, though it had only taken a few minutes, seemed to Katharine to go on forever, but then two lines appeared on the screen, showing the results of the inquiry, and her hopes leaped again.

X:\serinus\artifact\Philippine\skull.jpg
X:\serinus\artifact\Philippine\video.avi

"If the directories are set up with any kind of logic, at least we know where the skull came from," Katharine said as she gazed at the screen. "But what does 'serinus' mean?"

"It's one of Yoshihara's projects," Rob Silver said. "It has something to do with pollution. Serinus is the genus designation for finches. Specifically, *Serinus canaria*—canaries."

"Canaries?" Katharine repeated. "I'm not sure I see the connection."

"The connection comes from the old practice of lowering canaries into mine shafts. If the birds came up alive, it was safe for the men to go down. If the birds were dead, then there were dangerous gases in the mine." He paused. "I don't know much about that particular project, but I suspect Yoshihara's looking for new ways to stop killing canaries, as it were. Hence the name of the project. Corporate cute, if you ask me. Let's see if we can take a look at those files."

With growing anticipation Katharine watched as Rob pulled up a viewer, then copied in the full path of the jpg file. Almost there, she thought, we've almost got it. Until the screen went blank and a new message appeared:

PLEASE ENTER YOUR PASSWORD NOW

Rob had tried a few possible passwords, ranging from anagrams of the words "artifact" and "serinus" to Takeo Yoshihara's name spelled backward. To neither his nor Katharine's surprise, none of them worked. "Who knows?" he'd finally sighed. "It could be someone's mother-in-law's birthday, or a random sequence of letters and numbers. And I suspect that if I just keep trying to break in, the computer will notice what's going on and report me to someone."

Katharine gazed dispiritedly at the monitor, unable to shake from her memory the disquieting images recorded on the strange video. "It's probably not the right file anyway," she said, disappointed. "What on earth would a tribe slaughtering some kind of primate have to do with air pollution?"

Rob shrugged. "I'm afraid you'd know a lot more about that than I would. You're the bone person, remember?"

But Katharine had no answer. They spent a few minutes poking around in the directory named Serinus, but quickly discovered that without the password, only a single file was open to them.

A file that confirmed that Takeo Yoshihara and Mishimoto Corporation were indeed embarked on a major research project aimed at tackling the problem of global pollution head-on. "And making a fortune with whatever they discover, no doubt," Rob remarked as they finished reading the file.

They'd abandoned the computer then, but for the rest of the afternoon, as Katharine concentrated on reconstructing the skeleton that had been exhumed from the ravine, the first faint tendrils of an idea kept reaching out to her. When Rob finally interrupted her to suggest they have dinner together, she realized that the afternoon had slipped away.

Though she was no closer to gaining access to the files containing the image of the skull and the video, the skeleton was almost complete. And the idea, though not yet fully formed, was starting to come together in her mind. "I think I'm going to finish this," she said. "You go on, and I'll see you in the morning."

After Rob left, she called Michael and told him she'd be late.

"How late?" he asked.

"Only a couple of hours," she promised. "And then we'll go out for pizza, okay?"

"I guess," Michael replied, and she heard the anxiety in his voice.

"Are you okay?" she asked. "Is something wrong?"

There was a long silence, then: "I'll be okay. See you when you get home."

She hung up the phone and hesitated, wondering if she shouldn't call it a day and go home now. But even as that thought came to her, the idea that had been poking at the edges of her consciousness all afternoon suddenly came together.

Once again she replayed the video in her mind, but this time, instead of trying to decide what kind of creature it was that she'd seen, she concentrated on how old it might have been.

If it was some kind of small primate, it would have been full-grown.

But if it wasn't a primate?

More images flashed though her memory.

The way the tribesmen had stared at it.

The way its fear seemed to grow, and the look almost of surprise when the tribesmen had begun chasing it.

It had been so much smaller than the men.

And the woman had acted like . . .

The woman had acted like a distraught mother who had just lost a child.

A mutant?

Could what she'd seen on the video have been a mutated human child?

Mutated by what? Pollution?

Even as the question formed in her mind, so did a possible answer.

Mount Pinatubo.

The volcano that had erupted in the Philippines less than ten years ago, spewing enough ash and poisonous gas into the atmosphere to make dozens of villages uninhabitable.

If alcohol and tobacco could harm a fetus, what might the gases disgorged from an active volcano do? Katharine's eyes fixed once more on the skeleton on the table, but now her mind's eye no longer saw the fire pit next to which the body had been buried, but the sulfurous vent a little farther up the ravine. What if the remains she'd unearthed were of someone who'd been born only months after an eruption of Haleakala?

Suddenly it became imperative to determine the age of the bones as exactly as possible, and try to correlate them to one of the last eruptions on Maui.

Or on the Big Island, where even now new vents were opening, releasing gases from the bowels of the planet?

She worked for three more hours, preparing bone samples and searching the Internet for the labs that could do the work most quickly and efficiently.

And now her mind was starting to fog with exhaustion and her whole body ached.

And she was already hours later than she'd promised Michael.

Leaving everything as it was, Katharine began closing up the workroom. She'd just turned the lights off and was about to lock the door when a sweep of headlights across the window caught her eye.

Leaving the lights off, she went to the window and looked out.

*   *   *

Michael sat staring at the television, trying to concentrate on the characters on the screen but unable to keep his attention on the movie for more than a few seconds at a time.

He kept thinking about Josh, clutching the bottle of ammonia in the rest room, sucking the fumes deep into his lungs, struggling to hang on to it when he'd taken it away from him.

And he remembered the look in Josh's eyes just before he'd fled from the locker room. For a moment Michael hadn't been able to recognize his friend at all. Josh had completely disappeared, replaced by . . .

What?

A *wild animal.*

The words came unbidden into Michael's mind, but the more he thought about them, the more he realized that was exactly what Josh had looked like: a trapped animal, searching for a way to escape.

And for just a second, Michael recalled, he'd been afraid Josh was going to attack him, going to try to recover the bottle he'd yanked from Josh's hands.

After school Michael had waited as long as he could, hoping Josh would come back, but when the bus had been ready to leave, he'd finally climbed onto it. All the way home he'd kept half an eye out, thinking he might see Josh's truck racing up to overtake the bus, hear his horn blaring, and then find him waiting at the stop where he got off. But another part of him was just as sure that Josh's pickup was not going to appear, that something terrible had happened to his friend.

Should he call the police?

And tell them what?

Repeat the weird story Josh had told him about Jeff's strange behavior and his own flight from the cane field last night? But that would only get Josh in even more trouble than he was already in. And if something had happened to Jeff Kina in the cane field, wouldn't someone have heard about it? After all, he'd heard the names of the two men who had died in the cane fire before he'd left school: fire workers on a routine patrol, killed in a freak accident. One of them had been the uncle of one of the guys on the track team. But nobody had heard anything about Jeff Kina.

When he'd gotten home, he called Josh's house, but Sam Malani

answered, sounding drunk, and ranting that when Josh got home he was going to beat the crap out of him.

Michael hadn't called again.

Then, about an hour ago, he started feeling kind of funny again. It wasn't
too bad—not at all like when he'd had asthma—but for a minute he'd been
tempted to call his mother. He'd chucked that idea as soon as it crossed his
mind. If she didn't make him go to the hospital tonight—"Better to be safe
than sorry"—she'd definitely drag him back to Dr. Jameson tomorrow.

Better not say anything; he'd probably be fine by morning anyway.

He scrunched lower on the sofa and once more tried to focus his mind on
the movie he was staring at.

Stop it, he told himself. *Just stop it. Nothing's wrong with your lungs, and
Josh is just pissed off, and you hardly even know Jeff Kina.*

Except no matter how much he tried to tell himself that nothing was
wrong, he kept remembering the one thing that gave the lie to that thought.

Kioki Santoya had died the night before last.

What if Jeff and Josh were dead, too?

What then?

To that question, he had no answer.

By the time Katharine's eyes adjusted to the dim lights that illuminated the
grounds of Takeo Yoshihara's estate at night, the vehicle had stopped near
one of the doors in the other wing of the building. As Katharine watched, the
security guard who normally sat at the desk in the lobby emerged from the
building and walked quickly to the vehicle, which Katharine could now see
was a small van. As two men got out of the van, a second man came out of the
building, and a moment later the four men had opened the back doors of
the van and were unloading a box from it.

A box that appeared to be about three feet wide, three feet high, and perhaps seven feet long.

The image of a coffin came instantly into Katharine's mind, and though
she tried to reject it, the image wouldn't let itself be so easily banished. Instead, the vision of the coffin was immediately reinforced by her recollection
of the skeleton in the next room.

The skeleton that, though not of the species Homo sapiens, had been laid out for burial as if it were.

Leaving her office, Katharine strode down the long corridor to the lobby, then hesitated.

What was she going to do? Walk down the opposite hall, trying doors until she found one that was unlocked, and go in? Hardly, since the fact of the van arriving in the middle of the night suggested that her presence might not be welcomed.

The same reasoning also precluded going outside and simply walking up to the van to ask what was going on.

Changing course, she moved toward the security officer's desk, a big wooden cube whose surface was bare save for two identical computer monitors. Circling the desk as warily as if it were a tiger ready to spring at her, Katharine perched nervously on the guard's chair and studied the two monitors.

The first one—on the left—displayed a view of the area just inside the estate's main gates. Though she could remember no light fixtures around the gates, the image on the screen was almost as bright as if it were full daylight.

So, the security cameras were equipped with a light-amplifying device, she realized, making the darkness around the gates utterly deceptive.

The other screen displayed nothing more than a series of images of sculpted buttons, some of them labeled, others bearing nothing more than graphics that identified their use in manipulating the camera. Reaching out, Katharine touched the screen where a button framing a magnifying glass was displayed.

Instantly the image on the other screen enlarged as the camera's lens zoomed closer to the gate.

Now Katharine examined the labeled buttons, touching the one marked "North Wing."

All the buttons except those that controlled the cameras disappeared, and in their place appeared a floor plan of the building's north wing. Picking a room she thought was close to the area where the van had parked, Katharine touched the screen again.

The display monitor immediately responded, showing the interior of Stephen Jameson's office.

His empty office.

She touched the room two doors farther down the corridor, and was rewarded by a view of the two men from the van and the two security guards placing the box onto a gurney. As the men from the van departed, the guards pushed the coffinlike box through the office and into the corridor. Switching the monitor to a view of the north corridor, Katharine froze as she saw the guards, one at each end of the gurney, apparently moving straight toward her. A split second later, when the guard who would normally be sitting in the seat she herself was now occupying looked directly into the camera, Katharine had the horrible sensation that he could see her as clearly as she could see him. Her heart pounded and she had to fight an urge to bolt in the opposite direction, fleeing back to her office. But when the guards and the box disappeared from her view—and didn't come through the double doors at the end of the lobby—she realized they hadn't been coming toward her at all. In fact, they were moving in exactly the opposite direction.

But where?

She studied the control screen again, and discovered a button marked "LL."

Lower Level? Of course! The "downstairs" Dr. Jameson had mentioned just this morning.

She touched the button. It seemed to produce no effect.

The same floor plan and control buttons showed on the right-hand monitor, and the same image of an empty corridor was displayed on the screen on the left.

Yet she'd been all but certain that both screens had flickered slightly, as if their displays had in fact responded to her touch. Then, as she examined the control screen more closely, she realized that one thing had changed: the "LL" button was now labeled "UL."

So there *was* another level beneath this one.

As if to confirm the thought, the two guards reappeared, now moving in the opposite direction, away from the camera. Halfway down the corridor a door opened, and the guards maneuvered the box through it. Once again Katharine had to press two of the rooms depicted on the control monitor before she found the right one, and the image on the camera monitor changed again.

The room was obviously a laboratory of some kind. As Katharine watched, two men wearing orderly uniforms started to unscrew the top of the box. Katharine's fingers moved to the buttons that gave her control over the camera, and she zoomed in on the box. As the lid was raised, wisps of fog curled from the container.

Dry ice?

The lid came free, and Katharine could see that whatever was in the box was wrapped in plastic.

She watched as four hands, clad in rubber surgical gloves, worked at the plastic, loosening it.

Four hands.

Where were the other four, the hands that belonged to the security guards?

Katharine zoomed the camera to its widest angle.

The two guards were gone.

Touching the control screen again, she found them.

In the corridor, once again walking toward her.

No! Away from her, by the far end, where apparently there was an elevator. How long did she have before they would be back on this level and coming toward the lobby?

A minute?

Two?

Certainly no more.

She touched the screen again, and once more the orderlies appeared. They had finished unwrapping the outer layer of plastic and were taking out what was left of the dry ice the contents of the box had been packed in. Silently urging them to work faster, wanting to reach through the camera and tear the second layer of plastic from whatever lay within, Katharine could barely contain her impatience.

Her nerves screaming, she switched back to the corridor. The security guards were still standing there, waiting for the elevator. Then, just as she was about to click back to the room where the orderlies were working, the guards stepped out of her view.

They were in the elevator, and the elevator would already be moving.

How fast?

She had no idea.

She switched the screen back to the laboratory. At last, the orderlies seemed to have finished with the dry ice. Unconsciously holding her breath, Katharine gazed into the container. One of the orderlies reached for the layers of almost transparent plastic—all that remained to block Katharine's view of whatever had arrived at the estate in the middle of the night. Then, in a movement that made her want to scream with frustration, the orderly suddenly pulled away.

The zoom!

Her fingers trembling, she touched the adjustment buttons for the camera. It zoomed in and refocused slightly. For just a moment, before one of the orderlies abruptly leaned in and blocked her view completely, she thought she saw something.

A face.

A human face?

The glimpse had been too brief, the distortion of the wrinkled plastic too much.

How much time did she have left? If she could get just one more look—

She touched the UL button, then the hallway.

The guards were on their way back down the hall!

Her heart racing, Katharine rose from the chair and started back toward the double doors leading to the south corridor and Rob's office.

The display! As soon as the guards came in, they'd see what she'd been doing! Whirling around, nearly stumbling in her haste to get back to the desk, she searched the screen again, finding a button marked "Main." She hit it, and instantly the menu that had been displayed when she'd come in no more than five minutes earlier reappeared.

The gate!

Where was the button for the gate?

There—down near the bottom, at the right!

She stabbed at it, waited just long enough to see the image on the display monitor change, then fled across the lobby. Pushing her way through the double doors, she paused to make them stop swinging, then dashed down the hall to Rob's office, slipped inside, and switched the lights back on.

Leaning heavily against the desk, she waited for her heartbeat to return to normal and her breathing to even out, then picked up her purse. Switching the lights out, she left the office for the second time in ten minutes, locked it, and started toward the double doors.

For a moment she had the terrible feeling that the two guards would be waiting for her, knowing what she'd been doing. If they questioned her, what could she say? That she'd been worried when the guard hadn't been at his post and was looking for him?

Would they believe her?

Pushing the doors open, she stepped into the lobby. To her vast relief, the two guards were not waiting for her. One of them, the one who had been there before the van's arrival, was seated behind the desk again, thumbing through a magazine. As she entered the lobby, he looked up.

"Dr. Sundquist. I thought you'd left."

Was there suspicion in his voice? "Just finishing up a few things," she replied. Then, when she was halfway across the lobby, she suddenly knew exactly what to say to put any suspicions to rest. "What was that van that came in a few minutes ago?" she asked, turning back to face the guard. "Isn't it awfully late for deliveries?"

The guard smiled. "One of our trucks," he said. "The driver just stopped to find out where we wanted him to park it."

"Well, it's nice to know we're not the only ones working late," Katharine said, returning the guard's smile. "But how come that doesn't make me feel any less tired?"

The guard chuckled. "Doesn't ever make me feel less tired, either."

With a final good night, Katharine left the building and hurried toward her car.

The guard had lied.

Obviously, something was going on she wasn't supposed to know about. But what was it?

And how could she find out?

Was the corpse that had been delivered tonight—if it truly was a corpse—somehow connected to the alarming video and the skeleton in Rob's laboratory? That was ridiculous. There was no reason to make such a connection.

But the images of the anomalous skull from the Philippines and the film of the slaughtered creature were also still fresh in her mind. An image and a film that were stored in files locked away behind a password, just as whatever had arrived in the van was now hidden away in a lower level she hadn't known existed until tonight.

Every instinct she possessed told Katharine that somehow all these things were related.

The body—if that's what it was—that had been delivered just now.

The mutant—if that's what it was—that had been killed in the Philippines. And the skeleton she herself had excavated right here on Maui.

But how was she going to find out what the connection was? As she drove through the darkness toward the gates of the estate, she wondered how she might gain access not only to the files hidden away in the computer, but to the lower level of the north wing as well. Slowing to let the gates open, she came to a disturbing realization: security here was far tighter than Rob Silver had told her.

Just as she'd remembered, there were no lights illuminating the gates, yet she was positive that as her car passed through them, the guard in the lobby was watching her as clearly as if it were high noon. The thought sent a shiver down her spine, and though she kept telling herself that she was being silly, she couldn't rid herself of the eerie feeling that she was being watched until she emerged from the narrow road from the estate onto the Hana Highway. Even then it didn't quite leave her, and as she sped toward Makawao, she continued to glance in the rearview mirror, searching for some sign that someone was following her.

Though she saw nothing, the creepy feeling stayed with her.

Though the television was droning as Katharine entered the house, Michael was not watching it. Sprawled out on the sofa, he was fast asleep, and when she bent down to kiss his forehead, he barely stirred. Dropping her leather bag on the floor next to her sleeping son, Katharine used the remote control to turn off the television, then went into the kitchen to find something to eat. The remains of a pizza—not quite half of it—sat on the kitchen counter, cold in its grease-stained box. Transferring two pieces to a plate and slipping them into the microwave, Katharine poured herself a glass of wine while the pizza heated. Taking the pizza back to the living room, she set it down on the coffee table, but then, before settling down onto the floor to have her meal, she moved though the house, locking the doors and windows.

And pulling the curtains.

Before she pulled the last one, she stared out into the night, nearly shivering with the strange sensation that someone was watching her.

But that's ridiculous, she told herself. There's no one out there. No one's watching you!

Repeating those words to herself, though, did nothing to dispel the paranoia that had come over her as she'd left the research pavilion that night. She closed the curtain before going back to the coffee table to eat the pizza Michael had left for her.

She was just finishing the first piece when Michael stirred on the sofa and the rhythm of his breathing changed, taking on a labored quality. Within seconds his feet began kicking and his arms thrashed in the air. Katharine tensed, terrified that the awful scene of last night, when he'd fled into the darkness and not come back until hours later, was about to be replayed. Getting up from the floor, she went around the coffee table, crouched down, and laid a gentle hand on him. "Michael? Michael, wake up! You're having a bad dream."

He moaned and tried to turn away from her, but she put her hand firmly on his shoulder and shook him. "Michael! Wake up!"

Abruptly, Michael's whole body convulsed, and then he was sitting up, instantly awake. Startled, he stared at her.

"What was it?" Katharine asked. "What were you dreaming about?"

"The night di—" Michael began, but instantly cut himself off.

"The what?" Katharine asked. Her eyes fixed on him as she tried to figure out what the word was that he'd cut off.

Michael, reddening, knew by the way his mother was looking at him that there was no point in trying to lie about it. "I went on a night dive," he finally said.

"A night dive?" Katharine echoed uncertainly. Then, as the meaning of his words sank in, her eyes widened. "You mean you went scuba diving at *night*?"

Michael hesitated, then nodded unhappily. "With Josh Malani, and some other guys."

"What other guys?" Katharine asked.

Michael hesitated. "Jeff Kina and Kioki Santoya. And Rick Pieper."

The first two names rang a faint bell in Katharine's memory. They sounded familiar, but where had she heard them? Before she could even ask the question, Michael answered it.

"Kioki's the guy whose mom found him in the cane field yesterday morning."

Katharine remembered the radio report they'd heard that morning. "It was the night before that, wasn't it?" she asked. "The night you came home late."

Michael nodded.

"And that's what you dreamed about last night? And tonight?"

Again Michael nodded.

Katharine's eyes fixed on Michael. "Did something happen?" she asked. "On the dive?"

Michael thought quickly, but he'd hesitated just long enough to let her know that the forbidden dive had not been uneventful. "It wasn't anything serious," he said. "The tanks weren't quite full, so we had to quit early, that's all. No big deal."

"But it's given you nightmares," Katharine told him. "And after what happened to—"

Michael groaned. "Aw, come on, Mom. They don't even know what happened to Kioki!"

Katharine studied her son. Not only had he lied to her, but what he'd done had been both stupid and irresponsible. She should ground him, she thought, take away all his privileges, do whatever it took to make certain he'd never do anything like it again. But right now, after having been up almost all last night, she was too tired to cope with it. Besides, he was alive, and at home, and nothing terrible had happened to him. And maybe the fact he hadn't told her what he was planning was partly her own fault—after all, she'd been overprotecting him for years. If it hadn't been for Rob Silver, she wouldn't have let him go scuba diving at all.

The exhaustion that had been crawling through her body all day finally caught up with her, and she decided that this, at least, could wait until another time. "Go to bed," she told him. "Go to bed, and get some sleep." Then an idea came to her. "And Michael? You're the one who screwed up, so *you* decide how you should be punished. I'm just too tired and too angry to deal with it. So you figure it out. Okay?"

Michael looked at her for a long time, and she could see by the expression on his face that she'd come up with the right answer: she was certain that whatever punishment he finally decided to mete out to himself would be far worse than anything she could have come up with.

"Okay," he said at last. "I guess that's only fair." He got up and had almost reached his room when he came back, bent down, and kissed her cheek. "I'm sorry," he said. "I shouldn't have done it, and I should have told you." He straightened up. "G'night," he said softly as he started once more toward his room.

"Michael?"

He turned to face her.

"Try not to be too hard on yourself. A year's grounding will be way too much."

By the time she collapsed into bed a few minutes later, Katharine's exhaustion had reached the point where she was too tired even to sleep. Finally, feeling the house grow stuffier, she got up and opened all the windows. Not that it helped much; a kona wind had begun carrying a faintly acrid, smoglike miasma in from the erupting volcano on the Big Island.

Before she went back to bed, Katharine paused to listen at Michael's door. Though she herself was wide-awake, her son was sleeping peacefully.

CHAPTER
22

Takeo Yoshihara awoke, as he always did, as the first glow of dawn was lighting the eastern sky. As fully awake now as he'd been deeply asleep the moment before, he rose immediately from his bed and, dressing in the aloha shirt, white pants, and sandals that were his standard uniform on Maui, he went to the small dining pavilion. His breakfast of miso soup, fish, and tea was waiting for him, just as always when he was in residence at the estate.

As he ate he reviewed the conditions of the financial markets and scanned the stack of reports that had come in from all over the world during the night.

It appeared that he was thirty million dollars richer than when he'd gone to bed last night.

Finishing the reports as he drained the last drop of tea from his cup, Yoshihara left the dining pavilion to make his way through the gardens to the research center, stopping only once to remove a wilting orchid bloom that the Filipino gardeners had overlooked.

Entering the research pavilion through the main doors, he nodded to the guard as he passed the desk, pushed open the double doors leading to the south corridor, and strode quickly down the long passageway to the elevator at its far end. Pulling his wallet from his pocket, he passed it over a nondescript gray plate above the call button, and the red light at the top of the plate immediately blinked green. A moment later the door slid open. Yoshihara stepped into the car, and the door closed behind him.

Less than a minute later he was in the laboratory to which the large wooden crate had been delivered late last night. The crate, though, had long since been taken away, as had the remnants of dry ice in which the contents had been packed, and the plastic sheeting in which it had been wrapped.

Only the body itself remained, and it was all but unrecognizable.

Stephen Jameson looked up as the laboratory door opened. Surprised to see his employer coming into the room, he glanced at the clock.

Nearly six-thirty.

Suddenly feeling the fatigue of the long night of dissection, Jameson took off his glasses, rubbed his eyes, and stretched.

Nodding a greeting to the doctor, Yoshihara stepped closer to the table and looked down at what was left of the body that he'd had removed from its grave and shipped to Maui. If the sight of the carnage caused Yoshihara any discomfort, he gave no outward sign.

The corpse had been laid open from the crotch to the neck, and what few organs still remained in the thoracic area lay in confused disorder, like the pieces of a quickly disassembled jigsaw puzzle. The ribcage had been split and spread wide to allow easy access to the lungs and heart—both of which were missing entirely—so all that now remained was a great yawning cavity that, since it was entirely free from blood, gave the body the odd appearance of never having been alive at all. Rather, the remains of the cadaver had an artificial and strangely impersonal look to them, as though what lay on the table had been sculpted of wax rather than flesh and blood.

Yet Yoshihara knew that such was not the case, for he himself had seen pictures of the boy taken only a few weeks ago. A white male, seventeen years old, he'd stood a little over six feet tall, with the broad shoulders and narrow hips of an athlete. In one of the photographs Yoshihara had seen, the boy was smiling broadly, showing perfect white teeth, deep dimples, and a slightly cleft chin. In combination with his blue eyes and blond hair, he'd been the perfect example of the California surfer.

Oddly, the boy's good looks remained.

His blond hair, neatly combed and sprayed for his funeral, had been slightly mussed by the packaging, and before Yoshihara realized quite what he was doing, he found himself reaching out to smooth the stray locks back into place.

The pallor of death had been expertly covered with makeup, and the boy's cheeks showed a rosy glow, as if he might wake up at any moment.

The cleft in his chin was as clear as it had been in the photo, though in the solemn expression of death, he showed no signs of his dimples.

Yoshihara turned his attention back to Jameson, who now held a manila folder in his hands. "Have you determined the exact cause of death?"

Jameson opened the folder, scanning its contents. He'd had a team of laboratory assistants working all night, analyzing the tissues that Jameson himself had taken from each organ as he'd performed his dissection of the body.

As Jameson had expected, most of the boy's organs proved to be as healthy as they'd appeared. The lab tests showed no signs of disease or toxic substances.

Or at least there were no signs of any substances that one might have expected would kill a seventeen-year-old boy.

No strychnine, or cyanide, or any other poisons.

No drugs, either. No heroin, no cocaine, no uppers or downers.

Not even any alcohol or marijuana.

Yet the boy had died, and the lab report in Stephen Jameson's hands clearly showed why.

"The cause of death," he said, "was a violent allergic reaction to the substance in question." He gave Yoshihara a smug smile. "When the ambulance arrived, his mother was trying to get him out of his car, which was running in the garage with the door closed."

Yoshihara nodded. "And so they gave him oxygen."

"And he died," Jameson said.

"And the weather in Los Angeles that day?" Yoshihara asked.

Jameson smiled thinly. "Close to perfect. A Santa Ana condition had developed; the weather reports spoke of a crystalline day such as Los Angeles hardly ever experiences anymore."

"But not good for our subject," Yoshihara observed. "What would the result have been if they hadn't applied pure oxygen?"

"It's hard to say," Jameson replied. "But it appears that our latest subjects are doing better. So far, four of the five seem to be doing fine. Of course, the air in Mexico City has been particularly bad the last few days, but in Chicago it's been pretty good."

"And how long have they been in place?"

"Only two days," Jameson told him.

"Interesting," Yoshihara mused. "What about the local boy who died? What was his name?"

"Kioki Santoya," Jameson replied. "He wasn't given oxygen, of course—he was already dead when his mother found him. But our lab work shows that his lungs are in very much the same condition as this subject's." He nodded toward the cadaver on the table.

Takeo Yoshihara was silent for a moment, thinking. "The other two locals," he finally said. "I would like to see them. Not on the monitors. I wish to look at them directly."

Stephen Jameson's eyes clouded. "I'm not sure that's a good idea," he began. "If either of them recognizes you—"

"It won't matter if they do," Takeo Yoshihara cut in. His expression was grim. "After all, it's unlikely they'll be leaving here, isn't it?"

Stephen Jameson tilted his head noncommittally. It would not do to expose his feelings to his employer. "As you wish," he said, leading Takeo Yoshihara through a door. They passed through a chamber filled with tanks of compressed gas and a large pump, and then into yet another room.

This room was empty, except for a large Plexiglas box.

The box was filled with a brownish fog.

Barely visible through the haze were the figures of two young men. Naked, they lay sleeping on the floor, their heads resting on their arms. But as Takeo Yoshihara stared at them, the eyes of one—the larger of them, and as Yoshihara could now see, a Polynesian by ancestry—suddenly snapped open. In an instant he was crouched low to the floor, as if ready to spring.

Like an animal, Takeo Yoshihara thought. Like a wild animal sensing danger. Yoshihara stepped closer, exactly as he might have to get a closer look at an ape in a cage at the zoo.

The figure sprang at him, his hands extended as if to seize Yoshihara's neck, until, crashing against the Plexiglas wall, he dropped back to the floor of the cage with a howl of pain.

Now the other, smaller specimen was awake, too, staring through the transparent wall, his eyes burning with fury.

"We still have no idea how they became involved in our experiments?" Yoshihara asked, turning away from the box to gaze once more at Jameson.

"Since I'm sure they don't know themselves—" he began, but once more Yoshihara cut him off.

"I'm not interested in what they know," he said. "I wish to understand how they became exposed to our compound. Find out. I want an answer by the end of the day. Is that clear?"

Stephen Jameson swallowed nervously, but nodded his assent, knowing no other response would be acceptable.

"Good," Yoshihara said softly. Then, without so much as a backward glance at the two boys imprisoned in the Plexiglas box, he made his way back through the series of rooms, rode the elevator up to the main floor, and left the building to stroll for a while in the gardens.

He had an hour before it would be time to leave. Except for the small hitch involving the local boys, things seemed to be progressing nicely. And even the problem with the locals was being contained.

"Contained," he repeated silently to himself. It would have been better if all the research subjects could have been kept far from Maui, as originally planned, but since the error had occurred—and he *would* find out precisely how that error had occurred—there was no point in not turning the mistake to his own advantage.

For as long as they lived, the two young males down in the laboratory would make valuable research subjects.

For as long as they lived.

For Takeo Yoshihara, the life spans of Jeff Kina and Josh Malani were of no concern. Far more important—indeed, the only matter of any importance— was the essential scientific data their corpses would provide.

CHAPTER
23

Katharine was just turning off the Hana Highway into the long dirt road that led to the estate when she heard the unmistakable whup-whup-whup produced by the whirling blades of a helicopter. Though the sound was ominously close, she could see no sign of the aircraft. Instinctively braking the car to a halt, she gazed up into the sky, using her hand to shade her eyes against the brilliance of the morning sun. Like an iridescent dragonfly, the helicopter appeared, skimming low over the trees, seeming almost furtive as it bobbed and wove over the contours of the landscape. As it passed low overhead she thought she recognized Stephen Jameson and Takeo Yoshihara peering out of the Plexiglas shell, and she turned to watch it, expecting it to bank around to the left, toward the airport at Kahului.

Instead it turned right and disappeared behind a rocky parapet that rose nearly two hundred feet from the floor of the rain forest.

Only when the sound of the chopper's blades had faded away did Katharine put the car in gear again and continue down the narrow road. Anticipating her arrival, as they did every morning, the gates swung open as she approached, and she barely had to slow the car as she rolled through. This morning, though, Katharine felt the tiny hairs on the back of her neck rise as she sensed the camera that she was certain was watching her, and as she drove through the grounds of the estate, she had to consciously force herself not to look around for more cameras. She was nearing the research pavilion that housed Rob's office when she noticed that most of the parking spaces in the lot behind it were empty this morning.

She surveyed the nearly deserted lot, an idea taking form in her mind. An idea that began to dispel the dark mood that had come over her during the long hours of the night when she'd lain awake, wondering how she might gain access to the laboratory under the north wing. Last night she had come up with nothing. But this morning things had changed.

First the helicopter, and now the all-but-empty parking lot.

Something, obviously, was going on.

Abandoning her intention to go out to the site in the ravine this morning, Katharine pulled the Explorer into one of the empty slots in the parking lot. Entering the main lobby—and again resisting the urge to look for security cameras—she started toward the doors leading to Rob Silver's office, but then stopped abruptly, as if having just changed her mind. As she approached the security desk, the guard looked up, and she was certain she detected a look of surprise in his eyes. Perhaps she wouldn't have to pump him for information; with a little luck, he might just tell her what was going on without her even having to ask. A second later he spoke the words she'd hoped for: "Thought everybody'd gone up to the meeting in Hana."

She struggled not to betray her ignorance. Hana? What was he talking about? What was going on up there?

"I'm going up this afternoon," she said smoothly.

Why had she felt the need to lie?

But of course she knew—the paranoia she'd felt last night as she watched the clandestine delivery, then driven home with the feeling that eyes were watching her all the way, was creeping over her again, wrapping its coils around her like a boa constrictor.

But at the same time, the inkling of an idea that she'd had in the parking lot was quickly taking shape. "Has Dr. Jameson already gone?" she asked, her mind working quickly as she tried to inject a note of anxiety into her voice.

The guard nodded. "Took off in the chopper with Mr. Yoshihara a few minutes ago."

"Damn," Katharine muttered, carefully setting her features into a mask of annoyance.

"Pardon me?" the guard asked.

Katharine sighed heavily. "My son thinks his keys might have fallen out of his pocket yesterday. I was going to ask Dr. Jameson if he found them." She opened her mouth as if about to say something else, then closed it again, indicating a change of mind.

She hesitated, then fed out a little line, as though playing a fish: "Of course, he's blaming it all on me. Kids." She turned away as if having no expectation that the guard might offer to help her. But as she started toward the double doors leading to the north wing, she could almost feel him sniffing the bait, considering whether there was a hook in it.

"Maybe I could let you in for a minute, Dr. Sundquist," he suggested.

Katharine turned back as if she could hardly believe what he'd said. "I couldn't let you do that," she said, risking everything to set the hook firmly. "With him being gone—"

"No problem," the guard told her. "And I've got a sixteen-year-old of my own. I know how they can be. If the keys are there, we should be able to find 'em in a couple of minutes."

As she trailed along, the guard led Katharine down the north corridor. When he stopped, searching his ring for the key to Stephen Jameson's office, she glanced at the elevator at the far end. Above the call button was the drab gray plate, its red light glowing mockingly at her.

"Where should we start?" the guard asked.

Katharine shrugged a display of helplessness. "The examination room, I suppose. That seems the most likely place for him to have dropped them, doesn't it? Why don't I check the chair he used in Stephen's office while you look around the examining room? It's just a ring with half a dozen keys on it." As they entered Jameson's office, Katharine made a show of searching the chair while the guard went into the examination room. Alone then, she darted to the credenza, praying the drawer would not be locked.

It wasn't. There, in plain sight, was the gray plastic card, not even concealed under so much as a sheet of paper. Snatching it up, she slid the drawer silently closed, then joined the guard in the examination room. "Well, they weren't in the chair."

"And I'm not finding them in here, either." He nodded toward a cabinet containing half a dozen drawers. "Why don't you go through those while I take these? Did you look in his desk?"

"If anyone's going to prowl through someone else's desk, it's going to be you, not me," Katharine replied. "I'm the new kid around here, remember? I just barely got my key to the elevator. I'm not about to start rifling through desks."

They left Jameson's office a few minutes later, chatting cordially.

The key to the elevator was in Katharine's pocket.

And Michael's keys, she assumed, were still in his pocket. As far as she knew, he'd never lost them once in his whole life.

She waited half an hour before setting out for the north corridor, pausing only to exchange a few words with her new friend, the guard. "Well, down to the salt mines," she said, winking at him before pushing her way through the double doors and walking purposefully toward the elevator. It took all her self-control not to look back and glance up at the security camera she suspected was trained on her. When she took the card from her pocket and held it over the gray sensor plate, she prayed the trembling of her hand was not visible.

The light turned green. A moment later the elevator doors slid open. She stepped in and pressed the Down button, then tried to judge how far the car traveled. The ride was so smooth, though, that she had almost no sensation of movement; when the doors slid open fifteen seconds later, she could have been fifteen feet down, or fifty.

Or a hundred.

The corridor was deserted. Katharine walked along it as purposefully as she'd strode down the hallway above a moment ago, though she had no idea of precisely what she was looking for.

First, of course, she wanted to find the object that had been delivered last night. In her mind's eye she summoned up the floor plan of the lower level as it had appeared on the security monitor, and tried to remember in which room she'd seen the coffinlike box being opened.

Third door on the right, she was almost certain.

When she came to the third door, she paused, resisted an overpowering urge to glance back at the camera above the elevator door, then twisted the doorknob. To her vast relief, the door opened.

She recognized the room the instant she stepped inside: immaculately clean, its floor was covered with white tile, a white-enameled metal examination table stood in its center, and there was a large lab bench against one wall. Another wall was lined with three rows of large drawers.

Drawers she immediately recognized from the morgue scenes in countless television shows.

Steeling herself, Katharine crossed the room and stood before the bank of drawers.

She was wrong, of course. She *had* to be wrong! It couldn't possibly be a morgue.

Unsettling thoughts were tumbling through her mind. What if someone came in?

What if the guard was watching?

What if the room was alarmed?

Get out, a voice inside her head whispered. *Get out, and go back upstairs, and mind your own business.* All you have to do is work on one skeleton. One skeleton that Rob found two miles away. Whatever is in here is none of your business.

Get out.

Get out!

But even as the voice kept whispering to her, she reached out with a trembling hand and pulled one of the drawers open.

Empty.

The tension in her body easing only a fraction, she moved her hand to a second drawer.

Empty.

So was the third, and the fourth.

Now her hand was no longer trembling, and she was starting to feel a little foolish. Whatever she'd seen last night, it couldn't have been a—

The thought shattered in her mind as she pulled open the fifth drawer and found herself staring into the face of a boy.

A boy of seventeen or eighteen, perhaps, with strong features, blond hair, and a cleft chin.

And dead blue eyes that stared unblinkingly up at her from sockets that were sunk deep into his gray, expressionless face.

Katharine stood rock still, fighting the nausea that had risen in her belly. *Don't react*, she told herself. *If they're watching you, you mustn't react at all. You must act like you belong here.*

Pulling the drawer all the way open, she gazed into the great Y-shaped incision that had been cut in the boy's torso. What few organs remained were in a chaotic jumble, as if having been hastily put back after an autopsy. His lungs, though, had been completely removed.

His lungs?

Suddenly the description of the single file she'd been able to read in the Serinus directory came back to her.

Pollution? Could this boy have died from pollution poisoning?

She pulled the drawer farther open, looking for something—anything— that would identify the corpse. And then, as the drawer reached the limits of its extension hardware, she saw it.

A tag was attached to the big toe of the boy's right foot. Tearing the tag loose, she dropped it into her pocket, closed the drawer, and was about to leave the room when she noticed a door in the left-hand wall, toward the back of the room. Moving close to it, she listened for a moment and heard a humming noise. She hesitated, then tried the knob.

It turned, and she eased the door open enough to see inside.

It was some kind of equipment room, filled with tanks of varying sizes, all of which seemed to be connected to a central tank with a series of hoses and valves. From the central tank a series of large ducts ran in several directions, passing through two of the walls.

Then she saw the source of the humming sound: a pump next to the large tank, apparently moving the tank's contents through the ducts.

Both the wall opposite Katharine and the one at the far end of the room were pierced by doors as well as by the large ducts, and she quickly moved to the closest one, listened, and tried the knob.

Locked.

She moved to the other door, only to find it locked, too.

Frustrated, she rattled the knob hard. She searched for a card scanner, but there was no sign of one. Should she try to find a key? What if one of the cameras was watching?

She twisted the doorknob one more time, then gave up and went back to the autopsy room. She was tempted to return to the elevator right then—to press her luck no further—but when she stepped out into the corridor, its row of closed doors drew her like a magnet.

Deciding, she turned away from the elevator and moved slowly toward the far end of the hallway. Thirty feet farther on she saw a door that bore a plaque:

The Serinus Project

She stared at the sign, the realization slowly sinking in: she no longer needed the password to the protected directory that had so utterly frustrated her yesterday afternoon. Steeling herself, she reached for the knob, all but certain that this door, like those inside the morgue, would be locked.

It wasn't; apparently, Takeo Yoshihara considered the elevator's security system sufficient, for this area of the facility, at least.

She stepped into a wood-paneled anteroom, empty but for a deserted desk and a display case. As she realized what was in the cabinet, Katharine's heart began to beat faster.

The skull?

Could it be the same skull she'd glimpsed on the monitor in Rob's office? Katharine moved closer to the case, a sealed Plexiglas box fixed to the top of a black lacquered pedestal. As she studied the skull from every angle, her excitement grew. It *was* the one she'd seen! It *had* to be! And it appeared to be exactly like the skull she'd found in the ravine, in every aspect. Tearing her eyes away from it, she searched for something that would identify its provenance. For a moment there seemed to be nothing, but then she found it: a small plaque very much like the one affixed to the door through which she'd come in a moment ago. It identified the skull only as having been discovered in a village in the Philippines on a date two months earlier. Committing the name of the village to memory, Katharine studied the skull once more, then moved on.

And stopped in shock as she came to the next room. For a split second she had the strange sensation that she'd stepped into a veterinarian's office, since one entire wall was lined with animal cages. Except they weren't quite cages at all: rather, they were boxes made of Plexiglas. She moved farther into the room, her eyes rapidly taking in the details of its equipment. The cells—the word popped into Katharine's mind out of nowhere, but even as it formed in her head she had the distinct feeling that it was exactly the right word to describe the plastic cages—were airtight, with what were apparently remotely operated systems allowing food and water to be provided to the animals isolated within each of them.

Each cage had a ventilating system that kept the atmosphere within the cells constantly circulating, and a large computer monitor displayed the composition of the atmosphere within the confines of the plastic boxes. In an instant Katharine understood: the tanks in the equipment room she'd found a few moments ago were supplying the atmosphere for the boxes.

She moved closer to the wall of cages.

The cells were of varying sizes and contained various species.

In the smallest were mice, a few of them alone, some in pairs. In one there was a nursing female, with half a dozen babies suckling at her teats.

A row of larger cells contained cats and dogs. They were all caged singly, and most of the cats were curled on the floors of their prisons, some licking at their fur, others sleeping.

Or perhaps they had died?

Katharine's gaze shifted to one of the monitors; the display, a series of letters and numerals, indicated the composition of the atmosphere within the confines of the plastic box. She picked out familiar chemical designations: NH_3, CH_4, CO.

Ammonia.

Methane.

Carbon monoxide.

There were half a dozen other chemical formulae, a few of which she was familiar with, most of which she was not.

But all of them, she suspected, were equally deadly gases. Dear God, what was going on here?

Katharine moved closer to one of the cages and rapped on it sharply. The cat within stirred, then settled down and appeared to go back to sleep.

All but one of the dogs were awake. Two of them sat staring at her, but with none of the eagerness of puppies hoping to be played with. Rather, their eyes seemed oddly empty, as if they understood they would never be released from the plastic boxes in which they were imprisoned. The other three were sprawled out, apparently looking at nothing at all. With a shudder of revulsion, Katharine recalled the meaning of the project's name: canaries in the mines—that's what these poor animals were! Impulsively, she reached out, opened one of the cages, and lifted the puppy inside into her arms, then quickly closed the cage door against the foul-smelling fumes that spewed from it.

The puppy, wriggling gratefully, snuggled against her bosom, and as she stroked its soft fur, outrage at the experimentation going on in this room rose inside her. How could anyone *do* something like this? To subject all these innocent animals to—

Her thoughts were interrupted by a strange wheezing sound from the puppy in her arms. Then it was wriggling, as if trying to escape her hold on it, and when she looked down, it was gazing up at her with frightened eyes, its mouth gaping as it gasped in a struggle to catch its breath.

Dying! The puppy was dying in her arms!

She cuddled it close, trying to ease its fear, but a moment later it was over. The puppy lay limp in her arms, silent and still. Katharine stared at it numbly for a moment.

What should she do with it?

And then she remembered where she was and what she was doing. If someone found her—

Quickly she returned the lifeless puppy to the cage from which she'd taken it.

She should leave—leave now, before she was discovered. But there was another room beyond this one, and even as she tried to bring herself to leave the strange laboratory complex, she knew she could not. She had to try to find out exactly what they were doing down here.

How was it possible that any of the caged animals remained alive, given what they were breathing?

She moved on through a series of laboratories that were deserted but for a few technicians in white lab smocks, most of whom seemed to be concentrating on their work.

She barely paused, and asked no questions, determining to go unnoticed as long as she possibly could.

And finally she came to the last room.

It was a small chamber. In its center, enclosed in a thick glass case, was a sphere, perhaps three feet in diameter, made of a gray-black substance that could have been either metal or stone. From the sphere a tube protruded, which curved around, then went straight down, apparently through the case and into its base.

On one wall of the room was an instrument panel that appeared to be monitoring every possible condition within the case, from temperature and humidity to air pressure and the presence of trace elements within the atmosphere itself.

Katharine circled the case, studying it from every angle, but each aspect of the sphere inside appeared to be the same as every other.

Her back was to the door when a voice startled her.

"First time you've seen it?"

She whirled around, realizing a second too late how guilty she must look, then did her best to recover. "My God! You have no idea how you startled me!"

"Sorry," the technician replied. Then he smiled. "I suppose you're pondering the eternal question?"

"Excuse me?"

" 'What is it?' " the technician asked.

The question caught Katharine off guard. "That's just what I was going to ask you," she replied.

Now the technician's expression turned slightly quizzical. "That's what we're all trying to find out, isn't it? I thought maybe a new face might have a new idea."

Katharine floundered for a moment, then composed herself. "I wish I did," she said. "But I'm afraid I'm as puzzled as everyone else. Actually, I was just looking for Dr. Jameson."

"Not here," the technician replied. "He went up to the meeting at Hana." Now the last of his smile disappeared, and his eyes narrowed with a hint of suspicion. "Why aren't you up there?"

Katharine decided simply to tell the truth. "I wasn't invited," she said. "And since Dr. Jameson isn't down here, I suppose I might as well go back to my office and do something useful, huh?" Feeling the technician's eyes watching her every step of the way, Katharine quickly retraced her steps, again resisting the urge to look over her shoulder.

But even when she was back in Rob's office, the feeling that eyes were watching her every movement lingered on.

In a private conference room at the Hotel Hana Maui, tucked away at the end of thirty-five miles of some of the most winding highway in the world, Takeo Yoshihara faced the seven members of the Serinus Society who had flown in over the last thirty-six hours from every continent on the planet.

"I have good news," he began. "Four of our latest canaries have not died. One of the two new subjects in Chicago, along with the newest ones in Tokyo and Mexico City, seem to be doing well."

A murmur of excitement rippled through the room, which Yoshihara silenced with a slightly raised hand.

"We also have a problem. A boy died here on Maui two days ago, apparently after having been exposed to our compound."

The excitement in the room turned to consternation.

"And there are three other boys here, all of whom are—" He hesitated, searching for the right word, then smiled faintly as he found it. "All of whom are, shall we say, 'faring better' to varying degrees. Dr. Jameson will tell you about them."

Accompanied by uneasy whispers from the audience, Stephen Jameson rose to his feet. At the same time, photographs of Josh Malani, Jeff Kina, and Michael Sundquist appeared on a screen hanging on a wall behind him. "As you know, it was never our intention to carry out any of our human experimentation so close to our research headquarters. Be that as it may, at least four boys on Maui appear to have come in contact with the substance with which we are experimenting." He glanced up at the three faces on the screen, then fixed a laser pointer on the image of Jeff Kina. "This is a seventeen-year-old male of Polynesian heritage. He is six feet two inches tall, and weighs 225 pounds. He was apprehended in a burning cane field some thirty-six hours ago, breathing comfortably in an atmosphere that was heavily polluted with smoke. He is now in our lab, and doing well." The pointer moved on to Josh Malani's image. "This is another seventeen-year-old boy, five feet eight, and weighing 135 pounds. Mixed heritage. Less than twenty-four hours ago, while under our surveillance, he collapsed in a parking lot near one of the beaches. He was kept alive by administration of a mixture of carbon monoxide, methane, and ammonia, and is also now doing well in our lab."

"And the third boy?" someone asked from the back of the room.

Jameson studied the image of Michael Sundquist for several seconds. "This one is most interesting," he finally said. "This is a sixteen-year-old Caucasian of Swedish descent, and though we didn't specifically choose him for our project, any more than we chose the other three locals, he is proving to be one of our most intriguing subjects. We do not expect complete success with him, of course, but I think that at such time as he dies, his autopsy will greatly advance our understanding of precisely how the substance affects the human body."

A heavily accented voice spoke from the back of the room. "And if, by chance, he *doesn't* die?"

Jameson smiled, but there was no warmth in it. "Believe me, Herr von Schmidt, one way or another, *all* these boys will die."

CHAPTER
24

"Mrs. Reynolds?" Katharine said when a woman's voice answered the phone. Katharine, seated in Rob's office, was staring through the French doors at the idyllic scene outside: flowers everywhere, filling the balmy Hawaiian morning with a rainbow of colors that stood in stark contrast to the cold, gray fear that had cloaked Katharine in the half hour since she'd emerged from the laboratories on the lower level of the research pavilion's south wing.

The first thing she'd done upon returning to Rob's office was to locate the village in the Philippines from which the skull had come. Exactly as she guessed yesterday, the skull had been collected from the slopes of Mount Pinatubo. And if it was, indeed, the skull of a child, it had been breathing fumes—pollution—from the volcano its entire life.

Then, from the depths of her pocket, she'd retrieved the identifying tag she'd found on the toe of the corpse. The boy's name, neatly typed on the cardboard tag, was Mark Reynolds. Along with his dates of birth and death, the label revealed an address on North Maple Drive, in Beverly Hills, California. Right in the middle of metropolitan Los Angeles—one of the most polluted cities in the country. But polluted enough to have killed him? She had to know. First she'd called the hospital where Mark Reynolds had died, only to be told that she could be given no information over the phone. Perhaps if she'd care to make a request in writing?

No, she had *not* cared to make a request in writing. And so, reluctantly, Katharine dialed the number she'd found on the card, part of her burning to find answers to her questions, but another part hating to make this call to Mark Reynolds's mother, who was listed as his next of kin. The phone had been answered on the second ring. Now there was no backing out.

"Elaine Carter Reynolds?" she asked, repeating the name into the telephone exactly as it was written on the piece of cardboard.

"Yes," a voice replied, desolation so clear in the woman's tone that Katharine wanted to hang up.

But she knew she couldn't. "You had a son named Mark?" she asked.

A silence, then, again, a single word: "Yes."

Katharine took a deep breath. "Mrs. Reynolds, my name is Katharine Sundquist. I need to talk to you about Mark. I know it's going to be very difficult for you, but I need some information and I hope you'll be able to give it to me."

What sounded like a stifled sob came through the phone, but then Elaine Reynolds spoke again, and for the first time there was a trace of life in her voice. "It can't be any more difficult than what I've already been through," the woman replied.

"I don't think there can be anything worse than having a child die," Katharine said.

"Mark didn't just die, Mrs. . . ." She faltered, unable to remember the name she'd been given.

"Sundquist," Katharine said quickly. "But please call me Katharine."

"Thank you," Elaine Reynolds murmured. Again she was silent for a moment, and Katharine waited, sensing that the older woman was working her way up to something. Finally Elaine Reynolds blurted it out. "My son committed suicide, Katharine," she said. "Mark killed himself."

The words stunned Katharine. Killed himself? "I—I'm sorry—" she stammered. "I thought—" She fell suddenly silent, having no idea what to say.

"What did you think, Katharine?" Elaine Reynolds said, and now there was more than just a faint hint of interest. When Katharine finally voiced her idea that Mark's death must somehow have been related to the polluted air in Los Angeles, a single bark of bitter laughter erupted from Elaine Reynolds's throat. "I suppose some people would call carbon monoxide pollution," she said. Her voice catching on almost every sentence, and having to pause twice to regain control over her emotions, Elaine described to Katharine Sundquist the scene of her son's suicide. "But they got there too late," she said. "They gave him oxygen, but it was too late. He died on the way to the hospital."

An image of the puppy that had died in her arms a little while ago—a puppy that suddenly had trouble breathing the air outside its cage full of poisonous gases, rose in Katharine's mind. "Your son died while they were giving him oxygen, Mrs. Reynolds?" she asked, praying that she'd heard wrong.

Her voice breaking, Elaine recounted Mark's struggles in the ambulance. "He fought them," she finished. "I'm sure he had no idea what he was doing, but he fought against the oxygen mask. And there was nothing I could do. You have no idea how helpless I felt." She paused, then: "Katharine? What is this about? You still haven't told me exactly why you called me."

"I'm calling from Hawaii," Katharine began. "I'm working for a man who's very interested in pollution—"

"In Honolulu?" Elaine Reynolds interrupted. "I would have thought the air there would be as clean as anywhere in the world. Although actually the vog was pretty bad for a day or two while Mark and I were on Maui over Christmas."

Katharine froze. "Maui?" she echoed. What was going on? Could it possibly be only coincidence that Mark Reynolds had been on Maui a few months ago? "Mrs. Reynolds—Elaine—what were you doing on Maui?"

"Just vacationing. Why?"

"Elaine, I'm on Maui, not in Honolulu. And I've come across something. . . ." She paused, not wanting to cause Elaine Reynolds any more pain than she absolutely had to. "Well, something strange," she finally went on. "It appears that for some reason your son's lungs are being studied."

"But how could they?" Elaine asked. "I mean, without his body, what are they studying?"

Katharine hesitated, but quickly realized she had no choice but to tell the woman the truth. "His body *is* here, Elaine," she said.

"I'm afraid there's been some mistake," Elaine Reynolds said after Katharine's words had sunk in. "Mark's body was buried right after his funeral."

Buried? What was she talking about? Was it possible that she was wrong? That she was somehow talking to the wrong person? "Mrs. Reynolds," Katharine said, unconsciously slipping back into the more formal term of address, "would you mind if I—well, if I told you what the boy I saw today looked like?" There was a long pause, but finally Elaine Reynolds murmured her assent. Katharine summoned an image of the face she'd seen in the morgue drawer downstairs, and began describing it as dispassionately as she could. It was when she mentioned the cleft in the boy's chin that a soft but agonized moan came from the woman at the other end of the line.

"Why?" Elaine whispered a moment later. "Why would they have taken him out there? And why would they have lied to me about burying him?"

"I wish I could tell you, Elaine," Katharine said softly. "But I'm afraid I don't know any more than you do." Then: "What about when you were out here? Did anything happen then? I mean anything unusual?"

"No," Elaine sighed. "It was a wonderful trip. Except for the dive, of course."

Katharine felt a chill pass over her. "The dive?" she repeated.

"Mark went out with some other boys, and they had some trouble with their tanks. Some of the boys had to come up fast, and I guess it was pretty scary. Anyway, it scared me enough that I didn't let Mark go again. And I still keep wondering if that was what started his breathing problems."

Katharine's chill worsened as she heard the last two words, and the knot of fear that had been in her stomach since last night tightened. The night after he'd gone diving, Michael had had breathing problems, and even last night—

And then she remembered. Kioki! What about him? Why had he died? And Jeff Kina. Had he come home yet? Or had the same thing happened to him that had happened to Kioki Santoya? But even as the questions tumbled through her mind, so also did a memory of Michael's voice: "Aw, come on, Mom. They don't even know what happened to Kioki!"

"Elaine?" she said, her voice quavering. "What about the other boys who went on the dive with your son? Do you remember any of their names? Or where they might have been from?"

"I don't think I do," Elaine began. "But maybe—wait! There was a boy named Shane, from New Jersey, who Mark palled around with a lot after the dive. Hold on a minute." After what seemed an endless wait, Elaine came back on the line. "I found it," she said. "Mark had it written down on a scrap of paper in his wallet. His name is Shane Shelby and he lives in Trenton, New Jersey." As Elaine read her the address and phone number, Katharine scribbled it down on the back of the tag she'd taken from Mark Reynolds's body. "Let me know if you find anything out, will you?" Elaine asked.

"I will," Katharine promised. "Of course I will."

Immediately, she dialed the area code and number Elaine Reynolds had given her. On the fourth ring a man's voice answered.

"Keith Shelby."

Katharine struggled to keep her voice from breaking as she asked her question. "Mr. Shelby, my name is Dr. Katharine Sundquist. Are you the father of a boy named Shane?"

A long silence echoed hollowly from the receiver, and for a moment Katharine was afraid the man had hung up. But then Shelby spoke again, his voice betraying uncertainty. "Who did you say this is?"

Once again Katharine identified herself. "I know it sounds strange, Mr. Shelby, but I have to know if your son is all right."

There was another long silence—far longer than the last—and Katharine had a terrible premonition about what he was going to say. Finally, she said it herself. "He's not all right, is he, Mr. Shelby?"

"He's dead, Dr. Sundquist," Keith Shelby said, his tone one of utter defeat. "It was his lungs. They never found out exactly what it was. The best guess was that it was some new kind of virus or something. I don't know anything at all about things like that, but they tell me those things mutate all the time. We thought maybe he picked it up on the flight back from Maui. After that, he was never really very well."

When the call was finally over, Katharine sat numbly, staring out the window.

What on earth was going on?

Was Shane Shelby's body hidden away somewhere on the estate, too?

For several long minutes Katharine sat gazing out the window into the garden, but she saw nothing. Her mind was starting to feel fogged, partly with the exhaustion of the last two nearly sleepless nights, but just as much with strange bits and pieces of information that floated just out of her grasp, parts of a single puzzle that she couldn't quite fit together.

Think! She told herself. The answers are here. Find them!

Pushing her fear and exhaustion away, Katharine went to work.

In the conference room at the Hotel Hana Maui, Takeo Yoshihara felt the cellular phone in his jacket pocket vibrate. Stepping out into the corridor, he flipped the phone open and held it to his ear. "Yes?" He listened for a moment, then spoke again: "Exactly whom did Dr. Sundquist call?" he asked the caller who had just interrupted his meeting with his associates in the Serinus Project.

As he broke the connection several seconds later and returned to the conference room, Takeo Yoshihara was already considering the most efficient way to deal with Katharine Sundquist. And her son.

From the moment he woke up that morning, Michael hadn't felt right. His chest felt tight, and his whole body hurt, but he didn't want to complain to his mother, who would hustle him back to Dr. Jameson. So instead of saying anything, he'd taken the bus to school, where the first thing he'd done was hunt for Josh Malani.

Josh was nowhere to be found. Finally, Michael called his house. His father—sounding as if he were still sleeping off a binge from the night before—growled that Josh wasn't home, but when Michael asked if he'd been home at all last night, Sam Malani only mumbled something about not caring where the hell Josh was and hung up. Through the rest of the morning, Michael grew more and more worried about Josh, and his chest kept getting worse as well.

During third period, when he was starting to wonder if maybe he was going to have an asthma attack, he'd barely been able to breathe. Trying to work the tightness out in gym glass didn't do any good.

At lunchtime Rick Pieper tried to convince him to see the school nurse, but Michael knew what would happen if he did—the nurse would call his mother; his mother would come pick him up and haul him to Dr. Jameson, who would start jabbing needles in him and sticking things down his throat.

And he'd feel worse than he already did.

After lunch he barely made it through his last two classes. Fortunately, the windows of both rooms were wide open, and in both classes he sat close to them, struggling to suck as much of the fresh air into his aching lungs as he could.

By the time the last bell rang, his chest was still hurting and he was starting to feel kind of weak. Dizzy.

Maybe he should just skip track practice and go home.

He rejected the thought in an instant, as old memories rose in his mind. There had been times back in New York a couple of years ago when the asthma was so bad he'd had to catch a taxi just to get the five blocks from school to their apartment. Well, he'd worked for too long to get past that to let it start screwing up his life again. He'd grit his teeth, ignore the pain and the weakness, and break through it on the track. He'd start running, and keep going until the pain either went away or he couldn't feel it anymore.

As the clanging of the bell faded away, Michael packed his books into his bag and joined the throng of students pushing their way out the door. Emerging onto the covered walkway that edged the building, he had to pause to catch his breath before trusting himself even to make it to the locker room next to the gym.

Pulling open the door, he stepped into the humid room. The air was redolent with the mingled odors of perspiration, soap, disinfectant, and half a dozen other chemicals. Michael went to his locker, opened it, and stripping naked, pulled on the gym clothes that were still damp from his fourth-period workout. Then he fished around for a pair of clean socks, unwilling to subject his feet to the stinking pair he'd used earlier in the day.

As he put on his track clothes, he began to feel a little better, and flushed with pride for resisting the urge to skip practice. Finished dressing, he headed toward the rest room.

It was as he was standing at the urinal that he became aware of a new odor drifting into his nostrils. Instinctively, Michael expanded his chest, drawing it deep into his lungs. The pungency of the scent almost made him dizzy, but the constriction in his chest immediately eased and he felt some of the fatigue leave his body.

Glancing around, Michael searched for the source of the odor, but all he saw was the closet in which Josh Malani had found the bottle of ammonia yesterday. The door was slightly ajar. Finished at the urinal, Michael adjusted his shorts and pulled at the lever that flushed the porcelain basin. He moved to the sinks, which stood between the urinals and the closet, and the scent grew stronger. Unable to contain his curiosity, he approached the closet and pulled the door wide open.

The cleaning supplies were lined up on the shelf, just as they'd been yesterday. There were nearly a dozen different containers, holding chemicals ranging from window cleaner to scrubbing powder, from toilet cleaners to solvents powerful enough to remove practically anything from the school's walls, be they painted, tiled, or bare concrete. But there was nothing that could account for the peculiar odor he'd been breathing for the last couple of minutes.

His eyes fell on the ammonia bottle that Josh had been sniffing. Almost without thinking, he reached out, picked it up, unscrewed its cap, and sniffed at it.

The odor grew stronger, and he felt a heat spread through his body.

Frowning, Michael studied the label. Something had replaced the familiar acrid ammonia odor he would ordinarily have recognized.

All the label contained was the usual list of warnings against using the product in an enclosed area, inhaling its fumes, or ingesting it.

Picking up the bottle's cap to screw it back on, he hesitated. His frown deepening, Michael held the bottle to his nose and took another sniff, breathing more deeply this time. The warmth spread through him, setting his whole body tingling.

Was this what Josh had felt yesterday? Glancing around the rest room as furtively as if he were about to shoot heroin into his veins, Michael sucked the fumes in again, and then yet again. With each breath he felt more strength surge into his body, and the last of the fatigue and pain he'd been feeling all day evaporated. He drew a dozen more breaths, and was still holding the bottle in his hand when the rest room door slammed open.

"Jesus! It stinks in here!"

Quickly putting the cap back on the bottle, Michael stepped out of the closet to find himself facing the janitor. "Someone left the cap off the ammonia bottle," he said.

"Musta been Joe," the janitor said, so quickly that Michael was sure that Joe—whoever he was—got the blame for anything that went wrong in the maintenance department. "Christ! How can you stand to even be in here?" Obviously neither expecting nor wanting an answer to his question, the janitor propped the door open to let the fumes out of the rest room and started pulling supplies out of the closet.

"See you later," Michael offered as he walked back out into the locker room. The janitor barely grunted a reply.

Ten minutes later, the wondrous effects of the ammonia fumes still infusing his body with a strength he'd never felt before, Michael ran his first timed one-hundred-meter sprint of the afternoon.

He beat his own best time by nearly three-fifths of a second, and the school record by thirty-eight hundredths.

CHAPTER
25

The French doors to the garden outside Rob's office were wide open, but Katharine felt as if the walls were closing in around her. All day—ever since she'd arrived at the estate's gate that morning—she'd been unable to rid herself of the feeling of being watched. Indeed, the creepy sense that unseen eyes were following her every movement had grown stronger with each hour that passed, until finally she'd found herself suspecting that even the gardener, who appeared after lunch with a rake and a broom and proceeded to remove every fallen leaf and blossom from every square inch of garden she could see, was there solely to spy on her. That she had never once been able to catch him even looking at her, let alone snapping pictures of her, or aiming something that could be an amplifying microphone in her direction, had done nothing to dissuade her. Not that she had any idea what an amplifying microphone would look like, even if she tripped over one. She had been unable to bring herself to make any more phone calls for fear that the instrument was bugged, and before lunch, she had actually unscrewed the handset of Rob's phone, examining the inner parts for something that might be a tiny extra microphone, but had given that up, too.

The day had turned into an eternity, and if she hadn't also convinced herself that leaving early would be considered suspect, she would have fled right after talking to Elaine Reynolds and Keith Shelby.

Instead, she had stayed in Rob's office, her paranoia in full bloom, attempting to appear to whoever might be watching her as if she were proceeding with her normal work, establishing an identification for the skeleton from the site near the fumarole. But what she had actually been thinking about for the last three hours was what she'd seen in the Serinus Project laboratory.

And what Rob had said yesterday about canaries being lowered into mine shafts. The more she thought about it, the more certain she had become that the animals in the cages were precisely that. They were being used to test the levels of toxins that oxygen-breathing creatures could withstand in the atmosphere.

But there was a question that kept haunting her:

Given what they were breathing, and the levels at which they were breathing it, how were any of the animals surviving at all?

In mid-afternoon she'd gone onto the Internet, where she spent some time hunting for information about the effects on animals of the various chemicals being circulated through the Plexiglas boxes. The conclusions she came to were inescapable: given the levels of poisonous gases she'd seen on the gauges, every one of the animals should have been dead.

But they weren't.

The only logical conclusion, then, was that the Serinus Project was far more than simply a study of the effects of pollution on various life-forms.

There must be experiments going on, as well. Experiments in which the animals were being treated to make them resistant to pollutants in the atmosphere.

Her thoughts kept returning to the strange object she'd seen in the last room she explored, and the odd thing the technician had said: "I thought maybe a new face might have a new idea."

It hadn't taken her long to figure out that the technicians in the lab knew only as much as they needed to know in order to do their jobs, and obviously Yoshihara had decided they did not need to know the precise nature of the spherical object or its contents. Yet he'd made no attempt to conceal the sphere.

Their job was to tend the animals, and, she suspected, administer doses to them of whatever substance was being obtained from the tube protruding from the sphere.

A gas? Possibly. Both the object's spherical form and its heavy-looking metallic composition seemed designed to withstand tremendous pressures. Such as those that would emanate from a liquefied gas.

Though it seemed almost impossible to her, the logical conclusion appeared to be that whatever was being given to the animals was intended to counteract the effects of the poisonous gases they were breathing. And, since some of them were still living, it must be working, at least to some extent.

But if the gaseous contents of the sphere could change the metabolism of the animals, enabling them to survive in a poisonous atmosphere, what might the side effects be?

She stared at the strange skeleton she'd unearthed. Could it be some kind of anthropoid that had been altered right here in Takeo Yoshihara's research pavilion, and simply been buried after it died?

But as she gazed at the skeleton, noting yet again that it was far more humanoid than anthropoid, and remembered Mark Reynolds's body lying in the drawer downstairs, and the protected files on the computer, an insidious idea began to form:

Was it possible that it wasn't simply animal experiments that were protected in the files of the Serinus directory?

What if the research was being carried out on people as well?

What if Mark Reynolds's body hadn't been brought to Maui because he had died from the effects of prolonged inhalation of carbon monoxide?

Her mind raced. More and more of the pieces of the puzzle began to fall into place:

If you wanted to administer a gas to someone, how could it be done?

Tanks, of course.

There was certainly no reason that air tanks couldn't be filled with something other than air, and both Mark Reynolds and Shane Shelby had been scuba diving when they'd been on Maui.

What if Mark Reynolds and Shane Shelby weren't the only ones?

The files! The damned protected files that she had no way of getting into! But surely she knew someone —

Phil Howell!

He was on the computer all the time!

She reached for the phone to call him, but instantly changed her mind as paranoid thoughts of cameras and hidden microphones rose up, stopping her. Except, she thought, if there was even a scintilla of validity to the horrifying theory that had taken shape in her mind, then there was nothing paranoid about her fears at all.

She glanced at the clock—nearly four.

A perfectly reasonable time to leave, and plenty of time to get to Phil Howell's office in Kihei. If he weren't there, surely she'd be able to find him at the Computer Center across the street. She prepared to leave Rob's office, doing her best to appear as if nothing were amiss.

Every move she made seemed self-consciously overcasual, and in her own mind she gave herself away a dozen times. When she wrote a carefully worded note to Rob—"Meet me at Phil's office. I've had an idea"—she could almost feel a camera peering over her shoulder, not merely reading the words, but translating their meaning as well. But when she finally passed through the lobby a few moments later, the guard only nodded to her, barely looking up from his magazine.

She kept the car at exactly the speed limit as she started toward Kahului, and was about to pass the shortcut to Makawao when she thought once more of Michael.

For the last hour, since she began to consider the possibility that Mark Reynolds and Shane Shelby had inhaled something other than air from their scuba tanks, she'd been trying not to think about the possibility that the same thing could have happened to Michael.

And one of the boys with whom he'd gone diving was already dead!

She told herself that she was letting her paranoia get out of control, that Kioki Santoya's death was just a terrible, but meaningless, coincidence. But as she came to the turnoff to Makawao, she knew she had no choice. Michael had track practice this afternoon. He should still be out on the field. If he was there, she would continue on to Kihei. If he wasn't . . .

Her skin crawled and her heart pounded as she tried to reject even the thought that what might be happening to Michael was what had already struck Mark Reynolds and Shane Shelby.

As the school came into view, she slowed the Explorer, pulling to a stop as close to the track as she could get. There were a dozen boys standing along the track on the opposite side. For a moment Katharine couldn't make out Michael at all. Then she saw him, crouched low, his feet braced against a pair of starting blocks. A man she assumed must be the coach was holding his hand high in the air, and then, as the man's hand dropped, Michael took off, pushing off the blocks and sprinting down the track, the other boys cheering him on.

As she watched him run the hundred meters, Katharine felt at least part of her fear finally begin to diminish.

No matter what had happened—no matter what might have been done to Mark Reynolds and Shane Shelby and Kioki Santoya, Michael was safe.

In fact, it looked to her as if he was in better condition right now than he'd ever been in his life.

As she pulled away from the curb she barely noticed the dusty sedan that had been parked ahead of her.

She certainly didn't notice that the man sitting behind its steering wheel had also been watching Michael.

Watching him even more carefully than she.

Michael released the breath he had unconsciously been holding as he watched his mother's car pull away from the curb and head toward the Haleakala Highway. At least she hadn't gotten out of the car—that would have been all he needed! It had made him self-conscious enough when the rest of the team stopped practicing and lined up along the track to watch him run, but if his mother had actually gotten out of the car and come over to watch, too . . .

Just the thought of it made him flush with embarrassment.

On the other hand, if she'd stayed around and watched, then at least he'd have had a chance of convincing her he was telling the truth when he told her about the records he'd set today.

Though the times were unofficial, he'd broken the school records in the fifty-, hundred-, and two-hundred-meter sprints, and though he'd had to go inside and breathe a little more ammonia before the last run, he still felt really good. As his mother's car disappeared around a bend, he turned his full attention back to the track.

Even after having beaten every sprinting record for the school, he still felt totally terrific. So terrific, in fact, that maybe he'd just try some of the longer runs.

He set out down the straightaway, pacing himself carefully to make it all the way around the the quarter-mile loop of the track. Settling into a comfortable jog, he wasn't even breathing hard as he turned into the first curve. He held his pace steady until he came into the long straightaway on the opposite side of the field from the bleachers, but then put on some speed as he started down the backstretch.

A month ago—even a week ago—he would be feeling it by now. His breath would be getting shallow, and his legs starting to burn, and by the time he got to the far end, he'd have to slow down to a walk, if he didn't collapse onto the ground, gasping and panting until his breath finally returned to normal. Today, though, there was no pain in his legs and his breathing was still regular, though he was finally starting to feel the effects of the stress he was putting his body under.

Mostly it was just the beginning of a slight heaviness in his chest. It didn't hurt, really. It was just a feeling that something wasn't quite right.

Moving into the turn, he stepped up the pace a little more; whatever was going on in his chest would go away if he just ignored it. Shifting from the jog into a fast trot, he came out onto the stretch in front of the empty grandstands. As his gaze swept across the bank of empty seats, Michael imagined them filled with cheering people, and once again he upped his pace, the fast trot giving way to a lope that was easier on his legs but required more work by his lungs.

He made it around the second lap, and finally he was starting to feel a little heat in his legs. And his chest was hurting, too, but it wasn't the same as the asthmatic agony he'd grown up with.

This felt like the healthy pain of exertion, and he was sure that if he didn't give in to it—if he just kept his pace steady, or even increased it a little—he might break right through the pain and, for the first time, experience the high he'd heard long-distance runners talk about since he was a little kid, but which he had never felt himself. As he finished the third lap, his coach fell in beside him.

"What's going on, Sundquist? You said you couldn't do distances."

Michael flashed the coach a quick grin. "Just feel like running, that's all."

Peters shot him a quizzical look. "You been taking something?"

Michael felt an instant stab of guilt. What should he say? Should he lie? But ammonia wasn't a drug! It was nothing but cleaning fluid.

All the warnings he'd read on the label flashed through his mind. But if it was really as poisonous as the label had claimed, how come he was still feeling so good?

Except that suddenly he wasn't feeling so good.

The breakthrough he'd been expecting—the surge of pheromones that he'd been sure would wash the pain from his chest, giving him a second wind that would send him sprinting around the last quarter of the mile run he'd set out to do—hadn't come.

Instead, the pain in his chest was worse, and now the burning in his legs was starting to feel like fire.

The ammonia! That was it!

It had to be!

The pain was increasing by the second now, and he felt himself falter.

Keep going. If you can just keep going, you can get through it!

The coach, still keeping pace beside him, spoke again. "What's going on, Sundquist? You don't look so good."

So the pain was starting to show in his face now. If he got caught—if the coach found out what he'd been doing in the cleaning closet—he'd get kicked off the team for sure!

Run, he told himself. *Just keep on running. It'll be okay!*

But as he turned into the curve leading to the backstretch, his stride was way off and he could feel himself losing the pace.

His breath was getting ragged, too, and now every time he expanded his lungs, it felt as if knives were thrusting into his chest.

Stumbling, he lost his pace completely, regained it for a couple of steps, then stumbled again. This time, knowing he was going to fall, he veered off onto the grass of the football field, and finally collapsed onto the ground.

"Sundquist? Sundquist!" Jack Peters was crouching beside him now. Michael was lying on his back, and as he stared up into the sky, he saw it darken, lights darting around the edges of his vision, as though he was about to black out.

Or die.

No! He couldn't be dying. Not now! Not after he'd just been feeling so good, and running better than he'd ever run in his life!

He had to get back on his feet, keep going, get through it. He rolled over, tried to pull himself into a crouch, and flopped back onto the ground. Then he felt the coach's hands on his shoulders, turning him back over.

"Just lie there," he heard the coach say. "What is it, Sundquist? What happened?"

Darkness was closing in on him now, and no matter how hard he tried to catch his breath, he couldn't seem to get any air.

Then he felt another pair of hands on him and heard another voice.

Rick Pieper's voice.

"Michael? Michael, what's wrong? What is it?"

Feeling the strength ebbing from his body, Michael struggled to form a word. His lips worked, but as the seconds ticked by, no sound came out.

Rick Pieper looked up at the coach, his eyes filled with terror. Kioki Santoya was already dead, and Jeff Kina and Josh Malani had both disappeared. And now Michael looked like he was dying right in front of his eyes. "Do something!" he begged. "For God's sake, can't you do something?"

The coach leaned down. "What is it?" he demanded, speaking directly into Michael's ear. "What are you trying to say?"

Michael's tongue felt thick, but he struggled hard, and in a whisper he managed to stammer out a single word.

"A-Ammonia—"

Exhausted by the effort it took to utter the word, he gave up his struggles and concentrated what little energy he had left on the normally simple task of breathing.

A task that was now nearly impossible.

Takeo Yoshihara and Stephen Jameson were in the helicopter when the call came through that Michael Sundquist had collapsed on the field at Bailey High School.

"Where are we?" Yoshihara demanded, speaking into the headset that allowed him to communicate with the pilot despite the thundering racket of the rotor spinning overhead.

"We can make it there in five minutes," the pilot responded.

"Do it," Yoshihara ordered. Then he turned his attention to Stephen Jameson. "Will he make it?"

"If we get there before the ambulance does," Jameson replied. "But if they give him the same treatment they gave the boy from Los Angeles, they'll kill him."

"Then speak to the rescue crew," Yoshihara ordered. "Tell them you are the boy's doctor and that they are to do nothing until you arrive."

The pilot's voice came over the headsets. "We can't do that. We don't have the same frequencies the ambulances use. And speak of the devil—take a look!" He was pointing downward and slightly off to the right through the helicopter's Plexiglas bubble. Speeding along the road below them was an ambulance; even from here they could see its lights flashing.

"Faster," Takeo Yoshihara ordered. Though he didn't raise his voice a single decibel, there was a note of total authority in the command that galvanized the pilot.

Tipping the chopper forward, he increased the speed of the rotor, and with a lurch that brought a sickening bile into Stephen Jameson's throat, though Takeo Yoshihara seemed not to notice the motion, the aircraft shot ahead.

They reached the school thirty seconds before the ambulance. By the time the medics appeared with a stretcher, Stephen Jameson was in full control.

Obeying the doctor's orders without hesitation, the paramedics strapped Michael onto a stretcher and loaded him into the helicopter.

"Maui Memorial?" the pilot asked, already revving the engine in preparation for lifting off.

Takeo Yoshihara shook his head. "Home."

The pilot, like the ambulance crew, obeyed his orders without a single question.

CHAPTER
26

Phil Howell's right shoulder felt as if it were on fire, his eyes were gritty, and the images on the computer screen he'd been staring at through most of last night and all of today were blurring in front of him. But finally it was all coming together.

It had begun late yesterday afternoon, when he'd forced himself to admit that there was no way he could have the supercomputer compare the string of strange nonmelodic tones the radio-telescopes had been picking up to every file in every computer in the world. Finally he'd had the computer assign letters to the tones, choosing the four notes that came closest to matching the tones: A, B-flat, D-sharp, and G. Even as he'd done it, he was skeptical that it would lead anywhere: after all, there were no four-note musical scales that he knew of, and certainly no reason to think that a civilization — if there really was one — fifteen million light-years away would have any sense of earthly music anyway.

It was just that he hadn't been able to think of anything else to do. But then, as the notes had streamed across the screen, something had begun rising out of the fog swirling in his mind. At last he'd punched the Pause key at the top right of his keyboard and sat gazing at the screen.

Nothing more than a string of the four notes, one following another randomly, as completely free of a recognizable pattern as the sound—now emanating from the terminal's speaker—was free of a repeated melody.

Yet something about it looked oddly familiar. Then it came to him. Opening a new window on the monitor, he searched the web until he found a site that displayed a certain kind of code.

Genetic code.

A moment later Phil's eyes fixed on a long sequence of code. Not presented as rungs on the double-helix of chromosomal structure as it usually was, the code had simply been typed out in sequence, each of the nitrogenous bases—adenine, guanine, cytosine, and thymine—reduced to single letters.

A, G, C, and T.

His heart began to beat rapidly as his eyes went to the other screen, displaying the signal from deep in space.

A, B-flat, D-sharp, and G.

Substitute C and T for B-flat, and D-sharp, and—

—and it was so obvious.

He thought of the rocket NASA had sent out into deep space years ago, bearing a plaque with simple stick figures of a man and a woman, and some mathematical symbols.

But if you really wanted to communicate with another life-form—a life-form similar enough to yours so that your two races might have some slight hope of communicating—what better symbol to send out than an exact depiction of the sort of being you were?

Particularly when the very definition of your being could be conveyed in a simple code of four symbols, issued in a specific sequence?

Surely any culture that found such a signal, and was far enough advanced to recognize it, would also have had to develop in a way so similar as to make communication between the two species not only possible, but comprehensible as well.

Phil's eyes shifted back and forth between the two windows on the screen. The more he stared at it, the more certain he became.

He was right. He had to be!

The signal wasn't music.

It was code.

DNA code.

A full set of blueprints for a species.

His mind had begun racing then. First he'd have to convert the signal from the notation he'd assigned into genetic notation. That was a simple matter of substitution.

But which notes to substitute for what protein? It was purely coincidence that two of the notes from the signal happened to correspond to two of the letters that human beings use to symbolize the substances that comprise DNA. He hadn't wanted to try to calculate the odds that an alien race would not only have come up with the same musical scale that was native only to certain parts of planet Earth, but would also have assigned the same symbols to the proteins that dictated their own anatomic structure, whatever it might be.

By ten o'clock he'd given up and called a mathematician at the university who had been able to come up with a simple program to construct an entire directory of new files. Each file would differ only in the notes for which the letters A, C, T, and G were substituted. In all, there would be twenty-four files representing every possible combination of substitutions.

Then the supercomputer could begin comparing each of those twenty-four files to every file containing DNA data on every computer within its reach.

Even the mathematician had been unwilling to venture a guess as to how long it would take. Though Phil was nearly ready to pass out from exhaustion, he had been sitting in front of the computer most of last night and all day today, unable to tear himself away for more than a few minutes at a time for fear of missing the moment when a match was made.

If a match was going to be made. The mathematician had told him a match was statistically so improbable as to be virtually impossible. "But that's not to say you won't find something similar," his friend had gone on, confusing the issue even further. "In fact, I'd be surprised if you didn't. After all, if space is truly infinite, then somewhere there has to be an exact match. In fact, there has to be an infinite number of exact matches. But of course the likelihood of your finding one would be one in—what? An infinity of infinities?"

All day long Phil Howell watched the letters stream by, and he was no closer to the answer he was looking for than when he'd started.

But he'd find it. If it was there, he'd find it.

                         *   *   *

All the way from Makawao to Kihei, Katharine rehearsed what she was going
to say to Phil Howell, and in her own mind it sounded perfectly reasoned,
perfectly logical.

And utterly insane!

Takeo Yoshihara was one of the most respected men on Maui. Why
should Phil Howell—or anyone else—believe her?

If only Rob were with her!

What if he didn't find her note? What if someone else found it, and figured out what it meant, and—

Stop! She spoke the word so sharply to herself that she reflexively stamped
on the brake pedal, eliciting an instant and angry response from the car behind her. *Paranoia,* she reminded herself as she got the car back under control, moved into the left lane of the Piilani Highway, and turned up Lipoa
Street. *It was just an innocent note!* And if Rob didn't get there, she'd just
have to convince Phil by herself that she wasn't crazy.

But when she reached Howell's office, he wasn't there. She felt a moment
of desperation as she thought of how far she was from the top of the mountain, but then the receptionist told her he hadn't gone up Haleakala to work
with the telescope. "He's right across the street at the Computer Center."

Relief flooded through Katharine, and she hurried out of the building.
Just as she was crossing the street, a horn honked and she heard Rob Silver
call out.

"Kath, what's going on? I found your note and—" She turned around, and
he saw the look on her face. "Katharine, what's wrong? What is it?" A moment later he was out of the car, his arms around her.

She let her head rest against his chest a moment, then took a deep breath,
trying to remember the words she'd so carefully rehearsed, and failing utterly.
Instead she blurted, "Rob, something horrible is going on, and we have to
convince Phil Howell to help us find out exactly how bad it is."

For the next ten minutes she talked steadily, trying to separate what she
knew from what she only suspected; trying to knit the fragmentary pieces of
the story into a coherent structure. But even as she talked, she could see the

doubt in Rob's eyes. "You don't believe any of it, do you?" she asked when she was finally done.

Rob took a deep breath. "It's not that I don't believe you, Kath," he said carefully. "It's just that so much of what you say is—well, it's supposition."

"I know what I saw in the lab, Rob," Katharine said, her voice taking on an edge.

"I'm not questioning what you saw," Rob went on quickly. "But the conclusions you've come to—I mean, what you're implying about Takeo Yoshihara—"

"That he could be experimenting on human beings?" Katharine broke in. "Why is that such a difficult concept to accept? There have always been people willing to experiment on other people. And maybe I'm wrong. God, you have no idea how badly I want to be wrong. But I have to know, Rob. I have to know exactly what's going on down there, and I can't do it by myself. And I'm sure it's all in that damned Serinus directory that we can't break into! So you have to help me convince Phil to hack into it, or—" Katharine's voice broke as all her pent-up fear crashed over her like a great wave bearing down, crushing her beneath its weight. Her eyes welled with tears and her body began to tremble. For a moment she felt as if her legs were going to give way beneath her and she was going to collapse, but then Rob's arms were around her once again.

"It's all right, Kath," he whispered in her ear, his fingers gently stroking her hair. "It's all right. Of course I'll help you. Just don't worry anymore, all right?"

Katharine's arms went around him and she held him tight. "I'll try," she breathed. "But I've been so frightened that something terrible is going to happen to Michael—"

Rob pulled her closer. "It won't," he told her. "I promise you. Nothing bad will happen to Michael."

Katharine listened to the words and tried to cling to them as she was clinging to Rob himself, but as they started across the road to the Computer Center and she struggled to put her faith in what he'd said, another voice was speaking to her.

That voice was telling her that despite what Rob was saying, and despite the clear evidence of Michael's well-being, which she'd witnessed at the school only an hour earlier, it might already be far too late.

*   *   *

Phil Howell was still staring at the screen when he slowly became aware that he was no longer alone. When he looked up and saw Katharine's ashen complexion and the worry in Rob's eyes, he knew something had gone wrong.

"We need your help, Phil," Rob said quietly. "And we need it now."

Phil frowned, his eyes returning to the screen. If a match was found and he didn't see it—

"Please?" Katharine begged. "I'm afraid—" Her quavering voice was enough to convince Phil that she was truly frightened.

Certain that whatever Katharine and Rob wanted of him involved the computer, he opened yet another new window on his monitor.

The signal was already fifteen million years old.

It could wait a little longer.

Katharine, clearly, could not.

A tiny point of light glimmered faintly in the darkness, so dim that at first Michael was barely aware of it. As it slowly began to brighten, he found himself fastening onto it as the watchman on a ship might fasten on a beacon signaling safe shelter from a storm. He concentrated on the glimmer of light, willing it to grow larger, burn brighter, and wash away the darkness that had enveloped him.

The empty silence that had embraced him along with the darkness was also starting to give way. At first all he could hear was what sounded like a distant droning coming from some unidentifiable source. But as the light expanded and the blackness began to gray, the sound grew louder, and finally he could distinguish a variation in it.

Whup-whup-whup-whup.

It was a sound he'd heard before, a sound he should be able to identify in an instant. But dark tendrils were still wrapped around his mind, confusing him, and it wasn't until the sound became loud enough to frighten him that he finally recognized it.

A helicopter!

It grew louder and louder, but he couldn't see anything at all, for the blackness had now been washed away by a brilliance that blinded him as completely as the total night of a few moments before.

The roar of the helicopter's blades was deafening now. He knew he had only another second or two before those blades would surely crush him.

Run!

He had to get up and run!

But his entire body felt leaden. He could barely flex his muscles.

He tried to breathe, but his lungs hurt, and there was something over his face.

Was that why he couldn't see?

He tried to twist his head away, and then, over the roar of the helicopter's rotor, he heard something else.

A voice.

"Don't, Michael. Don't try to move. Just relax."

He knew the voice, but he couldn't quite place it. Dimly, he began to remember fragments of the last few minutes before the terrible blackness had closed around him.

He'd been running. And running better than ever. Running better because—

Ammonia!

He'd been breathing ammonia, and the coach had been asking him—

But this voice wasn't Coach Peters's. It was someone else, someone who—

Dr. Jameson!

That was it. When he'd gotten sick and passed out, they must have called Dr. Jameson.

The thing on his face was an oxygen mask, and they were taking him to the hospital.

No! He hated the hospital—from the very beginning, when the asthma had seized him in its grip for the first time and his mother had rushed him to the emergency room, he had hated everything about the hospital.

Not just the smell and the sickly green paint and the terrible food. The worst was the way they'd treated him, sticking needles in him, shoving pills in his mouth, doctors and nurses, all of whom he had learned to distrust, talking about him like he wasn't even there. And there was nothing wrong with him today—not really. He had fainted, that was all. He could tell, because he was already feeling a lot better, and when he'd had asthma attacks, the oxygen they'd given him had barely helped. But now the pain in his chest was almost gone, and it wasn't hard to breathe! If he could just get the mask off his face and tell them—

He struggled harder, and for the first time realized why he couldn't move his arms or legs: they were strapped down, immobilized.

He twisted his neck, trying to struggle free of the mask, and realized with astonishment what the blinding light was.

The sun, shining down from out of a blue sky through—

The bubblelike windshield of a helicopter! He could see the blur of the propeller spinning overhead, and feel the swaying of the machine as it hurtled through the sky.

"It's all right, Michael!" He could make out a tinny quality to Dr. Jameson's voice, and realized he was wearing a headset, as well as an oxygen mask. "If you can understand my voice, nod your head. Not hard, just a little."

Without thinking, Michael nodded.

"All right. Now, someone back at the school said something about ammonia. Did you drink it?"

Michael froze for an instant, then shook his head.

"Then you breathed it."

Not a question. A statement. But how did Jameson know?

"It's all right, Michael," Jameson told him. "We know what's wrong. Just relax. You're going to be all right."

Again Michael struggled to speak, but couldn't find the strength. Then he heard Jameson's voice again, urging him to relax, not to fight against the straps that held him to the stretcher or the mask that covered his face. "Relax," Jameson repeated, his voice taking on an almost hypnotic quality. "Just relax, Michael. You're not going to die. Do you hear me? You're not going to die."

Concentrating on the voice, Michael felt himself begin to drift back into the darkness, and the steady whupping of the propeller began to fade. But as he drifted back into unconsciousness, he heard another voice.

A voice he didn't recognize.

"Why do you say he isn't going to die, Stephen? Why should he be different from all the others?"

"I am a doctor, sir," he heard Jameson reply. "I believe in comforting my patients, even if it means lying to them."

The words rang and echoed in Michael's mind. He wanted to cry out against them, to struggle one more time against the bonds that held him and the mask that was pressed to his face. But his strength was gone.

He let himself sink back into the darkness.

It was edging toward six o'clock. Katharine Sundquist and Rob Silver were
still in the Computer Center, Rob watching patiently as Phil Howell worked,
while Katharine paced, her frustration ballooning with every minute that
passed. To her it seemed the computer itself had almost become an enemy.
Her eyes hurt from having stared at the monitor for so long. "Now do you believe me?" she sighed. While one of the windows displayed on the monitor in
front of them was filled with the unending stream of random combinations of
the letters A, C, G, and T, another window—the one in which Phil Howell
had been working for almost an hour—was flashing the same infuriating message that had been the result of everything the astronomer had tried so far:

Password Incorrect.
Please Enter Password:

The vertical line of the cursor blinked tauntingly just to the right of the
colon on the second line of the message, as if daring them to try one more

time to solve the puzzle of the elusive password that would allow them access to the Serinus directory.

"Well, I certainly believe your boss doesn't want us getting into that directory," Howell agreed. "But I still can't believe it's the only one guarded by a password. The man has business all over the world, and you can bet he wouldn't want anyone to see most of what he's doing. Even if all his transactions are perfectly legal—which I doubt—there must be an enormous amount of proprietary information in his memory banks."

"But this computer is only for the research pavilion," Rob Silver reminded him. "The business stuff is somewhere else. Japan, probably."

"Cayman Islands would be more like it, if you ask me," Howell muttered, then typed *Cayman* into the computer, pressed the Enter key, and watched the same box instantly reappear, flashing the same message. "That's it for me," he sighed. "It's going to take a lot better hacker than I am to get into that directory."

"Do you know one?" Katharine asked.

Howell thought for a moment. "No," he said glumly. His gaze shifted to the window on the monitor that was displaying his own project, but nothing seemed to have changed, and he felt the gnawing pangs of hunger that reminded him he'd completely forgotten to eat today. "What do you say we break for something to eat? Then we'll come back and try again."

Katharine's first impulse was to object that there wasn't time for food, but with a glance at the dark circles under Phil's eyes and the tight lines of his face, she knew his endurance was almost gone. "Maybe we'd better," she said, rubbing the back of her neck to ease the soreness of straining to watch the changing display on the computer screen. "I want to see what Michael's up to," she said aloud, turning to Rob. "Have you got your cell phone?"

Rob fished the flip phone out of his pocket. "You want to go someplace in Makawao, and take Michael, too?"

When the answering machine at home picked up on the first ring, signaling that there was a message waiting, Katharine assumed it would be Michael, telling her his own plans for the evening. But when she punched in the playback code and the impersonal electronic voice announced, "Seven . . . new . . . messages," a current of panic surged through her.

The phone at home rarely got even one message, let alone seven. She quickly punched in the code to play all the messages back. The moment she heard the tone of voice of the first caller, she knew it was about Michael.

And it was bad.

"Dr. Sundquist, this is Jack Peters, the track coach at Bailey High. I—I'm real sorry to have to tell you this way—I mean, I wish I could talk to you directly, but . . ." The voice trailed off, then started up again. "Michael collapsed on the track this afternoon. I don't know exactly what the problem was, but we called the EMTs. The ambulance was just arriving when Dr. Jameson showed up in Takeo Yoshihara's helicopter. I assume they took him to Maui Memorial. I just called there, but they haven't admitted him yet. I'll keep trying, though, and if you want to call me after you get this message, I'll be at 555-3568. I just can't figure what happened. I mean, he was running better than ever, and then . . ." For the second time, Jack Peters's voice trailed off. "Anyway," he continued, "I'll keep trying the hospital, and if I find anything out, I'll leave another message. I—well—God, I hate these things!"

By the time the next message began playing, Katharine's tiny cry of anguish when she'd heard Peters's words had brought Rob to her side. She tipped the phone enough so he could listen, too. They heard the voice of a frightened-sounding boy.

"Mrs. Sundquist? My name is Rick Pieper." As the boy began to repeat what she'd just heard the track coach say, she pressed the code to advance to the next message.

"This is Yolanda Umiki, Dr. Sundquist. From Mr. Yoshihara's office? He asked me to call you and tell you that your son is ill, and that he would like to talk to you as soon as possible. If you could call me as soon as you get this message, I can put you directly through to Mr. Yoshihara."

The panic that had seized her when she was told that Michael was ill turned to terror when she heard that Takeo Yoshihara was somehow involved. And why had Dr. Jameson shown up in the helicopter?

There were two more calls from Yolanda Umiki, and then another one from Rick Pieper:

"It's Rick Pieper again, Mrs. Sundquist, and I'm at Maui Memorial Hospital. I came to find out how Michael is, but he's not here! I mean, they say he hasn't even been here! But where else could they have taken him? Oh gosh, I'm sorry—I'm just—well, I guess I'm scared. I mean, I thought they'd bring him here, and—look, I'm really sorry, Mrs. Sundquist! But Michael said something just before he passed out, and I thought you should know! He said something about ammonia before he fainted. I don't know what he meant, or anything, but that's what it sounded like he said. Just 'ammonia.' "

The last message was from Jack Peters again, and it was almost a duplicate of Rick Pieper's: "I don't get it, Dr. Sundquist. If they didn't take him to Maui Memorial, where—" he broke off abruptly. "Christ, I must be scaring you half to death! He probably woke up and it turned out it wasn't anything serious and there wasn't any point in taking him to the hospital at all. Anyway, if you can let me know what's going on, I'd sure appreciate it."

The electronic voice came on once more:

"End . . . of . . . final . . . message."

"He's at the estate," Katharine said. "They didn't take him to the hospital! Oh, God, Rob, what if he's—" Even if Rob hadn't put his finger to her lips, she couldn't have brought herself to finish the sentence. Michael couldn't be dead! He just couldn't be!

"Call the woman in Yoshihara's office," Rob told her. When Katharine seemed unable to cut off the connection to the answering machine, Rob took the phone from her, punched in the number he'd memorized after Yolanda Umiki had left it the second time, and pressed the Send button. Then he handed the phone to Katharine.

When the assistant answered on the second ring, Katharine identified herself, then: "Is my son there? Is he at the estate?"

"Dr. Jameson thought he could treat him better here than—"

"No!" Katharine snapped. "I want him taken to Maui Memorial immediately. Or flown to Honolulu. But I don't want Dr. Jameson to—"

"I'm afraid I don't have the authority to do any of that, Dr. Sundquist," Yolanda Umiki replied in a voice that made it clear that she took orders only from Takeo Yoshihara. "If you will come out to the estate, Mr. Yoshihara will explain the situation to you."

Katharine hesitated, not wanting to ask the next question, not knowing whether or not she would believe the answer she was given, but knowing she could not end the call without asking it. Finally she forced the words out. "Just tell me one thing. Is Michael still alive?"

Takeo Yoshihara's assistant hesitated, then said, "I've heard nothing to the contrary."

As Katharine terminated the connection, she tried to tell herself she'd heard a note of sympathy in Yolanda Umiki's tone. But the woman's words were so . . . peculiar.

Was she trying to tell her that Michael was still alive without violating some edict Takeo Yoshihara had laid out against giving out any information? Or had she simply not wanted to be the one to tell her the bad news? Katharine's eyes, glistening with tears, fixed on Phil Howell. "Please," she whispered. "Keep trying. I don't know what they're doing, but if we can't find out, I think my son is going to die."

Numb, Katharine allowed Rob to lead her out of the building. Less than a minute later, with Rob driving her car while she sat trembling in the passenger seat, they were speeding back across the island.

Josh Malani leaned against the Plexiglas wall, glowering through the brownish haze that swirled around him at the empty room beyond the confines of the huge box in which he and Jeff Kina were imprisoned. He'd lost track of how long he'd been here, for the light in the room never changed.

No clock hung on the wall.

No window betrayed the changing light between night and day.

The last thing he truly remembered was going to the beach at Spreckelsville, thinking that just being outside and maybe going for a swim might make him feel better.

The memory was faint, but he thought he'd fallen, collapsing next to his truck. He'd felt terrible—worse than he'd ever felt in his life.

He'd felt like he was dying.

Then someone had been there, picking him up and putting him in the back of a car.

The next thing he remembered was waking up, and feeling good.

The tightness in his chest was gone, and his whole body had been tingling with energy. But when he'd opened his eyes, he knew instantly that something was wrong.

First, there'd been the haze; and then he realized he was naked.

And he wasn't in a hospital room.

He wasn't even in a bed.

He was lying on a cot, and the brown haze had made it hard to see; except for that, he felt all right. He'd sat up, looked around, and realized he wasn't alone.

There was someone else, stretched out on another cot about six feet away. As the last foggy wisps of sleep lifted from his mind, he'd recognized Jeff Kina. Jeff, also naked, had been sound asleep, but when Josh touched him, he'd come awake, springing off the cot to crouch on the floor, his eyes fixing on Josh as if he were about to attack.

"Jeez, Jeff, it's me!" Josh said, instinctively pulling back from Jeff's tense body. At first it seemed to him that Jeff didn't recognize him at all, but then he'd slowly relaxed, dropping from the crouch into a sprawl on the concrete floor. For a long time he'd simply stared at Josh, and when he finally spoke, his voice had a rough, almost guttural note. Though Jeff no longer seemed on the verge of attacking, his unblinking eyes were fixed on Josh with the concentration of an omnivore targeting its prey.

"They got you, too."

For a moment Josh had no idea what Jeff was talking about, but then it came to him—the cane field!

The car parked at the mouth of the dirt road, which shot into the field as he'd come out.

And the other car—the one with flashing blue lights that he'd been sure was a police car, but which hadn't turned around to chase him as he'd sped down into the valley, ignoring the speed limit in his race to escape the fire in the cane field.

The fire to which he'd abandoned Jeff Kina.

"I—I'm sorry," he whispered. "I shouldn't have—" He hesitated, then: "I shouldn't have left you there."

"You mean you shouldn't have run away," Jeff growled. Once again his body tensed, his thick muscles knotting under his skin, and Josh braced himself for the attack.

Jeff Kina was at least six inches taller than he was, and nearly twice as heavy, but until now Josh had never felt even slightly threatened by Jeff.

Now he could almost feel Jeff struggling to keep himself under control. "What did they do?" he whispered, making no effort to mask the terror he was feeling. "Where are we? What did they do to us?"

For another terrible moment Josh watched the conflict that was raging inside Jeff. Finally, slowly, Jeff's big body relaxed again.

"We're gonna die," he said. "Just like Kioki, man. We're just gonna die."

"Why?" Josh demanded. "What happened?"

Jeff shrugged. "I don't know. I don't know anything, and there's no one to ask."

As Jeff watched, Josh began prowling along the sides of the Plexiglas enclosure, examining every inch of it, touching every surface he could reach, searching for a way out. Again and again. Around and around. Like a rat in a maze, Josh kept moving, circling the perimeter of their prison.

For maybe an hour.

Maybe two.

Maybe more.

For a long time Josh had felt Jeff's eyes on him, watching his every move. At first he made sure he didn't turn his back on the other boy. But as the minutes dragged by and Jeff remained motionless on the floor, Josh focused more of his attention on the Plexiglas prison and less on Jeff Kina.

Finally, Jeff crept back onto his cot and fell asleep.

Yet Josh could still feel eyes watching him, and he'd moved his focus from the confines of the enclosure to the room outside.

He'd seen the cameras then.

Four of them, all pointing toward the box, watching every move he made, from every angle.

There was nowhere to hide, nowhere to escape from the all-seeing lenses.

After a while Josh, too, had fallen asleep, but suddenly come wide-awake, coiling his body tight in an instant, then springing away from the cot and whirling around, crouched low to the ground.

Jeff Kina was poised over his cot. "It's all right," he said. "I wasn't gonna hurt you, man."

From then on they'd been like two caged animals, warily watching each other, sleeping only fitfully, slinking around the perimeter of their prison when they weren't stretched on the floor or the cots, dozing.

Twice, a man clad in white entered the room, put food in the air lock of the seamless Plexiglas box, and left, without uttering a word.

Eventually, hunger overcame them, and they ate.

Then, a while ago—Josh had no way of knowing exactly how long it had been—someone tried to turn the knob on the door to the room beyond their Plexiglas prison.

This time, though, the door didn't open and the white-clad man with food didn't appear. Josh realized what the brief movement of the doorknob meant—someone who had no key was trying to get in.

"Help!" he shouted. "Help us!" But even as he yelled the plea, he had the feeling that whoever was outside the room couldn't hear him, that the Plexiglas and the walls of the room beyond composed a soundproof barrier. If they didn't want them to see outside, or to know where they were, or even what time it was, surely they wouldn't allow them to be heard, either.

Still, he'd tried again.

"Please!" he called out. "Please let us out!"

The knob had wiggled one more time, but that had been it.

Whoever was out there had gone away.

Since then, Josh had been slumped on the floor, staring at the door, waiting.

Something, he sensed, was about to happen, although nothing in the room had changed; the light was as glaring and shadowless as ever, the walls as featureless, the haze inside the box the grimy brown that he'd become so accustomed to that he barely noticed it anymore. He knew that Jeff Kina could sense the tension, too.

Like him, Jeff was on the floor, his back against one of the walls, his legs drawn up so his knees were pressed against his chest.

His eyes, like Josh's, were watching the door.

Time slowed; silence hung over the room.

Josh's eyes never wavered from the door.

When the knob moved—barely a fraction of an inch at first—Josh noticed it immediately. Shifting into a crouch, he felt the muscles in his body tense and the heat of adrenaline stream through his body.

The doorknob turned, the latch clicked, and the door swung open.

Two men came in, neither of them the white-clad attendant who brought them their food.

One of the men was a *haole*, the other Japanese—the same two men who had appeared outside the cage a few hours ago.

Both were dressed in suits, and though Josh had never seen the Japanese before, there was an aura of power about him that told him who the man was, now that his mind was clear enough to think.

Takeo Yoshihara.

Josh's eyes narrowed and his muscles tightened even more.

"Are they dangerous, Dr. Jameson?" he heard Yoshihara say. Even through the heavy panel of Plexiglas, he could hear no nervousness in the man's voice, only casual interest.

"It doesn't appear so," Stephen Jameson replied. "They both seem nervous and wary, but except for this morning, neither of them has shown any true signs of aggression. It's more as though some of their senses have been heightened."

"Interesting," Takeo Yoshihara mused. He circled the box, and Josh's eyes followed him, his body turning as he tracked the man's path. "Very interesting," Yoshihara remarked when he'd completed his circle. "I saw a tiger in a cage in India a year ago. He watched me with the same intensity." He smiled, but there was no warmth in it. "I suspect he wished to eat me." His eyes fixed on Josh. "I wish we had more time to do psychological studies," he went on. "But perhaps the researchers will be able to learn as much from the dissection. Instruct them to pay particularly close attention to the brain structures."

As the words penetrated his mind, Josh felt a shiver jolt through him. His whole body began to shake.

No! He must have heard wrong!

But then he caught sight of Jeff Kina, and knew he'd heard perfectly. A look of fury contorted Jeff's face, and his muscles had corded into tight knots. A howl of rage erupted out of Jeff Kina's throat, and he hurled himself at the Plexiglas with enough force to make the entire structure shake. Collapsing to the floor, his nose bleeding from the impact against the plastic wall, Jeff lay still for only a second before gathering himself and hurling himself again against the transparent barrier.

"No!" Josh yelled as a gout of blood erupted from Jeff's mouth. "Jeff, don't!"

Jeff, too caught up in his rage even to hear Josh, crashed to the floor once more, only to attack the wall a third time. His fingers, stiffening into claws, raked across the surface of the Plexiglas, but barely left a mark. An eerie screech of frustration bubbling from his throat, he kicked at the wall with his bare feet, his howl ascending to a shriek of pain as the agony of his smashed toes crashed through his rage.

"Stop it!" Josh yelled, throwing himself on Jeff, trying to pin him to the floor.

Jeff knocked him away as if he were no more than a yapping puppy, and returned to his attack on the Plexiglas wall.

Outside the plastic cell, Takeo Yoshihara and Stephen Jameson watched Jeff Kina's attack.

Yoshihara spoke. "Flush the enclosure."

Josh, the wind knocked out of him by Jeff's casual blow, lay on the floor, trying to catch his breath. And then, as Jeff kept smashing at the wall, leaving reddish-brown smears everywhere his bleeding hands struck the greasy surface of the plastic, the atmosphere inside the chamber began to change.

The brown haze cleared away.

And Josh Malani felt his chest begin to hurt.

He tried to struggle to his feet, but couldn't. Scrabbling across the floor, he instinctively stretched a hand out toward the two men who stood safely beyond the confines of the Plexiglas. "Help us," he pleaded. "Please? Just help us . . ."

Jeff Kina, writhing on the floor now, was clutching at his chest as he struggled to breathe the oxygen-rich air that was quickly replacing the noxious fumes with which the box had been filled only a moment ago. Josh crawled toward him, his hands closing on Jeff's wrists.

"They're killing us, Jeff," he whispered. "Oh, God, they're killing us."

Once more Jeff Kina tried to heave himself up, tried to launch one final attack, but already the strength was leaching from his body and darkness was closing in on him. "Mama . . ." he whispered. "Mama . . ." His voice trailed off, his body convulsed, then relaxed, and he lay still.

"Interesting that the bigger one died first," Josh Malani heard Takeo Yoshihara say. It was the last thing he heard before the darkness conquered him.

"I still don't understand why they brought him up here," Rob said as he steered the Explorer through the gates of Takeo Yoshihara's estate.

"She didn't tell me," Katharine said. She sat tensely in the passenger seat, arms wrapped tightly around herself, as if to contain the anxiety within. Her mind was reeling with images of Michael hidden away in one of the subterranean rooms below the south wing of the research building; Michael imprisoned like the poor puppy that died in her arms. "All Yolanda Umiki said was that I should come to Yoshihara's office."

Leaping from the car a moment after they pulled up, she ran across the gardens that separated the research pavilion from the collection of structures that made up Takeo Yoshihara's personal residence, as Rob followed—and stopped, realizing that she had never seen Takeo Yoshihara's office, and wasn't certain where it was. She looked about in confusion just as a servant materialized and bowed respectfully to them.

"Mr. Yoshihara is waiting in his office. This way, if you please."

A small bridge led to an Oriental-style building like a perfect teahouse,

floating in the center of a pond. Inside were the two rooms that Takeo Yoshihara used as an office on the estate. The smaller, rather cramped anteroom held Yolanda Umiki's desk, two ornately carved teak chairs, a tonsu,
and several filing cabinets. In Takeo Yoshihara's own office there was only a
simple table of highly polished wood that served as a desk—bare save for a
telephone—and a single chair. Several cushions were scattered on the floor.
Takeo Yoshihara himself stepped into the room through an open shoji that
led to a veranda that overlooked the mirrorlike surface of the pond and the
perfectly tended garden of bonsai conifers that lay beyond. Sliding the screen
closed, Yoshihara approached Katharine, his hand extended, his expression
grave.

Katharine was tempted not to take his hand at all, but thought better of it
at the last second.

Why warn him of her suspicions?

"Dr. Sundquist, I can't tell you how sorry I am about your son."

"Where is he?" Katharine demanded. "I want to see him."

"I shall take you to him myself in just a few moments."

"A few moments?" Katharine repeated, her voice rising. "Mr. Yoshihara,
you're talking about my son! My son! From what I already know, he collapsed
on the playing field at Bailey High. Why wasn't he taken to Maui Memorial
Hospital?"

Takeo Yoshihara tried to gesture her onto one of the cushions on the floor,
but when she remained standing, he did, too. "It was upon my orders that he
was brought here," he explained.

"Your orders?" Katharine shot back. "Who are you to be giving orders as to
what is to be done with my son? And how did you even know something had
happened to him? Have you been watching him?"

If she expected him to flinch at the accusation, she was disappointed; far
from being taken aback by the question, Takeo Yoshihara appeared to welcome it. "As a matter of fact, we have," he said. "Ever since Kioki Santoya
died, I have been concerned not only about Michael, but about his friends
Josh Malani and Jeff Kina, as well." He hesitated, then: "I'm not sure how
to tell you this, Dr. Sundquist, but the Malani boy died on the beach at
Spreckelsville yesterday afternoon."

The words stuck Katharine like a physical blow. Instinctively she reached out to Rob for support. As Rob took her arm, Takeo Yoshihara brought the chair around from behind his desk. "I can have Yolanda bring you something," he offered as Katharine sank onto the chair.

She shook her head but could say nothing. Josh? Dead? How could it have happened? And if Josh were dead . . . "How?" she asked, the bravado of a moment before gone from her voice, her hand slipping unconsciously into Rob's. "Dear God, *why?*"

"Dr. Jameson isn't yet certain where the problem began," Takeo Yoshihara said, leaning back against his desk. "But he was very interested in what happened to the Santoya boy, particularly the condition of his lungs. When he analyzed the lung tissue, it appeared that the boy's lungs had somehow become incapable of allowing oxygen to be absorbed into the blood. In fact, it was as if he had become allergic to it. When it was determined that your son was having respiratory problems but seemed not to be having difficulty in moving air in and out of his lungs, Dr. Jameson thought it imperative that Michael not be given oxygen."

Katharine's fingers clamped down hard on Rob's hand as she struggled against the terrible panic rising inside her. Rob tightened his arm around her, as if to protect her from whatever Takeo Yoshihara might say next. "But you still haven't told us exactly what's wrong with Michael," he said.

"In order to do that, I have to explain to you about some experiments that are going on here," Yoshihara replied. His gaze shifted to Katharine. "Dr. Silver has already signed a confidentiality agreement. It was part of his employment contract. I'm afraid I shall also have to ask you to sign one." He pressed a button on the telephone, summoning Yolanda Umiki, who appeared with a single sheet of paper in her hand.

Rob Silver's eyes narrowed. "Is this really necessary?" he asked. "Given the circumstances, I can't believe—"

"I'm afraid I shall have to insist." Taking a silver pen from the pocket inside his jacket, Yoshihara handed it to Katharine.

Without reading a single line of the document—not caring at all what it might say—Katharine scribbled her signature on it and handed it back to the woman.

As silently as she'd come in, the secretary left, quietly closing the door behind her.

When the three of them were alone, Takeo Yoshihara turned to Katharine. "As Dr. Silver may have told you, we are doing a great deal of environmental research here. What he hasn't told you, because until now he hasn't known, is that we have been working with a substance that appears to give oxygen-sustained, carbon-based life-forms—which comprise most of what we have on this planet—the ability to sustain themselves on gases other than oxygen. Gases that would ordinarily be poisonous to them."

"Are you saying you've developed a compound that would let people survive in badly polluted air?" Katharine asked, carefully keeping any clue that she had seen the subterranean labs out of her voice.

"We haven't developed it," Yoshihara explained. "We found it."

"Found it?" Rob echoed. "You mean you're mining it?"

Yoshihara shook his head. "One of my research teams—a group of divers—was working off the Big Island, along the Kalapana coast."

"Where the black sand beach used to be," Rob interjected. "But it's all under fresh lava now."

"Exactly," Yoshihara said. "At any rate, they found what appeared to be a geode near a lava vent, which they brought here. But instead of containing the typical crystals of most geodes, this one contains some kind of liquified gas. We began experimenting with the substance, and have discovered that when it is administered to oxygen-breathing animals, it has the effect of allowing them to thrive in an atmosphere containing what would normally be lethal doses of various gases and contaminants."

"I'm not sure I'm following you," Rob Silver said.

Takeo Yoshihara smiled. "I'm not surprised—I have only the most tenuous of grasps on it myself. But Dr. Jameson tells me our research animals seem able to function perfectly normally on an atmosphere that is heavily laden with such things as unburned hydrocarbons and oxides of nitrogen. Also ozone, sulfur dioxide, and hydrogen cyanide."

"Cyanide?" Rob said in disbelief.

The thinnest of smiles passed over Yoshihara's lips. "I can assure you, Dr. Silver, most of us breathe such things every day, but in amounts so slight as to be harmless. Except, of course, in areas of very heavy pollution. But this compound seems to make our lab animals immune to the effects of such pollution, even in the heaviest of concentrations."

"It sounds like a miracle," Rob said.

"Perhaps it is," Yoshihara agreed. "Except that there is a side effect. Our laboratory animals all have become allergic to oxygen. Once the compound has been administered, they are no longer able to breathe what we consider to be an unpolluted atmosphere."

The puppy, Katharine thought. She had killed the puppy by taking it out of the box. She felt a chill spread through her body as she anticipated Takeo Yoshihara's next words, and when they came, she heard them as an oddly distant echo of what her own mind had already told her. Yoshihara's features settled into an expression of utmost concern, though Katharine found that even as he mouthed the words of sorrow, his eyes seemed to betray no emotion.

"I'm so very sorry to have to tell you this, Katharine, but I'm afraid your son and his friends have become exposed to the compound inside the geode. We've no idea yet how such an accident could have occurred."

The dive! But nothing terrible had happened on the dive! Michael had said so. The only thing that went wrong was that some of them had run out of air, but even that hadn't been a problem.

"We think Michael and his friends must have come across another geode," she heard Takeo Yoshihara say.

A geode! But it wasn't a geode! She'd seen it herself, and it was a perfectly round sphere, the contents of which, she was absolutely certain, had been cooked up right here on Takeo Yoshihara's own estate!

"I want to see him," she said, her voice calm, though her mind was still reeling. "I want to see my son."

Katharine had to use every bit of her self-control not to scream when she saw Michael.

His room was on the subterranean level, and while it was neither a part of the complex that made up the Serinus Project nor a part of the laboratory she had discovered, it was, if possible, even more horrifying than what she'd seen before.

He was in a bed, but the bed was in a box.

The same kind of Plexiglas box she had seen in the Serinus labs, housing the animals which, though still alive, had seemed listless and ill.

The box was equipped with a pair of large ducts, as well as a variety of air-locked access ports that would allow food and drink to be passed inside without contaminating the internal atmosphere.

The atmosphere inside the cube was actually visible, swirling around Michael like smoke, filling the box with a brownish haze. The sight of it made Katharine feel like choking, though it was completely contained inside the plastic walls.

Michael, propped up against a pillow that rested on the raised head of a hospital bed, was awake. His face looked deathly pale to Katharine, but he managed a smile as she came into the room, followed by Rob Silver, Takeo Yoshihara, and Stephen Jameson.

"I guess I had a major attack of asthma this time," he said. His voice emerged from a speaker that was invisible to Katharine. It sounded both tinny and hollow, as if it were coming from a long distance away.

Don't cry! But even as she silently issued herself the order, Katharine felt her eyes welling with tears. She took a step toward him, wanting to put her arms around her son, to hold him, to tell him that everything was going to be all right.

The box stopped her.

Suddenly she felt helpless, unable to do anything for Michael or even to comfort him.

"Oh, Michael," she whispered. "What happened? You've been feeling so good. I thought . . ." She shook her head and bit her lip against the tears threatening to overwhelm her.

"I *was* feeling great," Michael said. "You saw me, Mom!"

"I sure *did!*" Katharine told him. "And you looked fine! I even stopped worrying about you." Once again she instinctively reached toward him, this time actually touching the hard plastic that separated her from her son. "Darling, what happened?"

Michael shrugged. "I—I'm not sure," he stammered. Haltingly, he told her that it had been getting harder and harder to breathe all day. "But then I found a bottle in the closet in the boy's room," he finished. "And as soon as I sniffed it, I felt great!"

Rick Pieper's broken message echoed in Katharine's ears.

Ammonia! He'd been breathing ammonia! Of course he was sick!

But no sooner had the thought occurred to her than she knew it was simply a straw she was grasping at to avoid facing the truth.

The ammonia hadn't made him sick. In fact, it had made him feel better. Her mind spun as more and more pieces of the puzzle clicked into place. Mark Reynolds—the boy from L.A.—hadn't been trying to kill himself; he'd been trying to *save* himself, and the medics who came to his rescue had unwittingly killed him by administering oxygen.

Oxygen!

For the first time since she'd entered the room, Katharine's eyes strayed from Michael's face as she took in her surroundings.

A computer monitor was mounted in the wall, its screen divided into a series of windows; some displayed a continuous graph of Michael's vital signs, while others monitored the makeup of the atmosphere within the box. Some she could identify: CO, SO_2.

Carbon monoxide.

Sulfur dioxide.

Most of them, long strings of atomic symbols designating complex chemical compounds, possibly hydrocarbons, she guessed, might as well have been written in Greek.

"Can I be alone with him for a few minutes?" she asked.

"Of course," Takeo Yoshihara agreed. "I have some business that must be attended to immediately. Dr. Silver can wait for you with Dr. Jameson."

When they were alone, Katharine moved as close to Michael as she could, placing her hands on the plastic as gently as if it were his skin she was touching. "I'm so sorry, darling," she whispered. "It's my fault. If I hadn't brought us here—"

"It's not your fault," Michael said. "It's just something that happened. It must have happened on—"

Katharine briefly held a finger to her lips, and as Michael fell silent, she pulled her pen and notebook out of her bag. The cameras might see— Katharine knew sharp lenses must be monitoring this room—but perhaps they would not *read*. It was a chance she had to take. There was no other choice. She began talking as she quickly scribbled on the pad. "They think you must have gotten exposed to something they found in a geode," she said out loud.

What happened on the night dive? she wrote. *I don't believe a geode was involved.* Opening the access lock, she put the notebook and pen inside. The air in the lock was instantly evacuated, and replaced with the toxic atmosphere inside the Plexiglas chamber.

"What kind of geode?" Michael asked, quickly reading the note, then scrawling a response. *There wasn't anything like a geode*, he wrote. *Four of the tanks ran out of air, and we started choking on something. Mine, Jeff's, Kioki's, and Josh's.* He passed the notebook and pen back through the air lock.

"I'm not sure Mr. Yoshihara even said," Katharine replied as she read what he'd written. Then she wrote: *Where did you get the tanks?*

"I don't remember ever seeing anything like a geode," Michael said. *Kihei Ken's*, he wrote. *Josh said it would be okay.*

After she'd read his last entry, Michael said, "Mom? Am I going to be all right?"

Katharine could contain her tears no longer, and even before she could speak, Michael read the truth in her expression.

"I'm going to die, aren't I?" he asked. His voice sounded very young.

Very young, and very frightened.

CHAPTER 29

There was nothing unusual about the car; it looked like any one of the hundreds of medium-sized, neutrally painted, minimally equipped sedans that make up the majority of the car rental fleets of Maui. Nor was there anything unusual about the two men in the car. Both of them were middle-aged, and both were dressed in the standard tourist uniform—polyester slacks and inexpensive aloha shirts like those sold out of the shops in Lahaina and in the malls along the Kihei strip.

Like tourists, they drove too slowly along South Kihei Road, as if unsure of their destination, or maybe just taking in the sights.

But the car was not a rental, and neither of the men were tourists. Both of them had lived on Maui for years, though neither had been born there.

And they knew exactly where they were going. Their destination was currently one block ahead of them, tucked back in a corner of one of the strip malls where it would be relatively hard to find unless you knew where you were going. Half the shops in the mall had already closed, and most of those that weren't were clustered around an ice cream shop near the southern end of a long row of storefronts.

Kihei Ken's Dive Shop was at the opposite end from the ice cream shop, and occupied all of a small freestanding building that appeared to have been set down on the mall's property almost as an afterthought. The two men parked their car in the middle of the parking lot and started slowly toward the dive shop, pausing to examine the merchandise in a few of the windows along the way.

Just as they'd been told, the CLOSED sign was hanging inside the glass door, but the lights were still on and they could see someone standing behind the counter, apparently filling out some kind of form. As one of the men held the door open, the other walked into the shop. "You Kihei Ken?" the first man asked.

"In person." The man abandoned the cash sheet he'd been working on and stepped out from behind the counter to extend his hand in welcome. "You must be the guys Mr. Yoshihara's office called about."

The second man had now come into the shop, and the door swung closed behind him. "Don't know anyone by that name."

The smile on Ken Richter's face faded to puzzlement as the first man ignored his proffered hand. "I'm sorry," he said, his eyes uncertainly scanning the parking lot in search of the men he'd been told to expect when the man from Takeo Yoshihara's office had called fifteen minutes ago. "Actually, I'm closed. I was just catching up on some paperwork while I waited for—"

"Us," the first man said.

Something in the tone of that single word rang an alarm deep in Ken Richter, setting off a jangling of nerves. "Look, I really am closed—" he began again. This time it wasn't a word that silenced him.

This time it was the gun that appeared in the hand of the second man. Only a moment ago, he'd been no more menacing than a curious tourist. Now there was nothing left of the tourist except the polyester aloha shirt. His eyes had a hard look that told Ken Richter he wouldn't hesitate to use the ugly black pistol that was held so easily in his right hand that it might have grown there.

"L-Look," Ken said, instinctively backing away, "if it's money you want, just take it, okay?"

While the man closest to Ken held the gun on him and said nothing, the other stepped into the back room to make certain it was empty, then locked the front door of the dive shop and snapped off the lights, leaving only the sickly blue glow of a neon sign that portrayed the outline of a diver in mask and fins.

The man with the gun spoke again. "In the back, please."

They're not going to kill me, Ken thought. If they were, they wouldn't be polite. Clinging to the thought, he edged nervously toward the back room. "Look, why don't you just empty out the cash register and leave? There's no cash in back—I haven't even got a safe. I won't call the cops. I—"

"Sit down, please." The man with the gun nodded toward a small step stool that served both as a place to perch while trying on fins and as a ladder to the higher storage shelves.

They're going to tie me up, Ken thought as he dropped onto the hard surface. They'll tie me up, and maybe clean the place out, but they won't hurt me.

The second man had now come into the back room. Ken watched as he circled the space.

Inspecting the shelves?

Looking for something?

"Don't watch him, please," the first man said. "Watch me."

Ken was confused. What did they want? If they were going to steal something, why didn't they just take it?

There was a moment of silence, interrupted twice by what sounded to Ken like the snapping of some kind of rubber.

Then came the distinctive click of metal on metal, as if an animal trap had just been set.

Though he kept his eyes on the man in front of him, as he'd been instructed, he sensed the second man directly behind him, and very close.

The hair on the back of Ken Richter's neck stood on end. Suddenly he understood.

But it was too late. Even as the flash of understanding came into Ken Richter's mind, the man behind him squeezed the trigger of the silenced pistol in his hand.

There was a soft—almost gentle—snicking sound as the hammer struck the cartridge and the carefully carved lead slug shot out of the muffled barrel.

Ken Richter felt nothing as the bullet drilled through his skull, then split open, tearing through his brain like the blade of a Cuisinart. He was already slumping to the floor when the bullet exploded out of his forehead, tearing half his face away.

Katharine didn't want to leave the estate—didn't want to leave Michael alone even for a minute. But she knew she couldn't tell Rob about the night dive until she was certain she wouldn't be overheard. The last thing she wanted was for Takeo Yoshihara to find out just how much she knew. Composing her face into a perfect mask of trust in the doctor and fear for her son, she told Stephen Jameson that she needed to go home and get some things for Michael; she would be back within an hour—no more than two. And would it be all right if she stayed with Michael through the night? He'd spent so much time in hospitals, and he hated them so much, and he was so frightened. . . . The improvised tale rolled off her tongue with the genuine sincerity of truth, since truth was exactly what most of it was. But as soon as she and Rob were away from the estate, she told him about the messages she and Michael had exchanged. Immediately, he used his cell phone to call Ken's Dive Shop.

"Something's not right," Rob said as he steered Katharine's Explorer into the parking space next to Ken Richter's aging Volvo. Though he shut off the engine, neither he nor Katharine got out of the car. Instead, both of them stared at the darkened dive shop. It looked as if it had closed hours ago.

"Maybe he went somewhere," Katharine suggested, still praying they would find Kihei Ken, and that he would have some reasonable explanation for what had happened to Michael on the dive. "Couldn't he be having dinner? Maybe he went to a movie?"

Rob shook his head. "The movies are down at Kukui Mall, so he would have taken his car. And the first time we called, he should have been here. I've known Ken Richter for years—we've dived together dozens of times—and he's the most reliably scheduled person I ever met. He closes the shop at seven every night, but he's always here until at least seven-thirty, closing up and getting ready for the morning. And if he has a dive scheduled, he's often here till nine or ten. I'm going to take a look."

They got out of the car and approached the building. Despite her suggestion that there could be a perfectly reasonable explanation for Ken Richter's failure to answer his phone, Katharine had the queasy feeling that something was not right. Both of them cupped their hands over their eyes to peer into the shop. The murky darkness within was broken only by a dim blue glow from a neon sign.

Nothing appeared to be amiss until they circled around to the side of the shop and Rob pointed to a counter clearly visible in the blue glow from the sign, on which a number of papers were strewn in disarray.

"Ken never leaves anything undone," Rob said. "That's what makes him a great diver. He hates for anything to be out of place." Moving to the back door and squatting down, he slid his fingers under a big metal drum that sat, slightly elevated from the ground, on four small wooden blocks.

"What are you looking for?" Katharine asked.

"Same thing Michael and his friends were looking for the night they went diving. The key." A second later he found it, hidden in the same magnetized metal box in which Josh Malani had discovered it a few days ago. Inserting the key into the lock on the back door, Rob twisted it, then pushed the door open. Reaching inside, he groped for the light switch, found it, and flipped it on.

For a second, half blinded by the sudden blaze of light, Rob didn't realize exactly what he was looking at. But as his eyes focused and he saw the red pool of blood that was spread around Ken Richter's head, his stomach churned. "Oh, Jesus," he whispered, his voice catching as his throat constricted.

"What?" Katharine asked from behind him. "What is . . ." The question died on her lips as she caught a glimpse of what lay on the floor. The vision of carnage froze them both for a moment that seemed to stretch into an eon. Katharine instinctively put her hand into Rob's. "It's him, isn't it? It's Ken Richter."

Rob tried to speak and couldn't. He made a move toward his friend.

Katharine's hand tightened on his and she held him back. "No," she said. "Don't touch him. Don't touch anything, Rob. Let's just call the police." As the seconds ticked by and Rob neither spoke nor moved, Katharine wondered if he'd heard her. Just as she was about to speak again, he found his voice.

"Go back to the car and call on the cell phone. Then come back here."

"Come back? We should wait for the police outside."

Rob shook his head. "Once the police get here, we won't be allowed to look at anything. They'll have the whole place taped off, and the first thing they'll want to know is why we're here."

"Can't we just tell them?"

Rob managed to pull his eyes away from the grisly scene on the floor of the dive shop's back room. Putting his hands on Katharine's shoulders, he looked directly into her eyes. "Tell them what, Kath?" he asked. "Tell them the truth? Do you really think we're going to walk away from here if we tell them we think Takeo Yoshihara had something to do with this? Believe me, they aren't going to be happy to hear us accuse one of the richest men on Maui of murder. We might as well accuse one of the Baldwins or the Alexanders, for God's sake! And the minute we make any kind of accusation, Yoshihara's going to hear about it. If he was willing to have Ken Richter killed to protect whatever he's up to, do you think he'll worry about you, or me, or Michael? Michael would be dead within the hour, and I'd be willing to bet you and I would have an accident—a fatal accident—before morning. All we can do is play dumb and find out everything we can. And we can't waste any time being questioned by the police. One slip and it'll all be over. Michael won't have a chance."

The warm Hawaiian evening seemed suddenly to have taken on a terrible chill. Katharine felt her whole body shiver as she realized the truth of what Rob had just said.

Returning to the car, she punched 911 into the keypad of Rob's cellular phone and pressed the Send key. As she made the hurried call, hesitating when the operator asked her name, then ending the connection, her whole body was shaking.

All she could think about was Michael—getting back to the estate, getting Michael, and getting him out of there.

But she knew there was no way that Takeo Yoshihara's security force was simply going to let her pick Michael up and drive him away. Even if they did let her take him, what good would it do? He'd die as soon as she took him out into the clean, fresh air.

For a moment she almost gave in to the sense of utter helplessness that washed over her, but then the thought of Michael in his Plexiglas prison coalesced her frustration and fear into a cold fury.

Michael wasn't dead yet. So far, Takeo Yoshihara had no idea how much she really knew.

And the night wasn't over yet, either.

Her body stopped shaking and the terrible cold loosed its grip. Still clutching the phone, she went back to the dive shop. This time, at the sight of Ken Richter's body, the horror she felt was tempered by something else.

Rage.

"What have you found?" she asked Rob.

"Not much," he admitted. While she'd been gone, he looked around the back room of the shop, but had neither touched anything nor gone into the front of the store. "There's not much back here except the rental scuba equipment."

"What's that?" Katharine asked, pointing to a large white board on the wall, marked off into a grid filled with names.

"The dive schedule," Rob said, looking carefully at it for the first time. "He always kept it—" His eyes widened and he moved toward the board, reaching out to it, pulling his fingers back just before he touched it. "Oh, Jesus! That's it! Look!"

Katharine moved next to him. "Look at what?"

"It's the board!" Rob said again. He was pointing to a section of the grid. "Look!" he repeated. "He had a VIP dive, the morning after Michael and his friends went on their night dive."

Katharine frowned. "VIP? What's that? Movie stars?"

Rob shook his head. "It was his special code. Every now and then Takeo Yoshihara's office would call and set up dives for the kids of some of his business associates."

"I still don't see—"

"It wasn't just that Yoshihara set up the dives," Rob went on. "He sent over special equipment, too. Fins, masks, regulators, the whole works."

"Including air tanks," Katharine whispered, suddenly understanding.

Rob nodded. "If the boys took the tanks that were already here for the next morning's dive—" Rob began, but Katharine was ahead of him.

Her notebook was out and she was already copying down the names of the five boys who had been scheduled for the dive that Ken Richter had designated as VIP.

Four of those boys, thanks to Michael and his friends, had undoubtedly escaped the fate Takeo Yoshihara had planned for them.

The fifth one might already be dead.

She had just slipped the notebook back into her purse when the first police siren wailed in the night.

CHAPTER 30

"What if he can't do it?" Katharine asked. They were driving up Lipoa Street toward the Computer Center. In the fifteen minutes since they'd left the dive shop, Rob Silver had made two phone calls. Nick Grieco hadn't answered, but Al Kalama had. On a terrible hunch, Rob had decided to swing by Nick's apartment building. The presence of three police cars confirmed that his hunch had hit a bull's-eye.

"I don't think we have any choice," Rob said, his voice grim. "You can't leave Michael alone up at Yoshihara's any longer, and there's no way Phil Howell and I can find what we're looking for by ourselves. We've got to have an expert."

"But you said he's a dive guide—" Katharine began.

"He's also a computer freak. When he's not diving, he's messing around on the Net. If he can't find the information we need, then it's just not there. I don't know why I didn't think of him an hour ago."

"If he's such a genius, then why doesn't he have a job?"

Rob glanced over at her, one eyebrow lifted. "Come on, Kath—this is Maui. Haven't you noticed how many jobs only exist to pay for the rent and the sports equipment? Besides, Al had a little problem a few years ago. Something to do with hacking into a government computer where he wasn't supposed to be. The way he tells it, the only reason he didn't go to jail was because no one was willing to acknowledge that what he'd done was possible. It's hard to convict someone of a crime if you won't admit it was committed."

The light at the Piilani Highway changed. As Rob pressed on the accelerator, a horn blasted behind them, and an ancient Honda Civic, its caved-in passenger door tied shut with a frayed rope, and a surfboard strapped to its top, shot past them. "Hey, man! Quit blockin' the road with that beater, huh?" A hand appeared from the driver's window, thumb and pinkie waggling.

Katharine's heart sank. "That's Al Kalama, isn't it?" she asked.

"Believe me, he knows what he's doing," Rob insisted, but a quick glance at Katharine told him she didn't believe him. A few seconds later Rob pulled the Explorer up next to the Honda.

Al Kalama, wearing nothing but a Speedo, a pair of sandals, and a grin, was already leaning against the door of his car. "So what's the rush, man? The way you were talkin', it sounded like someone was dyin' or something."

Rob Silver's eyes fixed on the beach bum. "Ken Richter's already dead, and I think Nick Grieco is, too."

The grin wiped from his face, Kalama listened to what they had found, first at the dive shop, then at Nick Grieco's condo complex. When Rob finished, he uttered a low whistle. "Jesus! What the hell's goin' on?"

"That's why we need you," Rob said. He handed Kalama the list of names Katharine had copied from the board in the back room of the dive shop. "We need to find out where these five people are, or at least if they're still alive."

Al Kalama paled as he read the names. "I was on a dive with these guys a few days ago."

Rob glanced at Katharine. "Are you sure?"

"Sure I'm sure! I remember the kids 'cause most of them were assholes. Plus, one of them had some trouble with his air tank, which was really weird, 'cause it was brand-new equipment that guy Takeo Yoshihara sent down."

The words struck Katharine like nails being pounded into a coffin.

Michael's coffin.

Until that moment she had been clinging to the hope, no matter how slim, that Michael's illness was an accident, as Takeo Yoshihara had insisted.

Now there was no more room to deny the truth. "The one who had trouble," she said, her voice trembling, "is there any way you can find out if he's still alive? Is he still on the island?"

Kalama shrugged. "Should be a piece of cake. All the kids on that dive were leaving that afternoon or the next morning. The guy who had the problem was from Chicago, and it seems like if he died, there ought to be some mention in the local papers."

"Do it," she said. "Please do it." She turned to Rob. "I have to get back up there. I have to get Michael out." She moved to get behind the wheel of the Explorer, but Rob stopped her.

"Katharine, are you crazy? How are you going to get him out?" he asked. "And even if you can, where are you going to take him? He can't breathe outside that box, remember?"

Katharine brushed the questions aside. "I don't know," she said. "I'll find a way. But I have to get back to him! My God, Rob, don't you see? Takeo Yoshihara doesn't want him alive! He just wants to find out how Michael and his friends got into that stuff, and when he does, he'll kill him!" Even as she spoke the words, new questions—questions Rob hadn't yet thought of—came into her mind.

What if they wouldn't let her back into the estate?

What if Michael were already—

She cut the last question off, unwilling even to let the thought come into her head. "Find out everything you can," she begged Rob. "Find out what's in the files. Find out what they're really doing!" Putting her arms around him, she pressed close to him for a moment, then broke the embrace and got into the Explorer. She was just about to pull out of the parking slot when Rob produced his cellular phone from his pocket and shoved it through the open window.

"Take this," he said. "I have a feeling we're going to need to talk."

"But if I have your phone—" Katharine began.

Rob cut her off. "I'll find another one. Phil Howell has one—his car's still here, so I'll bet he is, too. I'll call you with the number as soon as I get it."

As Katharine's car sped back down toward the Piilani Highway, Rob and Al Kalama hurried into the computer center.

In less than a minute Al was seated in front of the terminal next to the one at which Phil Howell was still working. Barely acknowledging the introduction Rob made, Kalama's fingers were tapping at the keyboard even before the monitor had fully warmed up.

While Kalama navigated through the Internet, Rob turned to Phil Howell. "I need to borrow your cell phone, Phil," he said. When he got no response, he glanced at the monitor in front of the astronomer, where the results of the substitution program he'd been running had finally come up. The screen was now displaying a new window, and inside the box was a list of the twenty-four files the computer had generated, each of them containing the results of one of the twenty-four possible substitution equations that could be applied to the original sequence of four letters.

Next to each file was the probability that the letter sequence could represent DNA code.

The fourth one from the bottom was highlighted, and read: ninety-seven percent.

Rob frowned, then felt his pulse begin to quicken. "Does that mean what I think it does?" he asked Howell.

The astronomer nodded. He had broken out in a cold sweat a few moments ago when the window opened and he'd seen the fourth line from the bottom of the report. He spoke, his voice quavering with excitement: "I think so. At least the computer thinks so." He slowly shook his head, as if still unable to accept what he was seeing. "My God," he breathed. "What if it's really true?"

"What if what's true?" Al Kalama asked from the next terminal, but Phil Howell had already returned to his work, so engrossed that he didn't even hear the question. Then, before Al could repeat it, a window on his own terminal filled with a brief paragraph—an obituary from the *Chicago Tribune* noting the death of Kevin O'Connor, a sixteen-year-old boy, from an unnamed "respiratory problem."

"You want to tell me what's going on?" he asked Rob.

Rob Silver, who had been staring at Phil Howell's screen in fascination, turned back to Al. "Takeo Yoshihara is experimenting on people," he said without preamble. "Katharine's son is one of the ones he's experimenting on."

Al Kalama uttered a low whistle, but he made no argument, asked no questions. Instead, he simply said: "So how do we nail the prick?"

"There's a directory on the computer up at his estate," Rob told him. "Those are the files Katharine was talking about just before she left. We think those files hold all the information on the project."

"What about the kid?" Al Kalama asked. "What are we going to do about him?"

To that question Rob had no answer.

Knowing there was no chance of regaining Phil Howell's attention for something as trivial as a cellular telephone, Rob began searching for it himself, and when he found it—in the right front pocket of Howell's shirt—the astronomer didn't even notice as he fished it out.

"Kath?" Rob said a moment later after he'd dialed his own number. "It looks like you're right. Be careful." Giving her the number of the phone he'd just appropriated, he hung up.

And still had no idea of what to do about Michael Sundquist.

Katharine was being followed.

She knew it, as surely as she knew her own name.

The car's lights had switched on as she'd made a left turn in Puunene. She watched in the rearview mirror as it pulled up behind her, following closely when she took the quick right onto Hansen Road, the shortcut to the Hana Highway.

How had he known she'd be coming this way?

Was the car bugged?

Of course it was—the same device that automatically opened the gate no doubt sent out a signal that Takeo Yoshihara's men could home in on.

Twice she considered turning off Hansen Road to take one of the narrow cuts through the cane fields that would lead her up toward Kula, but both times she lost her nerve as she slowed the Explorer to a near stop to peer up the long stretches of deserted road that quickly disappeared into the blackness of the night.

A blackness that seemed far darker than usual.

If she took one of these roads and got lost, she could poke around in Kula or Pukalani for an hour and never find the road to Makawao. Worse, if the car that was following her overtook her, and forced her off the road—

She cut off the thought, telling herself her sense of being followed was brought on by paranoia, but, unbidden and unwanted, an image of Ken Richter's body sprawled in a pool of fresh blood rose up in front of her, and the terror that had been escalating inside her all day notched up yet again. If they hadn't hesitated to gun down Ken Richter, why would they hesitate to kill her, too?

When the car behind her blasted its horn and ducked around her to speed away into the night, Katharine's body jerked so convulsively that she wrenched her shoulder against the restraining seat belt.

That's it! she scolded herself. *If you don't calm down, you don't have a hope of saving Michael.*

Bringing the Explorer back up to speed, she held it steady until she came to the intersection with the Hana Highway, then turned a few hundred yards farther on, where the road ascended the slope of Haleakala. She remained steadfastly calm until she neared the Haliimaile cutoff that wound through the cane fields to the left and would eventually take her to Baldwin Road, just a mile or so below Makawao.

Almost involuntarily, her eyes went to the pair of headlights glowing in the polarized glass of the rearview mirror.

Biting down hard on her lower lip, Katharine moved into the left turn lane.

The car behind followed.

She let the car continue to slow until she was almost into the intersection, then pressed the accelerator hard and swerved back to the right, shooting into a break in the uphill traffic that was small enough to make the driver of the car she'd cut off blast furiously on his horn. Ignoring the sound, Katharine glanced in the side mirror.

The other car was just completing its left turn, its taillights disappearing down the road toward Haliimaile as she watched.

Feeling both relieved and a little bit foolish, she managed to keep the paranoia firmly in check until she came to the turnoff from Olinda Road into the dark, narrow lane that led to her house.

As if acting under its own volition, her right foot left the gas pedal and moved to the brake. The Explorer rolled to a stop, its headlights aimed down the drive, washing the shadows away as far as the first curve in the road that wound through the eucalyptus trees.

The road appeared to be deserted.

Too deserted?

Images flashed through her mind of a dark figure lurking in the shadows within the forest, peering through the windows as she quickly packed a bag so that the watcher would believe she was planning to spend at least this night at Takeo Yoshihara's estate.

When would they come for her?

Would they use the cover of darkness to close in on the house, while she was helplessly blinded by the false security of the electric lights?

Or would they wait until she was at the estate itself?

No! No, no, NO!

No one had followed her; no one was waiting for her!

Then, just as she was about to move her foot back to the gas pedal, the cellular phone rang, startling her so badly she yelped out loud. Fumbling in her purse, she found the instrument, flipped it open, and held it to her ear. "Rob?"

"It's me," his familiar voice confirmed. "Two things. First, Al can't get into the Serinus directory from any computer outside the estate. But he says there's a work-around. Once you get there, get to any computer terminal— try the one in my office—and connect to this number. Got a pen?" Katharine rummaged in her purse, then told him to go ahead. Rob gave her a telephone number, then repeated it. "Once you hook up to him from my office, he should be able to use my terminal as a slave, and Yoshihara's central server won't realize he's coming in from the outside."

"What's the other thing?"

"Michael," Rob said. "We need a place to take him."

"We have to get him out first."

"We think we can do that. But the big question is, where are we going to take him?"

It was the question Katharine had been avoiding all the way home. Now she could put it off no longer. If Michael truly could no longer breathe fresh air, then where could they possibly go? Anywhere they took him, anywhere at all—

And then it came to her: the skull.

The skull from the Philippines—and the reason it was of such interest to the Serinus Project. The mutant boy—and Katharine was now convinced the murdered child had been a mutant—had been living on Mount Pinatubo, breathing the fumes spewing from the volcano. "The Big Island," she said. "If we can get him to where the eruption is going on, he might be able to breathe!"

There was a silence, then Rob spoke again. "It might be possible. But he's going to have to be able to breathe long enough for you to get him out of the building, plus maybe ten to fifteen minutes. Can he do that?"

Katharine didn't hesitate. "I'll make sure he can."

"How long before you get back to the estate?"

Katharine glanced at her watch. It was just past nine-thirty. "I'm just getting home," she said, calculating the time it would take to grab a few things, then drive to the estate. "I guess I should be there by ten. That's if they let me get in at all."

"Don't talk that way," Rob told her. "Don't even think that way. Just get what you need and go. If we're lucky, we'll have what we need within a few minutes after you get online with Al. How much time will you need to figure out a way to get him out of the building?"

"How much can I have?" Katharine countered.

"I wish I knew."

"All right. I'll let you know when I get there. Will I be able to talk to Al on the computer?"

"Absolutely." He paused. "It'll be just like passing messages in school."

In the darkness Katharine smiled bleakly. "Why don't I quite believe that?"

"Well, I thought I'd give it a shot, anyway." There was a short silence, then Rob spoke again, his voice suddenly shy. "Katharine? Be careful, okay?"

It wasn't just the words, but the way he said them. A tiny bit of Katharine's tension eased, and she finally started the car slowly down the long driveway. "You have no idea how careful I intend to be," she said softly. "And you also have no idea how much courage it will give me if you just keep talking while I drive down this road. Remind me never to take another house that's at the end of a long, narrow, dark road."

"What do you want me to talk about?"

"I don't care. Tell me I don't have to be scared, and that there's nobody waiting in my house, and that Michael's going to be all right, and that when all this is over you're going to marry me and take me away from all this like a good knight in shining armor."

"All right," Rob said.

"I beg your pardon?"

"I said all right. To all of it. You proposed. I accept. Consider it a done deal. Listen to me carefully, Kath. There is no one in your house. You're going to get what you need, and you're going to go up to the estate, and we're going to crack into the computer and find out all of Takeo Yoshihara's dirty little secrets. Then I'm coming to get you and your kid, who is going to have to learn to like me, and we're going to live happily ever after."

Katharine was silent for a moment, then: "Promise?"

"Promise."

The car emerged from the woods into the clearing. Katharine carefully swept the darkness with her eyes. There were no other cars in the clearing.

"I'm gonna hold you to that," she said. "Call me again in half an hour. If I don't answer, then you lied to me and there was someone in the house."

"I wouldn't lie to you. I love you. I always did."

"Hell of a time to tell me." Katharine sighed. "Still, it does make me feel better. Talk to you in a while."

Breaking the connection, she sat in the car for a few more seconds, summoning the nerve to go into the house. Switching on the lights as she entered, she glanced around, half expecting it to look like a scene from a movie after the Mafia had paid someone a visit.

It was exactly as she'd left it.

Nothing had been moved.

Nothing had even been touched.

Katharine quickly threw enough clothes into a small suitcase to make it look as if she was prepared to stay at the estate for several days. Then, thinking about what she had to do in the hours to come, she added a few more items to the suitcase.

In less than five minutes she was back in her car, driving steadily toward whatever awaited her at Takeo Yoshihara's estate.

CHAPTER
31

The cellular phone buzzed. "I'm almost at the gate," Katharine said before Rob had even spoken.

"Is it opening?"

"I'm not worried about getting back in," Katharine told him. "I have a feeling it's getting back out again that's going to be the neat trick. And I have no idea how I'm going to be able to communicate with Michael." The murder of Kihei Ken proved to Katharine that the camera's eye had seen the notes she and Michael had passed. No doubt they could hear every word she might say, as well.

"You'll find a way," Rob assured her, and she prayed he was right.

Ahead of her, the gate was swinging open, just as it always did when her car approached.

Katharine took a deep breath as the car passed through, then said, "I'm going through the gate, Rob. I'll call you again if I can, but don't be surprised at anything I might say. And I might not say anything at all."

"I'll do my best to decode."

Shutting off the cellular phone, she caught herself watching in the rearview mirror as the gate swung closed behind her.

Like the gate of a prison?

Though the parking area next to the research pavilion was far emptier than it ever was during the day, it still held more cars than Katharine would have expected. For a moment she felt the courage she had carefully nurtured during the last half hour begin to crumble.

Not until Michael and I are out of here, she told herself. *After you get him out, you can turn into a whimpering idiot, and it won't matter. But not now!*

Pulling the Explorer into an empty space, she took the suitcase out of the backseat, locked the car, and went into the lobby of the research pavilion. Perhaps, if she was lucky, the guard on duty would be the one whose friendship she had enlisted—dear God, could it really have only been this morning?

As the lobby door swung closed behind her, the guard at the desk looked up. She was looking into the face of a stranger. Then, as he rose to his feet and spoke, she realized that she was not a stranger to him.

"Dr. Sundquist. They said you'd be coming back tonight."

They. Who were *they?* The security staff?

Stephen Jameson?

Takeo Yoshihara himself?

"My son," she said, for the first time hoping she looked every bit as worried as she was. If she was going to get Michael out, she would have to appear to be so upset as not even to be thinking straight. "He—he's . . ." She pretended to flounder, letting the words trail off as if she weren't certain how much she should say in front of the guard.

"It's all right, Dr. Sundquist," the guard assured her. "They told me what happened to your boy. I'll just let you into the elevator, and you can go right down."

The elevator! She'd completely forgotten about the elevator.

But it was all right—she still had Stephen Jameson's card.

Unless Jameson had noticed that it was gone? Would he have reported it already? Would the gray plastic square still activate the elevator, or would they have removed its code from the computer? *Don't worry about it now,* she told herself. *And don't even think about trying it first. If they see that on the security cameras, it will be over before you can even start.*

The computer! She had to get to Rob's computer, even if only for a minute or two. She offered the guard a distracted smile and set down her small suitcase. "Could I leave this here a minute? I need to go to Dr. Silver's office for a second."

"No problem," the guard replied, dropping back onto his chair.

Was he going to watch her on the monitor? Should she offer him some excuse? No! Why should she be explaining her movements to him? It would only make him wonder why she'd felt the need to explain herself.

Leaving the suitcase next to the guard's desk, she strode down the north corridor to Rob's office, turned on the lights, and switched on the monitor attached to his terminal. Finding the communications program, she quickly entered the number Rob had given her and touched the Enter key. The connection was completed almost instantly, and she heard a brief exchange of static as the computer on her desk established a link with the one in Kihei. A window containing two lines of text opened. A cursor flashed at the end of the second line. As she watched, the last digit of the first line changed as each second ticked by:

> **Pick-up 04:00:00   Current time is: 22:16:53.**
> **Enter to Confirm.**

Understanding the message immediately, Katharine glanced at her watch. It was almost exactly two and a half minutes ahead of the time displayed on the screen. Adjusting her watch to synchronize to the time on the screen, she hit the Enter key again. A new window opened and letters appeared as Al Kalama began his first efforts to open the Serinus directory. Before he'd finished typing the first line of his instructions, Katharine used the mouse on her desk to minimize the program so that all that showed on the monitor was the normal desktop screen.

Shutting off the monitor, she turned off the lights in the office and started back down the corridor.

"All set?" the guard asked as she reentered the lobby.

Katharine nodded and picked up her suitcase, glancing at her watch one last time as she followed the guard through the doors that led to the south corridor and the elevator at its far end.

"Nothing worse than having your kid get sick, is there?" the guard asked as he passed his card over the gray panel next to the elevator door. Katharine shook her head but made no reply. After what seemed to her to be an eternity, the elevator car arrived and she stepped inside.

To her relief, the guard remained where he was, nodding his head a fraction of an inch, then turning away as the doors slid closed.

Glancing at her watch, she saw that "eternity" had amounted to fifty-two seconds.

Katharine counted the seconds it took for the car to descend to the lower level.

Fifteen, including the time it took for the doors to open.

Leaving the car, she moved down the corridor to the door behind which Michael lay.

An anteroom guarded the chamber in which Michael had been put. Behind a desk, empty of anything except a telephone, a woman sat. A nurse, or a guard? Though she wore a white uniform, her posture and her steely gaze told Katharine that here was no angel of mercy. This woman would not simply sit still as she and Michael walked out of the room.

If Michael could walk.

"You can go right in, Dr. Sundquist," the woman said. "Dr. Jameson is with your son."

She went through the door into Michael's room, and felt a terrible fury begin to rise in her as she looked at her son.

The atmosphere inside the box was now so foul that a brown film was building up on the inside of the Plexiglas. In places, it had grown so thick that it was actually running down the surface of the plastic, leaving behind long, slimy-looking trails.

And Stephen Jameson actually had the nerve to smile at her as he looked up from the computer terminal at which he sat. "He's doing very well," he said. "You have quite the boy here."

As if Michael had just won some kind of race! Katharine thought, her anger threatening to overwhelm her.

For the first time, then, she knew with absolute conviction that she would get her son out of the vile box in which he lay. Somehow. Even if it meant killing Stephen Jameson and the female guard. And anyone else who tried to stand in her way. Indeed, right this instant, she would take a distinct pleasure in ending the life of this man who regarded her son as nothing more than a lab specimen. "He's always had a lot of courage," she said, revealing nothing of her thoughts. "May I talk to him?"

"Certainly."

She glanced around the room as she moved closer to the Plexiglas box, searching for the camera she knew was hidden there. As before, she saw nothing.

"Hello, darling," she said softly. "Are you all right?"

Inside the box, Michael nodded. "I think so." Then: "Am I ever going to be able to breathe regular air again?"

The question wrenched at Katharine's heart. *Tonight!* she wanted to scream. *I'm going to get you out of here, and I'm going to take you to a place where you can breathe until we can fix what they did to you!* But she could say none of it.

Then, as her silence stretched, she noticed that Michael's head was moving. He seemed to be nodding toward his own lap.

Looking down, she saw the forefinger of his right hand moving. For just a moment she didn't understand what he was doing.

Then it came back to her.

He was forming letters with his fingers, tracing them on the sheet so casually that no one who wasn't looking for it would have realized what he was doing. "Of course you'll be able to," she said. "And Dr. Jameson says you're doing very well."

GET ME OUT, his fingers spelled.

Glancing quickly to be certain that Jameson was still concentrating on the computer screen, she nodded once. "Tonight," she said, raising her right hand to her stomach, its four fingers extended while the thumb remained folded under the palm. Her eyes fixed on Michael, willing him to understand that she was responding to the plea he'd traced on the sheet. She spoke again, almost immediately repeating the word. "Tonight, I'll stay right here with you. Okay?"

She was almost certain she saw his eyes flick to the four fingers she'd displayed at the instant she uttered the word "Tonight." Would he understand that she was giving him the time of escape—four A.M.?

His wink confirmed that he did.

*   *   *

"Got it!"

For several seconds Al Kalama's shout didn't register on Rob. Over the last three hours, as Al had worked patiently at the terminal next to the one at which Phil Howell labored, Rob had become increasingly fascinated with the innumerable lists of files that scrolled on the terminal in front of the astronomer's monitor. Hour after hour it had gone on as the supercomputer in the room a few yards away reached out into every other computer it could find, hunting for files containing DNA sequences, and whenever it found one, comparing its contents not only to the single file that the supercomputer had calculated bore a ninety-seven percent probability of listing the DNA sequence of an unknown organism, but to the other twenty-three files it had generated as well.

By the time Al Kalama spoke, thousands of files had been put through the process, and each of them had been added to the ever-lengthening list of digitally stored DNA sequences—the genetic codes for the tiniest single-celled organisms, for thousands of species of algae, mosses, ferns, bushes, and trees, as well as for additional thousands of worms, insects, spiders, reptiles, amphibians, fish, and every species of warm-blooded creature known to man.

The astonishing result was that there were sequences—some short, some long—in every single file that perfectly duplicated one or another sequence that could be found in the file the computer had generated from the signal from the far reaches of space. A signal, Howell had told Rob, that had come from something called the Whirlpool Galaxy. In every case, the computer dutifully reported the exact percentage of match it had found. Though there was no complete match—not even anything the computer considered significantly close—more and more segments of the sequence from the galaxy fifteen million light-years away were matching to one or another segment of the DNA of some organism on Earth.

Cumulatively, Howell was already nearly certain, the proof would be irrefutable: not only was life not unique to Earth, but its basic building blocks, the four nitrogenous bases found here, were found on other planets as well.

Not only was life universal, but its forms, when they were finally found, would be familiar. . . .

Rob's thoughts were shattered by a hand roughly shaking his shoulder. "Rob," Al Kalama was saying, "what do you want me to do now that I've cracked it?"

Rob whirled around, fixing his attention on the screen Kalama had been slaving over for the last few hours. The Serinus directory was open at last, displaying several more subdirectories. Under each subdirectory were dozens—in some cases hundreds—of files.

"Can you search them?" he asked, his eyes scanning a small portion of the long list of cryptically named files that filled the screen.

"No problem," Al replied. "What are we looking for?"

"Names," Rob replied. "Michael Sundquist, Josh Malani, and Kioki Santoya, for starters. Also, look for a kid named Mark Reynolds, and another named . . ." He hesitated, searching his memory for the name of the boy from New Jersey, then found it. "Shelby. Shane Shelby. Start with those."

Al Kalama's fingers flew over the keyboard as he activated a search program, typed in the names Rob had just given him, and pressed the Enter key. A list of fifteen files appeared, five in each of three subdirectories of the main Serinus directory.

As Rob was studying the list, trying to decide which of the files to look at first, a soft chime sounded from the terminal in the next carrel, and he heard Phil Howell utter a single quiet phrase in a tone barely above an awed whisper: "Oh, Jesus."

For a moment Rob wasn't certain what the chime meant, but then it came back to him.

Phil Howell had set an alarm.

An alarm that would go off if the supercomputer found a match for the file it was comparing to hundreds of thousands of others.

Not a partial match.

Not even a ninety-nine percent match.

Only a perfect match.

But it was impossible! They knew what the sequence was, and knew that there was no possibility of a perfect match—at least not on this planet! Yet the alarm had gone off.

His pulse quickening, Rob moved over to gaze at the screen in front of Phil Howell.

A single line was highlighted. The moment he looked at it, Rob felt a sensation of déjà vu, as though he'd seen this display, this file name, in precisely this configuration, before. It took him an instant to realize it was not the name of the file that was familiar.

It was the name of the directory it was in.

The Serinus directory.

"Al," he said softly, "take a look at this."

Al Kalama, still in his chair, slid over and peered at the screen on which Rob Silver's eyes remained fixed. "Jesus," he whispered, unconsciously echoing Howell's exclamation as he read the full address of the file that was highlighted on the screen. "What the hell is going on?"

Half an hour later, all three of them knew.

Takeo Yoshihara had not been lying after all when he said his people had found something resembling a geode containing an organic substance. But Rob knew now that neither Yoshihara nor the team of scientists he had put together to analyze and find a use for the substance—the group he had called the Serinus Society—could have had any idea where the substance within the sphere had come from.

Though it had emerged from deep within the crust of the Earth, spewed up by violent volcanic activity far beneath the ocean floor, its source was a mystery only the conjunction of Phil Howell's accidental discovery could unravel.

And suddenly Rob understood: the object at the heart of the Serinus Project wasn't a geode at all.

It was a seed.

A seed that had arrived sometime so far in the past as to be almost beyond comprehension, from a planet so far away as to be entirely invisible. Indeed, a planet that had ceased to exist fifteen million years ago.

A seed that was undoubtedly one of many—thousands, perhaps even millions—that had been sent out into the universe like spores riding on the wind. Most of them would have floated endlessly in space, moving through the freezing void for millennia upon millennia.

Some would have fallen into stars, to be instantly burned.

But a few—the most minuscule of fractions—would have fallen onto planets, burying themselves far below the surface. And there they would have lain, dormant, waiting. Every now and then one would have risen to the surface, carried by rising tides of magma, and broken open.

If conditions were wrong—if the chemical makeup of the atmosphere was improperly balanced—the life within the seed would die.

But sometime, somewhere, one of the seeds would open, and find an atmosphere that nurtured its contents, and the life contained within would begin to reproduce.

A new planet would be seeded, and evolution would begin.

And the life of the dead planet—the planet that had long ago been destroyed by the explosion of the star around which it orbited—would go on.

"How many planets?" Rob finally mused, barely realizing he was speaking out loud. "How many planets do you suppose received them?"

For a moment Phil Howell was silent. When he finally spoke, the awe in his whispered voice told Rob that he, too, had realized the truth. "Not them," he said. "Us. We're what evolved from the first of those seeds." His eyes fixed on Rob. "It wasn't some kind of aliens that sent out that signal, Rob. It was us."

Midnight.

Four more hours.

How was she going to make it?

I *will* make it, she told herself. I won't let Michael die. Not here, not anywhere!

Inside the Plexiglas box, Michael seemed to be asleep, though Katharine suspected he wasn't. Stephen Jameson was gazing down at her son with no more concern than if Michael had been suffering a minor case of the flu. "I think our patient is doing quite well, all things considered," he said in the professionally comforting tones Katharine thought he must have learned in medical school.

Patient? How could he call Michael a *patient? Victim* was more like it! She felt like smashing her fist into his face, like locking him into the box in which Michael was trapped, and letting him breathe the deadly atmosphere that was suddenly the only thing that could keep her son alive.

Why wouldn't he go home? What if he was planning to stay up with Michael all night? What would she do?

Though she managed to keep her own mask in place—a mask she'd carefully composed of equal parts concern for Michael and appreciation of the doctor's efforts—her mind was racing. But then she heard the words she'd been waiting for.

"I think maybe I'll see if I can catch some shut-eye," Jameson told her, scanning the monitors that were keeping track of Michael's vital signs one more time. "Everything seems to have stabilized. If there's a problem, LuAnne knows how to reach me."

LuAnne, Katharine repeated silently to herself. One look at her hard gray eyes had told Katharine that, despite the nurse's uniform, the primary job of the woman who sat in the anteroom outside—perhaps her only job—was security. Carefully concealing her true feelings, Katharine tried to inject exactly the right mixture of worry and confidence into her voice. "Do you really think he's going to be all right?"

"He'll be fine," Jameson assured her.

As if I'm a child! Katharine managed a sigh she hoped sounded like relief. "Well, I hope you get enough sleep for both of us," she said. "I just don't think I'll be able to sleep a wink tonight." Oh, God. Had she overplayed it? Jameson, though, seemed willing to accept her at face value.

Or did he simply know there was absolutely nothing she could do to extricate Michael from this room? She instantly rejected the question, unwilling to deal with its implications.

Fifteen minutes after Jameson finally left, she set off on the first of what she'd begun to think of as reconnaissance missions. Certain that every word she spoke was being overheard, every move she made watched, she forced herself to tell Michael not to worry and try to get some sleep. Hoping the words didn't sound as ludicrous to whoever might be listening as they did to her, she took a Ziploc bag out of her suitcase, left Michael's room, and asked the "nurse" if there was a kitchen on this level. "If I don't get some coffee, I'm never going to make it through the night," she said, sighing.

Eyeing her sharply, LuAnne hesitated, then pointed toward the end of the corridor. "But there's no coffee," she said.

"Not to worry." Ignoring the woman's coolness and holding up the Ziploc bag, which contained a fistful of single-cup coffee bags still in their foil packets, Katharine explained, "I brought my own."

LuAnne made no reply, so Katharine proceeded to the kitchen. As she passed the door behind which lay the Serinus Project laboratories, she noticed that the brass plaque was gone, and had to resist an urge to try the knob to see if it was locked.

In the kitchen she put a kettle of water on to boil, then washed out two cups, dropping one of the coffee bags in each of them. After the coffee had steeped, Katharine fished out the bags, then carried both cups back to the anteroom in which the nurse was stationed. "I made you a cup, too," she announced, setting both cups on the nurse's desk and willing herself not to react to the look of suspicion that immediately came into the other woman's eyes. "This one's Chocolate Mocha, and the other's French Vanilla Bean."

"Which one's your favorite?" the nurse asked.

"I think maybe the vanilla."

"Maybe I'll try that one."

Picking up the other mug, Katharine took it into Michael's room. Though he appeared still to be asleep, she was almost certain he was pretending. Grateful for his pretense, which removed the need to make up conversation that would undoubtedly sound as false to whoever might be listening as it would to them, she turned off the light. The room was plunged into near blackness, save for the glow of the monitors that still displayed Michael's vital signs, and the chemical makeup of the atmosphere inside the plastic box.

Even the darkness has eyes, Katharine thought, remembering the cameras at the gate. She settled down to wait, hoping that by four in the morning the darkness and silence of the room would have lulled the watchers into sufficient inattentiveness to let her make the final move in the game she'd planned.

Moving surreptitiously, she fished the cellular phone from her pocket and switched it over so that instead of ringing it would vibrate silently.

Forty minutes later, playing out the script she'd devised while packing her suitcase a few hours earlier, she got both herself and the nurse a second cup of coffee. This time, though, she lingered at the desk in the anteroom long enough to find out that LuAnne's last name was Jensen, that she had no family, lived alone, and seemed to take no interest in any subject on which Katharine tried to engage her.

But she accepted the second cup of coffee, which she finished in less than ten minutes.

The same thing happened with the third.

On none of the trips to the kitchen did Katharine hear or see anyone else. Nor was there any sign of a security guard, if she didn't count LuAnne Jensen.

Which meant one of two things: either they thought she'd bought Takeo Yoshihara's story, or they were so supremely confident of their security that they simply weren't worried.

When Katharine finally saw the minute hand on her watch creep toward five minutes past three, she picked up her empty cup and stepped out into the anteroom one more time.

LuAnne Jensen actually smiled at her. "I was just about to come in and see if you wanted me to fix it this time."

"Not a problem," Katharine replied, picking up the empty mug from the desk. "Michael's still sound asleep, and I'm tired of sitting in the dark. Any particular flavor this time?"

"Maybe another Chocolate Mocha?"

"Coming right up."

Heading for the kitchen for the fourth time, Katharine once again set about making two mugs of coffee. But this time she removed one more tinfoil packet from the Ziploc bag.

This one, though, contained more than coffee, for before she left her house, she'd carefully slit it open and added to the original contents three of the Halcion tablets that her doctor had prescribed for her more than a year ago. That had been during one of Michael's bad periods, when she'd worried so constantly about his asthma that she couldn't sleep. Though she'd never taken the pills, she'd kept them, superstitiously, as though their mere possession would act as a charm against needing to use them.

"Does it ever seem like the nights will never end?" she asked now as she set one of the coffee mugs on LuAnne Jensen's desk.

"Every one of them gets longer," the nurse agreed, picking up the mug, blowing on the steam for a moment, then taking the first sip. "You have no idea how much this helps."

"Have as much as you want," Katharine replied. "I brought plenty." Leaving with her own mug of coffee, Katharine went back into Michael's room.

In the darkness, she stripped off the clothes she'd been wearing all day and put on the jeans and shirt she'd brought from home. The cellular phone went into one of the front pockets of the jeans, where she'd feel its vibration if Rob tried to call her.

At three-forty she cracked the door to the anteroom open just wide enough to allow her a glimpse of the desk. LuAnne Jensen was still in her chair, but her head had rolled forward so her chin nearly touched her chest, and a rhythmic snoring was emanating from her open mouth. Katharine silently closed the door.

At three forty-five she felt the cellular phone vibrate in her pocket. Slipping it out, she flipped it open and was about to utter Rob's name when she thought better of it. "Michael?" she asked. "Are you awake?"

Instantly, her son's voice crackled from the speaker. "Uh-huh."

At the same time, she heard Rob's voice coming through the telephone: "If you don't say anything, we'll pick you up in exactly fifteen minutes. If there's a problem, speak to Michael again."

Katharine hesitated. She had a plan, but she had no idea whether it would work. If it didn't. . . . But what choice did she have?

Silently, she pressed the End button on the cellular phone, closed it, and returned it to her pocket. Then she went over to the bed. In the dim light emanating from the monitor, she could barely make out Michael's face. But he was staring at her, his eyes wide open, and she no longer had any doubt that he'd been as wide-awake as she through the long hours of the night.

She held a finger to her lips, then took the bundle of clothes she'd brought for him out of the suitcase and pushed them into the air lock. He immediately began wriggling into them, staying under the covers and doing his best to move as little as possible. When he was done, she signaled him to pull the covers up and pretend to go back to sleep. Then she stepped out into the anteroom.

"Are you ready for—" she began, then cut herself off. "LuAnne? LuAnne, what's wrong?" Moving around behind the desk, she shook the nurse, who slid off the chair onto the floor. Straightening, she looked wildly around the anteroom as if uncertain what to do, then picked up the telephone and pressed the button that was labeled "Lobby Desk." Someone picked it up in the middle of the second ring.

"Jensen?" a voice asked.

"It's Dr. Sundquist," Katharine said. "Something's happened to LuAnne. I just came out to make us some more coffee, and I thought she'd fallen asleep. But when I tried to wake her up, she slid off the chair."

"Oh, Jesus," the guard swore. "I'll be right there."

Katharine darted back into Michael's room and took three more items out of the suitcase.

Two of them were large plastic garbage bags.

The other was the fossilized femur of an anthropoid that had become extinct several million years ago.

Shoving the garbage bags into the air lock, Katharine finally risked speaking to Michael out loud. "Hold these up to the intake tube," she said. "Get them as full as you can." Then, taking the femur with her, she went back to the anteroom and once again pressed the Lobby Desk button on the phone. When there was no answer by the second ring, she hung up, left the anteroom, and went to stand by the elevator door, her back pressed against the wall.

As she counted the passing seconds, she prayed that the camera above her was being monitored only by the guard who should be stepping out of the elevator in five more seconds.

In at least partial answer to her prayers, the doors slid open exactly five seconds later and the guard stepped out.

As the second hand of Katharine's watch ticked one more time, she raised the femur high, then brought it down on the back of the guard's neck as hard as she could.

Grunting, he dropped to his knees.

Katharine smashed the fossilized bone down one more time.

The guard sprawled out on the floor, facedown, and lay still.

Grabbing both his hands, Katharine dragged him down the hall and into the anteroom. Closing the door, she tied his hands behind him with the telephone cord, then pulled his wallet out of his back pocket.

If the elevator card stolen from Jameson didn't work, the guard's would.

Rising to her feet, she looked once more at her watch.

Seven minutes had gone by.

Going back into Michael's room, she finally turned the lights on. Inside the plastic box, one of the garbage bags was inflated, and Michael was pulling its drawstrings tight.

"Don't tie them," she said. "Hurry, and get the other bag filled, and—" Her words died on her lips as she realized for the first time that none of the corners of the Plexiglas box had hinges.

"My God," she whispered, staring at Michael in horror. "How am I going to get you out of there?"

Holding the second garbage bag up to the intake tube, Michael jerked his head toward the corner of the room. "Over there. There's a button."

Katharine searched the corner where he'd gestured, saw nothing for a moment, then spotted a small button mounted flush into the wall. When she pressed it, nothing seemed to happen, but then she saw Michael pointing toward the ceiling.

A small panel had slid open directly above the center of the Plexiglas box. From it a stainless steel rod, perhaps an inch thick, was descending. A knob on the rod slipped into a socket on the box's top. She heard a click as something locked in place.

A second later the box began to rise up off the floor. Instantly the room filled with the noxious gases with which the cube had been filled. Katharine, already coughing from the fumes, lurched toward the anteroom door.

"Take one of the bags," she heard Michael say as the box cleared the bed. Grabbing the strings of the bag he had shoved in her direction, she darted out into the anteroom, yanking the door shut behind her.

Nine minutes had gone by.

She waited as another minute passed, and was about to go back into the inner room when suddenly the door opened and Michael, clutching the second garbage bag, came out.

"Follow me," Katharine told him. Pulling the door to the hallway open, she raced down the corridor to the elevator, the key card already in her hand. Holding it up to the panel, she uttered a silent prayer.

The light on the gray panel changed from red to green, but nothing happened.

The doors remained closed.

Then she understood: the elevator had returned to the upper floor.

The fifteen seconds it took for the elevator to arrive back on the lower level seemed to take forever, but at last the doors slid open.

Katharine almost shoved Michael inside, stepped in after him, and pressed the Up button. Then, as the doors began to slide shut, she saw someone come out of one of the doors down the hall.

The door to the Serinus Project.

The man stared at her in surprise and started toward her, but the elevator doors closed before he could get to them.

The elevator was only halfway up when Katharine heard the faint ringing sound. An alarm.

As the doors slid open at the top and the sound of the alarm battered against her eardrums, Katharine looked at her watch again.

Ten minutes left.

"Come on," she told Michael.

She raced down the corridor toward the double doors at the far end, the inflated garbage bag bouncing clumsily behind her. Michael, pausing only to suck a deep breath from the second bag, ran after her, catching up to her just as she came to the lobby doors.

She pushed them open.

Here, the sound of the alarm was even louder, but the lobby was still empty.

"Outside," she said.

They ran for the front door, and a few seconds later burst out into the night. For an instant, seeing no pursuers, Katharine dared to hope that, after all, they might escape. Then the blackness was washed away by a brilliant beam of white light.

Like two insects caught on a pin, Katharine and Michael cowered in the brilliance.

Over the alarm, Katharine heard another sound.

The familiar *whup-whup-whup* of a helicopter.

Shielding her eyes against the glare of the light, she looked up. As suddenly as the beam had appeared, it disappeared, and finally she saw it.

The helicopter dropped down no more than twenty yards away.

She froze in horror, thinking:

Takeo Yoshihara.

Then, as lights all over the estate began to go on, she caught a glimpse of a face inside the chopper's cabin.

Rob Silver's face.

Grabbing Michael with one hand and still clutching the garbage bag with the other, Katharine stumbled toward the hovering aircraft and shoved Michael inside.

As Rob's strong hands closed on her wrists and began to lift her into the cabin, she heard the helicopter's engine roar.

Even before she was fully on board, it lifted off, wheeled around, and began racing away into the darkness.

From the lanai outside his bedroom, Takeo Yoshihara watched the helicopter disappear into the night, then spoke into the telephone he had picked up the instant the alarms had wakened him from sleep.

"Track them on radar," he ordered. "Find out where they are going. We will bring them back. Do you understand? Both the mother and the son." Before hanging up, he spoke once more: "And when we go, I shall want a special guard with us. One who has been trained as a sniper."

CHAPTER
33

The headset that Rob clamped over Katharine's ears the moment after he dragged her into the helicopter's cabin cut the rotor's roar just enough so she could make out that he was trying to talk to her, but the words themselves were lost in the din coming from above. When she finally trusted herself to speak after the sickening series of dips and turns the helicopter made as the pilot raced it away from the estate, she had to raise her voice to a shout, even though the headset's microphone hung only a fraction of an inch from her lips.

"I said, how long will it take to get to the Big Island?"

Rob started to reply, then went silent as the pilot jerked on the joystick and the helicopter yawed sharply to port as it banked away from the face of a cliff. It plunged straight down, then stabilized and began to rise, finally cresting the top of the cliff and swooping away to the west.

"Maybe forty minutes," Rob finally answered.

Forty minutes? But before, she recalled, Rob had said Michael would have to breathe for only ten or fifteen minutes! And though one of the two plastic bags was still full—she herself was clutching its top to make sure none of its contents could escape before Michael needed them—the bag Michael had carried out of the research pavilion was already nearly half empty. He'd never make it! Before she could say anything, though, Michael spoke.

"I'm gonna try breathing regular air!" he shouted into his microphone. "Maybe I can save what's in the bags!"

Katharine nodded vigorously, then shouted into the microphone again: "Just don't waste any of it trying to talk!"

Michael made a thumbs-up sign. Then, as she watched, he exhaled the last breath he'd taken from the bag, and inhaled his first breath of air from the cabin.

For a second, just a second, Katharine felt a surge of hope. Then a fit of coughing seized Michael, and she could see the pain he was experiencing. He buried his face in the mouth of the bag, sucked in some of the gas it held, and the coughing subsided.

The bag, though, had collapsed still further. When Katharine glanced at her watch, she saw that only three minutes had gone by since they'd left the estate. At this rate, both the bags would be depleted before they were even halfway to the Big Island. "What are we going to do?" she asked, struggling to control the panic rising within her. Michael couldn't die now! He couldn't! They were supposed to be rescuing him, not killing him!

"Don't worry!" Rob shouted over the noise of the rotors. "By the time he finishes them, we should be okay!"

Katharine gazed out through the Plexiglas bubble into the darkness outside. The route they were taking was leading them up the side of the mountain, and the pilot was keeping the chopper low, hugging the ground. The rain forests around the estate had already given way to the lush pastureland above Makawao and Pukalani, and just ahead and off to the port side Katharine could see a few lights she assumed must be at Kula. In the distance, strung along the edge of Maalaea Bay like a string of glittering diamonds, were the lights of Kihei and Wailea.

Farther to the south there was a vast expanse of darkness, broken only by a faint glow from the Makena Surf Condominiums and the Maui Prince Hotel, then a scattering of glimmers marking the dozen or so houses strung along the beach until the beach itself ended abruptly at the lava flow. Beneath

the helicopter the landscape was changing again, the lush up-country pas-
turage giving way to the scrubby ranch land that dominated the leeward side
of Haleakala. Even in the starlight she could make out the dense thickets of
prickly pear cactus and scraggly kiawe trees that made up much of the sparse
vegetation that grew there.

She glanced over at Michael; the first of the two bags was all but depleted,
but as his body began to recover from the burst of energy he'd expended during the escape, his breathing, like her own, had started to return to normal,
and the remaining gas contained in the bag had lasted far longer than she
would have thought possible. But even so, the bag was deflated long before
they had even crossed over the coastline and started out over the broad channel that separates Maui from the Big Island.

As Michael discarded the first bag and took his first breath from the second, she realized that instead of turning southeast, en route to the Big Island,
the helicopter was still moving southwest. In the darkness, she could see the
silhouette of a small island etched against the night sky. But there were no
small islands between Maui and the Big Island. A glance at the compass confirmed her suspicion, and a new fear took root inside her as she searched for
some plausible reason that they would be going in the wrong direction.

And why had Rob assured her that Michael would have to breathe no
more than fifteen minutes?

Then, as the helicopter held a steady course almost ninety degrees away
from the only place where Michael had a chance of surviving other than in
Takeo Yoshihara's laboratory, the truth dawned on her.

Rob was still working for Takeo Yoshihara!

Not only was he still working for him, but he'd led her—and Michael—
directly into a trap.

Frantic, she looked wildly around, trying to decide what to do. Should she
attempt to take control of the helicopter herself? She dismissed the idea the
instant it occurred to her—perhaps in the movies someone who'd never
flown a helicopter before could simply take over the joystick, but in real life it
simply wasn't possible.

"Why aren't we going to the Big Island?" she demanded, shouting to make
herself heard over the din of the rotor.

Rob cupped his hand over his ear, as if he hadn't been able to hear her.

But he must have heard! How could he not have? Furious now, she jabbed her finger toward the compass, then the island beyond. "That's not the Big Island, God damn you! You lied to me! You're going to kill us, aren't you?" As Rob's eyes widened in the face of her fury, she shouted at him again. "Why? Why are you doing this?" Suddenly it all made sense: of course she'd managed to pull off the escape—they'd always intended for her to! And they'd timed it perfectly:

The man from the laboratory appearing in the hallway just seconds too late to prevent her from using the elevator.

The alarms going off just seconds too late for the guards to prevent her from getting to the helicopter.

Even the arrival of the helicopter itself, unchallenged, its searchlight blinding her, confusing her, scaring her into shoving Michael into it with no questions at all.

An idiot! She'd been a complete idiot! Her frustration and fury overwhelming her, she lunged at Rob, wanting to smash him even harder than she'd smashed the guard with the fossilized bone half an hour ago. She wanted to hit him, to strangle him, to shove him out the door of the helicopter. "Damn you!" she screamed. "Damn you, damn you, *damn you!*"

Rob's hands instinctively came up to defend himself, then his fingers closed on her wrists, holding her arms immobile. "What are you talking about, Katharine?" he demanded. "What's wrong?"

"What's wrong?" she screamed. "For God's sake, Rob! How stupid do you think I am? Don't you think I've figured out why you told me Michael was only going to need to breathe for—what did you say? Ten to fifteen minutes, wasn't it?"

"Kath—"

"I should have known then, shouldn't I? I should have been able to figure out there was no way to get to the Big Island in that short a time. But I thought you had a plan! I trusted you, God damn it! I trusted you!"

"Stop it!" Rob shouted, so loudly his voice carried over the roar of the motor even without the help of the headsets. "Will you tell me what the hell you think is going on?"

"I don't think!" Katharine bellowed back. "I know!" She jerked her head toward the vista beyond the bubblelike cabin. They had crossed the coastline now, and the helicopter was speeding low over the water, directly toward the small island she had seen. "That's not the Big Island, Rob. What is it? Does Yoshihara have another lab down there? Or are you just going to dump us into the ocean?"

Michael, his complexion going ashen in the face of his mother's fury, loosed his grip on the neck of the plastic bag, and the cabin began to fill with choking fumes.

Instantly, one of Rob's hands released Katharine's arm and closed around the bag. "Careful with that!" he yelled. "You need that for about five more minutes. Don't let it escape."

As Michael, almost hesitantly, took the half-deflated bag back from him, Rob swung around to face Katharine again. "It's the wind!" he shouted. "We can't go directly to the Big Island—Michael would never make it! But the wind's carrying fumes from the eruption almost due west, so we should be able to catch the worst of them just on the other side of Koho'olawe. Then we can turn and fly due east, right into the fumes. It might be rough for the rest of us, but Michael should be able to breathe on his own. It's longer, but at least he has a chance!"

Katharine's eyes bored into his, trying to read the truth.

And what she saw was love.

Love, and the agony that her doubt had caused him.

Then, as if what she saw in his eyes might not be enough to convince her, she felt a shift in the attitude of the helicopter and heard the pilot's voice coming through the headset.

"Someone open a window. Let's see if our boy can breathe."

His hands dropping away from Katharine, Rob twisted around and slid his window open. Instead of the fresh sea air Katharine would have expected, the air that filled the cabin was so laden with volcanic fumes that her eyes immediately began stinging.

"Bingo!" the pilot yelled. "Don't you love that vog?"

As the helicopter finished its swing, Katharine searched for the great mass of the Big Island that should be rising out of the sea ahead, but Rob, reading her mind, shook his head. "You won't be able to see it through the haze. But wait ten or fifteen minutes. Believe me, it's still there." Then he said to her son: "Well, what about it, Michael? Can you breathe, or did we take the wrong gamble?"

Katharine turned to look at Michael. Once more, as he had shortly after the helicopter took off, he exhaled the fumes from the bag and inhaled the cabin's air. He coughed once, hesitated, and tried again. After a long pause, while Katharine waited anxiously, he stuck his right hand out, thumb up. "It's not great," he said. "But I'm not feeling as bad as I did at school yesterday."

"Hang on to the bag, but just use it when you have to," Rob told him. Then he grinned at Katharine. "And as for you, I forgive you your suspicions," he said, as he drew her close.

Half an hour later the helicopter, with both its windows wide open, was cruising along the Kalapana Coast southwest of Hilo. The entire mountainside was pocked with glowing vents, and Michael gazed in awe at the lava flows that oozed down the mountain's flank like slithering, flaming serpents.

Bathed in the eerie silver light of the moon, he could see the stone cliffs of the coastline being battered by the heaving ocean—an ocean made angry by the mountain's attempt to invade its realm with spreading fingers of molten rock. The Pacific was waging an unending counterattack, hurling vast masses of water against the intruding rock and casting spume high into the sky like spent artillery shells being ejected from machine guns.

Here and there along the battle's front line, enormous plumes of steam gushed up where the ocean quenched the mountain's fire, and from behind the lines, on the mountain's slopes, clouds of smoke arose.

The helicopter crossed the coastline and began moving up the flank of the mountain. Below, most of the terrain was barren lava without so much as an inch of topsoil covering it, though here and there a few scrubby bushes had gained a foothold. Almost everywhere Michael looked, steam or smoke belched forth from deep within the mountain's bowels. The air reeked with the acrid smell of sulfur.

He sucked it deep into his lungs, feeling the warmth that spread through his body as he absorbed the fumes. "Where are we going?" he shouted.

"The pilot says there's a clearing where he can set the chopper down," Rob told them. "The idea's to get you as close to these vents as possible."

In the distance, and two hundred feet above them, flames rose out of a crater like a beacon. As the pilot guided the chopper higher, rising above the caldera, they saw for the first time its demonic contents. Lava boiled with the fury of hell, flames leaped across its surface, evil fountains of molten rock shot high into the air, some of them breaking apart to drop back into the churning caldron, others exploding into brilliant bursts of sparkling embers that drifted on the wind before cooling to the point where their fiery glow died away.

The heat rose in waves, and above the gaping, hellish maw into which Michael was gazing, the air itself shimmered and danced. The flames took on a hypnotic quality that wrapped itself around Michael's mind until he was staring at the spectacle with unblinking fascination.

Only when the helicopter began to drop down toward the ground, and the lip of the caldera once more hid its fires from his view, did Michael finally turn away to see where they were going. A minute later the helicopter settled into something that seemed to him like an oasis in the desert of fire and lava. Somehow, in the vagaries of its flow, the lava had left a clearing in which stood a grove of scraggly kiave trees. On the ground, miraculously, a thin covering of grass still survived.

Near the center of the clearing there was a fire pit, built of a circle of rocks very much like the one in the ravine where his mother had uncovered the skeleton.

Beyond the fire pit were the ruins of a hut, its walls also built of lava, its roof long since caved in.

The chopper settled onto the ground and the pilot cut the engine. As the roar died away and the great rotor slowed to a stop, an eerie silence fell over the four people inside.

"What is this place?" Michael finally asked.

"Used to be a campground," the pilot explained. "This is all that's left of it. It's about the only place around here that's still safe to land. Everywhere else, you don't know what's under you."

Katharine, feeling oddly disoriented by the sudden quiet, looked uncertainly at Michael, as if perhaps his breathing might have been somehow dependent on the power of the helicopter's engine. "Well?" she asked.

Pushing open the door, Michael scrambled out of the cabin and dropped to the ground, then turned and grinned at his mother. "I can breathe!" he yelled. "It worked! I can breathe!" Almost as quickly as his grin had come, though, it faded. His eyes flicked around the desolate landscape, taking in the darkness that was laced with patches of glowing fire and swirling smoke and fumes. "Is this the way it's going to be from now on?" he asked, his voice quavering despite his effort to control it. "Is this where I'm going to have to live the rest of my life?"

Katharine's eyes met Michael's and she felt a terrible sense of dread come over her.

She had no answer for him.

CHAPTER
34

Katharine and Rob sat side by side, very close together, a few feet from the small campfire the helicopter pilot had built. The pilot himself was hunkered down opposite them, poking at the fire with a stick. He was a lanky man, tall and skinny, named Arnold Berman—"but everybody calls me Puna"—whom Katharine judged to be in his mid-twenties.

The wind had shifted, flushing some of the fumes from the small clearing, and Michael, his chest starting to hurt, had gone off in search of a fumarole, where the smoke and gases boiling up from deep beneath the crust of the earth would ease the pain in his lungs and give him the strength that oxygen no longer could. Katharine, terrified of losing sight of him even for a moment, wanted to go with him, but Rob stopped her.

"Let him be, Kath," he'd said. "Whatever happens to him—however this turns out—he's going to have to deal with it. And so are you and I."

As exhausted mentally as she was physically, Katharine had reluctantly settled back, but ten minutes later she wished she hadn't, for as the first flush of victory at having rescued Michael from Takeo Yoshihara's estate began to fade, the full horror of her son's condition set in. The alien landscape seemed to be closing in on her, with its perimeters oddly lit by tongues of flame that flicked up from the fire pits, while all around her there was a strange pulsating glow from the lava flows. When Puna had built the small fire, she'd been drawn to it less for its warmth than for its familiarity, and as the little fire seemed to hold the demons surrounding them at bay, she looked at the man who had flown them here, studying him for the first time.

His dirty-blond hair was long, and he wore the standard Maui uniform of shorts, T-shirt, and sandals. He looked far more like a beach bum than a helicopter pilot. "Is there any way I can ever thank you enough for what you did tonight?"

Puna shrugged. "Ken Richter was my best friend. We came to Maui together. If what Rob says is true, I wish I'd had a bomb to dump on that prick's place after we picked you up."

"It's true," Katharine sighed as Rob slipped his arm protectively around her. "It's all true." She pressed closer to Rob and looked into his face. "What are we going to do?"

"For the moment, all we can do is wait," Rob told her. "But the way I figure it, as soon as it gets light, we should have some company."

Katharine shuddered. "Yoshihara's going to come after us, isn't he?"

"Probably," Rob agreed. "But if he thinks we're going to be all by ourselves out here, he's going to find out he's wrong." His arm tightened around her and his eyes rose to scan the sky. And there it was, right where Phil Howell had told him it would be. Glimmering in the blackness of a sky that had been washed all but bare of stars by the light of the fires burning around them, a single light hung far above them.

A light that would shine more brightly with each passing night, but then— in a week or perhaps a month—would disappear.

Disappear forever.

The nova.

"Look," he said softly, guiding Katharine's eyes to the brightening star. "That's where it all came from." Then, choosing his words very carefully, Rob began explaining to Katharine exactly what he and Phil Howell had discovered that night.

*   *   *

The first light of dawn was washing the blackness from the eastern horizon when the sound intruded on Katharine's dream.

She was back in the Serinus laboratory on Takeo Yoshihara's estate, but instead of rats, hamsters, monkeys, and chimpanzees, the cages each contained a little boy.

The rows of Plexiglas boxes seemed to stretch on forever, and each of the aisles opened into another, forming a labyrinth that went on into infinity. Katharine saw herself running through it, searching for Michael, but there were too many cages, too many children, and all of them were reaching out to her, begging her to help them.

She stopped finally, and opened one of the cages, but the moment she did, the child inside began to cough and choke, and when she picked up a little boy—a boy who looked exactly like Michael had when he was six—his coughing became convulsive.

And the child died in her arms.

She began running again, but now something was pursuing her, coming closer and closer, its sinister noise building to a crescendo.

Whup-whup-whup . . .

She tried to run faster, but the aisles stretched longer and longer before her, and with every turn, there were more of them to choose from. But no matter which way she turned, how many times she dodged from one aisle into another, her pursuer drew ever nearer.

Whup-whup-whup . . .

She cried out Michael's name, praying he would answer her, that she would be able to find him before—

"Katharine!"

Her name! Someone was calling her name! But not Michael!

"Katharine!"

She jerked awake, the dream dissolving around her, and with a start remembered where she was. She'd escaped from the estate, and Michael was with her, and so was Rob, and they were safe.

WHUP-WHUP-WHUP-WHUP!

The noise was still there, and now that she was wide-awake, she knew exactly what it was.

She struggled to her feet, ignoring the stiffness that had crept into her body as she'd dozed against Rob's shoulder, still huddled close to the small fire

Puna was nursing. "Where is it?" she asked, searching the brightening sky for the source of the noise.

Then she saw it. Flying high and coming in from the direction of Maui, she instantly recognized Takeo Yoshihara's helicopter. "Michael," she whispered, clutching at Rob's arm while her eyes remained fixed on the aircraft. "Where's Michael?"

"He hasn't come back yet," Rob told her. "Let's go find him."

"There!" Takeo Yoshihara said, pointing to the slope of Kilauea where Arnold Berman's helicopter was clearly visible in a small clearing.

"Shall I land?" the pilot asked.

"Not until we find the boy!" Takeo Yoshihara, a satisfied smile curling his lips, gazed down at the landscape below. Though the glow of the lava flowing through the cracked and fissured tubes was fading in the breaking dawn, the flames dancing above the fire pits and calderas were still visible, as were the plumes of smoke and steam from the fumaroles that lined the great fissure — the point where an immense chunk of the island of Hawaii would eventually slide away into the sea, creating a tidal wave a thousand feet high. It wouldn't happen this morning, or tomorrow, or this year or next. Indeed, it probably wouldn't happen in Takeo Yoshihara's lifetime, or for generations to come. Which was too bad: a natural phenomenon of that magnitude and the devastation it would wreak, was something he would like to see. This morning, though, there were more important things to do than contemplate the scene below.

The timing, as he had intended, was perfect.

They'd taken off from Maui in darkness, but by the time they found the boy—and they *would* find him—it would be light.

Light enough to pursue and capture him.

Or to kill him.

But still so early that there would be few witnesses. Only the mother, the besotted Dr. Silver, and their pilot, none of whom would survive.

"Fly lower," he ordered. "We should be able to see . . ." His words died on his lips as he caught a flicker of movement that was neither flame nor smoke

nor any of the churning gases that swirled up from below. Raising the pair of
Leica binoculars that hung from his neck, he peered downward. "Yes," he
said softly. "There he is."

Keeping the binoculars fastened on Michael Sundquist, Takeo Yoshihara
began guiding the pilot toward the spot where the boy stood.

Nearly two hours had passed, but Michael, mesmerized by the undulating
rhythm of the fires dancing above the caldera's surface, had long ago lost any
sense of time. After he'd left the small oasis in the lava where the kiawes grew
and the others could still easily breathe the air, he'd moved quickly through
the tortured landscape. His senses, heightening every minute as his lungs
absorbed the nutrients his body now craved, guided him from one vent to
another. He'd stopped at each of them, breathing in the thick fumes that
steamed out of the cracks in the earth's crust, inhaling the pungent odors issuing forth from the fumaroles. Finally he'd come to the caldera. There,
crouched at its rim, the night had closed around him, wrapping him in a
blanket of darkness from which he watched in silent wonder as the fires
boiled up from deep within the earth. Through the hours, the flames danced,
weaving intricate patterns above the molten rock that seemed to Michael to
throb like the heart of the planet itself. Now, as the black mantle of night began to lift from the mountain, he sensed a change coming.

The rhythm of the flames seemed to intensify, as if they had some urgent
message to impart before the brilliant fires of the sun made their own lumi-
nescence fade to invisibility.

As he was released from the folds of darkness, Michael flexed his body, but
found no stiffness in it, despite the hours of crouching near the edge of the
caldera's lip. Then he felt, more than heard, a new rhythm beat into his consciousness. At first he tried to ignore it. Finally, it became so strong that he
tore his eyes from the pulsating flames and gazed upward.

The helicopter hovering in the distance took on an iridescent glitter like
that of a dragonfly searching for prey in the first rays of the rising sun. Michael watched it in fascination, but as it swooped down, moving steadily
toward him, his fascination gave way to a tingling uneasiness.

It was, indeed, a predator out hunting in the morning sun like a dragonfly. Hunting for him.

But at the same time that he realized he was the prey for which the great metal dragonfly searched, so also came an absolute conviction that he must remain where he was, close to the fires, where smoke and fumes sustained him, and would also now, somehow, protect him.

Rising to his full height, Michael waited.

Katharine, with Rob right behind her, was stumbling along the rocky path that led out of the oasis and onto the lava flow when suddenly a shadow flicked over her. Reflexively, she looked up into the sky, then stopped in her tracks as she watched Takeo Yoshihara's helicopter, hovering high above for the last several minutes, make a sudden descent.

"They've found him!" she told Rob. "Hurry!"

"Land!" Takeo Yoshihara commanded.

His employer's command ringing in his ears, the pilot searched for a likely looking spot, but found nothing. Already he was beginning to feel the effects of the churning thermals rising from the shattered landscape below, some of them so strong that they shot the helicopter straight up, but at the same time so narrow that by the time he'd adjusted for the added lift he was out of it, and the aircraft would yaw giddily, or plunge for a second or two like an out-of-control elevator. "There's no place to land," he finally replied.

"Find one!" Yoshihara demanded, his eyes fixed on Michael Sundquist, who was standing near the edge of the caldera's highest wall, only a few yards from a hundred-foot vertical drop into a lake of seething lava.

"No chance," the pilot replied. "My job is to fly you, not kill you."

Takeo Yoshihara's eyes went flat and the single brief look he gave the pilot was enough to tell him that this might be his last flight. After raking the pilot, Yoshihara's glare shifted to his chief of security.

"Shoot the boy," he ordered.

The security man reached behind the seat and picked up the laser-sighted rifle he'd brought on the flight for exactly this purpose. Placing its stock firmly against his right shoulder, he switched on the laser, kicked open the door of the cabin, then peered through the telescope mounted above the barrel. The helicopter, now buffeted not only by the thermals, but by the rising trade winds as well, was swinging far too wildly for him to get anything resembling a clear shot at Michael. "Too high," he said.

"Lower," Takeo Yoshihara commanded the pilot.

The pilot, weighing the dangers to the craft against the loss of his not-inconsiderable salary, carefully began to drop the helicopter toward the lacerated surface of the mountain.

Yoshihara's sniper, still peering through the telescope, saw the red dot of the laser flick across Michael Sundquist's face far too quickly for him to squeeze the rifle's trigger.

Better if he'd brought an AK-47, he thought, or even an Uzi.

"Lower!" Takeo Yoshihara demanded again, understanding that the flatter the angle, the better the chance of hitting his target.

Michael gazed up at the rifle barrel protruding from the door of the helicopter and instantly knew that the man holding the gun intended to kill him. For some reason, though, the thought did not disturb him. The calmness that had come over him as he'd watched the fires boil remained intact. Instead of turning in an attempt to flee the hunter, he moved closer to the caldera's lip, as though something deep inside him had instructed him that the fires of the earth were his protection, not his enemy.

"Good," Takeo Yoshihara said to himself as he watched Michael move closer to the edge. Now, when the boy dropped from the single shot that was all that would be required to execute him, he would pitch forward, plunging into the sea of churning molten rock, his body instantly incinerated. "Lower!" he again commanded the pilot.

The pilot, hands tightening on the controls, peered down into the fiery hell below, then looked away as he felt himself losing his nerve.

Only ten more feet.

He would drop only ten more feet, and that would be it. Even if it cost him his job, he would go no lower.

His eyes glued to the altimeter, he nudged the helicopter downward.

He could feel the heat now, even through the protective bubble of Plexiglas that formed the cabin.

Six more feet.

Five.

Only three more, then he would hold steady, and rotate the cabin around to give the marksman a clear bead on the boy who still stood on the edge of the caldera, calmly watching.

Why didn't he run?

Was he crazy?

Three more feet . . .

Michael felt no fear as he watched the helicopter hover over the caldera, dropping lower and lower. He could feel something in the ground now, a slight tremor, as if the earth itself were about to come alive. Then, as the helicopter edged lower, the glowing surface of the lake inside the caldera awakened.

The level of the lava rose steeply, the oddly rhythmic undulations of the boiling rock suddenly interrupted by a column of fire that fountained out of the caldera's throat, hurling rock, ash, and fire into the air in a burst that seemed to come from nowhere and everywhere simultaneously.

Michael ducked beneath the cover of a thick lip of lava, but his eyes remained fastened on the spectacle in front of him.

For the helicopter, there was no place to hide, nor time to flee.

The sniper saw the flicker of red on Michael's face as the laser sight found its mark. But in the instant before he could squeeze the trigger, a fragment of molten lava struck the helicopter's enormous propeller. One of its blades broke free of the shaft, and as the helicopter yawed wildly in response to its injury, the metal blade boomeranged back, lashing through the open cabin door, severing the marksman's arm just above the elbow, and sending him, screaming, into the maelstrom below.

Blood from the severed arm splattered across the Plexiglas cabin, blinding the pilot, who was still trying to control the mortally wounded aircraft.

A terrified howl issued from Takeo Yoshihara, his self-control deserting him as he looked down into the yawning hell into which the helicopter was plunging. His scream, unheard by anyone beyond the confines of the Plexiglas cabin, was suddenly cut off as the fuel tank, heated beyond endurance by the all-consuming fire welling up out of the mountain, exploded into yet more flames, blowing the helicopter into a thousand pieces even as it plummeted into the depths of the churning lake.

The fire spout, as if sensing that it had completed the mission for which it had been summoned, subsided back into the bowels of the mountain. Beneath Michael's feet, the trembling of the earth began to subside.

By the time Katharine and Rob reached Michael, the helicopter and its occupants had vanished, incinerated as completely as if they had never existed at all.

"It's beautiful, isn't it?" Michael asked, still gazing out over the caldera's surface.

Katharine slipped one arm around her son, the other around Rob Silver. "It is beautiful," she agreed. "It's the most beautiful thing I've ever seen."

EPILOGUE

TWO WEEKS LATER

It didn't seem like two weeks. It barely seemed like two days. Yet the exhaustion that had become Katharine's most familiar and constant companion since the night she and Michael had fled from Takeo Yoshihara's estate told her that the time had, indeed, passed.

She was back on the estate, now in an office of her own, though not in the north wing of the research pavilion.

The entire north wing had been turned over to the army of press that had descended on the estate. Katharine and Rob had moved into what had been the Serinus Project laboratories, and found it ironic that Takeo Yoshihara's security system now served to protect them from the swarm of reporters upstairs, freeing them to concentrate on finding a way to reverse the damage that had been done to Michael and a dozen other adolescent children scattered around the globe.

Wherever the victims were found, fumatoria had been immediately set up, funded by the companies that Takeo Yoshihara had controlled, to keep them as comfortable as possible until an answer could be found.

If there was an answer.

Most of the scientists who had been involved in the Serinus Project, acting on the advice of their attorneys, refused to discuss anything about the sphere—or the Seed, as it was still called, the press having latched onto the term the moment they heard it—let alone the project that had been centered around it.

"We knew nothing of it until two days ago," Herr Doktor Wolfgang von Schmidt had insisted. "As far as we knew, we were called here to be briefed on a new project that Takeo Yoshihara had in mind. Needless to say, when we heard of his plans to indulge in human experimentation, we were all appalled. And we all refused."

Juan-Carlos Sanchez and all but two of the other scientists who had been housed at the Hotel Hana Maui had clung to von Schmidt's position, though now they were protesting their ignorance from prison cells in Honolulu rather than hotel suites on Maui.

The laboratory staff, save for the one man whose job it had been to fill the scuba tanks before they were sent to Kihei Ken's Dive Shop, was still intact, now working under the supervision of Katharine and Rob and the team of biologists and geneticists they had assembled to reanalyze the compound within the Seed and attempt to find a way to reverse its effects.

Thus far, no progress had been made. Though Katharine was doing her best to remain optimistic, with each day that passed a little more of her hope faded. This morning, when one of the lab technicians rapped on her open door, she looked up from the data she'd been studying and braced herself for more bad news.

"There's something I think you should see, Dr. Sundquist," he said. "Right away."

Following him out of the office, she threaded her way through the laboratory and then into the room in which the walls were lined with the Plexiglas boxes where the animals waited for death.

The technician stopped in front of a cage. Katharine herself had paused at this box earlier this morning to try to comfort its sole occupant, a chimpanzee whose energy seemed finally to have been sapped. The animal, so heartbreakingly close in appearance to a human child, was still breathing, but seemed unaware of her presence, its dull eyes staring off into space, as if looking at something that wasn't there. Katharine had talked to it for a moment or two, but it gave no more sign of hearing her than it had of seeing her. Finally, knowing there was nothing she could do for the creature, she'd turned away.

But even as she'd gone on toward her office, a thought had lingered in her mind:

Is this the way it will end for Michael?

Now, standing in front of the cage, she made herself look at its occupant, certain it must have died.

Instead, the chimp was sitting up on the floor, scratching itself with the fingers of its left hand while it clung to a banana with its right. Catching sight of her, it chittered softly, then held out the banana as if offering it to her.

Katharine's eyes shifted to the gauges monitoring the atmosphere inside the cage. As the significance of their readings slowly sank in, she knew what she had to do.

And she had to do it right now.

Phil Howell, as overwhelmed by the army of reporters as Katharine and Rob, had moved onto the estate, too, hiding out in one of the subterranean offices while he worked on a monograph concerning the origin of the Seed. Now, with the monograph finally completed, he stood nervously behind the podium of the largest conference room on the estate, trying to quell the attack of stage fright that had seized him the moment he'd entered the room and been surrounded by the pack of journalists, all of them jamming microphones at him, calling out a barrage of questions.

Shaking his head, hand held up as if to ward them off, he fought his way to the front of the room. There, he waited silently until the crowd of reporters had quieted down. Then he began:

"The civilization that created the Seeds knew what was going to happen to them, just as we know how much longer our own sun is going to last, and how it is going to die. For us, that event is so far in the future as not even to be a factor in our thinking." He paused, then went on. "But they, fifteen million years ago, knew that their sun was going to explode. They knew that their planet was going to be incinerated, and that they were all going to die.

"Not slowly.

"Not over a period of centuries, or decades, or even years.

"They were going to die in an instant.

"And so they prepared. Probably for hundreds of years; perhaps for thousands. They knew they couldn't prevent their sun from exploding, nor save their planet. So they did something else. They escaped."

Someone at the back of the room rose to her feet. "But they didn't," she said. "The Seed isn't viable here. Whatever might have hatched out of them couldn't live in our atmosphere."

Phil Howell's gaze shifted to Rob Silver, who was standing against the wall just inside the conference room's door. "Perhaps you could comment on that, Rob."

Coming to the podium, Rob looked out at the faces, some expectant, some skeptical. "The fact of the matter is, we feel fairly certain that the contents of the Seed may be perfectly viable." The murmuring crowd grew silent as the import of what he was saying slowly sank in. "Right now, Michael Sundquist is living on the slope of Kilauea, thriving in an atmosphere that would poison the rest of us. And in the basement of this building there is a skull and a skeleton, both of which bear very close resemblance to early hominids. Preliminary tests show that the DNA of both of them are a very close match to that of the organic compound inside the Seed. Though we can't yet prove it, we are fairly certain that the beings whose bones we are currently analyzing must have been affected by the contents of one of the 'Seeds' at a very early age, possibly even before birth, through a mother who came into contact with one of them. The atmosphere of this planet, like everything else in the universe, is constantly changing and evolving. If there are areas on this planet right now where organisms such as those who created the Seed can survive, think of how many such areas there would have been eons ago, when life here was just emerging."

Rob paused, fixing his eyes directly on the woman in the back row who had posed the question. "Except, of course, that life was not emerging at all."

The reporter frowned. "I beg your pardon?"

"Isn't it obvious?" Rob replied. "Life on this planet did not emerge," he said again. "It adapted."

For a moment the silence in the room held as the reporters digested what Rob Silver had just said, and then a dozen of them were on their feet, all shouting questions at once.

Rob waited until the furor died away, then dealt with all the questions in one statement.

"It's very simple," he said. "Life did not *arise* on this planet—it *arrived*. Before that planet was destroyed fifteen million years ago, the essence of its life force escaped; this is where it came. Here, and perhaps to hundreds—even thousands—of other planets." His tone changed, almost as if he were no longer speaking to the people in the room, but to everyone, everywhere. "When you look up into the sky tonight, and see the one star that is brighter than all the others, understand what it is. Or what it was."

A silence fell over the room, and finally the woman in the back of the room, still on her feet, spoke a single word.

"Home."

"That's right," Rob said softly. "Home."

Then, seeing Katharine waving to him from the door, Rob turned the press conference back over to Phil Howell and left the room.

Michael had awakened before dawn that morning, his eyes snapping open in the darkness and immediately fixing on the nova that was now the brightest star in the sky. For him, the brilliant beacon of light had taken on a special meaning, appearing for the first time on the night he had been delivered from the confines of the Plexiglas box and brought to the oasis in the lava shield covering the flank of Kilauea.

The oasis was still his headquarters, and in the two weeks that had elapsed since the helicopter deposited him here, a tent had been set up. There was a picnic table and benches, and half a dozen folding chairs stood in a loose circle around the stone ring in which a small fire always smoldered.

A makeshift kitchen had even been constructed, with a Coleman stove for cooking, and an enormous cooler, its ice replenished every three days. They had offered to bring a generator to the oasis, but Michael himself had begged them not to, unwilling to have what little quiet remained on the mountain-side destroyed by the constant roar of another machine.

The helicopters overhead were bad enough.

A crowd of reporters had set up camp farther down the mountain, held back only by a team of rangers whose sole job had become to protect the small amount of privacy Michael had, and the reporters had brought their own generators up. When the winds were right, Michael could hear them all too clearly, and when he went to the caldera at night to watch the flames dance over the surface of the boiling lava, the comforting blanket of darkness in which he'd wrapped himself that first night was gone, torn to shreds by the brilliant halogen lights with which the reporters lit their camp.

Visitors came to see him every day, and every day his mother and Rob came as well, if only for an hour or two. Most days, the three of them had sup-per together, and often one or the other of them spent the night with him, sleeping in the tent while he himself lay outdoors, savoring the expansiveness of the sky.

Each day, he felt a little stronger, and each night the star grew a little brighter. Three days ago, for the first time, it had remained visible into the dawn, only disappearing when it inevitably dropped over the horizon.

But the star, he knew, was eventually going to fade, and though he'd said nothing to either his mother or to Rob, he had begun to fear that day.

This morning, when he'd come awake before dawn and looked up into the sky, something had changed: the nova had been less bright than the night before. He'd gazed at it for a long time, silently willing its brilliance to grow, before he drifted back into a fitful sleep.

When he awoke again, the sun was rising, and the stars, except for the nova, were gone.

And he felt a tightness in his chest.

All morning long he told himself it meant nothing, that he'd simply caught a cold, and that by tomorrow or the next day it would be gone. But he knew better; knew that tomorrow, and on every tomorrow to come, the nova would have dimmed, and the pain in his chest would have spread.

The night it disappeared, he was certain, would be the night he died.

He spent the day alone, hiking on the mountain, visiting all his favorite places, inhaling the smoke and fumes, praying they would banish the pain in his chest and replace the flagging energy in his body.

They did not.

It was nearly three o'clock when he heard the roar of rotors and looked up into the sky to see Puna's helicopter cruising above him, then dropping lower, and finally landing in the oasis. Even before the blades stopped spinning, his mother and Rob scrambled out. Then his mother's hands were on his shoulders, and her eyes intently studying his face, and she asked the questions she asked every day since he'd come here.

"How do you feel? Are you all right?"

Michael hesitated, then decided there wasn't any reason for her to be as frightened as he'd been when the pain in his chest persisted throughout the day. "I'm fine," he said. There was a flicker of something in his mother's eyes, and when she spoke again, she almost sounded disappointed.

"You're sure? You aren't in any pain? You have plenty of energy?"

Michael's smile faltered. "I—I'm okay, Mom. Really!"

For some reason, his words didn't seem to make her feel better. She took a deep breath. "I brought you something," she said.

Michael glanced at the helicopter, but saw nothing except Rob and Puna unloading some kind of box from behind the aircraft's rear seats.

A Plexiglas box.

A Plexiglas box that looked big enough for him to get into.

Involuntarily, he took a step backward. His mother grabbed his arm. "No!" he said. "I won't—" He fell abruptly silent when he realized the box wasn't empty.

Inside it was a chimpanzee.

"She's from the laboratory," he heard his mother say as Rob unlocked the door to the Plexiglas box. "This morning I thought she was dying."

Rob opened the lid of the box, and the chimpanzee, as if surprised to find its prison door open, hesitated, then slowly came out. It looked curiously around for a moment, and then its eyes fixed on Michael. In two short bounds it crossed the space between them and leapt up, its arms encircling Michael's neck as it sniffed at his ear.

"But how can she breathe?" Michael asked, certain that at any second the chimpanzee would begin gasping. As if on cue, the chimp began to wheeze. "Put her back in the box," Michael pleaded. "She's going to die!"

Katharine shook her head. "She's not, Michael. She's going to be fine."

Michael blinked. "I don't understand—" he began, but then his mother's arms were around him again, hugging both him and the chimpanzee.

"It's over," she said. "The reason the animals in the lab have been dying is because the effect of the Seed doesn't last! It wears off, and when it does, the animals can only survive on oxygen again. Even this morning I was afraid this baby wasn't going to make it through the day. But in the middle of the morning, someone changed her atmosphere and started giving her oxygen again. And look at her! She's all right!"

As the words slowly sank in, Michael pulled away from his mother and looked into her eyes. "How long?" he asked. "How long before me did they give it to her?"

"Not quite two weeks," Katharine told him. "And it was just about a week ago that she started failing. We thought she was getting sicker, but it was just the opposite. She was getting better, but we kept on poisoning her."

Michael was no longer listening. Instead, he was gazing up at the nova, and remembering what Rob had told him about how long it would take before it began to die.

A couple of weeks.

Perhaps a month, or even more.

But now it no longer mattered, for long after the star had died, he would still be alive.

A sheepish smile came over his face. "Mom?"

Katharine looked at him.

"When you asked me if I was okay and I said I was fine?"

Katharine nodded.

"Well, I lied. Actually, I've been feeling kind of lousy all day, and breathing fumes and smoke hasn't helped much at all!"

Darkness was falling as the helicopter took off from the Big Island for the last time, carrying Michael, Katharine, and Rob back to Maui.

Below them the glowing vents of the volcano were brightening, and the flames above the caldera were beginning their nightly dance, but Michael could see that the lake of lava was beginning to recede, and the writhing serpents of molten rock were slowing in their progress toward the sea. The eruption was ending; the mountain was slowly dropping back into an uneasy slumber.

Above them the nova hung alone in the sky, but other stars were beginning to appear as well.

And soon—very soon—the nova would fade away.

Unlike the volcano, it would never awaken again.

More than a year and a half ago the idea for *The Presence* came to me while I was walking on the beach near my home on Maui. Here, on this island paradise, exists one of the finest astronomical observatories in the world, as well as one of the most powerful computers on earth. And, within a few short miles, an active volcano, Kilauea, sends forth continual lava flows. From these intriguing, disparate-seeming ingredients, the basic concept began to take shape for a book of "speculative fiction."

Little did I know as I began to write that my "speculative" fiction might turn out to be not quite so speculative. First it was discovered that there may well have been life on Mars, and the remnants of that life may have been carried to Earth within the core of a meteorite. On the heels of that discovery came new photos from the spacecraft *Galileo*, revealing that Europa, a moon circling Jupiter, may well have water and volcanic action beneath its covering of ice. More than one scientist has theorized that these conditions could presage the presence of life.

Just three months prior to publication of *The Presence*, *Smithsonian Magazine* reported that at the American Association for the Advancement of

Science meetings in Seattle, there was discussion of very unusual life-forms living on the floors of our own oceans, near hydrothermal volcanic vents: life-forms surviving and developing with *no* oxygen, *no* sunlight; life-forms thriving in 500° F. heat, on gases such as hydrogen sulfide—the very "poisonous" gases that would terminate life as we have previously known it. Additionally, many scientists now believe that volcanoes deep under the ocean may not simply harbor life, but be the very place where life *began*.

Suddenly, all our presumptions about the source of life have been turned upside down. So, now that I have finished writing *The Presence*, and you have finished reading it, the question arises: Is this truly *speculative* fiction?

Or is it possible that perhaps things might have happened just this way?

John Saul

Somewhere in the Arizona desert
April 30, 1997

ACKNOWLEDGMENTS

Many thanks go to John L. Africano, Astronomer and Senior Engineering Specialist at Rockwell International Corporation, and Paul W. Kervin, Chief Scientist at Phillips Laboratory, for their assistance and time. *Mahalo*, guys, for the tours, the stories, and your work.

Much appreciation is extended to David Fisher, Center Director of the Small Business Development Center at the Maui Research and Technology Park. Thanks for showing me around and introducing me to a group of fascinating people.

I am grateful to A. Keith Pierce, Designer of the McMath-Pierce Solar Telescope, for the time he spent guiding me around Kitt Peak. Thanks, Keith, it was lots of fun.

Special thanks also go to Les Horn and William Longacre, who connected me to the right people.

ABOUT THE AUTHOR

John Saul's first novel, *Suffer the Children*, published in 1977, was an immediate, million-copy bestseller. He has since written eighteen successive best-selling novels of suspense, among them *Guardian, The Homing, The God Project, Nathaniel, Brainchild, Hellfire, The Unwanted, Creature, Darkness*, and, most recently, *Black Lightning*. He is also the author of the *New York Times* bestseller, *The Blackstone Chronicles*, a serial thriller in six parts, which was published in monthly installments earlier this year. Mr. Saul divides his time between Seattle, Washington, and Maui, Hawaii.

JOIN THE CLUB!

Readers of John Saul now can join the John Saul Fan Club by writing to the address below. Members receive an autographed photo of John, newsletters, and advance information about forthcoming publications. Please send your name and address to:

The John Saul Fan Club
P.O. Box 17035
Seattle, Washington 98107

Be sure to visit John Saul at his Web site!
www.johnsaul.com